Highland Sanctuary

Also by Jennifer Hudson Taylor

Highland Blessings

Highland Sanctuary

Jennifer Hudson Taylor

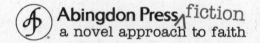

Abingdon Press fiction
a novel approach to faith

Nashville, Tennessee

Highland Sanctuary

ISBN-13: 978-1-4267-1421-4

Published by Abingdon Press, P.O. Box 801, Nashville, TN 37202

www.abingdonpress.com

Published in association with the Hartline Literary Agency.

Library of Congress Cataloging-in-Publication Data

Taylor, Jennifer Hudson.
  Highland sanctuary / Jennifer Hudson Taylor.
    p. cm.
  ISBN 978-1-4267-1421-4 (book—pbk./trade pbk., adhesive—perfect binding :
alk. paper)
  1. Heirs—Fiction. 2. Outcasts—Fiction. 3. Secrecy—Fiction. 4. Greed—
Fiction. 5. Betrayal—Fiction. 6. Scotland—History—15th century—Fiction. I.
Title.
  PS3620.A9465H547 2011
  813'.6—dc22

                                     2011023829

Scripture on page 7 is from the King James or Authorized Version of
the Bible.

Printed in the United States of America

1 2 3 4 5 6 7 8 9 10 / 16 15 14 13 12 11

To my sweet daughter, Celina,
You make me so proud of all you've overcome
and the young lady you're becoming.

And to the wonderful Lord,
Thank you for healing Celina from her seizures
and wrapping her in your loving arms.

Acknowledgments

I would like to thank so many people for their help and encouragement to make this dream of a novel into a reality. To Dwayne, my husband, thank you for not only reading this book once, but twice, to make sure my men characters aren't *too sappy*.

To my beta readers, the Faith Girls, and HisWriters, thank you for your continued support, excellent historical wisdom, and encouragement.

To my editor, thank you for taking the time to meet with me in-person to discuss the changes. It made a HUGE difference.

To my agent, thank you for always believing in me.

To those who created and maintain www.caithness.org, thank you for a wonderful site full historical details and information that led me to even more references.

"Honour and majesty are before him: strength and beauty are in his sanctuary."

Psalm 96:6

1

Scotland

1457

The ordeal over, fragmented tremors still quaked through Evelina Broderwick's body. She gazed down at her new daughter. Now, she'd finally have someone who would truly love her. Tiny fingers curled. Evelina marveled at the wee nails. The other hand tightened into a fist and flew into the bairn's mouth as she sucked on her knuckles.

"She's beautiful, is she not?" Tears clouded Evelina's vision, overwhelming her by the magnitude of God's gift of life.

Gunna, her wet nurse, peered closer at the babe swaddled in a warm blanket. "Aye, she is at that."

"I believe I shall call her Serena after my Spanish grandmother. The lass has an English da and a Scottish mither—a mixture of noble blood from three countries."

"Not a verra common name here in the lowlands," Gunna's round cheeks swelled in a smile as she nodded in agreement, "but lovely just the same."

The bedchamber door swung open, casting dim light from the hallway candles. The shadow of a man's tall frame bounced on the dark pine walls. Evelina tensed as her husband, Devlin

Broderwick, strode in with his usual frown. A dent marred his forehead. He towered over the bedside.

The midwife followed him and stood at the foot of the bed, folding her hands in front of her. The woman appeared to be in her mid-fifties, personally chosen by Devlin and quite loyal to the Broderwick family. Her dark gaze traveled from Evelina to Gunna and down at the infant.

"I've heard the unfortunate news." Devlin's sharp tone cut through the room like a blade through a gentle lamb.

Was a lass so terrible? Evelina glanced at the only window on the far right. The shutters were closed, blocking the night sky from view. She would like naught more than to escape the confines of her marriage, even if it meant taking sanctuary behind the walls of a convent for the rest of her days.

Devlin cleared his throat. He wore a black tunic with blooming sleeves narrowing at the cuffs. Black suited his dark moods. His hair hung straight in the shape of a downward bowl. He crossed his arms, taking an authoritative stance. "Fortunately, you're still young and healthy. You can try again when you're well enough."

Evelina stayed her tongue. Over the last eleven months of their marriage, she had come to despise him. She had tried to love him, tried to win his affection, but he had been most impossible to please. No wonder her kinsmen hated the English. He had wounded her feelings more times than she cared to count. She'd begun to resent her parents for arranging this union and forcing her into a lifetime of sorrow.

"I'll love her." Evelina held her daughter against her bosom. She stared at the wine-colored blanket covering her bed, tracing a finger along the raised flower pattern stitched into the thick fabric, a gift from Devlin's mother.

"I'm sure you will." He pointed at their daughter. "Now lay her down so I can see her."

Cradling her child's unsteady head, Evelina lowered Serena onto her back. She unwrapped the white blanket from her squirming body. Devlin leaned close.

The bairn's rosy glow turned red then deepened to a shade of purple. Serena's head twisted at the nape, her face almost level with the bed. The child's eyes glazed over, twitching into the corners, only the whites visible.

"What's the meaning of this?" Devlin jumped back in alarm.

Though Serena's entire body had grown stiff, it quivered in spasms. The area around her lips faded to white and the rest of her skin melted from purple to an ashen gray.

"She's not breathing!" Evelina turned to the midwife. "Do something!"

"I deliver wee bairns. I don't cast out demons." The midwife's fearful eyes met hers.

Evelina gripped her husband's arm, but he pulled away. "Devlin, please do something. She's stopped breathing! Save her, please?"

He only stared at the helpless babe with disbelieving eyes.

Evelina reached for her daughter's seizing body. Not knowing what else to do, Evelina turned the child over on her stomach and patted her back. She willed her babe to breathe. She blew air in Serena's face, hoping to startle her into breathing. White foam leaked over Serena's colorless lips. Evelina laid her down and plunged her finger into the tiny mouth, pulling with all her might against the curled tongue. Serena coughed, moaned, and screamed into a blessed cry.

"Oh, thank God!" Evelina collapsed, lowering her head next to Serena and letting silent tears fall in relief. Their wee bairn would live.

Evelina kissed the thin layer of soft black hair on Serena's round head. Her tiny lungs panted for air as her breathing returned to normal. She touched Serena's sweet ears, her pug nose, and cheeks now gaining a rosy glow.

"What was that?" Devlin's voice flayed her nerves and she jumped. He stood with his hands on his hips, staring at the child in disbelief, his dark, condemning eyes narrowed.

"The babe was having some sort of fit," the midwife said. "I've heard of stories like this, but never seen one myself."

"Yes, I can see that. I want to know why!" Devlin took two menacing steps toward her.

"'Tis unexplained." She stepped back, tilted her head upon her shoulders, and looked up at him with wide eyes. "No one really knows what it is. Some call it the falling sickness."

Devlin paced across the chamber, rubbing the back of his head. The soles of his mid-calf leather boots clicked against the hardwood floor. "Why would a child have such a fit? How can ye stop it?"

"I don't know." The midwife shook her head and sank against the wall.

His gaze dropped to the bundle in Evelina's arms. "It's possessed." His lips twisted in thought. He paced again. "We'll call a priest to cast it out." He paused and shook his head. "No, we can't do that. How would it look if the Broderwick family produced a demon possessed child?" He shook his head. "I won't have the family name ruined." He turned and pointed at the midwife and Gunna. "No one had better speak a word outside this bedchamber. If you do, I'll make you sorry."

"I won't say a word," the midwife said, shaking her head.

"Aye, my lord," Gunna said, looking down at her feet.

"She isn't possessed," Evelina said, her heart pounding in worry. "She stopped breathing and nearly died."

Devlin strode toward her. He pressed his fists into the soft feather mattress and leaned forward. "There's no other explanation."

"Devlin, ye're mistaken. She couldn't catch her breath is all."

"Then why did she turn her head as if it would disconnect from her body of its own accord? Where did her eyes go? In the back of her head? What was coming from her mouth? Do ye call it somethin' from God?" He stepped back. "This isn't the work of God. I feel it in my soul. Something is wrong. As head of this household it's my responsibility to take care of it."

"Our child is not evil." Evelina moved Serena over her shoulder and patted her bottom.

"I make the final decisions in this house." Devlin's dark eyebrows knitted together in an angry line. "She may look normal now, but her body is possessed by somethin'. I'll not tolerate evil under my own roof. Do you hear me, woman?"

"Devlin, listen to yerself. She's our child." Evelina clutched the bundle in her arms, fear rooted in her heart. Was he completely mad?

"I saw the babe turn into a demon with my own eyes. I won't claim it as mine. I've made up my mind. I don't want it, and I forbid ye to keep it."

"I won't give her up!" Evelina moved Serena to the far side of her body away from him. "She's my bairn, not some animal to cast away."

"You're my wife, and you'll do as I tell you." He stepped toward her, grabbing for the child.

Evelina refused to relinquish her hold. Their daughter began to cry at their tug of war. He tightened his grip on Evelina's flesh until she could no longer feel. Fearing Serena would be hurt from their struggle, Evelina relented. He snatched Serena.

"I beg ye, don't take her away." Tears clogged Evelina's voice, choking her.

He strode from the chamber with Serena. The midwife made a "humph" sound and followed him.

Evelina tried to rise. In her weakened state, she fell to the floor.

"Oh, dearie me!" Gunna cried, hurrying around the bed to help her.

Evelina had forgotten Gunna was still in the room. Frantic hands pulled under Evelina's arms, trying to lift her as she struggled to her knees.

"Nay! Don't bother with me. Find out where he's taking her." Evelina nudged her.

"But—"

"Please? Do this one thing for me." Evelina sniffed back tears. "Go! Make haste before it's too late."

"I-I'll do as ye ask. Don't ye worry, lass. We'll save yer bairn." She fled the chamber, leaving Evelina alone in her anguish.

Evelina dropped her head upon her arms. Her eyelids fluttered shut. "Dear God," she whispered. "I dedicate Serena to Ye. She isn't evil. She's just the way Ye made her. Allow me to be her mither and I'll teach her Yer ways and raise her to be Yer child."

The room began to spin. Evelina clutched the bed linens for support. Darkness claimed her vision as the distant sounds of her child crying in another part of the house fell silent. "Please . . . God," she whispered, fading to unconsciousness.

Scotland 1477

Gavin MacKenzie and Leith, his brother, led fifty clansmen along the narrow dirt path, two men abreast, their conversation a gentle rhythm above the steady clip-clop of horses. The comfortable late-spring air made it a good day to travel.

Something moved ahead. From this distance it looked like a horse pulling a wagon. The sound of weeping reached his ears and then faded. Had he imagined it? He motioned to the men to be quiet. Their voices dropped to whispers before altogether silencing.

Sholto, his horse, grew restless and sidestepped. Gavin grabbed the reins with both hands. The animal snorted in obvious distress. To calm the beast, Gavin rubbed his mount's neck until his breathing evened and his gait steadied. Gavin's red and gray plaid fell over his right shoulder. Shoving it out of his way, he studied the layout of the land, looking for signs of a surprise attack.

They'd travelled for days, leaving the familiar glens and rolling moors with a sheltered forest for the flat peatland surrounding them in Scotland's northern tip of Caithness. With no place to hide, the element of surprise was not in their favor. The light wind carried the scent of the bog myrtle across the silver lochs. Purple heather dotted the land, its sweet scent mixing with the salty sea air. By this, Gavin knew they must be getting close to Braigh Castle. He was told it stood alone on the moss-covered rocky cliffs facing the sea—like a sanctuary.

The wagon up ahead moved. Gavin gripped the reins tight and hastened his mount. As he drew closer, a skittish horse hitched to a heavy laden wagon flung his tail in vexation. The animal neighed and pranced about as much as the load allowed.

More weeping carried from the opposite side of the wagon. Gavin motioned for his men to halt. He nodded toward Leith who dismounted and went to calm the beast. Gavin inched toward the noise.

A woman with a long braid of auburn hair streaked with gray bent over a lass lying on her back. He couldn't see much of the one lying down, but the weeping one wore a dark blue gown. She patted her unresponsive companion, speaking in a hushed, worried tone.

He cleared his throat, reining in his horse and sliding to the ground.

She gasped and turned a frightened expression toward him.

"What happened?" He nodded toward the unconscious lady lying in a bed of thick grass.

Her moss-green eyes watched him, assessing his character. She wiped at the tears staining her cheeks. "We must have hit somethin'. The wagon nearly tipped over. She fell from her seat and hit her head."

Gavin bent to his knees, surveying the unmoving lass and felt for a pulse in her neck. It beat steady. Her skin was warm and smooth. She was much younger than her concerned friend. "Have ye checked her head for bleeding?"

"It only happened a moment ago. I first tried to wake her." Alarm crossed her face as her eyes widened, and she grabbed the girl's hands between her own. "I do wish she'd wake. 'Twould put my mind at ease. She's my daughter . . . my only child." Her chin trembled.

"May I?" Gavin gestured toward her daughter. "I'd like to check her head for bleeding or lumps."

"Aye." She nodded. "Serena took many falls as a child. She was always so free-spirited. But I've never known her to be out this long."

Serena. He liked her name. It was different. Lying here, she looked serene. Although her skin was pale, he could tell she had spent time in the sun. Her dark lashes curled against her skin. Light freckles lay across the bridge of her nose. He took a deep breath and eased his hands in her black hair. It was thick and free of curls, reminding him of black velvet, though it felt more like smooth satin.

"It's right here." He found a bump forming on the right side of her head above her ear. "'Tis only a slight knot. I'm sure she'll be fine." Gavin glanced at the full wagon. "There's little room in yer wagon. Would ye like me to carry her to my horse?"

She graced her knuckles over her daughter's cheek. "I'm verra thankful for yer assistance. We live in the Village of Braigh about a mile ahead. Would ye mind carrying her there? We were just returning from the town market."

"We'd be honored," Gavin said. "We're on our way to Braigh Castle. Is yer village near the castle?"

"Aye." A smile brightened her worry-filled eyes. "Only a half a mile further beyond our village would be my guess."

Gavin crooked his finger toward his men, singling out Roan. As his friend dismounted, Gavin realized how much his tall frame would benefit them. His long blond hair was tied back at the nape. One thing he and his men lacked over the course of their travel was proper grooming. He hoped their ragged looks and overgrown beards wouldn't offend or frighten the lasses.

"I'm going to mount my horse, and I need ye to lift her to me as gently as possible."

"I got 'er." Roan said, bending to one knee and slipping an arm beneath her neck and behind her knees.

Once he was settled upon Sholto, Gavin secured the reins and held out his arms. Roan raised her up. Gavin settled her across his lap, hoping she would be comfortable and the ride wouldn't jar her wounded head too much. It helped that she wore a simple brown gown.

"Careful," her mother said, wringing her hands.

"Serena will be safe. Would ye prefer to drive the wagon or would ye like for one of my men to take over?" If she was too upset, he didn't want another mishap to befall them.

She shook her head. Pieces of hair loosened from her braid. "Nay, it helps me to have somethin' to do. Let me know as soon as she wakes. My name's Evelina Boyd, and I'm verra thankful for yer help."

Leith assisted her to better secure the horse to the wagon and checked the condition of the wheels. Once he and Roan were mounted on their horses again, they began a slow pace to match Evelina's wagon.

The men conversed in quiet tones. A bird flapped its wings above them and sang. A gentle draft kept the air from being too warm. The sun hid behind white clouds and burst out in brightness every once in a while.

Gavin looked down at the bonny lass in his arms, breathing in the feminine scent of heather and juniper. The aroma stirred forgotten memories of another lass he'd tried his best to forget. If she had lived, he'd be a married man by now, mayhap the father of wee bairns. To his bitter disappointment, his life had taken another route, which led him and his brother all over Europe to escape his grief and guilt.

"Could that be a patch of woods down yon in the glen?" Leith rode up beside Gavin and shielded his hand over his eyes.

"Looks like it." Relieved to be distracted from his thoughts, Gavin looked where his brother gestured. "That must be Braigh Castle."

Situated on a long, narrow rocky cliff sat a magnificent stone fortress that looked to be king of the sea. A wide tower stood tall above wings that stretched out on each side. "From here, it doesn't look like it needs to be restored," Gavin said, admiring the view. "How will we ever be able to improve upon it?"

"Ye're here to restore the castle, then?" Evelina rolled the wagon to a stop beside them.

"Aye." Gavin nodded, careful not to reveal the other reason they were there—to protect the new laird, his castle, and the village. He wondered how much Evelina and Serena knew concerning the truth behind the elder laird's death.

"The massive keep is at least two centuries auld and Vikings have attacked it on several occasions," Evelina said.

"Were they ever successful?" Leith asked.

"I don't think so." Evelina shook her head. "But I don't know the whole history." She glanced at Serena in Gavin's arms. "Will the restoration take long?"

Gavin shrugged. "We won't know 'til we see the damage."

"Oh." Her gaze shifted back to the castle as she pondered his words. Her expression tensed as the lines around her eyes and mouth deepened. She cleared her throat. "I suppose that means ye'll be here for quite a while then?"

"Aye." He nodded.

A strange silence followed. An eerie forboding crawled up his spine. He couldn't help sensing she didn't welcome their presence. He scratched his temple.

"Back in the town of Braighwick people called it the Village of Outcasts," Leith said. "Why?"

"Ye'll see soon enough." The warmth in her eyes faded to a reserved caution as she clicked to her horse and started forward.

As they approached the only patch of woods in the area, Gavin braced himself for what could earn this place the odd name. They crossed into the shade of the birch and hazel trees dotted among the dominant forest of pine. Brown needles cushioned the ground in a blanket of comfort, much like the serenity of snow he loved in winter. The fresh pine scent surrounding them appealed to Gavin as he breathed.

Small dwellings were scattered throughout the woods, made of stone and packed with peat bothy, straw, heather, and moss. The turf roofs contained a simple hole for the smoke that rose from the center where they built their fires. If the inside of these cottages were like the ones that belonged to his father's tenants at home, most were one-room dwellings with a dirt floor. The family slept on one side, while their cattle passed the night on the other. Having grown up in the luxury of his father's castle, it was hard to imagine enduring conditions such as these as a way of life.

A few people opened their doors to watch them pass. Compassion hit Gavin with a force he had not expected. Their clothes were worn through and tattered in places. Most were barefoot. Filth and grime covered their faces. The Boyds seemed out of place here with their clean clothes and appearance. Yet, in spite of these people's poverty, their eyes glowed with a passionate joy he couldn't fathom, not the listless melancholy one would expect.

"This is ours." Evelina stopped in front of one of the rectangular hovels. She secured the reins, set the wagon brake, and climbed down.

2

As Evelina's feet landed on the ground, the wooden door swung open and Gunna poked her gray head out. "What on earth?" Her face wrinkled in concern. She narrowed her gaze and patted her tight bun in place. "Evelina? Is it ye?"

"Aye, Gunna." Evelina knew the poor woman couldn't see their faces. Over the years her eyesight had grown worse. Evelina feared she would soon be blind. "Serena had an accident and these men have helped me bring her home," Evelina said over her shoulder as she rushed to Gavin. "I'll show ye where to take her."

Gavin handed Serena over to Leith so he could dismount.

"Oh, dearie me. How bad is she?" Gunna stepped outside, wringing her hands in distress. Her plump form blocked the entrance.

"Gunna, let us by," Evelina said. "He's trying to bring her in."

"Beg yer pardon. I didn't mean to get in the way." She touched her hand to her chest and moved.

Evelina followed Leith inside with a silent prayer on her tongue. She made the sign of the cross, touching her forehead, chest, and each shoulder.

"Ye can lay her here on my bed." Evelina pointed to a small box bed in the corner of the one-room cottage with an identical bed beside it. As Leith laid Serena down, she stirred, moaned, and rolled over without waking. Evelina's heart pounded against her ribs, a glimpse of hope in the slight movement stretching her faith. "I'm afraid the loft where Serena usually sleeps would be too difficult for ye to carry her up the ladder and for me to attend her."

"Good idea," Gavin said, stepping inside. His gaze slid to the wooden ladder nailed to the wall that led to the loft. He peered at the oak table with wooden chairs by the fireplace. She wondered what he thought, then dismissed the concern. Serena was the priority.

"Is there aught else we can do?" Gavin asked.

Evelina walked over the dirt floor to the end of the bed and removed her daughter's shoes. She pulled a blanket over Serena. "Would ye find Tomas for me?" Evelina straightened. "He should be at the kirk. If not, he might be tending to someone in the village. Just ask around for him."

"What does he look like?" Gavin asked.

"He's bald." She paused, realizing that wasn't entirely true. "Well, maybe a wee bit on the top." She patted her own head for emphasis. "He's average height, thin, and I'd say middle-aged."

"I'd be obliged to find him for ye." Gavin stepped back toward the door.

"And he's probably wearing a brown robe with a rope cord around the waist."

"He's a priest?" Leith asked.

"Aye." She nodded.

"Do ye plan to have her last rites read?" Gavin glanced over at Serena, concern apparent in his eyes as he raised a brow.

"Tomas is both priest and physician in our village." Evelina tucked the covers around her daughter.

"We'll be happy to find Tomas for ye." Leith said, grabbing Gavin's arm and leading him out. "Come on, Gavin. We'd better be on our way."

"Thank ye for yer aid." Evelina said to their retreating backs. Once they were gone, Evelina sighed and dropped to her knees. "Gunna, Serena had another fit. This one was the worst I've seen. We've got to pray she comes to—and soon."

"Once I find the physician, I'll join the rest of ye for supper." Gavin slapped Leith on the back.

They parted ways while Gavin headed to the only wooden building in the midst of the village with a crooked cross leaning to the right above the entrance. He walked up the four steps and opened the door aged with splintered wood. Rusted hinges groaned. No windows. The little sanctuary appeared as dark as tree bark. He blinked, allowing his eyes time to adjust.

"Hello!" Gavin called. Silence. "Tomas?"

Rows of benches ran on each side of the sanctuary creating an aisle up the center. He listened, but no sound save his own cautious footsteps greeted him. "Tomas, if ye're here, Serena Boyd has fallen and needs yer help." If the physician-priest was hiding, Gavin hoped he would show himself once he knew why Gavin sought him.

Gavin waited a few more seconds and walked out. As he bounded down the steps, he wondered where he should go next. He had no choice but to make an unexpected visit to each resident of the village until he found Tomas. Peering through the woods, he saw another dwelling to the right. He walked toward it, ducked beneath a low branch, his boots crushed over pine needles, cones, and fallen twigs.

A hand-carved slate that read "Cobbler" hung outside a small cottage. It didn't look like a cobbler shop. Gavin took a deep breath and knocked. No one answered. Hammering continued from inside. Mayhap they couldn't hear him. He pushed open the door as bells jingled from a string. The room was wide-open with a long table on each side. Shoes and boots for ladies, men, and children were stacked in neat rows across the carved shelves along the walls of the shop.

The cobbler worked on a pair of soles with his back to the entrance. Gavin cleared his throat, but the man didn't move from his practice.

"May I help ye, sir?" A young lass appeared through a long blue curtain from a back room and hurried toward him. Her soft brown eyes gaped up at him in curiosity. She couldn't have been more than ten and six. When she leaned forward with her hands clasped in front of her, long brown hair fell over her shoulder, down to her waist. She blinked, her eyelashes curling.

Gavin glanced over at the cobbler, who was still oblivious that anyone had entered his shop.

"Da is deaf." The lass followed his gaze. "That's why I attached the bells to the door, so I'd be able to hear while I tend to other chores. I'm Lavena, so do ye need some shoes made?"

"Nay, I'm looking for Tomas. Have ye seen him?"

"How do ye know Tomas?" She tilted her head. "Ye're new to the village."

"True. I don't know him. We ran into Serena and Evelina on our way to Braigh Castle. Serena was hurt and Evelina sent me to find Tomas."

"I hope she'll be all right." Concern flickered in her eyes as she blinked and shook her head. "I've not seen 'im, but let me see if either of my sisters have." She turned. "Rosheen! Birkita!" Gavin's ears rang, unprepared for the way she bellowed their names, quite a booming voice for such a young female of her small stature.

Another lass appeared through the curtain carrying a worn book with her finger pressed in the center of it. Her hair was a shade darker than her sister's. She smoothed her free hand across her gray wrinkled skirt and straightened to her full height, which was quite tall. "Birkita, this man is looking for Tomas. Did ye see him on yer walk earlier?"

"Nay." Birkita shook her head.

A third lass popped through the curtain and shoved her plump hips between her two sisters to make room for her grand entrance. A displeasing frown marred her forehead, as her dark eyes shifted to Gavin. "I heard, and nay, I've not seen 'im." She was shorter than the other two, and while she was heavier, Gavin could tell by her smooth, round skin that she was the youngest. Her dress pulled against the extra flesh folding around her neck and arms. "Why do ye want Tomas? Who are ye?"

"Rosheen, mind yer manners." Lavena scolded. "She doesn't trust strangers verra easily. Please forgive her rudeness. Ye must give Tomas my best when ye find him."

"Of course." Gavin said, backing up. He couldn't escape this odd place soon enough. He bumped into a solid figure who grabbed his shoulder.

"Ah! We've a customer, do we?" A man shouted in his ear. "My name's Girard, and I'll be glad to assist ye with a fine pair o' shoes this day."

Gavin resisted the temptation to poke his fingers in his ears. His sister had a brother-in-law who couldn't hear, but he didn't go around shouting like this man. He looked at Lavena for assistance. As if sensing his discomfort, she went to her father and removed his hand from Gavin's shoulder and shook her head.

"Oh, he's not 'ere for business?" Disappointment wrinkled his frowning expression. "Then why is he 'ere?"

Gavin closed his eyes. The cobbler's voice echoed through his head.

"Thanks for yer assistance." Gavin took advantage of the moment and made his escape. Outside, he breathed deeply and rubbed his sore ears. The refreshing pine scent gave him renewed energy. Determined to keep his word, he hurried to the next dwelling.

"Hold it up higher, Quinn. How ye expect me to get the wheel on if ye don't?" A whiny male voice complained.

A huge man who must have been close to eight feet tall held up a wagon, but as soon as he noticed Gavin, he lowered it. "We've company, Beacon." His deep voice sounded as menacing as he looked.

Gavin gulped. As a warrior who had been in his share of battles, he rarely quaked at the brawn of other men, but this man was a giant. He forced a friendly smile, knowing it was too late to turn around and retreat. Besides, cowardice wasn't in his blood.

"What do ye mean?" The other one stepped out from behind the cover of the wagon, rolling a wheel taller than himself. Gavin blinked at the wee man, standing no taller than three and a half feet. "What are ye staring at? Haven't ye ever seen a dwarf before?" He pulled out a short sword and held it up.

"Nay, Beacon. Calm yer temper." He laid a large hand on the dwarf's head.

"Afternoon," Gavin said with a nod in greeting. "Evelina sent me to find Tomas. He wasn't at the kirk. Do either of ye know where he might be?"

"What have ye done to the Boyds?" Beacon thrust his sword at Gavin, but he was too far away to touch him.

"Ye're a stranger." Quinn stepped forward, placing his fisted hands on his hips. "How do ye know Tomas?"

Gavin launched into the story of Serena's injury.

Afterwards, Quinn shook his head. "We haven't seen Tomas since this morn. But he mentioned he might visit Kyla this day."

"Who is Kyla?" Gavin asked.

"The village seamstress." Quinn scratched his brown head. "He worries 'bout her. She's not been the same since losing her husband and bairn to the fever."

"Fever? How long ago was that?" Gavin wondered if there might be some contagious disease spreading through these people. Mayhap that could explain the madness.

"At least a year ago." Quinn shoved a thumb over his large shoulder. "She's up this way. We can take ye there, if ye want."

"What?" Beacon looked at him, lifting a palm up. "We don't have time for that. We got work to do."

"Beacon, this wagon wheel will be waitin' when we get back. No reason why we canna help out. Ye're gettin' difficult in yer auld age."

"Auld age?" Beacon sheathed his sword at his waist and raised a wee fist at his giant friend. "I'm five years yer junior!"

"Let's go find Tomas." Quinn stepped over Beacon, ignoring him. Each heavy footfall he took pounded the earth.

Gavin had to run, taking two steps to each one of Quinn's. He glanced up at the trees above him. Now he knew why they called this the Village of Outcasts. It suited them. He took a deep breath as he struggled to keep up with the giant. He hoped they would soon find Tomas, but in the meantime, what else would he discover?

𝒵❧

Serena woke to whispered voices above her. She recognized her mother's soothing and peaceful tone, but the man now talking escaped her. Who was he? Their muffled words sounded as if they were behind a closed door.

She struggled to lift her heavy eyelids. Serena blinked a few times, allowing her vision to clear in the dim candlelight. Yawning, she stretched. Voices paused. Shadows shifted along the dark walls.

Her mother's concerned face leaned over her. She linked her fingers through Serena's. Faint worry lines edged her eyes. Tension hovered around her lips. She forced a smile as if the effort drained the last of her strength.

"What's wrong?" Serena tried to sit up, but her lack of energy prevented her.

"Nay, rest." Her mother's gentle hands pressed her back.

"Serena, ye've suffered a blow to the head." She now recognized the other voice as Father Tomas. "Ye've slept for several hours. Judging by the swelling on yer head, I'm afraid ye may have a cracked skull. Getting up and moving around could leak too much blood to the brain and make matters worse."

Easing back against the feather pillow her mother had made, Serena nestled into a contented spot and tried to remember.

They were returning from the town of Braighwick with supplies and one of her headaches began. Serena blinked, looking from Father Tomas to her mother. "How did it happen? Did I have another fit?"

"Ye did." Mother nodded and gripped her hand. "I'm sorry I didn't catch ye before ye fell. It all happened so fast."

"How could ye've known? I was still trying to figure out if it was only a headache or if I was about to have one of my fits." She turned to Tomas. "How long must I rest?"

"At least until the swelling goes down, lass."

Lying still when she felt fine might prove to be a hard challenge. Serena hated idleness. It allowed one too much time to dwell on things.

"Aye, Serena, 'twould be best." Mother patted her arm.

Another fit. Serena didn't dare question her faith aloud. It would distress her mother, who had tried so hard to build Serena's faith, but there were days when she couldn't help wondering why God would ignore her prayers for healing. If so many people thought her condition evil, why wouldn't God help her? Mother chose to blame ignorant people, but she questioned God since the Lord was the one who created her and seemed to be the one in control of everything.

"Ye've a visitor." Mother gestured toward the foot of the bed.

Feet slid across the dirt floor. Serena strained to make out the features of the person in the shadows. Her heart beat fiercely as she clutched the handwoven covers lying over her, waiting. Cara, her best friend appeared in the candlelight.

"Serena, I came as soon as I heard. We're all praying for a quick recovery." Cara held out her hands with each sliding step until her knees pressed against the box bed.

"Careful. Ye don't want to bruise yer legs," Serena said. "I'm so glad ye came."

"What a pair we make. Me, running into things with my blindness and bruising myself, and ye cracking yer skull with yer fits." She smiled, but Serena heard the sorrow in her voice.

"At least we have each other," Serena said. "As close as two sisters could ever be."

"True." Her bottom lip trembled as she brushed a wave of brown hair from her face. "How are ye feeling?"

"A wee bit tired is all."

"Are ye hungry?" Mother asked. "Gunna made a fire pit outside for some stew. Since it's a nice day out, we didn't want to smoke up the house or make it too hot in here."

"Aye," Serena said, glancing up at her mother. "My stomach isn't rumbling, but I believe a little nourishment will help build my strength."

"I agree," Tomas smiled. "That's the hearty spirit I want to hear from ye."

"If I canna go out, please open the door so I can at least see some light. I wish we had a window like the ones at Braigh Castle." She loved the long halls and chambers layered with windows that opened to the beauty and splendor of the outdoors.

"I'll take care of it," Cara offered, heading toward the wooden door. She splayed her hands across it and felt for the latch. With both hands she swung it open. Light poured in like golden rays of varying shades. Dust stirred, swirling in the air like snow flurries. It was a welcome sight compared to the contrasting darkness.

"We've company comin'. Looks like that fella was here earlier." Gunna's cheerful voice carried through the threshold.

Serena tensed. "What fellow?"

"After yer fall some men happened upon us on their way to Braigh Castle. They helped me bring ye home." Mother touched her arm in support. "Don't worry. They don't know about yer fits—only the fall and the injury to yer head." She pressed her palm to her forehead. "Oh dear, I believe I sent Gavin on a merry chase looking for ye, Tomas." She stood to her feet. "I hope he isn't angry with me."

She rushed outside to greet their guest.

Serena pushed herself up with Cara's help and brushed her fingers through her long hair, hoping to improve her unkempt image. She adjusted how her dress lay across her shoulders and took a deep breath.

"None of the villagers will say aught," Cara said. "Yer secret is safe."

"Aye, but now he must think me a blunderin' fool to fall off a wagon." Fear wound inside her nervous chest. It wasn't often she got the chance to meet new people. She could only imagine the impression she must have made. Her skin prickled as a small shiver raced up her spine and crawled around her neck.

"Stop fretting. I'm sure he's quite nice," Cara whispered.

"He must be of excellent character to perform the deed he did for both ye and yer mother." Father Tomas bent toward her. His bald head glistened from the angle of the light. "Indeed, I'm looking forward to meeting him."

"Evelina, I'm sorry," a man's voice spoke outside. "I tried to find Tomas, but I failed. I trailed him everywhere, but each time I arrived too late to catch him." His voice sounded winded as he puffed between words.

"Gavin, what happened to ye? Looks like ye've tangled with a bear." Her mother's concern heightened Serena's curiosity.

"I came across a white wolf. Thought he wanted to eat me alive. Turns out, he just wanted to play."

Serena smiled, covering her lips before her mirth could escape. So Gavin, whoever he was, had already met the village wolf.

"Oh, ye must be referring to Phalen," Mother said. "He belongs to Quinn. The wolf has determined himself guardian over our village." Her mother paused. "While Phelan can appear frightening to strangers, he's naught but a playful beast. At least that's what I'm told. I don't like animals with fangs. I tend to keep my distance."

"I'll keep that in mind when I don my ripped tunic on the morrow." A gentle laugh laced the man's good natured voice. "After all, he only drew a wee bit of blood out o' me."

"Let me see, laddie," Gunna offered. "I've sewn a number of wounds in my lifetime, but my eyes 'ave nearly given out. Evelina or the lass will need to tend to ye."

"Thank ye, but I'm fine. Speaking of the lass, how is she?"

"She's much better," Gunna said. "Asking fer my stew, she is."

Serena imagined the proud smile on Gunna's wrinkled face. Her heart brimmed with love for her old nursemaid. She'd been like a grandmother to Serena.

"She's awake?" The eagerness in his voice surprised Serena. Cara giggled, but Serena swatted at her arm. She covered her mouth to suppress further noise.

"Aye, would ye like to come in?" Mother asked.

"If it's no trouble. When I couldn't find Tomas I began to worry."

Tomas crossed to the doorway. "No need, lad. I'm already here." He pumped Gavin on the back as he entered. "But I want to thank ye for all the trouble ye went through to find me. If ye hadn't stopped at so many places, I wouldn't have run into the cobbler's daughters and known to come here."

"I began to wonder if ye were real or not." Gavin greeted Tomas with a nod. His tunic was indeed ripped, all the way across the front of his muscled chest and there was a claw mark on his upper right arm. Dirt smudges covered his clothes.

Portions of his red hair had fallen from the tie at his nape, revealing shoulder length locks. A day's growth of a beard graced his jaw as fiery a color as his hair.

Serena gulped. She wasn't sure what she had expected, but certainly not this handsome stranger who lifted blue eyes in her direction. They were as striking as her mother's sapphire ring she was forced to sell a few years ago. She wondered about his age and where he came from.

"Gavin, meet my daughter, Serena Boyd, and her friend, Cara Grant." Mother gestured to them. "Serena, this is Gavin MacKenzie. Since the wagon was full, he carried ye home on horseback."

"I owe ye a debt of gratitude," Serena said. "Thank ye."

"'Twas an honor. I wish I could have done more. How do ye feel?"

"A wee bit sore and tight just above my ear." She touched the side of her head. "But otherwise, I'm feeling much better."

"With a few days' rest, let's pray the swelling and soreness go away," Tomas said.

"I believe it will." Serena gave him a smile.

"Gavin, on the way here ye asked why they call us the Village of Outcasts. Have ye figured it out yet?" Evelina folded her arms as she regarded him, tilting her head.

"I believe so." He thumped a finger against his chin. "But I think they've given it the wrong name."

"What would be more fitting?" Serena braced herself to hear a hideous name that would be even more insulting to her beloved home.

"I think the Village of Hospitality is more appropriate."

Stunned, Serena could only stare at Gavin, waiting for him to burst into laughter or at least admit he was jesting. The few who had visited usually couldn't escape fast enough. The villagers' generosity was always overlooked for their flaws.

People in Braighwick teased and taunted them without mercy. Serena wasn't about to give up her guard so easily. Mayhap Gavin MacKenzie was a gifted charmer.

Horse hooves pounded the earth as a rider rode toward the cottage.

"Slow down there, laddie. Else ye'll end up in my stew." Gunna warned from outside.

"Is my brother here? I need to speak with him. It's important." A man's voice spoke between short gasps.

"Ye'll find 'im inside," Gunna said.

Gavin's blue gaze met Serena's before he strode to the door. "Sounds like Leith." A dark-headed man rushed in with wide, worried eyes. Standing at eye level with each other, Gavin folded his arms and waited while Leith took a moment to catch his breath.

"A giant is tearing down our tents. He has a vicious wolf following him everywhere. I assumed he might be from the village so we didn't want to harm him, but neither can we allow him to destroy our things."

"Is anyone hurt?" Gavin scratched his forehead and pinched his eyebrows.

"Nay, but at this rate, we canna set up camp. What do ye advise?" Leith asked.

Gavin shifted his weight to one leg and rubbed his red beard as he pondered what to do. This was only the beginning of the many challenges he would encounter if he intended to stay here long enough to repair Braigh Castle.

"Still think we're the Village of Hospitality?" Serena asked.

3

*G*avin strode beside Leith, pondering Serena's question about the village name. Even though he hadn't admitted it aloud, he could understand why this place was deemed as the Village of Outcasts. Most of them would have a difficult time fitting in with others—even among the low-class. The only exceptions were Serena and Evelina. Why were they here? They didn't appear to belong anymore than the rest of the villagers belonged in the town of Braighwick.

"Wait!" A woman's voice called from behind.

Gavin whirled. Serena held onto the door frame as she stepped over the threshold. Tomas supported her on the other side. Gavin dropped the reins on his horse and rushed to her.

"What's the meaning of this? Ye should be resting as Tomas advised." A surge of unexplained protection welled inside him. Mayhap it was from seeing her in such a weakened state when he'd carried her home.

"Aye. See?" Tomas glanced down at Serena with a disapproving frown, his tone a fatherly reproach. "Gavin agrees with me."

"Serena, I do wish ye'd go back to bed and rest," Evelina said from behind, hidden by the shade inside of their home.

"I'll be fine, Mither. I need to warn Gavin about Quinn. I won't be able to rest 'til I do." Serena lifed a pleading gaze. Her eyes reminded him of the color of fresh peat moss in the spring. His heart swelled with mixed feelings as he waited, the lure of her expression tugged at him. "Have ye met Quinn?"

"I have. He seemed like a pleasant man, but quite large."

"Aye, and his size alone seems a direct challenge to some. They pick and prod hoping to push him into a fight so they can say they've defeated the giant."

"I see. Ye think my men have provoked him?" Gavin raised an eyebrow, not sure whether he should be insulted or admire her loyalty.

"Please, I mean no disrespect, but I know Quinn—we all do." She glanced at Tomas and back at her mother. "Quinn is much like his wolf. He's lovable, sensitive, playful, slow minded at times, but verra protective of folk he cares about— that includes any of us villagers—especially Beacon and the wolf." She stepped forward, slipped her fingers around his forearm in a steady grip in spite of her weakened condition. "Don't let them hurt Quinn. If he's on a wild fit, it's because he feels the need to protect something or someone."

"I promise I'll do my best." Gavin laid a hand over Serena's warm fingers. He looked into her eyes. A current of understanding passed between them. "I give my word."

"And I know how important a Highlander's word is." She stopped worrying her bottom lip with her teeth and broke into a relieved smile. "Ye'll discover that we're not like other villages. Here, we're all family."

"True, but more than that, I believe in keeping the Lord's commandments. Breaking my word once I've given it would be the same as lying."

"Then God brought an honorable man to rescue us." Her hand trembled in his. "I pray the Lord's favor will continue with ye."

Pleased by her reaction, Gavin didn't want to let go, but he knew it was the right thing to do. He stepped back.

"Come on." Leith tapped his other arm. "Yer word will mean naught if the giant provokes our men while we're away."

"Indeed. We'd better hurry," Gavin said, striding to where Sholto was tethered to a tree. Gavin took the reins in his right hand and lifted his other. "I bid ye farewell."

She waved and his chest pounded in response. Leith took the lead as he knew the exact location of their camp. They arrived at a beautiful loch, its surface shimmering in the sun's rays as the water gently moved with the slight wind. Heather and an assortment of flowers he couldn't name dotted the wild grass in a mixture of peat moss.

In the midst of this pleasant beauty, men shouted. A group surrounded Quinn in a circle, closing in on him. Swords and bows aimed at the vexed giant as he raised a fist in the air. Two ripped canvas tents lay on the ground nearby. Gavin raced his horse toward them, hoping he could prevent anything they would all regret. Leith kept pace.

"Stop!" Gavin broke through the circle and faced Quinn upon his horse. "Quinn, who's in danger? Who are ye trying to protect?"

"They have Phelan. And I want 'im back." Quinn pointed in the distance at the white wolf he had seen earlier. The animal was bound in an iron chain to the trunk of an oak tree. He lay on his side.

"What do ye mean asking him who's in danger? It's us!" Roan said, his skin color nearly matching his shoulder-length red hair. His lips thinned to white and his green eyes glistened like emeralds. "That wolf started growling at me as if he was about to attack, and this big brute went crazy when I protected myself and hit him with a limb. He's lucky I didn't run him through with my sword."

"He was already down. Ye didn't have to chain 'im," Quinn said. "Let him loose!"

Roan pulled his sword and stomped toward Quinn.

"Stop, Roan!" Leith warned. "Hold yer temper."

The man paused in mid-stride, but his expression clearly showed his struggle to obey. He clamped his jaw and turned away to pace.

"Did the wolf physically attack anyone?" Gavin shielded his eyes from the sun to better see the men. Some looked at each other, shaking their heads, while others murmured among themselves.

"Nay," Craig stepped forward. "But the wolf was growling and snarling at Roan as if he might."

"Ye left out the rest o' it." Quinn said. "Roan called to Phelan and when the wolf ducked from his grasp, Roan cursed at 'im in anger. Phelan sensed he wasn't to be trusted."

"Roan, why would ye provoke a wolf?" Leith asked.

"I heard him say that the white fur would make a nice coat," Craig said, tilting his blond head toward Roan, who kicked his booted foot into the ground.

"What's wrong with Phelan? Why is he lying down?" Gavin looked at Quinn.

"Roan hurt 'im when he threw the stick at his head." Quinn clenched and unclenched his hands at his side. "I need to set him loose and take him home where I can tend to 'im."

"Verra well." Gavin nodded. "Craig, help Quinn set the animal free." He looked into the giant's eyes. "I'm sorry."

"Wasn't yer fault." Quinn cast a dark menacing gaze at Roan. "If Phelan doesn't recover, ye'll be the one who's sorry."

"Is that a threat?" Roan straightened and glared back.

"One that is well deserved. Ye had no right to do what ye did," Gavin said.

"How was I supposed to know he belonged to someone?" Roan crossed his arms.

"He didn't belong to ye, so it doesn't matter. Ye should have left him alone," Gavin said. "This isn't our land. We're the guests here. Naught on this land is yers to claim without the laird's consent and ye'd do well to remember it."

"Ye can handle Roan's punishment." Gavin faced Leith. "There must be a consequence for his thoughtless actions."

"Aye, I'll take care of it," Leith said.

Gavin turned his horse around, pleased he hadn't broken his promise to Serena. He would have to remember to thank her for the tip about Quinn. He smiled. It was an excellent excuse to stop by and see her on the morrow.

❧

Serena rolled over. Gray light angled through the open door. It was already daylight? She rubbed her eyes and sat up. No sign of Gunna or her mother. Cattle lowed outside. Chickens bawked and wings flapped. What happened to the rooster? He always crowed at dawn.

She tossed the covers aside and swung her legs over the box bed. A wave of dizziness gripped her. Serena wrapped her arms around her middle and paused, waiting for the world to right itself again.

The lump on the side of her head had gone down. Tomas said she could go back to a normal routine once the swelling faded. After waiting a few days, she was very eager to do just that. Easing her bare feet upon the compact dirt floor, Serena winced at the cold contact. Even though it was now late spring, freezing air was common at night or in the early morning.

Sheep bleeted in the distance. Embers simmered in the fire pit, but it didn't give much heat. Serena threw on some kindling and stoked the hot coals until a new blaze lit. She grabbed a log and threw it on. Now she could dress without feeling like an icicle.

By the time she donned a clean dress and fastened her plaid around her for warmth, her mother walked in carrying a pail of milk. She breathed heavy from hauling her burden.

"How are ye feeling?" She set the pail down and kneaded the back of her neck. "Yer not as pale as yesterday. It's good to see color back in yer face."

"I feel much better and the swelling is gone." Serena combed through her long thick hair, wincing as she tugged the tangles free. "It's time I get back to work. I hope the laird won't be angry I overslept this morn."

"We sent a messenger. He'll think naught of it." Mother pulled out a bowl. "Would ye like somethin' to break yer fast? I was about to make fresh bread."

"'Twould take too long to make from scratch. I'll just have some of the strawberries."

"Serena, I wish ye'd wait one more day. It's a long walk to the castle."

"I'll be fine." Serena strolled to the table and grabbed a small basket of the ripe red fruit. "Where's Gunna?"

"At the loch washing clothes."

"Oh, I'll see ye both this evening." She slipped out before her mother could protest.

Serena hurried through the village greeting people as she passed. Her thoughts drifted to Iain MacBraigh, the new laird of Braigh Castle. When he took ownership six months past, he had inquired through the village for someone to run his household. Tomas had recommended her. As the laird had no wife and was a private sort of man who wouldn't be doing much entertainment, he didn't require her to live at the keep.

Serena's only concern in taking such a position were her horrible fits. The last thing she needed was to be discovered. People didn't understand and would say she was demon possessed as her own father had done. Her mother finally told her about the story of her birth when she turned ten and six a few years ago, but she'd refused to give his name. All Serena knew was that her mother had chosen the name of Boyd from distant relatives.

Something wet nudged her hand. Serena gasped and pulled her arm against her chest. She glanced down to see Phelan. The animal lifted his head against her. He was so large, he knocked her off-balance, causing her to sidestep. Serena laughed. "I suppose Mither got her way. So I'll have company on my walk after all."

Serena frowned, remembering what Gavin had said about Phelan's injury. One of his men had hit him in the head with a stick.

The dog's yellow eyes blinked, begging for affection. "Are ye all right, laddie?" She rubbed him between the ears. His tail wagged in happy satisfaction. Her fingers graced a raised knot. "Looks like we've both been recovering."

They walked in silence through the forest. As she left the woods, Serena took a deep breath smelling the salty sea. She climbed down the twelve-foot drop to where Braigh Castle was situated. Her head only hurt once and the pain soon went away.

Seagulls flew about and squeaked above her. Waves pounded the rocky cliffs below. White clouds drifted over the bright sun until it burst through again.

Phelan followed her to the castle gate. She turned and patted him on the head. "Thank ye for keeping me company and watching over me. Go back to yer master."

The black iron gate rolled up. The turning wheel squealed as the ropes wound around the pulleys. Serena stepped into the courtyard and waved at Philip, the gatekeeper. "Good morning!" The gate crashed to the ground behind her and rattled.

He secured the thick rope and hobbled over. A huge grin brightened his weather-worn face, bearing yellow-stained teeth. A full gray beard peaked to his chest. "Serena, I'm glad to see ye, lass." His warm brown eyes sparkled. "The laird was askin' 'bout ye a short while ago."

"Oh dear. Is he angry? I didn't intend to oversleep." She swallowed the rising concern. "I'd better get inside, posthaste."

"He didn't appear to be."

"I'd better hurry just the same." Serena waved a hand in the air.

She lifted the hem of her dress and ran to the side entrance. A quick search of the library, drawing room, and art room showed no recent trace of the laird. She paused, her hands on her hips, trying to imagine where he might be. Mayhap she would encounter him later.

Serena decided to begin her chores in the kitchen. She would check the inventory and determine if a trip to the market was needed.

As she walked down the servant staircase, she hummed a melody her mother used to sing to her. The winding steps narrowed toward the bottom, preventing her from viewing around the curve. She slid her hand along the stone wall, wishing for a rail.

At a long arched window, she couldn't help glancing out to view the glorious sea. Continuing on to the next step, Serena gasped as she landed on a moving object. She lost her balance and would have tumbled forward if sturdy hands hadn't grabbed her shoulders and held her upright.

"Steady, lass. 'Tis only me."

She glanced up to see Gavin grinning down at her. She realized her palms pressed against his chest where his fast-beating heart now pumped under her fingertips. Serena breathed in the scent of pine and heather as she struggled to gain her wits.

Heat flamed her neck and face until even the top of her head tingled with shame. Serena didn't want to look up and see his reaction to her blundering mishap, but how could she avoid it?

"Ye always seem to be rescuing me." She attempted a half-hearted laugh as she leaned back. Brilliant blue eyes stared at her. He tilted his head, attempting to see her better. An expression of concern lingered in his eyes.

Not wishing to be studied, Serena tried to wrench free of his hold, but he held her tight. He swayed on his heels and reached for the stone wall with one hand, while maintaining a grip on her with the other.

"Uh, lass, I canna move. Ye're standing on my feet."

"Oh!" Serena's hands flew to her mouth in horror. She tried to back up, but the previous step dug into her calf. Careful not to tip him, she stepped to the side, feeling quite awkward. She leaned back against the opposite stone wall. "I'm sorry. Why didn't ye say somethin' sooner? I feel mortified." No sense in trying to hide her humiliation now. Her actions were far beyond justification. To think she had been standing on the poor man's feet! She shoved the heel of her palm against her forehead.

"Mayhap, I liked having ye so close." Gavin shrugged, a mischievous grin curling his lips. "Or maybe I wanted to see how long it took before ye figured it out."

"Ye're incorrigible! What kind of evil mind lurks beneath that red head of yers?" In spite of everything, Serena smiled. After all, he had saved her from falling. "I hope I didn't bruise yer toes?"

"Not at all." He shook his head.

"Not a wee bit?"

"Should ye have stomped them, ye think?" Gavin grinned, revealing a row of white teeth.

She wondered if he used sage powder and minted herbs on his teeth. It was a simple trick her mother had taught her.

"I suppose not. Thank ye for saving me—again," Serena said. "I must get back to my duties." She moved down the steps.

"Ye work here?" He followed close behind.

"Aye." Serena kept her gaze ahead of her to ensure proper footing. No doubt, Gavin thought her unable of much without the need of being rescued. To him, she must be the most blundering lass in all of Scotland.

"What do ye do?"

"I keep the laird's castle running smoothly."

"Have ye been in the position long?" he asked.

"Nay. Only six months. I never worked for the former laird, Iain MacBraigh's late uncle."

"I see." Gavin kept pace with her. "Did ye know the late MacBraigh? How did he die?"

"I'd only seen him a few times. He kept to himself." They reached the bottom steps, which emptied into a dark hallway. "As to how he died, I've heard two conflicting stories. One is that he died peacefully in his sleep. The other is that someone pushed him down the stairs. I've never asked the laird. 'Twould be above my station."

Torch light lit the walls. The floor was made of uneven brick. Serena hated it as she found herself tripping quite often. She hoped she didn't sprawl in front of him. Whenever Gavin was around, it seemed quite possible that she would make a spectacle of herself.

"I meant to ask ye before, but how is yer head? Have the headaches ceased?"

"I'm fine." The innocent question should not have irritated Serena, but it reminded her of her secret fits. "Forgive me, but why were ye on that staircase in the first place? I was led to believe ye'd be working on the north wing, and mostly on the outer defenses."

"We are. My brother will be directing that construction. I'll be handling minor repairs to the rest of the castle. Iain asked me to view the kitchen while he and Leith take notes on the courtyard."

"But I thought ye were the one in charge?"

"Essentially, I am, but this whole endeavor is to give my younger brother experience and skills in a trade. As the eldest, I'll inherit my father's castle and lands, and will likely be the next chief of the MacKenzie Clan. Leith needs to be able to provide for his family."

Gavin MacKenzie was full of all kinds of surprises. She would never be a suitable match for Gavin. She had no dowery, proper education, or a respectable, well-known family with desirable connections. *Oh dear, where had that thought come from?*

"Ye're verra quiet." He leaned close. She backed away. "What's wrong? Did I say something offensive?"

"Nay! Of course not. I was just thinking how good of ye to help yer brother like that."

"There ye are!" Iain MacBraigh and Leith hurried toward them. "Philip told me ye'd arrived. I figured I might find ye down here. I didn't know when to expect ye back. I thought ye'd send another messenger." The tone of the laird's voice changed, and Serena braced herself for the chastisement she feared would come.

Gavin knew the moment fear skipped across Serena's face. Her innocent, green eyes widened and her mouth formed into a perfect circle, but no words came forth as she glanced between Iain and Leith and back at Gavin.

"Well, no matter," Iain grinned. "Ye're back now, and I admit, I'm relieved. Mayhap, ye can soon restore order."

Serena's tense expression eased and a deep breath gushed from her full pink lips. A smile surfaced, brightening her face, and warming Gavin's heart. He didn't know why, but this woman did strange things to his insides. She could make his heart beat as if he had fought off a swarm of swordsmen. There was a mystery about her and it made him curious.

"I'm much better. I assure ye." Serena twirled thick black strands of hair lying over her shoulder.

Gavin hadn't noticed the small action before. Was twisting her hair something she only did when nervous, or was there a real attraction toward Iain MacBraigh? Disappointment sliced through his gut, splitting Gavin's mind in conflicting directions.

"Glad to hear it. Yer welfare is under my authority. I've offered all the villagers sanctuary on my land—and that includes ye." Iain winked in a light-hearted tease. "I would do no less for any of the villagers."

The way Iain soothed her sensitive feelings gained Gavin's respect. Serena needed someone to look out for her. Why then, did it bother Gavin that Iain seemed so perfect for the role?

He swallowed. The dryness in his throat a sudden discomfort. Gavin covered his mouth and coughed.

Iain glanced over at him then back at Leith. He nodded, stepped from Serena, and lifted his hand toward the kitchen. "Don't overdo it on yer first day back."

"Aye, my laird." Serena dropped her gaze, dipped her head, and bent into a bow. She glided down the torch-lit hall, leaving an awkward emptiness in her wake.

Gavin cleared his throat, gaining Iain's attention. "The brick floor along this hallway is verra uneven and eroding from cold moisture. We could dig out a more level surface and replace it with new brick."

Iain walked around, testing the floor surface. He nodded. "Aye, it wouldn't make sense to do all the other repairs and leave this area in such a state." He took a deep breath. "Now gentleman, let us go discuss our business." He turned the corner and climbed the stairs Gavin and Serena had descended moments earlier.

Gavin turned to Leith. "It'll be good experience for ye to negotiate the restoration contract. I'll handle the rest regarding the protection of the castle and grounds." Gavin slapped his brother on the back in good-natured support.

"It's about time we get to business," Leith said, moving past him to follow Iain up the stairs.

"Ye're young and impatient," Gavin said.

"Ye sound too much like Da." Leith's voice echoed above him.

Gavin paused where Serena had stood on his feet. No doubt, the memory would bring a fond smile to him for days to come.

Out of curiosity, he leaned over to peer out the window to see what had beguiled Serena. "Mmm. She has an admirable appreciation for God's creation," he whispered. The sun cast shimmering crystals upon the ocean as it danced in calm swells where it met the sky in the distance.

"Gavin, are ye comin'?" Leith called.

"Aye!" Gavin took comfort that the winding staircase afforded him some privacy. The other men hadn't seen him gazing upon the morning sunshine like a romantic fool. He tore himself away from the scene and hurried up the steps, his boots pounding against the hard stone like a hammer.

"Ye sound like a herd stampeding the castle," Leith said, a grin upon his face as Gavin reached the landing. "What were ye doing down there?"

"Paying attention." Gavin met Iain's hazel eyes. "Sorry to keep ye waiting."

"I like a man who takes his time to get things right," Iain said. He pointed down a hall filled with paneled walls containing painted portraits of long ago Scots and candelabra between the gilded frames. "My study is this way."

Gavin and Leith walked into the room he motioned to while Iain closed the door behind them. On the far side, a double door opened to a library with several rows of bookshelves. A red tapestry with a gold crest in the center hung above a simple oak desk. A fireplace with a granite mantle faced the desk. Gavin liked the unique layout of the study. It must have been brilliant at one time.

"Would ye like a drink?" Iain asked from behind Gavin, as he opened a table cabinet filled with wine bottles and pewter goblets.

"Nay, but thank ye," Gavin said.

Leith shook his head, also declining the offer.

Iain poured himself a goblet of wine and carried it over to a side table in the corner. He pulled out a few parchments with drawings. "I had these drawn up. Moisture from the sea has corroded much of the outer wall, especially along here." He pointed to the first drawing of the entire castle. "The repair work will be dangerous. Ye need to be prepared. Ye could lose a couple of men to the rocky cliffs."

"We don't intend to lose any men, but we'll take every necessary caution," Leith said.

Gavin allowed his brother to take on the leadership role, while he remained quiet. As he listened, Gavin was quite proud of how well Leith handled himself. He asked excellent questions, gave practical guesses on supplies and the time frame to finish each task. Iain seemed comfortable discussing business with Leith, which also pleased Gavin.

Once things were final, Iain wrote up an agreement. Both Leith and Gavin read it before signing. The laird strolled over to his desk. He opened a drawer, pulled out a pouch, and tossed it to Leith. "Here is the advance we discussed and there is extra to cover the supplies."

While Leith counted the money, Gavin ambled over to the laird. "I'd like to ask ye something about the village, but I don't wish ye to take it the wrong way."

"Ahh, the Village of Outcasts, is it?"

"Aye. That's what I've been told." Gavin grinned. "I've met some interesting individuals. I'm not quite sure what to think. Is Serena the only villager who works at the castle for ye?"

"Philip, the gate keeper came from the village. Serena is the only one who travels back and forth. I offered her and her mother a chamber here in the castle, but they declined."

"She's heard the rumor that yer uncle was pushed down the stairs. Mayhap she's afraid to stay here."

"I wouldn't doubt it. They're verra superstitious. My uncle's accident happened while I was still in England. As soon as he wrote me, I came home." Iain ran a hand through his auburn hair. "When my uncle was dying, I promised him I'd take care of the village as he had always done. I'd forgotten how strange some of them were since I'd been away for so long."

"They're a wee bit different to be sure, but they seem harmless enough," Gavin said.

"Let's hope so." A worried frown marred Iain's smooth features. "Ye sound like Serena. The lass is forever defending the whole lot of them. She's different and doesn't belong among them. If it wasn't for the sane conversations I'm able to have with her, I think I'd have gone mad in this place these past six months."

"I was wondering about her. She doesn't seem to have any of the same issues plaguing the rest of the villagers. Why is she in the village? Where did she and her mither come from?"

A pensive look crossed Iain's face as he stared down at his desk. "I've been wondering the same thing myself. The lass is reserved and doesn't trust verra easy. I've questioned the other villagers about her, and none of them seem to know her history." Iain met Gavin's gaze. "If they do know, they're saying naught."

"They're loyal. Ye've got to admire their spirit," Gavin said.

"As long as it also extends to me." Iain pointed his thumb to his chest. "Now, let's discuss the investigation of my uncle's murder and how ye plan to provide protection without the villagers knowing it. I don't want them to worry."

4

$\mathcal{S}$erena rushed into the kitchen and pressed cool palms to her hot cheeks. While the laird had made her nervous about her position, Gavin's lingering presence had made her worse, even in the company of others. She forced slow breaths to calm her erratic heartbeat.

Standing on Gavin's feet…being so close to him on the stairs . . . everything about the whole incident heightened her awareness of the man in a new way. After today, she would forever think of him when she smelled the mixed scents of pine and heather, especially since she lived in an area where they were abundant.

"Serena?" Doreen peered at her in concern from where she chopped carrots at a center table. Heat blazed from the burning fireplace, and Doreen paused to wipe a few brown strands of hair from her eyes. The curls had escaped her white cap. "Ye look a fright. Did somethin' happen?"

"Nay." Serena shook her head and straightened her shoulders. "Merely thinking is all."

"Ye ran in here like ye were runnin' from the devil hi'self." Doreen blinked her brown eyes, watching Serena's reaction. "I couldn't help wonderin' if ye'd seen the handsome men visiting the laird." A slow smile curved her mouth. A line of sweat formed across her upper lip and upon her forehead.

"Aye." Serena averted her gaze and strode over to the pantry, taking mental note of the items needing replacement. "They assisted Mither and me home when I fell and struck my head the other day."

"Did one of them pick ye up and carry ye in 'is arms?" Doreen's face lit like a torch in a dark cave. "I think that would be most romantic, don't ye?"

"Mayhap, but I was unconscious." Serena raised an eyebrow and wondered if her cheeks looked as warm as they felt.

"Which one carried ye? One of the two brothers or one of the others?" Doreen laid down her knife and abandoned the carrots, turning toward Serena. "Tell me the rest. There's more isn't it?"

"Did ye hear aught of what I said?" Serena asked. "I was out. Missed the whole thing."

"Ye had to wake up, didn't ye? Don't pretend one of them didn't catch yer eye. I know better. I saw the two brothers a wee bit ago. They're quite handsome, they are."

"Lass, ye need to get those carrots in the pot before the stew cooks without 'em," Malvina hussled by, carrying a black iron pot to the huge fireplace where she hung it on a peg. She spared Serena a quick glance. "I see ye're back to distract the help 'round here." Malvina thrust her thick hands upon her plump hips and glared at Serena.

Her lips twitched as if she wouldn't be able to hold the angry pose much longer. Serena knew she wasn't really cross. Malvina enjoyed teasing Serena and Doreen whenever she got the chance. Unmarried and well into middle-age, Malvina had no family of her own, only distant relatives who lived elsewhere. She made cooking for the castle residents and visitors her life's ambition and took pride when her meals pleased others.

"Not at all." Serena fixed a determined expression and pointed at Malvina. "I'm here to help. What happened to the laird's meal this morn when he broke his fast?" Serena tilted her head and regarded the flustered look crossing her friend's face. "He was most displeased."

Malvina's round cheeks darkened and her breathing increased to a rapid pace. Her brown eyes transformed to black coal as she folded her arms over her chest. "And what might he be complaining 'bout? I provided everythin' to 'is likin' as usual."

Serena couldn't hold her mirth a moment longer. She burst into laughter and leaned her elbows on the counter. Doreen gasped as if she too had believed Serena. "I'm jesting. Ye have a temper worse than Beacon's."

"Aye, that ye do." Doreen nodded.

Malvina released a huge sigh, relaxing her shoulders. "Lass, ye're too cruel to play with an auld woman's feelings like that."

"Ye're not auld." Serena opened a cupboard and counted small baskets of beans. They had used two baskets while she was out. She leaned on her tiptoes to peer over the next shelf. One basket of peas was empty.

"Serena has an eye for one of the laird's visitors." Doreen scooped a handful of chopped carrots and tossed them in the pot over the fire. She glanced over her shoulder at Serena, a slanted grin marking her mischievous ploy.

Closing the cupboard, Serena whirled, crossing her arms over her chest. She had hoped to distract Doreen, but apparently she hadn't succeeded and now Malvina would join Doreen in taunting her.

"If ye must know, I stumbled upon Gavin MacKenzie on the stairs and in my blundering effort to escape him, trampled his feet. I canna imagine what the mon must think of me." Serena touched her hand to her forehead. The simple memory made her cringe.

"Well now, this puts a whole new perspective on things." Malvina tapped her chin in thought. "Ye're such a level-headed lass. I've never known anyone to gain yer favor." She shrugged. "Although I suppose ye haven't had much to choose from in the village."

"The two of ye have verra active imaginations. I'd venture that the poor mon fears for his safety when I'm around. I nearly knocked him down the stairs." Serena glanced from Malvina's wicked grin to Doreen's dreamy expression. She threw her hands up in surrender. "I'll finish the inventory later. Right now, I think I'll inspect the vegetable gardens."

"Ye know what I think?" Doreen's voice rose, reaching Serena at the door.

Curiosity lingered over her will to depart, and Serena paused at the threshold.

"If ye won't have enough faith to believe in what ye think is impossible, then God will have to bring ye a miracle to make ye believe."

"What do ye mean?" Serena tilted her head, regarding Doreen with speculation, but interested enough to listen.

"It's simple." Doreen shrugged. "Ye've just met a live saint— the kind ye didn't think existed—a mere mon. He's twice rescued ye. I daresay, ye'll be seein' more of him while he's here. I hope ye decide to make the most of it."

"I've no such intention." Serena turned and strode away.

"Consider yer future and that of yer mither's." Doreen's words echoed after her . . . mocking . . . digging into the private places of her heart as a haunting reminder that she would never be like the other lasses.

Gavin MacKenzie could never know her humiliating secret.

❦

After an eventful day at Braigh Castle, Gavin and Leith rode back toward camp. As the sun descended, a crisp chill floated through the air gently lifting off the sea. They climbed the steep twelve-foot hill at a steady pace.

"I'll have the men start with building scaffolds on the morrow," Leith said. "We'll need to finish the outside walls first, while we have warm summer days ahead."

"Aye." Gavin nodded. "When do ye plan to visit the town merchants for supplies?"

"In the next few days, as soon as I have the men settled in their assigned tasks. I canna afford to wait too long or they won't have aught to do." Leith crested the hill first. He glanced over his shoulder with a wide grin. "Look who we have here." He tilted his brown head forward.

Curiosity prompted Gavin to move his horse faster. His pulse quickened at the sight of Serena thirty paces ahead. She walked toward the village and twirled a long stick in her hand. Gavin paused to watch her. "Has she noticed us yet?"

"I don't think so." Leith shook his head, a mischievous glint in his eyes. "I'd sneak up on her if I didn't think the horses would give us away. I wonder what she would think if she knew we were watching?"

"No doubt, she'll know soon enough. We canna stay here like two sorry souls at the King's court gaping at a selection of bonny lasses." Gavin allowed his eyes to feast upon her. Serena's long black hair hung down her back like a velvet curtain over her tan cloak. She entered the forest path, the center of a scene with pine needle branches enveloping her.

"That may be what ye're doing, dear brother, but I intend to be a gentleman. I'll make my presence known and talk to the lass." Leith directed his horse into a trot.

Serena looked natural in any setting he'd seen her so far—at home in a wee cottage surrounded by poor villagers—even in a large castle among fine things. He'd rather see her as mistress of such a grand place, not a servant. She deserved better. Her speech and manners pointed at an education. Evelina as well.

He tried to imagine her sitting at his mother's place in the great hall of MacKenzie Castle. Gavin shook his head. What was he thinking?

As Leith approached her, Serena smiled up at him. They talked until Gavin caught up. Her smile faded. Disappointment loaded Gavin's chest like a pile of stones. Did she not welcome his presence? What had he done? The idea of her disliking him churned his stomach and unsettled him.

Sholto snorted and pawed the dust in restless protest, as if determined to gain her attention. It worked. Serena turned and grinned at the animal, reaching toward him.

"Ye might be careful," Gavin warned as Sholto pranced in place and snorted again. "He's a bit spirited right now."

The moment Serena touched him, he calmed. She rubbed the side of his neck and crooned into the beast's ear as if he were a human bairn.

"Nonsense, he only needs a wee bit of love and attention." Serena scratched him between the ears, and Sholto's tail swung in a circle, content and happy.

Gavin watched, certain if his horse had been a cat, he'd be purring. She had favor with animals, he'd give her that. If only he could find a way into her good graces as easily as Sholto.

"I've a mind to admit that Gavin has worked many hours with Sholto and tamed him when no one else could," Leith said. "But I've never seen the beast calm at a few simple words as ye've done this day."

"'Tis naught." She looked down and jabbed the stick in the dirt and twisted it.

"Why do ye carry a stick?" Gavin asked.

"Sometimes Phelan walks with me. If he doesn't, I carry a stick lest I'm suddenly attacked. It isn't much, but it affords me something beyond my own two hands."

"Allow me to take ye home. It's getting dark." Gavin held out his hand.

"Nay, but thank ye." She stepped back, shaking her head. "Ye've come to my aid many times in the last few days. I wouldn't want to start relying on ye. Where would that leave me after ye've finished the castle repairs and gone home?"

Gavin lowered his hand.

"But that's so far away." Leith leaned forward. "We could be here almost a year."

"I enjoy walking in the fresh air." Her moss-green eyes met Gavin's, and he recognized a will of fortitude.

"Ye can ride Sholto, while I walk beside ye." He hoped to tempt her with what she liked—his horse. She reached up and stroked the animal again. While Gavin was relieved that Serena appeared to consider the offer, it wounded his pride that she would only do so if he didn't ride with her.

Just when he thought she would accept, the stubborn woman shook her head and backed away. "Please, I prefer to walk alone as I always do."

"Verra well." Leith nodded. "We'd be honored to escort ye in the mornings, or give ye a ride—especially if it's raining."

"Think about it." Gavin wanted to keep trying, but he took his brother's cue and relented.

"Thank ye. Good day." She dismissed them with a brief curtsy.

They rode in silence for a while, waiting until they were out of hearing. After rounding a corner, Leith glanced over his shoulder and cleared his throat. "With the exception of Lesley, I've never seen ye so taken before. She's comely and bright to be sure, but there's the question of her lineage and station."

"Don't fash yerself, Leith." Gavin sounded harsher than he intended. "I'm quite aware of what Da would say. But yer concern isn't warranted. I get the impression that Serena has no desire for me—at least not in that way. "

A scream echoed through the woods. Gavin straightened as he calmed Sholto. Female weeping followed. Gavin's blood raced. It didn't sound like Serena, but a strong desire to go back and see to her safety seized him.

"It's from up ahead," Leith said. "Come on. We might be of help."

"Ye go. I canna leave Serena unprotected in these woods." Gavin turned his horse. "I'm goin' back for her."

"Good idea." Leith charged forward, stiring up a cloud of dust behind him.

Gavin rode Sholto until he saw Serena walking with her stick. He slowed as she glanced up at his approach, an uncertain expression in her green eyes. Serena shivered.

"What was that?" She rubbed Sholto on the neck. Her hand trembled. "I thought I heard a scream."

"Ye did." Gavin grabbed her hand, leaned over, and met her gaze. "I've come back for ye. An' this time I won't leave without ye. These woods are too dangerous."

"What happened?"

"I'm not sure. Leith went on to check it out. We'll likely see for ourselves in a wee bit." Gavin offered her his arm. "Grab on. I'll pull ye up."

At first he thought she would refuse, but then she closed her eyes and clutched him. He lifted her and she gasped as she settled behind him. Her arms wrapped around his middle. He liked having her next to him—mayhap too much.

Gavin nudged Sholto forward. He galloped toward the sound of a weeping lass bent over a dead cow. She lifted her tear-stained brown eyes, her dark hair fell over her shoulder.

"'Tis Lavena!" Serena said.

Leith had dismounted and bent examining the animal. The blood still oozed to the ground, a recent kill.

"My sister didn't get around to her chores this morn, so I offered to help her this evenin'. We needed the milk. I couldn't find her an' now I know why." Lavena's lower lip trembled and fresh tears filled her eyes. "Who could do such a horrible thing? We depend on our animals. We don't have much as it is."

"Could it have been Quinn's wolf?" Gavin asked.

"Nay." Leith stood and stepped back, pointing at the carcass. "Look at the wound. The cut is smooth and clean. Only a sword or a dagger could have done that. Whoever it was didn't steal this animal for food or profit or they wouldn't have left it here." Leith met Gavin's gaze. "The question is—why?"

ℒ♥

Serena stepped into the small, humble home she had come to cherish over the years. Relief filled her aching muscles as she pulled off her cloak with a sigh. Her first day working back at the castle had tired her more than she thought it would, but the murdered cow had shaken her even more.

"Here she is." Tomas stood from the wooden chair he'd been sitting in at the table.

Her mother bent over an iron pot hanging from the hearth, stirring. Gunna stood kneading dough on the other side of the table from Tomas. The aroma of rabbit stew lifted in the air, a musky scent mixed with onions, carrots, and spinach leaves. Any other time she would welcome the smell, but for the moment, her stomach rolled.

"Did ye bring us another rabbit, Tomas?" Serena asked, hanging her cloak on a peg by the door.

"Aye." Her mother straightened, rubbing her hand on her lower back. "And a good thing he did or else we'd have no meat with our vegetable stew this night."

"I went hunting this afternoon with Quinn and Beacon. Surviving their boasting was quite an adventure. I thought the two of them would scare away the prey before they stopped arguing over who would bring back the most meat."

Glad to free her mind from the recent troubles, Serena grinned. The two behaved more like brothers, fighting one minute and planning events the next. She had no doubt they'd defend each other to the death.

"I caught two rabbits, I did. And I thought to myself," Tomas touched a finger to the side of his head, "who would enjoy such a fine feast and be so kind as to share their even finer cooking? That's when I thought of the three of ye." He bent in a mock bow, dipping his chin where she could no longer see his gray eyes. A thin layer of brown hair on his head reminded Serena of the peaches a peddler once brought to the village.

"Serena, I believe yer advice to Gavin about Quinn helped him handle things peacefully," Tomas said.

"Dearie me, but she preaches to all of us, ye know." Gunna covered the dough biscuits in the oven pan and carried them to the fireplace.

"That's not true. I merely give a wee bit of advice when it's needed." Serena clenched her fists at her side and pretended to glare at the sweet woman she thought of as a grandmother. "What can I do to help?"

"Ye can pour that pitcher of water over my hands outside. They need washing." Gunna headed for the door.

"And when ye finish that, ye can set the table. I think the rabbit stew is about done," Mother said.

Serena grabbed the soap and pitcher and followed Gunna out. A nip in the air made her shiver without her cloak. The skyline looked like a dark gray canvas with sparkling jewels. It was rare that clouds didn't congregate above them, hiding the stars.

"I think Father Tomas is verra lonely," Gunna said as Serena poured water over her hands. She lathered the soap and scrubbed the dough off with expert force. "I wonder if he ever regrets giving his vows to the church, especially after the way they treated him—sending him here."

"Well, I'm glad they sent him here. He's one of the best things that ever happened to our village," Serena said. "Although, I'm sorry he now has a speech problem when he's nervous and that's why he lost his other church."

"Loneliness has it's own grief." Gunna's voice faded as she paused. Serena knew she was thinking of her own dear husband, dead two years before Serena's birth.

"Let's not dwell on the past." Serena laid a hand on her shoulder. "Mither and Tomas are waiting."

"Aye, that they are."

To Serena's relief, Gunna's tone brightened in an instant. Serena disliked it when Gunna became distressed. It was like her own heart wept with her. Serena ushered her inside. "Warm yer hands by the fire, Gunna. It's cold out."

Gunna hobbled over to the fire.

Serena allowed her gaze to stray to Gunna's bulky form, her gray bun such a familiar and dear sight. The back of Serena's throat stung with the realization that Gunna was getting on in years and might not be with them much longer. Serena's heart swelled and tightened.

"Hurry, Serena. I've already flipped the bread cakes for Gunna," Mither said.

Launching into action, Serena dismissed her wayward thoughts. "I ran into Gavin MacKenzie and his men at the castle." Serena left out the part about actually running into Gavin and landing on his toes. She set out the wooden bowls and spoons, while her mother filled them with stew.

"Father Tomas, I'm sorry but water is all we have to offer." Gunna poured water into the cups.

"Ye know perfectly well that is fine by me." He rubbed his belly. "I feel blessed the three of ye took pity on me and let me have a wee bit of that delicious stew I've been smelling for the past hour."

Serena handed Tomas a warm bread cake. "And we enjoy the entertaining conversation."

"Oh, dearie me!" Gunna gasped, setting down the water. "Look what I've gone and done." She set the cup she had spilt upright. Water soaked the wood and leaked through the cracks onto the dirt floor.

"Don't worry, Gunna." Serena grabbed a nearby towel hanging on a wall peg and mopped up the access water. "I'll take care of it."

"I canna see like I used to." Gunna wrung her hands together and side-stepped from one foot to the other.

"Come, Gunna. Ye need to rest awhile. Ye've been up on yer feet far too long." Mother pulled out a chair and gestured to it.

Sighing, Gunna settled in the seat. She shook her head in disbelief. "I didn't used to be so awkward." She looked at Tomas. "I'm afraid I'm more of a bother than a help these days."

"There comes a time to be served. Ye've spent all yer years serving these two. Let them return the favor. It'll make them feel good," Tomas said.

"I agree with Tomas." Mother poured more water in Gunna's cup.

Serena sat across from Tomas, while her mother faced Gunna. They bowed their heads and closed their eyes. In silence she gave thanks for holding her tongue about the murdered cow. Gunna didn't need the stress.

"Father, thank ye for this meal and the friends we have. Please bless this family with yer protection, provision, and wisdom. In Jesus' name."

"Amen," everyone said together.

Tomas dug his spoon into the stew. He chewed and swallowed. "Gavin tells me he and his men will be attending kirk this Sunday. 'Twill be nice to have some visitors again. I only hope I don't shake and blunder my words."

"Even if ye do, I doubt they'll think much of it. They've already met most of the villagers. Surely, one more oddity will not alter their opinion." Mother sipped her water.

"Aye, but it was definitely enough to keep me out of the pulpit elsewhere, wasn't it?" Tomas raised a dark brow.

"But not here." Mother leaned forward and tapped a finger on the table. "This place has been our sanctuary in the Highlands all these years and likely will be. I think of it as God's saving grace—a holy place He's gifted to us and no one else."

Tomas linked his fingers. "Evelina, ye put too much value on a place. Our home here could be invaded as well as any other." Tomas shook his head. "Nay, this village isn't yer sanctuary from the cruel world. It's God Almighty. He's the only one who can protect ye. Change is comin'. The strangers who have come to restore Braigh Castle are proof enough. We must be strong in our faith."

"Which is why I wish they would all leave." Serena let her spoon drop against her bowl. "The whole lot o' them."

"Ye don't mean that." Mother turned to her. "Gavin and Leith MacKenzie have been verra attentive to ye."

"I do mean it, and I wish they wouldn't."

"Dearie me, lass, ye sound bitter." Gunna propped her elbow on the table and leaned her cheek on her palm. "If ye ask me, I think Gavin has taken quite a likin' to ye. He keeps comin' by to check on ye."

"Aye. He seems to stare at ye a great deal." Mother nodded. "And it would be a long-awaited answer to my prayers."

"Mither! How could ye?" Serena sat back in her chair and folded her arms. "What kind of life could I possibly have with a man like Gavin MacKenzie after he discovers my fits? If he doesn't think I'm demon-possessed, most likely his family and neighbors will."

"There are plenty of families and neighbors here who know. I believe God has a mate for ye, lass. Ye must have faith. Gunna and I won't live forever. I don't want ye to be alone."

"I won't be alone. I have the villagers. Mither, please, I couldn't take it if Gavin were to discover my secret and think evil of me. I'd rather die!" Serena stood. Her chair swayed. She strode over, grabbed her cloak, and ran outside.

5

As Gavin and Leith approached camp, scattered fire pits looked like orange globes against the dark. The smell of burning wood and peat moss teased Gavin's senses, while roasting meat turning on a spit churned his stomach in hunger and made his tongue ache for a taste.

Men's voices carried in soft tones, mingling with the nightly sounds of nature and crackling fires. The horses Gavin and Leith led breathed heavy like a continuous sigh. Their hooves clopped against the hard ground as if their legs were too heavy to lift.

"Is it ye, Gavin? Leith?" One man turned toward them.

"Aye," Leith answered. "What a day we've had, but first I want somethin' to eat. I'm starving."

"We went hunting and have some venison." Craig said, falling into step beside them. "One of the canvas tents the giant nearly destroyed has been repaired."

"How?" Gavin studied his friend in the firelight. "I thought they were beyond repair."

"Turns out one was. The village seamstress offered to work on it today. I believe her name is Kyla. That's all she would tell me. A strange creature, she is, but verra skilled with a needle and thread."

"Aye. I've met her." Gavin nodded. "When I was looking for Tomas. She wasn't overly friendly, but I hear she's a widow still grieving for her husband and bairn she lost to the fever last year."

"I suppose that would explain the sadness surrounding her," Craig said.

Gavin moved toward the fire as the men stepped aside to clear space for him. He held his hands out, seeking warmth. The flames didn't disappoint, warming his hands as well as the front of his body. He'd have to be careful not to burn his tunic or plaid.

"Will one of ye see that our horses are rubbed down and given water?" Leith asked, joining Gavin.

"Aye, I'll take care of it." A lad hurried over and led both animals by the reins.

"About time the two of ye got back. We were wondering if something happened. The place 'round here is a wee bit strange, ye know." Roan folded his thick arms over his chest, a firm expression marring his forehead. The thick red beard and mustache covering the lower half of his face glowed in the firelight, illuminating his frown.

"Something did happen," Gavin raised an eyebrow before launching into the tale of the murdered cow.

"Why would someone waste a good animal like that?" Roan asked. "At least when men reave cattle, it's with the intention of using the animals, not wasting them out of spite."

"Aye," Gavin nodded. "The poor lass was beside herself. We took her back to her da, but the man is deaf. 'Twas verra difficult to talk with him."

Craig brought some meat to Gavin and Leith. It was warm and tender, fresh from the flames. As soon as he took a bite, juice burst upon Gavin's tongue. Some of the other men had left the other fires and gathered around to hear the tale.

Leith swallowed and raised a finger. "The worst part is they've never had this happen before, so the cobbler immediately suspected us." The men murmured among themselves in anger. "Gavin and I proved we were on the way back from the castle and came upon Serena Boyd. But then he asked about the rest of ye."

"That's foolish!" One man yelled from the back.

Conversations buzzed. Gavin gulped water from his flask, washing down the meat. He wiped the back of his hand across his lips and replaced the top on the container, looping it back on his belt. His plaid shifted on his shoulder. He adjusted it as he listened to the mounting comments stirring from their wounded pride.

He lifted two fingers to his lips and blew a warning whistle. Their conversations instantly dissolved. Gavin held up his palms, motioning for them to listen.

"The cobbler's response is warranted. This has never happened before. Suddenly a group of strangers arrive and this happens. I'd be questioning the same thing. Did any of the villagers go hunting with ye?"

"Nay," Craig answered.

"Who stayed behind?" Gavin scanned the group of ten raised hands. "Were any of the villagers here?"

"The woman who sewed the canvas tent. She brought another lass with her," Roan said.

"A blind lass and the dwarf," another man said.

"From the time these villagers left, how long was it before dark?" Gavin asked, rubbing his eyebrows. He needed to find a way to cover his men from possible accusations.

"About an hour," Craig said. "Maybe a wee bit more. Gavin, do ye think that's sufficient enough to prove our innocence?"

"Don't know." Gavin stroked his chin in thought. "While the deed of killing the cow wouldn't take long, walking from here to there and back again would."

"Tomas stopped by as well. He was carrying two rabbits with him," Roan said. "He escorted the seamstress home. The dwarf took the blind lass."

"Even though no one has ever murdered a cow before, we're here to protect the villagers and the castle," Craig said. "Wouldn't the laird know we're innocent?"

"Aye, but the villagers wouldn't," Gavin said. "Since Iain isn't sure who in the village he can trust and who is in danger, we're going to have to keep quiet about our other purpose for being here a while longer."

"I think we have enough witnesses for today," Leith said.

"I agree." Gavin nodded. "But from now on we've got to be careful."

"Other than the laird, looks like we aren't welcome 'round here," Roan said.

"True. We aren't strange enough," said another.

Some men laughed.

"I say we find the person that did this before worse happens," Leith said. "The culprit is likely to strike again, but I canna understand why. What would someone gain from torturing these poor souls?"

"Murduring the elder MacBraigh makes sense if someone besides Iain believes he has a chance to inherit. Iain says he has a cousin who contested his uncle's will, but he didn't succeed."

"But no one stands to gain naught from these poor villagers," Craig said.

"Let's set the bait." Leith grabbed Gavin's shoulder. "When we're all in kirk on Sunday, leave a few men behind to scope out the village. 'Twould be the perfect opportunity for the guilty to do something."

⊱❧

Serena sat on the wooden church pew between Gunna and her mother, wishing for a feathered pillow under her backside. She shifted to ease the pressure. The bench creaked as if the wood were splitting in two. Her neck and face burned as all three of the cobbler's daughters turned to glance at her. She offered a smile to recompense for her disturbance. One by one they turned around.

Determined to pay better attention to the sermon, Serena fixed her gaze upon Tomas as he stood at the pulpit, facing their small congregation. He wore his usual brown robe with a rope cord tied around his waist. Light from the candles reflected off his balding head when he looked down at his notes.

"By grace we are saved through faith. Not by our power, but as a gift from God." Tomas held out his hand as if he were handing them a gift.

Gunna's chin dropped to her chest. Loud snoring erupted from her throat. Her mother spiked her elbow into Serena's arm. Knowing what she wanted, Serena poked Gunna in the side. Gunna awakened, swallowing and making a hissing sound.

Serena bit her bottom lip to hide a smile. She fixed her mind on Tomas and what he was saying. "Think of yer faith as a shield when evil attacks come against ye."

An image of Gavin MacKenzie came to mind as she thought of the shield she had seen hanging from his horse. Was he an evil threat against their village? By all appearances, he and his men seemed friendly, but what would happen once they spread the news of their strange village to people in their clan?

Her skin crawled with a shiver of fear. She wished they had never come.

The door burst open in the back and footsteps walked across the wooden floor, causing the boards to creak. The cobbler's daughters turned. Other heads whirled. Tomas's voice faded to stunned silence as he raised his head with wide eyes. His mouth dropped open.

Unable to ignore her curiosity, Serena glanced over her left shoulder. Gavin pointed his men to the empty pews in back. Once they were out of seats, the rest of them lined up against the wall to stand like an army guarding the congregation. She gulped, certain this wasn't the sort of shield God had intended for their small village. If anything, these men were strangers, a possible enemy for all they knew.

"W-welcome," Tomas said, reverting to his speech problem.

Serena clenched her teeth. Poor Tomas hadn't stammered through the whole sermon, until now. She glared at Gavin. He stood with his back to the wall, his hands folded in front. His red hair looked wet from a recent wash, the layered strands combed back from his face and down his neck. A few wayward curls hung over his forehead to the side. His striking height and broad shoulders once again reminded her of a shield. He wore a sea-colored tunic and matching plaid across his shoulders.

Gavin's gaze met hers. A slow smile curled his lips as he nodded in silent greeting. Serena's breath gushed in a sudden gasp. Not only had he caught her staring at him, but she had been thinking how handsome he was in spite of how he didn't belong there among them. A pool of warmth bubbled in the top of her stomach and fluttered up to her chest. Afraid he would see her blush, Serena faced the front.

Candle flames shimmered against the ceiling beams, much like the erratic pulse in her veins. Tomas stammered through the rest of his sermon, sparking her compassion. The situation only served to heighten her resistance to the strangers. Twice, she said a silent prayer of forgiveness. The first one was for not paying attention. The second one was for disliking the warriors and wanting them gone.

"Dearie me, but the whole lot o' them takes up the entire sanctuary," Gunna whispered aloud in Serena's ear as she glanced from side to side.

Serena nodded in agreement, not wanting to encourage further conversation while Tomas bowed his head in a closing prayer. She lowered her head and closed her eyes. One of the men broke into a fit of coughing and she missed most of the prayer.

". . . please protect and keep our visitors s-safe as they work to re-s-store Braigh Castle. In Jesus' name. Amen."

Serena lifted her head and watched Tomas in disbelief. He offered a warm smile as he stepped from behind the pulpit. What about the villager's safety? Most likely they would need protection from all the new strangers among them, rather than the other way around.

"By the way," Tomas raised his voice over the noise of people greeting each other and moving about. "Today we're having a pig roast at Quinn and Beacon's cottage. All our visitors are welcome to join us."

While she knew Tomas had done the right thing by inviting the MacKenzie men, Serena still wished he would use a bit of caution. Just because everyone else planned to go didn't mean they had to.

"I'm looking forward to an afternoon of fellowship and great food." Her mother stood. "No cooking this evening. Won't that be a treat, Gunna?"

Serena's words of protest died on her tongue.

"What?" Gunna wrinkled her brow and cupped her ear.

Serena's mother repeated herself, louder, as others filed into the center aisle.

"Allow me." Gavin appeared by Gunna's side holding out his elbow.

He winked at Serena. She pressed her lips together and looked elsewhere to avoid succumbing to his charm. He was only here for a short while. Heartache lay on the other side of risking her heart. She wanted no part of it.

✍

Something charged at the kirk door and rattled the building so hard it sounded like it would come right through. Gavin braced himself as several women screamed in fright. Men murmured and stunned expressions were exchanged among the congregation.

"What was that?" Leith stepped around Kyla and wiggled the latch. It was unlocked, but wouldn't open. He shoved his shoulder against the wood door. "We're barred in somehow."

Serena's breath hitched in her throat as she turned to Gavin. He tried to mask his confusion. Serena bit her bottom lip and twisted her hair around her finger in a nervous habit. "Could a large tree have fallen across the front entrance?"

"Mayhap," he said, unwilling to say anything further until he knew more. This wasn't what they had in mind when they decided to set this trap. And where were the men they left behind? Could someone have gotten to them as well?

"What's that smell?" Cara's voice carried above the grumbling murmurs throughout the sanctuary. "Something's burnin'!"

"She's right." Leith dropped to his knees. "There's a wee bit of smoke floating under the door."

Several women screamed in alarm. Other men rushed at the door. People moved in every direction.

"There's no windows." Rosheen pressed herself against the wall. "How will we breathe until we're rescued?"

Lavena went over to comfort her.

"Where is Quinn when we need 'im?" Birkita asked.

"We're in a bad way, aren't we?" Gunna looked at Serena, her eyes misting.

"We'll be fine, Gunna. Ye'll see." Serena clutched her arm, looking up at Gavin for confirmation.

"Aye, we've enough strong men to break through the door." Gavin assured her. "If the women and children will move to the other end at the pulpit, we can use one of the pews to bust through the door." Gavin raised his voice to be heard above the chaos.

"An excellent idea!" Father Tomas waved them toward him. "Come! This way."

The men rocked a pew until they ripped it from where it was nailed to the floor. They carried it up the center aisle. "All right, men," Gavin said. "On three. One. Two. Three!" They charged down the aisle. The pew cracked the door, but didn't break it. "Again!"

"I hear Phelan barking," Carla said.

"Then Quinn must be coming," Birkita said.

"Again!" Gavin directed the men forward.

"They better hurry." Gunna coughed. "The smoke is gettin' thicker."

"Ladies, let's pray," Father Tomas said, leading them in the Lord's Prayer.

The door gave way, splitting in two, revealing a wagon of burning hay that had been rammed at the front entrance. The wooden steps were broken and had taken the brunt of the blow. Phelan continued barking as Quinn shoved a plank from beneath the back wheels. "Hurry!" Quinn yelled. "Two MacKenzie men went for a couple of barrels of water I'd saved for the feast. We've got to keep the kirk from catching fire."

With the plank discarded, Quinn pulled the wagon away. While people escaped, the other two MacKenzie men who had not attended kirk returned with barrels of water on a small cart. They dumped it on the fire and wet their plaids to beat out the rest of the small flames. Within moments, the fire smoldered to ashes. They had saved the kirk and everyone's lives.

"Who would do such a thing?" Serena asked her mother once they were outside, breathing fresh air.

"I know not." Evelina shook her head, a sad expression lingering in her eyes.

"We have much to celebrate and be thankful for," Tomas said. "Let's go to Quinn's cottage and have our feast as planned."

"Someone just tried to murder the whole village," Kyla said, pulling her plaid tight around her shoulders, an angry glare in her eyes.

"But they didn't succeed, and we shouldn't let them. We canna allow fear to rule us. That's what they intended— to frighten us." Tomas looked at his congregation. "If they intended real harm, they would have set larger fires all around the kirk ensuring no escape."

"Tomas is right," Gavin spoke up. He looked at Quinn and the two men who had not attended kirk. "Did any of ye see aught?"

They shook their heads.

"We heard the wolf," one of them said.

"Aye." Quinn nodded. "I knew his bark was different this time. I left Beacon to tend to the roasting pigs and came to see what was wrong."

"I agree with Tomas," Gavin said, waving everyone toward Quinn. "Let's go have our feast."

As the others griped, but fell into step behind Quinn, Gavin grabbed the two men who weren't in kirk. "Where were the two of ye? What were ye doing while someone was ramming a wagon on fire into the kirk?"

"Ye said to check out the villagers that were left behind. We were in the woods watching Quinn and Beacon. Whoever did it, we can assure ye it wasn't them," one man said while the other nodded.

"Fine. Go with the others." Gavin rubbed his neck as he took a lingering look at what almost happened. "Lord, thank ye for protecting us all. Help us find out who is doing this. Reveal him to us. Give me wisdom in how to catch this person and how to protect these people. In Jesus' name. Amen."

He arrived at Quinn's cottage where two pigs churned on a spit over a fire. A couple of the village fiddlers perched on logs and belted out a lively ditty. Gavin watched as sad faces glanced around them in worry. It might take a while for them to get in a cheerful mood.

Quinn related the fire incident to Beacon, who paced in angry strides.

"Lads, the women and children are quite shaken. We need to show them a good time and get their minds off what happened," Tomas said. "Go find a partner."

A few minutes later, Beacon swung around in a circle, half-skipping and hopping with Rosheen. For a short lass, she shadowed him by more than a foot. The sight amused Gavin. He grinned as their free spirit soon spread to others. Soon Gavin's hand tapped his thigh in rythym to the fiddles.

Craig held Cara's hand and they joined in the dancing. She stared outward holding onto him, trusting his lead.

"Looks like people are beginning to recover." Leith stepped beside him. "I intend to find me a young lass to dance with and make merry."

"Be careful, Leith." Gavin warned. "Ye aren't home and the lasses here aren't used to yer charming ways."

"I'll be a perfect gentleman. Ye have my word." Leith grinned, spreading a hand over his heart in a gesture of good faith.

"Ye'd better." Gavin gripped his brother's shoulder. "In the meantime, I have my eye on a lass I've been hoping will agree to dance with me."

"Serena Boyd, no doubt?" Leith raised a dark eyebrow. "I'm surprised ye've waited this long. Better hurry. I think ye may soon have some competition." Leith nodded in the direction behind Gavin.

Iain MacBraigh rode up on a brown stallion. The animal looked to be the best piece of horse flesh he'd seen since they'd come to Caithness. People paused to stare. Gavin could only assume his appearance at such an event was rare in the village.

Iain dismounted and glanced in Serena's direction before striding over to Gavin and Leith. "Father Tomas told me about today's feast. I hoped to make it to kirk this morn, but I had a new foal born. I didn't like the idea of spending the rest of the afternoon alone."

"Loneliness has a way of eating at a man." Gavin nodded in understanding. "It can fill him with depressing thoughts that torment his soul."

"That's easy to fix." Leith beamed with confidence. "Find a bonny lass and dance."

Iain leaned over and patted Leith's arm. "Excellent advice, my friend." He looked around. "Serena doesn't seem to be taken. Mayhap she'll oblige me." He straightened his back, squared his shoulders, and took a deep breath. "Wish me luck, friends."

Gavin folded his arms as he watched Iain approach Serena. His gut twisted in regret that he hadn't acted sooner. "I'll wish ye no such thing," he muttered in a lowered tone.

"Ye waited too late, Gavin." Leith clucked his tongue, swinging his head from side to side.

"Aye." Gavin rubbed his chin. "Iain's the laird and her boss. 'Twill be hard for Serena to say nay to him, but she canna dance every song with him."

6

Serena could feel Gavin's gaze upon her as Iain swung her around to the fiddler's tune. While Gavin's red locks shone bright in the sun, Iain's auburn hair was a shade darker, matching his hazel eyes. He wore a mustache and no beard.

It felt strange to be dancing with the man she worked for, but he seemed not to notice as he laughed and enjoyed himself. They had little opportunity to talk as the rhythym kept them hopping to the beat. By the end of the dance, her heart pounded and she struggled to catch her breath. She touched her hand to her chest as she stepped to the side.

"Would ye like to continue on with the next dance?" Iain asked.

"Nay." Serena clutched her stomach. "I'd like to rest for the moment and mayhap I'll dance again later."

"If ye're quite certain?" Iain raised an eyebrow.

"I am." Serena nodded. "Thank ye for being an excellent partner."

Iain bowed and turned to ask Birkita for the next dance. She smiled and nodded.

Someone held out a wooden goblet of mead in front of Serena. She accepted the drink and glanced over her shoulder to see Gavin smiling down at her. "I thought ye could use this."

"Thank ye." She took a sip, letting the liquid burn down her parched throat. "Why haven't I seen ye dance?"

He glanced down at his feet and smiled, as if hiding something.

"Come now, Gavin. Surely ye can dance?" She laughed. "I canna imagine the next clan chief of the MacKenzies unable to dance a simple country dance."

"The truth, Serena?"

"Aye, sir." She nodded. "Confess the truth."

"I've been waiting," his blue gaze captured hers, "for ye."

How prophetic she could have taken that statement—after all, Leith had said Gavin was a score and ten years. Why had he waited so long to marry? What harm could it hurt to pretend for an hour that she was Gavin's divine appointment? Afterward, their lives would go in their separate directions once again.

But for now, she could pretend. Dream . . . that she was normal.

"Then I daresay yer wait is over." She took another swallow of the mead and set it down on a nearby table. "For on this day, I've decided I shall forget all of life's unkindnesses and enjoy myself."

"Don't worry. We'll figure out who blocked us all in the kirk and set fire to the wagon."

Serena nodded, content to let him believe she referred to the kirk accident. Instead, her mind drifted to that overcast day when she was eight and they were in Braighwick for supplies. A woman had been condemned as a witch, tied to a stake, and set on fire. Her mother had hidden Serena's eyes, but she couldn't stop the heart-wrenching screams, which continued to haunt Serena through adulthood.

In that moment, her faith that God would save and protect her vanished. He would no more save her than he had that woman. That was why her mother had moved her to the village and wouldn't allow anyone to know about her fits. The villagers didn't discover her secret until she had a fit in front of them during one of her fittings with Kyla when she was ten and three.

If her mother truly trusted God to take care of them, Serena knew she wouldn't be so fearful and dependent upon the sanctuary of their village. Serena feared a similar fate as that woman, and she'd do everything in her power to keep hidden and stay safe.

The current song ended. Gavin held his hand out to her and smiled. Serena placed her small hand in his, determined she would make enough memories of this day to last her a lifetime. It was the best she could ever do under the circumstances.

His warm hand circled hers in swaddled security, leading her to the line with the others. The fiddlers began a new song. Someone kicked off the dance with a loud yelp and everyone moved at the same time.

Gavin swung her around to face him and grabbed both her hands as their feet kicked and their bodies moved and swayed around the circle with other dancers.

Serena loved these gatherings in her village. Very few rules existed with the exception of having fun. Of course, they rarely had so many young men. Gavin and his warriors changed things—for her he changed everything.

She had never known a man to make her heart race or the blood pound in her head the way Gavin did. Since his arrival, she found herself more self-conscious of her blundering behavior, the condition of her windblown hair, and what he thought of her. No one else's opinion mattered as much, not even Iain's, except where her work was concerned.

Caught up in the delight of the moment, Serena swung on Gavin's arm and leaped in the air at the same time as the other women. He laughed as she bounced back into the fold of his arms. Together, they moved in harmony, lithe and free. She had never enjoyed herself so much. Gavin had a way of making her feel comfortable as he encouraged her into trying new steps in the next dance.

Serena didn't want to stop, but she was parched. When Gavin finally led her to the side, he didn't let go of her hand as Iain had done. He stared down at her, his blue eyes crisp and full of brightness that seemed to echo right into her very heart.

"Ye're an excellent dancer," he said. "I count myself most fortunate to be one of yer partners."

"And because of today's feast, I'll accept yer flattery." She smiled, aware that the pad of his thumb now circled over the top of her hand.

"Gavin!" Iain strode up. "Father Tomas told me about the kirk incident."

"Aye." Gavin nodded. "Serena, I enjoyed dancing with ye, but I regret that duty now calls."

"I understand." She turned to go, but Gavin didn't yet relinquish her hand. Instead, he lifted her fingers to his lips and placed a kiss upon the top of her knuckles and bowed. "Thank ye, my lady."

Her heart swelled with tenderness for this man. He knew very well that she wasn't a proper lady, but he understood that she had wanted to pretend just this once—and he had joined her in the the game—because he understood her.

Gavin told Iain all he knew about the fire at the kirk and then relayed the cow murder incident. Leith had joined them in Iain's library.

"I don't understand why someone would do this against the villagers." Iain shook his head as he paced in front of the unlit fireplace. "It doesn't make sense. What would anyone gain by it?"

"That's why we're so addled," Leith said.

"Do ye know if any of the villagers have enemies in the town of Braighwick? Mayhap someone from there could be doing all these strange things." Gavin peered at Iain, hoping something would bring about his memory. He crossed his booted ankle over his knee.

"I confess. I don't know as much about the villagers as I probably should," Iain said, rubbing his mustache in thought. "We may have to take Father Tomas into our confidence. I canna think of anyone who would know more about them."

"All right," Gavin said. "We'll visit him on the morrow." He cleared his throat. "What about this cousin who tried to dispute yer uncle's will? Do ye think it would benefit us to meet him?"

"Aye, he wrote a letter chastising me for not introducing him to the heir of Clan MacKenzie." Iain leaned his elbow on the mantle. "I suppose I'll have to invite them over."

"Does he live close enough to send someone to the village to do these things?"

"But why would he? It's my estate and castle he wants. What would the villagers have that he could possibly want?" Iain raised his hands and began pacing again. "Hogan Lennox is the Earl of Caithness. He already has a sizeable estate, but he only has a cozy stone manor. A castle like Braigh would make him look even more mightier than he already is."

"Granted, the issue with yer cousin could be unrelated to what is happening to the villagers." Leith scratched the side of his dark head. "I'm only sorry the two who stayed behind didn't see aught."

"'Twas an excellent plan, Leith," Gavin said. "We canna get discouraged and give up. The answers are somewhere around us. We must find them."

"The villagers may be a wee slow, but they aren't complete simpletons," Iain said. "They are bound to know something is going on by now—and mayhap frightened. And they have every right to be."

"We could station a few men to stay in the village on rotation." Leith leaned forward, elbows on his knees, and linked his hands. "That might ease their fears and instill a little more security. The rest would be here working on the castle and making sure things are fine here."

"Let's do that." Iain nodded, walking over to a chair and taking a seat. "I'll work on an invitation to bring my cousin and his family."

"And we'll talk to Father Tomas and see if there are any villagers who might have some enemies in Braighwick." Gavin stood. Leith followed.

"At least we have a plan to move us forward," Iain said. "Let's pray naught worse happens in the meantime."

The laird wanted to see her. The moment Doreen came for her, Serena fought a nervous foreboding. She fretted all the way up the stairs, wringing her hands like a lass in trouble. She searched her memory, but couldn't think of a task she'd neglected.

Her worn soles made no sound as she approached. The door stood ajar. She forced herself to step through it. Iain MacBraigh sat at his desk writing. He didn't notice her until he looked up to redip his quill and paused. His gaze traveled up the length of her, meeting her gaze.

"Why didn't ye make yer presence known?" He set the quill aside and leaned back, linking his fingers over his flat belly. A piece of auburn hair fell over his forehead, almost covering one hazel eye.

She disliked being studied, but what else could she do but bear it? Iain MacBraigh was her superior in every way. Serena cleared her throat. "Ye seemed so intent upon what ye were doing that I didn't wish to disturb ye. I'm sorry if ye feel I was eavesdropping, but I assure ye, I wasn't."

"So direct." A slow smile eased across Iain's face, relaxing his firm features. "That's what I like about ye, Serena Boyd. No airs. No silliness. Only honesty. Serenity—the kind a man like me craves. I think yer name suits ye well. It isn't Scottish, yet ye say ye've lived in the village yer whole life?"

"Aye, I have." Serena nodded, familiar with people's curiosity about her name. "I'm named for my grandmother. My mither's mither was Spanish. She married a Scot by an arranged marriage."

The laird stroked his shaved jaw. "An arranged marriage across country borders are usually only done by families of consequence. What of yer father? Did yer mither marry beneath her station then?" He raised a brow.

"I know naught." Serena lifted her chin and stiffened. "Mither dislikes talking about him. What I've learned doesn't make me wish to know more."

"Och! Forgive me for prying, but I canna help wanting to discover more about ye."

"My laird, Doreen said ye wanted to see me about something?" Serena hoped to distract him without encouraging his wrath or more curiosity. Could he not give new orders and allow her back to her duties?

"Such an eloquent way of forcing me back to the point." Iain tilted his head, steepled his fingers, and regarded her. "But first, tell me who educated ye. Lass, ye're not like the others in the village. Ye read as well as I do. Yer manners are perfect. Ye may live in a wee cottage, but ye know how to run the household of a castle and ye've only been doing so these past six months."

"My mither has been my only teacher."

"I see," Iain said. "As ye might have guessed or heard from the gossips, I was sent away to England to be educated by my uncle. To the merciless delight of others, I never lost my Scottish brogue and became the source of much taunting at social events. When it became known that I stood to inherit a large estate here in Scotland, only then did I earn the respect of my peers, but by then I no longer desired it."

He picked up a letter on his desk and stood, walking around to lean against the front of it. "I received this letter from my cousin, Hogan Lennox, the Earl of Caithness. He has heard that the sons of Birk MacKenzie are here, the Chief of the MacKenzie Clan. Since Gavin is next in line as the MacKenzie heir, my cousin has chastised me for not holding a welcoming party to introduce the MacKenzie brothers to him and other residents of influence in the shire of Caithness." The laird tossed the letter on his desk and folded his arms. "I'd hoped to be free of such organized events when I moved back here. I grew weary of all the social games people play among the elite in England."

"My laird, ye're a wealthy man in this shire, ye canna expect to remain hidden forever. People are too curious about ye." Serena stepped forward, wanting to encourage him.

"Lass, I see ye almost daily. Can ye not think of me as a close enough friend to call me by my given name? Please? I desire it." He raised his chin and looked into her eyes with such an earnestness that she faltered and looked toward the open window through the library doorway. Birds chirped in the distance and a slight draft lifted the white drapes.

"I fear that may be seen as disrespectful." Her voice sounded too low and less sure than she would have liked.

"Believe me, I understand yer concern, but I've asked the same of everyone who works for me here at Braigh Castle. We are so remote and rarely have out-of-town guests. I find such propriety too much of an inconvenience. Such formality makes me feel like a stranger to the people who share my home and to those I see so often—like ye."

She couldn't blame him for feeling that way. A sense of compassion stirred within her. Having her mother and Gunna to talk to and spend time with made a huge difference to a lonely existence, even though she'd claimed she wouldn't be alone because she would have the villagers.

"Verra well. Iain it is, then." Serena couldn't resist smiling at him.

"Good." His hazel eyes lit up like the morning sunrise. "Then we have an understanding." Iain's lips curled into a wide grin. "And I have another favor to ask of ye—the real reason I summoned ye."

"Aye?" Serena folded her hands in front of her and waited for him to proceed.

"I need yer help planning this party. I've no wife, mither, or sister to attend to such matters."

"Of course, I'll be happy to assist ye. I'll need a list of people ye plan to invite. I'll take care of everything. Don't ye worry none. "

"Fine." He shook his auburn head. "But I want ye there."

"Of course, ye'll need servants." Serena nodded. "I and the others will be prepared."

"Ye don't understand, lass. I want ye to attend the party— as a guest. I'd rather ye help me as hostess, but that probably would be unacceptable."

"Indeed." Serena gasped, and then covered her mouth at the sudden outburst. She stared at Iain in confusion.

"As a guest, then." He shrugged as if the matter were closed.

"That too would not be acceptable. I'm naught but a servant in yer household."

"I care not about such matters. Ye should know that about me by now."

"But I care. Nay." She shook her head and stepped back. "I'm not comfortable with it. Please forgive me."

"Bring yer mither. Mayhap ye won't feel so awkward then."

"Nay!" Serena backed away. "We've no proper clothing. A village lass would bring disrespect upon yer head. I care naught about myself for I'm quite used to being from the Village of Outcasts, but ye're the laird of Braigh Castle. One day ye'll want a mistress for it . . . and heirs."

"Aye, and I can promise it won't be Lady Fiona as he intends. I'll wed a lass of my own choosing. I don't care where she comes from, her station, or breeding. I'm only interested in her morals and good character. Is she a God-fearing woman who will be faithful to me as I age? Will she be a good mither and wife? Will she treat others with respect? I don't want a wife who only accepts friends based on their station in life as if no one else matters." Iain walked toward her.

Serena held her ground, swallowing. She licked her dry lips. "I admire yer decision, but I don't see what that has to do with my presence at this party."

"No one need know ye're from the village."

"I won't lie."

"Fine. As I told ye, I'm not the one who is concerned about what others think. I'd still like ye to be there. I plan to have dancing and there will be plenty of lonely men without a partner. Ye may bring a friend or two from the village."

A servant cleared his throat at the doorway. "Lord Lennox has arrived with his daughter."

Iain rubbed his eyes. "Now the man has taken to calling unexpectedly and this time he has brought his daughter, hoping we'll become better acquainted, no doubt." He looked over Serena's head at the servant behind her. "Show them to the drawing room," Iain said.

"Mayhap ye'll become more fond of her after ye get to know her." Serena offered him a hopeful smile.

"Hogan Lennox is second in line to inherit this estate if I have no heirs. He tried to prevent my inheritance and when the court didn't settle the appeal in his favor, he's now trying to throw his daughter at me. I need at least one ally I can trust at this party. Please? I need ye there."

"Verra well." Serena sighed. "But ye might regret it."

"I doubt that." He stepped around her and headed for the door. "I promised to show Gavin and Leith the lands. Will ye do the honor for me? Ye know the grounds as well as I. Give them my regrets and explain the plight of my unexpected visitors."

An image of Gavin's handsome face came to mind and her heart seized in a spasm. She wasn't sure if she nodded in agreement or not, but Iain still thanked her and walked out. Serena took a deep breath and patted her hot cheeks. She would have to gain better control of herself if she had to spend the rest of the afternoon in Gavin's company.

✍

Conversations filled Gavin's ears as he worked beside the men. Used to giving the orders, he found himself crushing his tongue and holding back his thoughts in order to give his brother a chance to lead the men and earn their respect.

He looked forward to the laird's tour of the estate, anything that would get him away from the temptation of taking over. Leith was doing well.

"How tall should we build this next scaffold, Gavin? Should they all be the same height?" Craig dropped a couple of poles on the ground and shoved his fists at his sides.

"Ye need to ask Leith. He's in charge." Gavin pulled a rope tight, making sure the two pieces of wood were sturdy and secure.

"I'm looking for Gavin MacKenzie."

Gavin paused, recognizing Serena's voice. Why would she be seeking him at this time of day? His heart raced as his mind sought various possibilities.

"Over there, lass," Craig said, pointing in his direction.

Turning, Gavin's chest tightened as he studied her. Serena's creamy skin and full pink lips beckoned into a smile, sending his pulse pumping at full speed. She wore a tan cloak over a simple brown gown.

"The laird sends his regrets. He has unexpected company and asked me to show ye and Leith the estate." She bit her bottom lip. "I hope ye don't mind?"

89

"Mind spending the rest of the afternoon with a bonny lass? I recognize a blessing when it comes my way." Gavin grinned, hoping he didn't sound like an addled fool. He certainly felt like one. Strange things happened to him when Serena was around. His breathing became erratic, his mind muddled, and his body warm.

"Yer flattery won't work on me, Gavin MacKenzie." In spite of her words, the color in her cheeks deepened. "Today we aren't dancing and having a feast."

"An' why not?"

She tilted her head as if considering the matter at great length. "Because that was a tale of pretend and today we're back to the real world—where ye're the MacKenzie heir and I'm a poor village lass."

The logic in her words clubbed his chest like an afflicted warrior losing a fight. Hadn't Leith said something similar? Still, Gavin didn't want to think about the obstacles. He'd rather think about the moment.

"Fair enough." Gavin crossed his arms. "How about we keep things simple? A friendship with no assumptions."

"Agreed. Iain gave me permission to ride one of his horses. Did ye bring Sholto?"

"Aye. He's at the stable." Gavin noticed she used the laird's given name. It was the first time he could recall her doing so. He tried not to let it bother him, but the change weighed on him. He disliked jealousy and had no right to muddle if Iain was man enough to ignore her low birth.

Gavin turned to Craig, who worked at tying the two scaffolds together, pretending he hadn't heard their exchange. "Craig, tell Leith he can join us on the tour of the grounds and to meet us at the stables in the next few minutes if he intends to go."

He and Serena walked across the courtyard to the stables. Their arms brushed. Unexpected warmth gushed through him. How could he ignore this glaring attraction to her? Serena kept moving as if oblivious to the mounting connection between them. He struggled with his code of honor. The odds stacked against them would be difficult, but not impossible.

"How well do ye ride?" A horse snorted and another one whinnied as they drew closer to the stables.

Serena tucked a strand of black hair behind her ear and stared up at him. Her mouth twisted as she raised her chin. "I suppose that's a fair question since ye've never seen me ride on my own."

"I didn't mean to offend ye. I merely thought to help ye find a proper horse." Gavin leaned one arm over an empty stall door and watched her.

She twisted the button on her cloak at her neck. Her gaze shifted around the stable. Was she afraid to ride and too proud to admit it? Such a thing would most certainly be the Highland way.

"In spite of what ye must think of me, I'll choose my own mount." Serena strolled down the aisle, her head turning from side to side, glancing in each stall.

"What must I be thinking, pray tell?" Gavin followed at a leisure pace, his hands linked behind his back. Something vexed her, and he couldn't help wondering what.

She smirked. "That I'm a feeble lass who canna stay seated upon a wagon, with spoiled feet that trample stranger's toes."

Ahh, her wounded pride was the barrier between them. Mayhap he could flatter his way past it. "On the contrary, I no longer consider myself a stranger. And nay, I think something unusual must have happened to unseat ye from the wagon. I imagine ye're used to that wagon and ye've probably made the trip to town on many occasions."

Serena whirled, her green eyes blazed with fire. He wasn't sure if it was anger or fear. "What unusual thing must have happened?" The question came out breathless.

Gavin blinked, trying to understand her curious behavior. He lifted his hands as if in surrender. "Only that yer horse must have stepped in a hole or tripped over a rock. What else could I have possibly meant?"

He stepped closer and trailed a finger over her cheek. "Serena, I could never think ill of ye. Indeed, I'm in awe of ye. I don't wish to argue, but ye seem determined to be angry with me. If I've done something, tell me. I want to make amends at once."

"Nay, I'm sorry." She blinked, but didn't turn away. "Ye've done naught to deserve my temper. I let my imagination get carried away is all."

"Glad to hear it. I've only had good, decent thoughts about ye. Don't ever think otherwise. I'll leave ye to choose a horse while I ready Sholto."

Gavin strode to Sholto's stall and unlocked the gate. He rubbed the animal's neck in greeting. Sholto leaned toward him, embracing the contact. Gavin smiled as Sholto's tail swung in an arc. He was ready for a vigorous ride.

A few minutes later, Gavin led his horse out at the same time Serena appeared with a brown mare. The two animals greeted each other with a snort. Sholto's white hair glowed in comparison. Much taller and filled with muscular strength, Gavin couldn't help thinking how each horse matched their rider.

"Has Iain told ye of the welcoming party he intends to throw for ye and Leith?" Serena glanced sideways at him.

"Aye." Gavin nodded. "That isn't necessary, though. He's given us plenty of hospitality. I've no wish for him to go to more trouble on our behalf."

"Too late. He's made up his mind. The Earl of Caithness wants to meet ye. I'll be in charge of planning it. We'll have a fine feast, music, and dancing."

"Serena, will ye be there?" The idea of dancing with her again warmed his blood.

"Aye, but I'm none too pleased by it." Her lips formed a thin line as they left the shadow of the stables.

"Why is that? Most women I know would be thrilled at a chance to wear their finest at a lively evening full of dancing and entertainment." He grinned, unable to hide his amusement.

She looked toward the castle where his men worked building the new scaffolds. "Mayhap those women have fine gowns, and they've been trained in courtship dances and the formal ways of such things. No doubt, they know what to say around educated men who have traveled the world. At my age, they wouldn't be attending their first formal dance—beyond the simple country dances."

"A fine gown is a material possession that can be bought quickly enough." Gavin wanted to give her the confidence she needed—to somehow ease her discomfort and fear. "The dances can be taught, but the rest is fear I hear in yer voice. I think ye're too strong a lass to let fear conquer ye like that. I'm an educated man who has traveled the world, and ye have no problem talking to me."

"Aye, Gavin." Serena brushed strands of hair from her face. "But ye're different. I've already trampled yer feet and still ye're my friend."

His smile faltered. His tongue burned with the desire to tell her he wanted to be more than her friend, but she was right. He had offered her his friendship with no assumptions. Instead, he shrugged and forced a smile. "Any man who denies ye his friendship for such a simple matter wouldn't be worth having as a friend. As for the dances, I'm willing to teach ye a few on one condition." He raised a finger.

"Which is?" Serena lifted a dark eyebrow, her green eyes glistening in the sun.

"Ye give me the first and the last dance at the party."

7

Serena rode along the border of the laird's property, pointing out memorable landmarks to Gavin. It included the whole village in the woods, the loch, and the rocky edge bordering the sea where Braigh Castle was situated.

She glanced over at Gavin. He rode like a warrior upon Sholto's white back, sitting tall, his broad shoulders stretched like an oak mantle. She loved the bright red of his hair and how it tapered down his neck. Gavin glanced in her direction, as if he sensed her studying him. He winked at her, a wicked grin spreading across his handsome face.

"What was that for?" Her neck heated, numbing her head. She gripped the reins tighter.

He pulled his horse to a stop and dismounted. They were at a grassy knoll overlooking the brilliant blue-gray sea. Below them, waves crashed against the rocks. The castle walls were high above them to the right. The wind sailed off the ocean, filling the air with the smell of salty seaweed and fish. It was wonderful.

"Ye're about to receive yer first dance lesson." Gavin strode toward her. "I canna think of a better place—or time."

What had she agreed to?

Gunna's voice came to mind, "dearie me."

The words dissolved from her thoughts as Gavin reached up and swung her down. Serena gasped, holding onto his powerful arms. It took her a few moments to realize she had landed on her feet and could let go of him. His blue eyes touched her face, kindling a spark of tenderness inside. She swallowed, unsure of her feelings.

He cleared his throat and stepped back, gesturing around them. "Pretend this area is surrounded by people. All of them will form a large circle. The first dance I'll show ye is the ring dance. Everyone will move this way." He stirred his arm like a clock.

Taking her hand, he skipped, hopped, and turned around. He pulled her along. By the time they completed the imaginary ring, they were breathless from laughing. Gavin pressed his palms to his knees and drew a deep breath. Serena touched her chest, as her fast-beating heart kept a constant rhythm with the roaring ocean.

"Do people always dance that fast?" Serena asked between breaths.

"Mayhap, not quite as quick on their feet." He straightened to his full height. "I could use some water." He whistled and Sholto came forward. Gavin unfastened a flask from the animal's saddle and held it out. "Here, drink from this and quench yer thirst."

Serena accepted the brown container and popped the cork. She lifted it to her mouth and welcomed the cool, refreshing liquid. It slid down her throat like a smooth waterfall. Wanting to save some for Gavin, she forced the tiny fountain from her lips and handed it back, wiping her mouth.

"Thank ye." The words came out in a breathless whisper. His fingers closed around hers, warm and full of strength as he gripped them. Their eyes met and once again she was struck by the handsome blue depths watching and assessing her.

"Ye have bonny eyes, the color of peat moss, which gives Scotland its natural beauty."

The seriousness in his tone broke through the icy walls of her heart, like cracking the surface of a frozen loch. The warmth of his touch melted her fears into a river that shivered throughout her body.

"I'm sorry, lass. Are ye cold?" His eyes flickered. He leaned closer.

"Nay." She shook her head. "The air is delightful after so much dancing." She couldn't tell him that he had made her tremble with a mere look. The last thing she wanted was for the man to think her daft.

He nodded, accepting her answer and raising the flask to take a drink. The corded muscles in his neck moved with each swallow. Once he had enough, Gavin slid the cork back in place and tucked the container away.

"Shall I teach ye another dance?" He grinned as if he took pleasure in the idea.

"Aye, but first let's talk a bit." She strolled to the edge and sat upon the grass, overlooking the sea. "Sit down." She patted the spot next to her. "Tell me of yer homeland. I've never been anywhere but here."

She wanted to know more about him. What was it like where he came from? What did he think of the Village of Outcasts—of her?

He sat beside her as a seagull flew over them, squealing. The waves below roared in constant motion, easing her into a peaceful state, almost tempting her to lie back and enjoy a nap.

Gavin crossed his ankles and leaned back on his palms. "MacKenzie lands are a couple hundred miles south of here in an area called Ross. I grew up living at MacKenzie Castle up on a brae."

"Our wee cottages must seem like a hole in the ground in comparison." Serena kept her eyes on the ocean, afraid of what she might see in his eyes.

"Some of our people live in similar homes. Ye must remember, Serena, it isn't the house that makes a comfortable, loving home. It's the souls that live in it."

"Is it better than Braigh Castle? I canna imagine aught larger."

"Aye." Gavin nodded. "And the stones are more sturdy and smooth. The foundation of Braigh Castle is decaying by the grit of the salt air and the cold, moist winds blowing off the north sea."

"Ye don't have the sea where ye're come from?" She lifted her knees and folded her arms around them as he shook his head. "That would be sad to me. For I dearly love the sea."

"We have lochs, plenty of moors and burns. The land isn't as flat as Caithness, and we have more woods. My part of the Highlands has it's own mysteries and beauty. I think ye'd like it if ye ever visited. My step-mither and da are verra friendly. They would treat ye like a queen."

"Me? A low-born lass?" Serena laughed. "I'm not that innocent, Gavin MacKenzie."

"But they would. Ye'd have just as much protection under my da's care. Mayhap even a better home. I could build one for ye and yer mither."

"Gavin! I'm not much impressed by things. We could have lived in a castle if we wanted."

He paused and leaned forward with a raised eyebrow. She longed to reach out and trace a finger along the golden-red arches above his intense eyes now staring at her, but she refrained, clasping her fingers tight.

"Aye." She nodded. "When Iain MacBraigh offered me my position, he gave us the choice to live at Braigh Castle. Even though the village is under his protection, he said he could keep us safer if we were behind the castle walls."

"I'd agree." Gavin's voiced turned rough. He looked away, plucked a handful of grass and tossed it. His lips formed a scowl and his jaw tensed. "Mayhap, ye should have taken him up on his goodwill. There's foul play about—with the cobbler's murdered cow and the kirk fire. I don't like ye walking back and forth to the castle. It's too dangerous."

"I'll be fine and Phelan is with me most of the time."

"Why won't ye let me carry ye back an' forth each day?" His thumb traced a circle on her cheek like light butterfly swirls, breaking her thoughts.

He inched closer. Serena's heartbeat quickened. His gaze lowered to her mouth. Fear of the unknown fluttered through her, along with a fierce curiosity to feel his lips upon hers. The war waging inside her didn't feel right, and she pulled out of his grasp, standing to her feet.

"Serena?" Gavin clambered to his feet after her. "I'm sorry. I shouldn't have allowed myself such liberties. Please forgive me, lass."

With her back to him, Serena closed her eyes and took a deep breath, feeling immense heat rise to her face. She turned, squaring her shoulders and lifting her chin.

"I'm not angry at ye, Gavin." She was furious at herself for wanting him to kiss her, knowing that a relationship between them could lead nowhere. How could she be vexed at him for desiring the same? "But our friendship must remain as it is."

"I don't know that I can do that, Serena. I crave more." Gavin paced before her. He ran a hand through his hair.

"Let me ask ye a question, Gavin. Ye said that yer parents would welcome me and offer me their protection in the clan?"

"Aye." He stopped pacing and watched her.

"Would someone like me be welcomed into yer family as well as the clan?"

His gaze faltered, unable to meet her eyes. Serena recognized the guilt in him, but the confirmation of what she already knew sliced through her hopeful heart.

"I won't lie, Serena. My family would welcome Leith forming such an attachment more so than myself. As the second son, he'll inherit lands, but not the castle estate or the chieftainship of the clan." He folded his arms and stroked his chin. "But that doesn't mean they would outright disown me. And if I were not elected as chief, I would survive."

Serena smiled. "Ye say that now, but ye might come to begrudge it later. Besides, ye haven't considered that I might not be willing to leave Caithness. I'm safe here. This place is my sanctuary."

"But I would protect ye." Gavin grabbed her shoulders.

"Gavin, there are things ye don't know about me. Everyone living in the Village of Outcasts has something different about them—including me. This burden I carry would be a much stronger obstacle for ye to overcome than my being a poor commoner."

"Whatever it is canna be that bad or I would have already recognized it." He tightened his grip on her shoulders. "It won't matter."

"Aye, it will."

"Gavin!" A voice called in the distance.

Serena stepped away and shielded her eyes. Leith rode toward them. He slowed his mount to a stop as he drew near. "I hope ye've finished touring the grounds. We've been summoned to the castle. The Earl of Caithness would like to meet us."

᪥

While Serena seemed relieved for Leith's interruption, Gavin was disappointed. He wanted to question her further on the secret she had mentioned, but sensed she wouldn't welcome such a discussion in Leith's presence as they rode back.

The near kiss . . . he couldn't bring himself to regret that action. She was lovely inside and out. He didn't feel compelled to impress her with displays of prowess. Serena made him see things differently. Her satisfaction in such a small cottage with a dirt floor shamed him for his desire of wanting more.

"Gavin, ye're not listening," Leith said. "Twice I've asked yer opinion of the grounds ye've seen today."

Springing to attention, Gavin cleared his thoughts. "Iain MacBraigh has a large estate. There's plenty of unused farmland he could rent out to the villagers if he wanted. The soil appears lush and fertile. He has freshwater lochs. It looks like Iain owns the only land in the shire with timber."

"Aye, that he does." Leith agreed with a nod. He turned to Serena. "Did my brother behave himself? Sometimes he has a way with the lasses that can leave behind many a broken heart."

"Leith!" Gavin raised his voice, but couldn't help the small grin that slipped through in spite of Leith's mischievous ploy. "The only brokenhearted lasses left behind are the ones ye've left. No one from home, and none of the men with us, would deny the truth in that."

"Rightly so." Leith lifted a finger and tilted his brown head. "A second son ought to have a wee bit of charm. How else am I to lure the fortune seekers out of yer clutches?"

"Ye're the third son or have ye forgotten?" A familiar pain shot through Gavin. Over the years, the death of their brother Elliot had diminished, but he refused to allow Elliot's memory to fade. Nor could he forget how different things might have turned out if he had gone with Elliot that day. Elliot had learned some news regarding a murdering traitor in the MacPhearson Clan their sister had married into, but Elliot never returned home.

"Nay, I've not forgotten, but there are times I wish I could." Leith's tone sobered. "Ye're determined to remind me often enough."

"I'm sorry." Serena said. "I didn't know ye had another brother."

"He was killed in a fight a few years ago." Leith said. "I was only a wee lad at the time. Elliot and Gavin were full-blooded brothers, while Akira and I are only their half-siblings through a different mither, the second wife."

"Who's Akira?" Serena looked from Leith to Gavin.

"Our sister," Gavin said.

"Mayhap that would explain why the two of ye look so different." Serena scraped her teeth over her bottom lip with a smile. "Although, ye both seem to have the knack of embellishment from what I can tell."

"What do ye mean?" The words were out of Gavin's mouth before he could hold them back.

"Which of us is the handsomest?" Leith leaned forward, no doubt expecting flowery praise. "Don't ye think Gavin has a bit of a rugged look to him?"

"Och, Leith." Serena shook her head and clicked her tongue. "If I didn't know ye better, I'd think ye were a wee bit jealous of yer elder brother. It's a good thing ye're only jesting."

Gavin's opinion of Serena grew even more. Most of the lasses back home either fell for Leith's bid for compassion or his charming wit. He could now add intelligence to her growing list of attributes.

They arrived back at the laird's stables and left their horses in the care of the stable lad. As they walked into the courtyard, Serena stopped. "Thank ye for the dance lessons."

Turning, Gavin watched her gather her cloak tight around her, as if she was uncomfortable. "Are ye not coming?"

"Nay. The earl has requested to meet the two of ye. I've no desire to see him, and he didn't ask for me. I've things I must do before the day's end."

"Mayhap we can escort ye home this evening?" Gavin lingered, not wanting to separate from her just yet.

"That depends." Serena backed away. "The laird may want ye to stay for dinner since he has guests." She turned and strode toward the opposite end of the courtyard, her brown gown rustling against her legs. Serena's boots crushed the pebbled dirt, fading with each step.

"Come on, Gavin. They're waiting." Leith prompted him. "Serena has work to do and we have business to attend."

"Since when did ye become so sensible and able to help me keep my priorities straight instead of the other way around?" Gavin strolled beside Leith, giving him a curious sideways glance.

"When ye became enamored with an innocent lass who doesn't deserve to be hurt. Ye're forgetting how loyal ye are to the family, the clan, and yer sense of duty. Ye may come to truly care for her and feel torn, but in the end, ye'll choose yer conscience in what ye believe is right."

Leith pulled open the heavy wood door. It groaned and squeaked. They blinked in the dark hallway, giving their eyes time to adjust. Their heels clicked against the hard floor.

"So that's why ye tried to make it sound as if I'm like ye, leaving broken hearts everywhere I go." Gavin shook his head in disbelief. He had never known his brother to be concerned about such matters before.

"That's the difference between us," Leith said. "Ye've always handled yer obligations. For me, it's a mere thought—at least it was until now."

"What's changed?" Gavin asked.

"I canna deny our birth order. I'll either have to make my own way or keep depending on yer good graces. I'm getting to an age where I need to make my own way."

"I'm glad to hear it. Ye're finally coming to yer senses. But as for the lasses, I still think ye'd break every woman's heart for the lust of travel in yer blood, while I could only do so for a moral obligation." He paused, considering his next words. "I'm a man with principles. I still believe a solution is obtainable where Serena is concerned."

"Ah, but does she? I get the impression she's quite attached to this place."

The question grated on Gavin's nerves as they entered the great hall where two long wood tables were arranged side by side. Another table of less length rested on a dais overlooking the hall. The seats were empty and the air drafty with no warm bodies in the room or a blazing fire in the hearth.

"Kind of eerie, isn't it?" Leith shook his shoulders and arms as if warding off a chill.

"Auld castles are like that. Ours doesn't have the same effect because we've grown up in it."

"True, but MacKenzie Castle isn't barren like this." Leith held out his hands and gestured to the dark corners and crevices. "Our rooms and hallways are filled with people, laughter, happy chatter, not this silence of the tomb."

Gavin grinned. One thing he could always depend on was Leith's lively outlook on life.

"Listen." Gavin strained to hear. The sound of a distant conversation echoed. A woman's high-pitched laughter ruptured. "This way." Gavin walked through a side door and followed a hall that emptied into a large room he assumed was the throne room.

A lady sitting in an elegant carved chair looked up from Iain MacBraigh standing above her. She wore a dark purple gown with a plaid underskirt. The large sleeves contained matching ribbon ties and puffed out in waving folds down to her wrists. She held a goblet in her hand as her gray eyes met his, and then turned to assess Leith. Her long, curly brown hair fell in ringlets around her shoulders.

While Iain made the proper introductions, Gavin noticed how her interest in Leith waned at the mention of the clan chieftainship and estate Gavin would inherit. She rewarded him with an even brighter smile. This time her eyes sparkled like diamond slits, but Gavin had no interest in a fortune seeker. Still, duty called for politeness and the best of manners.

"Pleased to make yer acquaintance, Lady Fiona Lennox." Gavin bowed.

"And I, my lady." Leith bowed beside Gavin.

"Ahh, so the MacKenzie brothers have finally arrived," said a male voice behind them. "I've been looking forward to meeting both of ye. Iain has told me such excellent things about ye."

Gavin and Leith turned. A middle-aged man stepped forward. He had gray hair and a full beard and mustache, and piercing brown eyes that measured them up and down. The man wore a tan tunic and a plaid of purple and dark blue as his daughter.

"May I present my cousin, Lord Hogan Lennox, the Earl of Caithness," Iain said.

While bowing, Gavin noticed the grim expression on the laird's face. His lips appeared tight and his tone harsh, as he cut a glance at the earl. "Thank ye for being understanding about my unexpected absence in touring the grounds. I trust Serena was able to show ye everything and answer yer questions?"

"Aye, she's a verra able lass."

"And may I ask who is Serena?" Lady Fiona looked from the laird to Gavin. She lifted her chin. "With a brood of brothers surrounding me each day, I welcome the acquaintance of another woman." She smiled, revealing a row of white teeth, but the warmth didn't reach her eyes. Gavin wondered if she struggled to hide something.

"Serena Boyd is a village lass who helps here at the castle," Iain said. "She's well-educated. She has a way with the servants in solving disputes. The lass has earned their respect and it seems that most would do almost aught for her." Iain sipped from his goblet. He motioned to the drinks on the side table. "Would ye like some wine?"

"Aye." Gavin nodded. A servant brought him a filled pewter goblet and handed one to Leith.

"So she's a commoner who works for ye. Mither doesn't allow me to associate with our servants. She says they'll teach me vulgar things."

"Fiona!" The earl's face darkened a shade. "That wasn't her exact words."

"Well, I can vouch for Serena's goodness of character," Iain said. "I've invited her to the welcoming party we're throwing on behalf of the MacKenzies. As my guest, I expect her to be treated with warmth and respect."

"Leith and I could put in a favorable word for her character as well," Gavin said.

"Indeed." Leith nodded. "I hope to take a turn with her upon the dance floor."

"Well, the first and the last dance are already promised to me." Gavin sipped his wine.

"However did ye do it?" Iain swung his head in Gavin's direction. "It took some time for her to agree to come. I thought I might have to resort to ordering her."

"Gentlemen, I'm not completely without charm." Heat burned Gavin's face, and he resisted the temptation to touch his flaming cheeks. He wouldn't be surprised if his skin color matched his hair.

"I must admit, I'm now quite curious to meet this Serena Boyd, especially since she has ye all enamored with her. She must be a verra special commoner." Lady Fiona exchanged a awry glance with her father. Gavin wasn't sure what it meant, but it put him on guard.

❧

Serena and Cara leaned over their washboards and scrubbed linens with the lye soap Serena's mother had made a few days ago. They were on their knees in the grass by the loch as the gray sky dawned into morning. Gunna wasn't feeling well, so Serena had offered to take care of the chore before leaving for the castle.

"Thank ye for going with Gunna to the loch each day. I miss the time I used to have with her," Serena said. She lathered Gunna's plaid and turned it over to scrub the other side.

"I enjoy it. She's a delight and full of the latest news about ye. How else am I supposed to keep up with what's happenin' with ye?" Cara held up the white tunic she had just washed. "Did I miss any spots?" She stared in Serena's direction, trying her best to do her part.

"It's good and clean," Serena said, leaning over and inspecting the garment. "And what news might Gunna be telling ye?"

"That the laird has invited ye to a feast and dancing." A proud smile lit her face. A piece of brown hair flew into her eyes, and she wiped it to the side. "What if he falls in love with ye, Serena? What a grand life ye'd have. All the burdens yer mither and Gunna suffer would be but a trifle load compared to what they endure now."

"There's about as much chance of that as there is of him wedding Phelan. Nay, I won't even waste my time on such thoughts. Iain MacBraigh is merely uncomfortable hosting parties and entertaining people. He only wants me there to help, naught more."

"Are ye nervous?" Cara dumped the clean tunic in a woven basket. "I'd be. But ye have such fine manners and all the learnin' yer mither taught ye. I think ye'll be like a princess."

"Far from it. I don't even have a decent gown to wear. I canna even make anything. I've naught but scraps of fabric from previous gowns—work garments, really. I was hoping to find a wee bit of satin so that maybe Kyla could improve one of my other dresses."

"Did ye ask Kyla if she has some fine bolts of fabric? Of anyone in the village, I'd think she'd be the one to have it. Don't ye think?" Cara raised a dark eyebrow.

"I thought of that, but who around here would have requested Kyla to make such elegant gowns? Besides, I couldn't possibly afford such material." Serena sighed and shrugged. "I'll simply tell the laird I canna go. I wouldn't want to shame him." Her chest felt like a heavy stone.

"From what ye've told me about the laird, I doubt he would feel that way. He's verra much aware of yer poverty. He knows where ye live and what ye wear each day."

"But he's a man. I doubt he's even thought much of it." Serena finished rinsing the plaid and wrung out the excess water, twisting it as best as she could. "Which is why I must tell him today that I canna go." Serena dropped the garment in a basket with the other washed clothes. She dried her cold, dripping hands on her blue and green plaid skirt. "Are ye ready? We'd best be getting back. I'll need to hang these to dry and hurry to the castle."

"Aye." Cara felt around for her basket, grabbed it, and climbed to her feet.

Serena hooked her own basket under one arm and looped the other through Cara's. That way it would be easier to guide her friend.

"Gunna said that Gavin MacKenzie offered to give ye dance lessons for the laird's celebration. Is that true?" Cara asked.

"He did, but now it won't be necessary."

"I think it was thoughtful and romantic." Cara tightened her grip. "How many men in our village would have offered to do such a thing?"

"Cara, most of the men in our village are auld, married, or wouldn't know how to dance."

"True. Mayhap that is why God has brought these other men to our village. To give us a chance at having our own families some day." Cara inhaled deeply and slowly released the air. "I confess, I'd almost despaired at finding a husband. Having a blind wife could be quite a burden to a man. But Craig, he doesn't treat me like that at all. He talks to me as if I matter." She smiled with a dreamy expression. "He even asks my opinion on things. He comes by and visits us often in the evenings."

Alarm bolted through Serena's heart. Cara had never confessed these secret desires. She got along so well in life with her blindness that Serena assumed Cara had accepted her limitations, as she had her shameful fits. Had they not jested about being two elderly maids, living together as sisters once their parents were gone? Serena had always believed it to be true. To now discover that Cara had been hoping and praying for a husband—a family of her own, stunned Serena. But why shouldn't she? Cara was a comely lass, intelligent, compassionate, and loyal. She would make a wonderful wife and mother. A sense of loneliness surrounded Serena.

"I haven't had much of an opportunity to talk to Craig, but if he has set his eyes upon ye, Cara Grant, then he is a man of excellent taste," Serena said.

Cara gasped. "I didn't mean to imply that he feels more than friendship. But I must admit, his attention and behavior toward me have awakened a new hope—that my blindness may not be the hindrance I've always feared. God works through people, Serena, even when they aren't aware of it."

"I confess—I've wanted them to leave, but it's only because I worry one of them might witness my fits."

"And that's what I mean." Cara tightened her grip on Serena. "If one of them does finally see a fit, it may prove to ye that someone other than us villagers might accept ye as ye are."

Serena felt like weeping. None of them had witnessed that woman being burned at the stake like she had. Most of the villagers were laughed at and teased, but none of them feared being murdered like she did.

8

*G*avin and Craig stood outside Serena's home. The weath-ered door stood ajar, but he felt uncomfortable barging in. What if one of them was dressing? It was merely a one-room cottage with a small loft where Serena slept. The design didn't provide much privacy.

It was about half past dawn. Surely they would be up by now, but wouldn't he have already heard conversation? He thought about the murdered cow and the kirk fire. Fear slith-ered through him.

He glanced at Craig, who shrugged his shoulders and nod-ded his blond head. "Ye might as well knock," Craig whispered. "Ye've come this far."

"Who's there?" Evelina appeared at the door, wearing a simple brown gown and a plaid shawl wrapped around her shoulders. She held a lit candle, the wax dripping on a brass holder. Her concerned frown relaxed into a welcoming smile as she held up the light and recognized Gavin.

"Well, this is a pleasant surprise. Come in. Come in." She opened the door wider and waved them through. "Both of ye."

She gestured to the table. "Please . . . sit down and break yer fast with us."

"Have we missed Serena?" Gavin glanced around the dark cottage and didn't see her. Snoring floated across from the bulky form on one of the box beds.

"Nay. Gunna isn't feeling herself today. She has a fever and so Serena did her laundry. She's out back hanging clothes. I just came in from collecting the eggs and milk. Ye're in time to join us. I hope Serena will eat before she leaves."

"We didn't mean to interrupt," Gavin said. "We're heading to town and wanted to stop by and see if ye needed anything."

"Thank ye for yer trouble, but we're fine," Serena said, standing on the threshold, an empty basket tilted to the side in her hand. She bristled as all eyes turned toward her. Gavin couldn't tell about the manner of her tone, but something seemed amiss.

"That's verra thoughtful of ye." Evelina awarded him with a smile. "I do believe there are a few items I'd like." She lifted her gaze to her daughter who still stood behind Gavin and Craig. "Serena, I hope ye'll stay long enough to eat. I was about to warm up some bread cakes and cook a few eggs."

Serena glanced at Gavin and then Craig. She chewed her bottom lip. "I'm already running late from doing the laundry."

"The laird is a reasonable man." Evelina bent, placing the bread cakes in a warming pot over the fire. "I'm sure if ye tell him about Gunna he'll understand."

"I agree," Gavin said. "Even though I haven't known him as long as ye, I've the same impression."

Gavin glanced at Craig and nodded toward the table. He strolled over and pulled out a chair, knowing Craig would follow his lead. "I thank ye for the offer of some bread cakes.

Save the eggs for yerselves. Gunna may need the nourishment when she wakes."

Sighing, Serena strode over to the milk pail and picked it up. "I'll prepare the milk. We like to sweeten ours a wee bit."

Evelina pulled an iron pan from the fire and broke the eggs into it. "Are ye sure bread cakes are all ye want?" She asked, placing another pot in the fire. "I'm warming some stewed apples from last night's dinner."

"That sounds good." Craig rubbed his hands together.

Gunna rolled over and the rhythm of her snoring changed. Serena smiled before covering her mouth. Gavin enjoyed her amusement.

"I do not intend to be rude." She said to Gavin in a lowered tone. "But ye're always trying to do things for us. We already owe ye a debt of deep gratitude as it is."

Gavin pressed his hand against his heart with a thump, turning to his friend. "Craig, the lass has mortally wounded me. I thought my chivalric attentions would have been more appreciated." He glanced up at her mother.

"A young lass often needs a wee bit of time to make up her mind about things." She smiled as she turned over the bread cakes, her gaze sliding to her daughter's with purpose.

If only he could break through Serena's walled fortress. "There are plenty who could vouch for my fierce prowess on the battlefield if that would gain yer admiration." Gavin pretended to puff out his chest and lifted his chin.

"Oh, hush!" Serena said, rolling her eyes and covering her mouth to keep from laughing, but a prevailing smile broke through to Gavin's delight. It was as if his heart sang a ditty. How he loved to see her smile.

"I'm only trying to lighten yer mood." Gavin scratched his chin, wondering what had dampened her spirits so early this morning. It encouraged him to know he had succeeded in cheering her—if only a bit.

Evelina brought over a steaming bowl of stewed apples that teased his nose until his mouth watered and his stomach rumbled. He and Craig exchanged a wide-eyed look of excitement. Craig wiggled in his chair like a small lad, while Gavin linked his hands tight in his lap under the table to keep from digging in.

Serena brought them wooden cups and poured the milk. She leaned over his shoulder, her black hair draping over his arm. He inhaled the feminine scent of heather and juniper, closing his eyes to savor the moment. As she pulled back, her elbow brushed his arm. His eyes popped open.

"I'm sorry." Serena's voice softened and her cheeks stained to a rosy glow. She stepped around Gavin to Craig's side and filled his cup.

Evelina set out the bread cakes before them on a wooden platter. Steam rose in the air as the smell of butter enticed them. Gavin realized he was licking his bottom lip like a man who had never tasted a warm cooked meal. He clenched his jaw and waited for the women to settle in their seats across the table.

Making the sign of the cross, Evelina bowed her head. Serena did likewise, preventing him from reading her expression. Gavin and Craig peeked at each other. He shrugged, touched his forehead, chest, and each shoulder before also bowing his head.

"Heavenly Father," Evelina said. "I pray that ye bless this family and our guests. Make Gunna well. Bless this meal for our nourishment. Please protect Serena as she walks to the castle and the villagers as they are out and about. We give ye thanks. In Jesus' holy name. Amen."

Evelina and Serena passed the food to Gavin and Craig before serving themselves. Once everyone had a full plate, they ate in silence for a few moments.

"This is verra good," Craig said, biting into his second bread cake.

"Thank ye. We're glad ye're here to share it with us." Evelina smiled, glancing between Gavin and Serena. "Will ye be giving Serena more dance lessons?"

The innocent question hung in the air. He met Serena's gaze. Her green eyes flickered before she glanced down at her plate. It wasn't like her to avoid eye contact, but she seemed to be doing so now. Gavin swallowed before turning to her mother. "I thought I might show Serena a few more dances this evening."

"Nay." Serena's voice carried across the table. "There's no need. I won't be going."

"Good morn, lass!" Philip greeted Serena with a warm smile buried in a gray bushy beard. His soft brown eyes averted one's attention from his yellow teeth. The wrinkles in his weathered face gave him a look of tenderness that Serena adored.

"Aye, it's an excellent morning. I must say, ye look bright and cheerful." Serena stepped under the raised gate. She never liked walking under the iron spikes. If Philip lost hold of the rope the heavy gate could crush down upon her.

"Aye, my wife is feeling much better. She hurt her back a few days ago and took to her bed, but this morning she rose with the sun." He laughed as he let go of the rope. The gate rattled, rolled, and crashed to the ground. "Does my heart good to see her up and about. I've reached the age where I don't know how many more years the good Lord has in mind for us. I treasure every moment now."

Serena tilted her head, regarding him with a new respect. It must be a wonderful feeling to love and be loved like that—to have one's life with someone so special.

"I had not known she was feeling poorly. Please tell her I'm glad she's better."

"She'll be 'appy to hear it." His grin broadened.

Serena hurried through the courtyard. She had tarried long enough. By the time she reached the main hall, she breathed heavy from her vigorous haste. Slowing to catch her breath, she paused as a door closed. Booted footsteps echoed toward her. Realizing the laird would be coming to break his fast, she pulled a stick from the mantle, lit it from the fire burning in the hearth, and carried it to the dais.

The laird entered as she lit the two oiled lamps in the center of the table. He wore a dark tunic that matched his hazel eyes. A plaid draped over his shoulder, fastened by a silver pin with the MacBraigh crest. When he smiled, she realized his auburn mustache had been trimmed. His jaw bore a fresh shave, and he smelled of lye soap and musk.

"Good morning, Serena. Ye certainly brighten this dreary hall. I wonder if I could have them put in a few windows?" He looked around as if contemplating the idea. "Mayhap up there. 'Twould be nice to have light from the ceiling. I've seen it done at other castles in England." He pointed to the top of the wall facing the front.

"I've never seen aught like it." She tried to imagine such a thing. "I think it would be interesting." She carried the burning stick to the wall candelabrum on each side of the dais and lit those as well. Waving the long stick, she blew out the flame. Lingering white smoke curled in the air as the smell of burnt wood drifted past her nose.

"I'll see what the MacKenzie brothers recommend." Iain walked around the table to his chair, but he didn't pull it out and sit down. Instead, he watched her replace the stick on the mantle. "Is that a new gown? I don't recall ye wearing purple before."

Serena glanced down at the material flowing over her figure like an elegant tapestry of plaid with dark blue and purple lines.

"Nay, I was looking for some fabric to make a decent gown for yer feast. I found an auld gown my mither had discarded years ago and altered it." She lifted the hem from the floor. "This is the result. Unfortunately, I couldn't find aught better. I don't wish to shame ye, so I've decided not to attend. Please forgive me."

Iain's lips dropped in a frown and his eyebrows wrinkled in concern. "Of course, how remiss of me. I didn't realize—" He rubbed his forehead.

"Please, it isn't yer fault." Serena twisted her hands in distress. "I'll make certain that ye have what ye need, that the cook prepares the proper food, and musicians arrive early, and I'll be here beforehand to direct the servants."

He grinned and stepped around the table toward her. "Lass, ye're always so eager and willing to serve others. I don't host many celebrations such as this. I want this to be an enjoyable event for ye as well. Ye've worked hard and deserve it."

"I don't understand." She was a mere servant. What should he care about her joy? A shiver of fear climbed up her spine like a foreboding shadow. "Ye said it's a welcome celebration for the MacKenzie brothers. Might I ask how I'm to be involved?"

"If truth be known, I was hoping to dance with ye, and I don't know any other occasion in the near future." Iain stepped closer and lowered his voice. "I hear ye've already promised the first and last dance to Gavin MacKenzie. Will ye save one for me as well?"

Serena's head spun until she felt dizzy. She had never thought of Iain MacBraigh as the romantic sort. He seemed so wealthy and above her. Surprise left her void of words. She stepped back and took a deep breath.

"I see I've stunned ye." Iain looked down and paced a few feet and came back. "Lass, I don't wish to alarm ye, but I mean to tell ye how I feel. These past few months, watching ye run my household with such perfection, I've come to enjoy yer company and believe ye'd suit me. We have similar tastes, likes and dislikes, and view things the same way. I've watched ye make decisions that I would have made. When ye walk into a room, ye brighten all the walls and people in it. It warms my heart to have ye near, and I've come to value yer opinions."

Unable to break eye contact with Iain expressing such thoughts, Serena's skin grew warm. She blinked several times as she tried to form a response. "I'm honored that ye're so pleased with my work, and if I were attending the celebration, I'd be most happy to save a dance for ye."

Iain's face transformed into a smile, and she noticed a few freckles across his nose. "If a gown is the sole reason for yer reservation, then allow me." He held out a hand, gesturing for her to leave the hall. "There's something I'd like to show ye upstairs."

Serena glanced back at the empty dais table. "But yer food will soon arrive. Ye don't want it to be cold."

"It'll be fine. Right now, it's more important that I do what I can to ease yer mind." He bent his fingers, waving her forward.

Like a wavering child who didn't want to obey, Serena took slow, deliberate steps. Where did he want to take her? Most of the rooms on the upper floors were bedchambers. Serena gulped. *Lord, please let him behave with moral character as he has thus far. Protect me.*

While she had no reason to fear Iain's intentions toward her, she figured a bit of cautious prayer wouldn't hurt. Her soft shoes were silent as she climbed the staircase, but Iain's boots were like a charging stampede upon her heels. When she reached the landing, she paused, waiting for further instruction.

"This way." The laird stepped around her, taking the lead along the banister rail overlooking the stairs they'd just climbed. They passed a maid carrying bed linens down to wash. Serena smiled and nodded in greeting. She had to hurry to keep up with Iain's long strides.

The dark walls gave the hall a primitive look of ancient mystery. A musty smell clung to the corners and to the carpeted tapestries hanging on the walls between the gilded framed portraits.

He led her past several doors that she assumed were chambers to a small door at the end of the hallway. She had never thought much of it as the entrance was quite small. Iain slid the iron lock back and pulled the handle. The hinges creaked like a wailing cat.

"I always thought this was storage space, but the other day I discovered it's a stairwell passage to a tower keep." Iain grabbed a lit candle, carefully removing the brass sleeve from the wall. He stepped into the black hole, ducking his head under the low threshold.

The deep abyss of the unknown caused Serena's heart to skip with fear. She hung back, afraid to go where it might not be safe. Iain held out his hand, but she didn't take it. Instead, Serena shook her head.

"I'd rather stay here." She crossed her arms in defiance.

"Trust me. It's naught more than a few steps to a sewing room. I believe it must have belonged to my aunt. The room is a treasure trove."

Serena leaned in and peered inside, but couldn't see beyond the three steps that the candle light afforded. Iain's description peeked her interest with the mystery of it. He held out his hand again, and this time she accepted it.

"Stay close. The light isn't much, and I don't wish ye to trip."

She clung to the stone wall as they climbed the spiral stairs, wide enough for only one. Iain's frame blocked most of the light, but Serena kept her footing by listening and sensing the rhythm of his feet upon each step.

They came to a small, narrow room filled with cedar chests, baskets of yarn and spools of thread, flax combs, a spinning wheel, and a weaving board. Two windows with closed shutters would produce a decent amount of light on a sunny day.

"It's more than a sewing room. This is a weaver's paradise." Serena strolled to a window and opened the shutters. Brightness nearly blinded her. She blinked and dropped her gaze, waiting for her eyes to adjust.

The laird bent over and blew at a layer of dust on top of a chest. Rather than ridding it of the unwanted dust, he ended up stirring it into the air like a fine mist clouding and settling back down. He unlatched the cover and lifted the lid. It squeaked and groaned. He shook out a lovely satin gown in a forest green shade.

"I realize that these are probably out of style, but I thought ye might find something ye like and could alter it. None of it will do my aunt any good now that she's departed this world." He waved a hand around the room. "Ye may use anything in here."

"Could I give some of it to Kyla, the village seamstress?" Serena asked. "She would have more use of it than I would."

Images of new dresses for Lavena, Birkita, and Cara came to mind. Her heart skipped to the beat of joy as she eagerly sifted through the other chests.

"On one condition," the laird said. "Ye have Kyla make a gown for ye and yer mither. Both of ye must attend my feast."

❦

Gavin drove the wagon that Iain had lent them. Craig sat beside him in lengthy silence, each man occupied with his thoughts. Of late, Serena consumed Gavin's mind. Having spent the morning in her company didn't help matters. She had taken him by surprise when she announced her intention of not attending the laird's feast. Gavin had been looking forward to dancing with her. The disappointment drained him, leaving him in a brooding mood, a rare thing since he disliked brooders.

Craig laughed.

Curious, Gavin abandoned his sour thoughts and glanced at his friend. Craig held a pensive grin as he shook his head.

"Och, mon! Share the jest," Gavin said. "I could use a wee bit of mirth about now."

"I canna believe how that wolf sat outside and whined for Serena. When she told him to wait, he laid down and dropped his chin over his paws like a wounded bairn."

"I've also seen how possessive that wolf is over the villagers." Gavin stretched his legs out over the wagon and propped his foot up on the side. The wood seat was much harder than his saddle. By the time they returned this evening, his backside would be sore.

"Still, ye'd think the animal belongs to Serena instead of that giant," Craig said. "I wouldn't mind the loyalty of a wolf like that."

"I would imagine it's the freedom Quinn gives him that gains his loyalty and trust," Gavin said. "Forcing him in a cage would rob him of the chance to choose loyalty. Come to think of it, I suppose that's how our Creator thinks about us."

"How did our conversation about a wolf turn into philosophy about religion?" Craig crossed his arms and averted his gaze upon the flat land layered with peat moss and heather.

"Think about it." Gavin leaned toward Craig. "God could have made us like puppets with no other thoughts or desires, other than to serve Him day and night in never-ending loyalty. But He didn't. God gave us the free will to choose as we please—to be loyal to ourselves or Him."

Craig blinked as he stared at Gavin. After a few seconds, his brows wrinkled, and he shook his head in disbelief. "Ye do realize ye just compared all of mankind to puppets?"

"Aye." Gavin grinned, scratching his temple. "But I think ye missed the point."

"I get it, my friend." Craig patted him on the back. "Ye just have a strange way of explainin' it."

For a while, they could see the outline of homes and buildings marking the town of Braighwick across the flat moors. As they drew near, the images grew larger and sharper. The sounds of rolling carts, horses clopping, children playing, and people talking mingled in every direction. A man chopped wood outside his house. On the other side of the dirt street another man hammered a hot iron, molding it to perfection. They passed a stable that reeked of hay, manure, and dust. Flies buzzed around the open gate. Gavin resisted the desire to cover his face with his plaid.

Most of the people were commoners dressed in simple, worn-out clothes. Dirt and grime covered their faces and hands. A handful of women gathered at the well. A few carried empty buckets. Others struggled with heavy burdens.

On they rode until they came upon merchant booths at market. Craig handled most of the bargaining for ready-made tools, while Gavin inquired about stonemasons and materials that would need to be ordered and custom made.

By the time their loaded wagon was piled high with no extra space, Gavin spotted a woman merchant with yards of fabric. He finished tying their supplies in place while Craig took care of the other side.

"Craig!" He tapped a barrel to gain his friend's attention.

"Aye?" Craig peeked around the corner, only the top of his head and eyes visible.

"I'll be right back. I need to see one more merchant before we leave."

"I thought we had everything?" Craig grunted as he pulled the rope tight in a secure knot.

"We do. This is for someone else." Gavin strode away before Craig could talk him out of his purpose.

He stepped around an elderly couple, avoided a horse, and nearly trampled a child who was after a sweet treat at the next booth.

"Robert, come hither!" the lad's mother scolded. She scooped the lad in her arms as he kicked and whined. "I'm verra sorry, sir." Her brown eyes searched Gavin's, seeking understanding as her skin darkened.

Gavin offered her what he hoped was a comforting smile. "Nay, the lad is fine, only quick and light on his feet as he should be. He's merely exercising a healthy pair of legs."

"Thank ye." She turned and fled before the bairn could wiggle out of her hold again.

Gavin fixed his attention on the fine fabrics laid out on the table. The merchant was a middle-aged woman who bent over a pile of goods showing them to a young lady near Serena's age. It gave him time to browse the choices.

There were various plaids, but Gavin paused to access the solid satin colors. He wished he knew Serena better. It would help to know what she would prefer. Instead, he would have to go with what he thought would look lovely on her and hope she liked it.

"Lookin' for some new gowns for yer lady?" a squeaky voice asked.

Gavin lifted his head to see the merchant standing in front of him, an eager smile showing a missing side tooth.

"I need somethin' special for a feast at MacBraigh Castle."

"The new laird finally entertainin' guests, is he?" The woman threw her hands on her hips and narrowed her eyes on Gavin as if he was a target. "'Bout time, I'd say. The mon's been a complete mystery ever since he moved in, six months past. I was beginnin' to think he'd be as much of a recluse as his uncle ever was." She made the sign of the cross from her forehead and over her chest. "God rest his poor soul."

Gavin cleared his throat. "Well, mayhap he's settled in now." He laid down the garment he'd been holding. "I'm not sure where to begin for a lady's wardrobe."

"That's where I'll 'elp ye. What does she look like?"

"Long, black hair. Fair complexion." An image of Serena came to mind, and he faded into silence, realizing he was about to describe her lips.

"Go on. What color eyes? How tall is she?"

"Green, like moss." He held up his hand, remembering that the top of Serena's head came to his chin when they had danced together. "About this high. She's thin around here." He patted his waist.

"Hmm." The woman tapped her chin with a finger. Her brown eyes brightened. "I've just the thing. Yer lady will shower ye with kisses when we're done."

Liking the sound of that promise, Gavin followed her at a quick pace. He kept telling himself that his flaming cheeks were due to curiosity and nothing more.

⌀

Serena sat beside Gunna and her mother, reading by the evening firelight. She was thrilled to discover that Gunna's fever had broken earlier in the afternoon. Gunna ate supper with them at the table and talked about a dream she'd had of Serena being in a fire. To calm Gunna's fears and to occupy her mind, Serena offered to read.

She turned to the first page of *The Canterbury Tales* by Geoffrey Chaucer. Before she began, Serena glanced at her mother. "I must admit, I began to wonder if Birkita ever intended to return this book."

"Serena!" The scolding expression on her mother's face didn't discourage her.

"Well, she kept it for the whole of winter. After I taught her to read a few years ago, she became as fast a reader as me. I canna imagine it taking longer than anything else she's borrowed." Serena turned it over and ran a finger along the worn spine. "Honestly, I wouldn't care except this is one of my favorites."

"And so ye have it now, dear one." Evelina leaned over and touched her arm with a soothing hand. "Now read. We're eager to hear what the knight has in store for us."

Clearing her throat, Serena began, "Here beginneth the Knight's Tale. As old stories tell us, there was a duke, Theseus, of Athens. He was lord and governor, and in his time such a conquerer."

The wooden door rattled in the frame as someone knocked.

"I'll get it," Evelina said, rising from her seat. The hinges squeaked as she opened the door.

"Pardon me, but the laird asked me to bring these chests to Serena Boyd."

"What chests? How many?" Her mother leaned her head outside.

"Over there on the wagon. I believe he sent two of 'em." The man pointed over his shoulder with his thumb.

Serena had seen him at the castle before, but had never conversed with him, as he mostly took care of the outdoor grounds. On occasion he travelled to town for supplies. Malvina often gave him the list.

Evelina turned to Serena, her eyes wide. "Serena, do ye know aught about this, lass?"

"Where would ye like me to put 'em?" The man's voice carried inside. "They're a bit heavy so ye might not want to move 'em again without a mon to 'elp ye."

Leaning over, Serena laid her hand on Gunna's arm. "I'll be right back." She stood, setting her book on the chair and hurried to her mother. "I'm not sure."

"Do ye know what's in them?" Serena asked, looking up at him.

"Nay, lass." He shook his gray head. "Do ye need me to 'elp clear a spot?"

Serena glanced around the small house. She pointed to an open spot by the far wall. "Over there will do."

"Aye." He strode out and returned a moment later hauling a bulky cedar chest in his arms. He grunted as he set it down, the wood structure thudded against the compact dirt floor. "I'll be right back with the other one."

"Dearie me, what's all this about?" Gunna twisted in her chair, her gaze following the man through the door as Evelina stepped out of his way.

The next chest was larger. He pulled it by the handle on the side, dragging it across the floor. It made an indention line in the dirt all the way to the wall where he shoved it next to the smaller one. Serena recognized two chests from many more in the castle sewing room.

"I'll be on my way." He straightened, nodded to each of them, and left.

"Are ye not goin' to open it, lass?" Gunna rose to her feet, wobbling like an old wheel.

"Exactly." Evelina spoke behind Serena.

Dropping to her knees, Serena slid the latch and lifted the dome-shaped lid. It creaked and groaned like the howling wind against an ancient house.

On top lay a folded piece of parchment paper. Serena picked it up, unfolded it, and read, "Dear Serena, I would like for you to have these garments to make a few special gowns. You may give the rest to your friends as you like. Iain MacBraigh."

"Well?" Impatience laced her mother's tone. "Why did the laird send these things? Were ye expecting them?"

"I told him I couldn't attend his feast because I didn't have a proper gown, and I didn't want to shame him." Serena thrust out the note to her mother. "Here, read it."

"That's more fabric in one place than I've ever seen afore." Gunna leaned over the open chest, a delightful smile showing her missing front tooth. She rubbed her palms together. "Dearie me, lass, ye'll look beautiful, ye will." Tears touched her brown eyes and her nose turned red. "I declare, but the laird must think highly of ye."

"I agree, Gunna." Evelina bent to her knees beside Serena and sighed. "I must admit that this comes as a surprise. I've always known ye were special and would one day catch the eye of someone, but I thought it would be a common man, so ye'd be out of sight of people—here where ye're safe."

"Why did ye encourage me about Gavin, then?" Serena turned, trying to understand.

"I only wanted ye to start accepting the idea that one day ye'll wed. I thought Gavin could help draw ye out of the shell ye've created around ye. I know he'll return home and ye'll remain here, but 'is friendship will be good for ye."

"Good in every way except for my heart." Despair twisted like a dagger in Serena's chest. She pulled out a bolt of lace and held it up to admire. "Ye can put yer worries to rest. I'm not going anywhere. I trust no one and love no one, save ye and Gunna." Using the chest as support, Serena leaned over and kissed her mother's cheek.

"Ye love not—yet." Lines of concern creased her mother's brows, pitching Serena's heart in a sea of doubt.

9

*G*avin hoped he had done the right thing in buying the fabric for Serena's new gown. She struck him as a proud lass, working at the castle to help her family. He prayed she wouldn't view his gift as charity and be offended. Gavin admired her too much for her to think anything else.

The horses pulled the wagon at a slower pace now that it was weighed down with heavy supplies. Someone would need to return for the materials still on order. The stone and bricks, at least, would be delivered to Braigh Castle.

"I know why ye bought all that fabric. Glad I'm here to witness the deed instead of Leith. He'd have no mercy with his teasing," Craig said, keeping his gaze ahead of them as he held the reins.

Gavin wasn't so sure he agreed with Craig. Leith had already warned Gavin about Serena, and he wasn't teasing at the time. Once he learned of this latest purchase, he might accuse Gavin of losing his wits.

"I won't be confessing my deeds." Gavin forced a light-hearted grin as he risked a glance in Craig's direction. "Are ye itching to see Leith torment me with his witty jests?"

Craig smiled, tilting his head. "I admit, the lad is quite entertaining, but nay." He shook his head. "I think ye know me well enough. I prefer tending my own business, while others take care of theirs."

"Aye, and that makes a trustworthy friend of ye," Gavin said. "Leith thinks I should leave Serena alone, but no woman has caught my interest since Lesley—until now. If I already have a secure inheritance, why should it matter about my bride's family and wealth? Do ye think me daft wantin' to break with tradition?"

"It's crossed my mind." Craig leaned forward, settling an elbow on his knee, and grinned. "But I understand how ye feel. A man wants to direct his own path."

"Precisely." Gavin assessed his friend. Did he feel trapped by obligations? "But then I'd be married to Lesley, and I wouldn't have the opportunity to consider Serena."

"Not necessarily," Craig said. "Ye might have been widowed. If it was her time to die. It was her time."

"We're never really in control." Gavin shrugged. "Mayhap we're given some choices and the rest is up to God."

Silence lengthened between them as Gavin turned his attention to the land and the late afternoon landscape. He had hoped to reach the village before nightfall.

White clouds dotted the blue sky. The vast openness took some getting used to without trees. The moors and glens cast a purple-brown hue. From this distance the loch's surface glistened like shards of glass in the sun's waning rays.

Another half-hour and they finally reached the cover of the forest hiding the village. The day's weather had been mild, but the cooler shade of the leaved branches above them made Gavin shiver. As they followed the narrow path, he blinked, waiting for his eyes to adjust to the contrasting darkness. The wagon wheels jostled them over roots and uneven ground, snapping a fallen branch. Barrels rattled in the back. Gavin gripped the wooden seat with both hands to keep his balance. He'd much prefer this part of the journey on horseback.

A deep growl bellowed from the thicket. Gavin looked to the left, seeing naught, he swung his head to the right. Foliage rustled. Out leaped a wolf, his yellow eyes fierce with warning. The horses whinnied, reared up, and pawed the air. They pulled against the harnesses as the wolf barked.

"Whoa!" Craig held the reins steady.

Gavin jumped down, hoping that the animal was Phelan, and there weren't any other white wolves around. He could try and lure him away from the horses. "Keep them calm, while I see to the wolf," Gavin said, training his eyes on the animal.

"That giant needs to do somethin' about him. He's a nuisance," Craig complained.

"Easy, Phelan." Gavin inched forward. "What is it, lad?"

Phelan stopped growling as he lowered his lips over his fangs and barked. Encouraged, Gavin stepped closer, but kept his hands to his sides. Phelan barked again and turned in a full circle, then whined.

An odd action for a wolf about to tear them apart only moments ago. The wolf stepped back into the woods. He popped his head through the leaves and whined again.

An eerie presence slithered up Gavin's spine, and he rubbed the back of his neck. His keen senses aware, he listened and watched, but saw no sign of an ambush.

Phelan barked, tilting his head, his yellow eyes never wavering. Gavin studied him. No beastly ambition lurked within those eyes as he'd thought, only a quiet intelligence that couldn't speak words.

"I think he wants me to follow him," Gavin said over his shoulder. "Stay here with the wagon. I'll be right back."

"What?" Craig twisted his mouth in disbelief and shifted in his seat. "Have ye gone mad, mon? That wolf can turn on ye in an instant!"

"If he wanted to attack me, he would have." Gavin turned back to Phelan and stepped toward him. He barked again and retreated into the woods. Gavin hurried after him.

He ducked below branches and leaves, leaning right, then left. His chest pumped in rapid breaths as he struggled to keep up. Phelan departed through the rough bushes. Gavin parted the leaves and peeked through, more woods greeted him. He listened. A flutter brought his attention upward to a bird flying from one tree branch to another.

A howl startled him back into action. He followed the sound, until he heard a weeping female. Fearing for Serena, he charged through the thick leaves, his hand on the hilt of his sword and his heart beating like a battling lion.

The lass in question screamed, cowering in a ball against the trunk of a tree. She crawled on her hands and knees away from him. While the blood in his head eased that she wasn't Serena, his heart lurched at the cuts, bruises, and distress of the young woman.

"I won't hurt ye." Gavin soothed. "I'm here to help. The wolf led me to ye."

In mad fear, she reached out trembling hands to feel her way as she hastened to her feet to run. Sobs shrilled as her breath caught in her throat, and she choked.

Cara! The realization hit him. He was determined to help her before she injured herself further.

"It's Gavin. Let me help ye."

She wasn't listening. The lass ran toward a tree branch unaware that she was in danger of busting her head. Gavin lunged after her, grabbing her around the waist before she could get away. She fought against him, pounding his chest with her tiny fists.

"I'll take ye to Serena."

"Serena?" The hopeful name hung like a lingering promise. She relaxed, the will to fight evaporating. Violent tremors shook her as silent tears streamed over the blood-stained gash on her right cheek. A bruise thickened under her left eye. "Ye know Serena?"

"Aye." Gavin held himself still in an effort not to alarm her. "It's Gavin. The wolf led me to ye."

"Phelan saved me." She sucked in air. "Someone was chasing me. Is he gone?"

"Who?"

"I don't know." She shook her head, her tussled brown hair everywhere. "He nary spoke a word."

"Then how do ye know it was a man?"

She touched her swollen eye, the cut upon the corner of her lip. Her fingers shook. "He had the strength of a brute, the arms of a tree trunk."

Crumbling in Gavin's arms, she burst into tears. "I thought he would kill me . . . or worse."

Not knowing what else to do, Gavin stood there, giving her the time she needed to collect herself. He scanned the forest for signs the man might return with others.

"Lass, do ye know if he was alone?" Gavin asked.

She took a deep breath, sniffled, and wiped her cheeks. "I heard no one else, but I canna be sure."

"We need to get out of here. I left Craig with the wagon. We need to go back in case there are more of them to ambush him."

"Craig?" She lifted her head, shivered, and stepped back. Brushing her hair from her face, she gulped. "I must look a fright."

"Ye're alive. That's all that matters." Gavin gathered her plaid and pulled it around to cover her. "Yer dress is torn."

She gasped. "Thank ye."

"Can ye walk?"

"Aye." She nodded, grabbing his arm. "I ran so far, I'm lost. God must have been looking out for me to send Phelan and then ye."

"Indeed, God is always with us, even when things look hopeless." Gavin led her back toward the wagon. Phelan followed close behind. The moment they emerged from the woods, Craig looked up. His eyes widened. He dropped the reins and hopped down.

"Cara!" Craig rushed over.

Gavin released her.

Craig pulled her into his arms. He took her face between his hands. He traced a tender finger over her wounds, swallowing hard. Gavin met his gaze over Cara's head. The intense pain in Craig's eyes was clear.

In that one expression, Gavin now understood the deep feelings his friend had for Cara. There'd be no teasing about Serena. Gavin's gut clenched. What if it had been Serena? An image of her smiling and dancing tugged and twisted at his desire to protect her.

❧

Serena leaned over Cara and wiped dry blood from her cheek. Tears stung Serena's eyes and her nose suddenly burned. "To think what could have happened to ye." She blinked to clear her vision. "The good Lord sent Phelan, of that I'm sure."

"Aye, Gavin and Craig as well." Cara's swollen lip barely moved as she spoke. She winced as Serena dabbed at the slit in the corner of her mouth.

"I'm sorry." Serena dipped the cloth in a bowl of water and wrung the excess liquid. "I'll have ye cleaned up before Gavin arrives with Tomas."

"Pray tell, where did Craig go? He was most attentive to me." Cara turned her head and stared at the dark wall. "Although, I wish he hadn't seen me in such a state."

"Dearie me, but the lad was in a desperate way, he was," Gunna said, shifting to the side in her chair. "He was beside himself with worry for ye. He paced outside afore Gavin asked him to fetch yer parents. He didn't want to leave yer side."

Serena glanced at Gunna. How was it she couldn't hear some things at all, while other sounds she picked up all too easily?

Cara clutched Serena's hand, gaining her attention from Gunna. "He went for my parents?" Her brown eyes widened. "If Mither sees me like this, she'll blame herself for letting me go to the well alone. I shouldn't have lingered."

"Cara Grant!" Serena gasped as she thrust her hands to her hips. "I'll not listen to such talk. A person should be able to walk wherever she pleases without being attacked and nearly beaten to death. There's naught ye could have done to deserve this."

"I agree." Evelina walked up behind Serena with a warm brew. "I've made somethin' to help calm yer nerves, but I can only let ye have a few sips. Tomas will want ye awake to answer his questions when he arrives. Then ye may drink the rest."

She slipped an arm around Cara, while Serena assisted from the other side to help lift her. Evelina tilted the cup to her lips. Cara sipped and swallowed. She laid her head back against the feather pillow.

"Thank ye." Her voice sounded weak. She tried to smile, but one corner of her lips remained still. "I know yer brews. At least I'll sleep well tonight."

Voices outside signaled that Tomas and Gavin had returned. A horse neighed and snorted. They knocked. Serena swung open the door. Tomas stepped in and strode over to Cara. Serena leaned outside, peeking to see Gavin tugging on a rope around a chest on the wagon.

"Gavin, won't ye come in?" Serena couldn't imagine what he was doing. Was he leaving now that he had delivered Tomas to them? Her heart pounded as she tried to think of how to encourage him to stay. "Yer supplies will be fine. Ye must be tired from the day's travels. Come inside, rest, and take refreshment. Surely ye'd like to hear what Tomas has to say about Cara?"

"Aye, I would, but I brought ye something back." He sighed. "I suppose now would be a bad time to bring it in. Don't know what I was thinkin', lass. Please forgive me."

His blue eyes met hers. A soft wind graced her cheek as a tremor pooled in the pit of her stomach and flooded her heart. Gavin MacKenzie was an honorable man, if only their circumstances were different. An aching pang braided inside her.

"Nay." She shook her head. "An apology isn't necessary. We're all feeling out of sorts."

"In that case, I shall join ye, then." Gavin met her at the threshold. Ducking inside, he stepped into a dark corner. Serena closed the door and slid the bolt in place. Gavin may be lurking in the shadows, but Serena was well aware of his presence as she stepped to the foot of the bed.

Having him near gave her strength and comfort. While she knew she should draw such security from the Lord, would it be wrong to rely on Gavin if God had brought him here for this purpose?

"I don't believe ye've any broken ribs. Merely bruised is all," Tomas said. "No doubt, ye'll be sore for a few days. Serena did a fine job cleaning all the wounds. Yer hands and arms took another beating from the limbs and briars ye ran through."

"What about her head?" Serena asked. "She complained of a headache when she first arrived." Serena helped Cara sip more of her mother's brew.

"Nay." Tomas pulled the blanket up to Cara's neck and tucked her in like a wee child. "No swelling or lumps that I could tell. Her pupils look fine." He paused, looking down at Cara. "With some rest, Cara, ye'll be right back to yer auld self again. The main thing ye'll need to overcome is the fright ye've had. It can make ye fearful of things ye weren't before. Only God and time can heal ye of that."

"Thank ye." Cara yawned, her eyes drifting closed. A few seconds later they fluttered open again as if she fought to stay awake.

"Yer brew is working, Mither," Serena whispered.

"I can . . . still hear ye," Cara murmured, her weary eyes shutting.

Soon, her chest rose and fell in a steady rhythm. Serena sighed, satisfied her friend would now sleep easy. She returned to her discarded sewing.

"Gavin and Tomas, please join us by the fire." Evelina said. "Would ye like somethin' to drink?"

Tomas took a seat at the table. Gavin's heavy boots pressed against the hard dirt floor as he sat opposite from Tomas.

"Nay," Tomas said. "But I'd like to know what ye gave her. It didn't take an immediate effect, but when it did, the brew worked well."

Evelina smiled, her cheeks a rosy glow from the praise. "I put a wee pinch of chamomile in some warm milk and honey."

"Ah, that explains it." Tomas nodded, folding his hands upon the table.

Gunna's head rolled back against her chair. She started snoring. Serena was torn between concern at her increasing naps and mirth. She grinned. "Mither, should I wake her before she falls?"

"Nay, she'll be fine. Of late, Gunna has perfected her talent of sleeping in awkward positions without mishap."

"And what are ye working on, Serena?" Tomas dropped his elbows on his knees. "Looks quite involved."

"I'm altering a gown for the laird's feast." Serena shook out the folds and held it up, proud of her handiwork. "I'm sewing in a lace border here." She pointed to the neckline.

"But I thought ye didn't have aught to mend." Gavin's tone sounded more like a protest as his back straightened and his chin lifted in speculation, his dark eyes assessing her.

Serena lowered the gown, feeling a sudden censure from Gavin. "I didn't misspeak ye, if that's what ye're thinking." Her throat went dry at the sudden change in his behavior.

"Gavin, the most wonderful thing happened," Evelina interrupted, walking over to the chests and opening the large one. "Ye know how Serena worried she didn't have a decent gown for the laird's feast? Well, the laird had these delivered from the castle yestereve. Both chests are filled with bolts of fabric, lace, satin and a few gowns like the one Serena is altering. He said she's to make herself a gown fit for the feast—a couple if she wants. Then she's free to give the rest to Kyla for other lasses in the village."

"I daresay, that's verra considerate of him." Tomas moved to the edge of his chair and angled to view Gavin. "Wouldn't ye say so, lad?"

"Aye, I would." Gavin stared at the chest as if it might burst into flames. He glanced at the empty table, preoccupied with his thoughts.

"Not only that," Evelina said, linking her fingers, excitement shining in her eyes and smile. "But the laird requested Serena save him a dance."

"I must be going." A chair scraped across the floor. Gavin stood with force. The wooden seat swayed on two legs. He grabbed the back before it could fall. Gavin cleared his throat. "Allow me to offer my earnest congratulations to the happy news."

"Ye're leaving so soon?" Serena bolted to her feet, crumpling the gown in her fists. Searching for a reason to detain him, Serena remembered what he had said outside. "What about the gift on the wagon?"

"Gift?" His blue eyes darkened as he gave her a direct look that resembled pain. He blinked and it was gone. Had she imagined it?

"Aye, ye mentioned something about a gift earlier." She nodded.

"Nay." He waved his hand. "'Tis naught of consequence. Mayhap, it should wait until Cara is awake to enjoy it as well."

"Verra well." Her hopes fell as she dropped her gaze, lest he see her disappointment that it wasn't something special for her.

"By the looks of it, ye've plenty of gifts from Iain MacBraigh to keep ye busy for a while. Good night." He left, the door shutting behind him. Serena stood for several moments, trying to make sense of his words.

"Serena, I'm so sorry, lass." Mother sank in her chair by the fire with a dazed expression. "I didn't expect him to . . . react like that."

"Aye." Thomas nodded, sitting back and crossing his ankles. "I do believe the lad is jealous."

"Of Iain MacBraigh?" Serena couldn't believe it. She lowered herself down and took up her sewing again. "That's the most foolish idea I've ever heard. Either way, as my friend, he should be most happy for me. And think how glad the other village lasses will be to receive a new gown." She pulled her needle through the material with a snap. "Indeed, I'm most disappointed in Gavin."

❧

He should have known better. Of course the laird intended to see to Serena's needs, especially since she was under his care. Now Gavin was stuck with a trunk of fabric he didn't need.

Hearing that Iain had asked Serena to save him a dance hadn't helped matters any. Gavin wasn't prepared to battle the assault of jealousy that consumed him, making him unable to think.

Anger, he understood. But jealousy? It didn't need sufficient motive. A simple dance could give rise to the unwanted feeling. Nor was there a target, as Iain MacBraigh had proven to be a good man . . . a friend. Serena deserved the best, all the happiness life could offer. If he truly cared for her, was it fair for him to get in the way?

Cracking twigs and branches caused Gavin to unsheathe his sword. He held the reins in his left hand and strained to listen through the dark over the rattling wagon. Movement shifted leaves and bushes at the right. The horse continued at the same pace, unaware. Had he mistaken a wild animal for a man?

His stomach churned in discomfort. The muscles in his neck and shoulders tensed as he braced for a blind ambush. The wheels rolled on beyond the trees and out into the open under the moon and stars where the loch glistened from the silver reflection. The burning camp fires among the tents were a welcome sight in contrast to the black woods. A chill in the air kept his men huddled around the flames.

"Gavin is back!" One of the lads hurried toward him. "Where's Craig?"

"Oh, there's much to tell, but first would ye secure the wagon and see to the horse?"

"Aye, but wait to tell the tale when I return." The lad reached up and held the animals while Gavin bounced to the ground.

"Where's Leith?"

"Over there." He pointed to the middle fire pit. "He has news for ye as well."

Gavin strode to his brother, greeting men along the way. Leith bent, warming his hands. He noticed Gavin and stood with a welcoming grin. "About time ye came back. I thought ye'd decided to take up residence in town." He leaned to the side peering around Gavin. "What happened to Craig?"

"He's fine, but first, I heard ye have some news," Gavin said.

"Iain MacBraigh has invited us to stay at the castle—you and I."

"What about the men?" When they had first arrived, Iain had offered a guest chamber to he and Leith, but Gavin had made it clear they would not depart from the men.

"He's offered a chamber to us and any men of rank, such as Craig and Roan. The rest may stay in the barracks inside the protection of the gate."

Gavin rubbed the back of his neck, considering this latest event. "Do ye have any idea what might have changed his mind?"

"Nay." Leith shook his head. "But mayhap it has something to do with the upcoming feast." Leith shrugged. "If his guests are residing outside the protection of the castle . . . in tents, it wouldn't look verra good."

"True." Gavin stroked his chin. How would they continue providing protection to the villagers?

"I thanked the laird and told him we'd have a ready answer on the morrow. If ye remember, the barracks are in poor condition. We'd need to make them fit to sleep in. Still, it might prove to be better than the hard ground and a canvas tent. What do ye think?" Leith raised a dark eyebrow, the firelight glowing upon his face.

"I think the move would be sensible, but I don't want to lose the ability to protect the villagers. Mayhap, we could change shifts staying with Tomas."

The other men gathered around.

"Before we make any final decisions, ye should hear what happened today." Gavin paused, meeting each man's gaze before launching into the story. After he finished, Gavin linked his fingers behind his back. "Until we can determine who might be behind these attacks, we've no idea what lengths he'll go to."

A scoff came from the midst of the group. Roan stepped forward. "Gavin, we were all here in the village and look what still happened to the lass. I don't know what else to do. What if it is a villager doing these strange things? Ye know these people aren't right."

"Aye," one man agreed.

"He has a point," another one echoed.

"I won't abandon them. We either do this in shifts or we stay here in the camp." Gavin looked around at the other men. "I think it's clear they canna defend themselves. We need to figure out what is going on. To do that we'll all have to become more involved with the villagers and learn what we can."

10

$\mathcal{S}$erena strolled beside her mother through the village. The afternoon air stirred against her face, a few degrees more brisk than earlier in the day when she had been at the castle. She pulled her plaid tight around her arms.

A hooded image cloaked in black appeared at the well. A cart rolled by and the person vanished. How could that be? Serena blinked, swallowing in discomfort. She glanced at her mother, who looked the other way. Not wanting to alarm her, Serena said nothing.

Her thoughts drifted to Gunna home alone. After what had happened to Cara and all of them at the kirk, Serena worried for her. "Are ye sure Gunna will be fine while we're gone?" Serena asked. "This morn she acted as if she'd never lit a fire in the hearth before."

"Aye, and she sleeps so much more than she used to. Most likely she'll nap in her chair and still be there when we get back."

"Snoring, no doubt." Serena smiled, trying to comfort herself that no one would want to harm a feeble woman. Yet, it hadn't stopped them from attacking an innocent blind lass. Serena shook her head as if to rid herself of the fearful thoughts haunting her.

"At her age, she's earned the privilege to do as she pleases." Evelina smiled, shaking her head.

Silence lengthened between them.

"Good day!" A female voice called.

Serena glanced up to see Birkita perched on a fallen tree trunk not far from the cobbler's house. She waved with one hand, while holding a book with the other.

Evelina and Serena waved back.

Birkita slipped her finger in the pages, marking her spot, and ambled over. "I'm supposed to be fetching a pail of water, but I'm so close to finishing this chapter that I couldn't help myself."

"What are ye reading?" Serena glanced at the brown leather volume in her hand, curious if Birkita had something new Serena could borrow. Books were such a rare item in their village. Outside of her mother and the laird, Serena didn't know anyone else who could read other than Birkita. When possible, they would buy new books from town and share them, although Serena suspected Birkita read some of them twice before she gave them over.

"It's the fourth volume of *The Canterbury Tales*." Birkita's eyes lit like a torch. "Da picked it up for me a sennight ago at the market. Ye can borrow it when I finish." A sly smile lifted the corner of her pink lips. She enjoyed being the first to read a new book.

Serena held up her hand. "In that case, I won't ask ye about it, for I want to be completely surprised when I get a chance to read it."

"Are ye going for a long walk?" From the advantage of her height, Birkita glanced over Serena's head to her mother and smiled in greeting.

"Only to Kyla's," Evelina said. "She invited us over for the afternoon."

"Oh, I long for a new gown. Even though Da sold a few new soles to some of the MacKenzie clansmen, 'twas only enough left over for a new book, not a gown. "

"Birkita!" A woman called from the house. A brown head appeared, leaning out the door to reveal Rosheen, their younger sister.

Looking back, Birkita sighed with a heavy spirit. "Good day to ye both. I'm needed just now. Enjoy yer afternoon walk."

Birkita picked up her pail of water and stomped toward the house. Serena glanced at her mother, struggling to hold back her mirth. A slight sound escaped as she covered her mouth.

Serena's mother gave her a stern look with her lips forming a thin line and her dark eyebrows rising. "It isn't like ye to laugh at others, Serena."

"I'm not." She shook her head as they continued walking. "I was only thinking that if given a choice between a new fine gown and a book, Birkita would still choose the book. Think how surprised she'll be to receive a new fine gown in addition to her new book."

"Aye, I believe ye're right on that account." Evelina nodded, her eyes on the well-worn path ahead of them.

As they passed the next house, Quinn's deep voice bellowed a greeting. He chopped wood on a stump by the shaded side of his tall but humble home. Phelan lay a few feet away, his ears pointed straight up, always aware of his surroundings. His tail flapped against the thick cushioned grass. A few seconds later he bounced to his feet and ran toward them.

"Oh, dear!" Evelina stiffened. "Ye know how I dislike animals."

"Brace yerself, Mither!" Serena warned.

Instead of leaping upon them as they feared, Phelan ran circles around them. He barked in a happy salutation. After a few laps, he calmed and trotted beside them. Her mother grabbed her arm, digging her nails in Serena's flesh.

"Mither, ye know he won't hurt ye." Serena pried Evelina's fingers loose and rubbed her sore arm. "He has a protective, but gentle spirit about him."

"Aye, but he doesn't know me as he knows ye. And I've seen him knock others over trying to play. The wolf doesn't know his own strength, much like his owner."

Serena linked her arm through her mother's and offered what she hoped was an assuring grin. "And that's exactly why ye're safe walking with me."

"Phalen, ye're naught but a traitor!" Quinn called behind them. In response, the wolf looked back at him, raised his snout, and grunted as if teasing him.

A while later, they reached Kyla's house. The front door stood ajar. Phelan barked, announcing their arrival and Kyla rushed outside to greet them.

"I'm so glad ye've come! I've got some good news for ye both." She crooked a finger for them to follow her inside.

Serena blinked, allowing her eyes time to adjust to the dark interior. Sunlight filtered through the door at an angle, illuminating a short path into the cottage. The walls and corners remained in the shadows.

"Please, sit down." Kyla motioned to two wooden chairs by the wall to the right side of the door. She hurried to a dark corner and carried two exquisite gowns, one a green satin with a plaid underskirt of dark blue with green and purple lines. The other gown was made of gold satin and white lace trimming and a plaid underskirt of brown with yellow and red lines. "With the last measure I took of ye, I've been working on these gowns. Which one do ye prefer for the feast?"

"They're beautiful, Kyla!" Evelina reached for the gold one.

"Indeed." Serena touched the smooth, thick material of the green gown. It was cool against her skin. *"Ye have bonny eyes, the color of peat moss, which gives Scotland its natural beauty."* Gavin's voice whispered to her heart's memory.

Serena thought back to the contents of the chests from Iain. "I don't remember the green fabric or this plaid among the materials I brought to ye."

"A fine gentleman brought the green by and asked me to make it for ye. He said it would match yer eyes. Lass, I believe ye've caught the eye of two admirers, ye have. Now ye'll have to choose. Which one will it be?" Kyla held a gown in each hand.

Without a doubt, she knew which one. Gavin had made a long trip into town. Iain had merely given her an old chest of fabrics in a sewing room he had found. Gavin had chosen the perfect material. Iain had no idea what the chests contained. She knew which man admired her eyes.

The gift! Gavin had said he'd brought back a gift for her, but among all of Iain's fabrics floating around he must have lost the courage to give it to her. Her heart swelled with love. Was it love?

Kyla laughed and looked at Evelina. "I do believe I'm enjoying this. Look at those rosy cheeks. Lass, it isn't often I've seen ye blush. After all ye've done to help me through my grief, I'm honored to be a part of such a thoughtful favor for ye."

"I know which one." Serena met Kyla's sparkling brown gaze. "The green."

❧

Gavin watched the entrance to the great hall, hoping Serena would be wearing the green gown instead of the red one he'd seen her sewing from the laird's chests. He didn't know why it mattered since she may not realize it hadn't come from the laird. Would Kyla have told her? His feelings were raw and foreign. Yet, he couldn't help it.

Servants rushed to cover two long tables and a shorter one upon the dais with white table linens. Torches burned on the walls on each side of the scarlet tapestry that had been hung for the occasion. Another servant lit candles on the tables.

The place had been transformed in one afternoon from the dark forlorn condition to a lively, cheerful hall. It now reminded him of home. A familiar longing for MacKenzie Castle pressed at him. He enjoyed traveling, had seen much of the world, but a lingering desire to settle down in his own home had begun to smolder in his heart.

"Gavin, what do ye think?" Footsteps approached from behind with Iain MacBraigh's voice. "Is the great hall not magnificent?"

Turning, Gavin witnessed a prideful smile on the laird's face. Iain leaned his head back perusing the high walls. He raised a hand, gesturing to their surroundings. "Serena Boyd was born to run a castle. She found this tapestry folded in an auld chest, had the servants clean and scent them. This place has long needed a woman's touch. I would have ordered the tapestry hung without any scents."

"I thought I smelled a light aroma of some sort." Gavin breathed deeply. Heather and juniper lingered of her scent. A deeper longing than he had felt for home seized his chest . . . longing for a wife. He could imagine no one but Serena in that role. He needed her.

They lived in separate worlds. She believed herself beneath his station, a step closer to Iain's world. Gavin's chest constricted, and he clenched his teeth, determined not to show his discomfort. The startling realization came at a great cost.

Would his family accept her? If not, could he give up his inheritance—his birthright?

Servants placed some flowers in a tall piece of pottery in the center of each table, followed by bowls of assorted fruits.

"The flowers are nice," Gavin said.

"Aye." Iain nodded. "Serena's idea. I ordered a fire in the hearth, but she reminded me that if there is to be dancing later, the guests may become overheated and the smoke would overtake the pleasant aromas."

More people arrived at the front entrance where a servant answered the door.

"Excuse me, Gavin. I must greet the newly arrived guests." Iain strode away, leaving Gavin to ponder his thoughts.

Craig and Leith talked in a corner. Several other members of his clan were scattered about the great hall. Gavin had never liked large events. He preferred conversing with people in more quiet settings, where the measure of a man's character could be better assessed. At large feasts as this, every word was planned with the goal of improving one's ranking.

"Here, ye look like ye could use this." Roan pressed a goblet of wine into his hand.

"And what am I doing to give ye that impression?" Gavin raised an eyebrow as he accepted the dark liquid. He sniffed the fermented brew, ensuring it didn't contain a sour smell. Good wine seemed to be scarce among so many these days. The sweet aroma made his mouth water.

"Yer scowl," Roan answered.

Lady Fiona appeared on Iain's arm, followed by her father escorting another young lass. Gavin tensed. The lady had struck him as a fortune hunter, intent to win a husband of quality birth and who had plenty lining the coffers.

She greeted Leith in a false pretense of interest. Gavin groaned, hoping the lad didn't fall for her forged charm. Raising the goblet to his lips, Gavin tasted the dark wine. It burned like a sore throat. He took a deep breath. His nose stung and eyes watered as the fiery liquid thrust his lively senses into a new zeal.

"I'm afraid Leith will soon discover Lady Fiona's venom," Gavin said.

Roan met Gavin's gaze, then turned to study Leith and Lady Fiona. "Could be a lesson well worth the risk." He grinned.

The knocker echoed through the great hall like a deep drum. The interruption gave Gavin time to consider the biting response about to roll off his tongue.

"So, this is the infamous Serena Boyd I've been hearing about?" Lady Fiona's tone rose to a high pitch.

Gavin froze. A vision of Serena in green satin and lace over an underskirt of a dark blue plaid with green and purple lines drained his throat dry. He felt like a parched man staring at a water fountain.

Satisfaction swelled in his chest, knowing she had chosen his fabric. While Iain introduced Lady Fiona, a shy smile crossed Serena's face as she shook her long black hair over her shoulder. It fell to her waist. Floral ribbons of ivory tied the strands on each side out of her face. Evelina stood beside her in the red gown that Gavin remembered Serena altering. A ravenous heat brewed in his lungs, robbing him of his next breath. He coughed, heading toward her.

At the sound, Serena's gaze lifted to his. The pulse in his throat quickened as her moss-colored eyes brightened. Her pink lips curled in a favorable smile. "Gavin! I see ye've already arrived."

"Aye, I've been eagerly awaiting yer arrival." He turned to Evelina and inclined his head. "Evelina, ye look lovely in red. It's a fine night for dancing after dinner. I understand a harpist will be playing soft melodies during dinner." Gavin motioned to a woman off to the side between the dais and the first long table. She sat in a wood chair, plucking each chord one at a time to fine tune her instrument.

"I've always enjoyed harp music. This will be a rare treat as no one in the village owns such a fine piece," Serena said.

"I should say not!" Lady Fiona narrowed her eyes and tilted her nose in the air. "An elegant harp would be out of place in those wee hovels. Where would one put it?"

"True." Serena spoke before Gavin could.

Gavin wanted to hurl Lady Fiona's insult back at her, but as the host it was Iain's place.

"Lady Fiona, I always thought yer gentle breeding would constitute compassion for those less fortunate than yerself." The laird's lips thinned and his eyes darkened like coal.

Serena met Lady Fiona's gaze. "Indeed, I suppose it would take a great deal of wit to organize such a wee space. Fortunately for ye, Lady Fiona, ye'll never be in such need." Serena turned to Gavin. "To answer yer question, aye, we both intend to dance. Right, Mither?"

Evelina turned her scowling expression from Lady Fiona and offered a forced smile. "After much persuasion from Serena, I finally consented."

"I didn't mean to imply that I possess a lack of compassion." Lady Fiona's complexion turned crimson, her gray eyes troubled. "Only that they're less likely to own such luxuries." She gave a nervous laugh. "And speaking of good manners, I need to find my cousin and make introductions for her. Please excuse me." She strayed away to where her father and cousin conversed with other guests.

"I must say, I'm quite impressed with how well ye handled her rude insolence." Gavin regarded Serena with even more respect. "Truth be known, I didn't think ye'd respond."

"Neither did I," Iain shook his head.

"Why not?" Serena's wide gaze snapped from Gavin to Iain and back again.

"I don't really know." Gavin shrugged. "I suppose because ye seem so reserved."

"Aye, but I'm more honest than reserved, which only means I don't have a quick temper. It doesn't mean I never get angry or that I won't defend myself."

He that is slow to anger is better than the mighty. A biblical proverb Father Mike had taught him when he was a child came to mind. He missed Father Mike's wise counsel. As the MacKenzie Clan priest, he had served their family's spiritual needs for many years. He was also one of the few who had a complete copy of the Latin Bible, rather than copied excerpts of ancient scrolls.

A servant announced that the feast was ready to be served. Gavin and Leith were seated at the dais table with the laird, the earl, and his family. Serena and her mother were placed at the lower tables with other invited guests from town and a few villagers, including Father Tomas.

Iain stood and raised his palms out. "May I have yer attention, please?" The sound of Iain's voice calmed the great hall, as conversations faded. All eyes lifted toward him. "I would like to introduce our guests of honor. Please welcome Gavin MacKenzie, the eldest son of Birk MacKenzie of Kintail at Eileen Donan, Chieftain of Clan MacKenzie."

Gavin stood and gave a bow. He forced a smile even though he disliked being noticed by everyone.

"And Leith MacKenzie, Birk's youngest son."

Leith, much more comfortable with the attention, stood and bowed with a broad grin.

"The MacKenzie brothers are here with an army of warriors making long-needed repairs to Braigh Castle. Gavin assures me it's a great way to keep unwed men busy in times of peace."

Some of the guests laughed and nodded in understanding, while clapping.

The meal was served consisting of pork roast, stewed carrots, potatoes, and bread. Gavin could hardly enjoy the fine food as he disliked being separated from Serena. She laughed and conversed with others as Gavin wished he was part of their lively table.

Lady Fiona tried to engage him in more conversation, but he kept his answers short, but polite, to discourage her. After three failed attempts, she finally turned to Iain, who couldn't escape as easily since they were sitting closer.

When Iain finally announced that the hall would be cleared for dancing, Gavin could hardly contain his excitement. He felt like a tender lad, ripe with the coming of age, not the one score and ten years that had branded him with plenty of experience. He paced back and forth as the tables were cleared and moved.

The musicians settled around the harpist, complete with fiddlers, drummers, pipers, flute players, and a bag piper. For a brief moment, Gavin thought of his lute at home, but one glance at Serena talking with Tomas and her mother on a bench by the hearth, and all he could think about was holding her in his arms for that first dance.

The music began. With his sights on Serena, he strode toward her. His heart pounded in time with the drums. Iain stepped in front of Serena, a few feet away, blocking Gavin's view.

"I'd be honored if ye'd share this dance with me, lass," Iain's voice spoke clear through the music around them.

Gavin stopped, his chest heavy with concern, as he waited for her response. Would she honor her promise to him or feel obligated to Iain since he was her host and laird? She faltered. Her silence lengthened. With a hammering heart full of disappointment, Gavin strode away.

Serena stared into Iain MacBraigh's expectant hazel eyes, awkward discomfort weighing a burden upon her. She hated to refuse the laird, but it would be much worse to break a promise to Gavin. Iain's auburn mustache moved with his upper lip as he smiled down at her . . . waiting.

Clearing her throat, Serena returned a smile. "I'm sorry, my laird, but I've already promised the first dance to Gavin. Mayhap later in the evening?"

"Of course." He frowned, nodding.

"I want to thank ye for the gowns and the materials ye so graciously provided. The colors are lovely."

"Ye're verra welcome. Serena, ye could have worn any color and ye'd still glow like an angel."

While his response was flattering, Iain lacked a certain depth that Gavin possessed. She struggled to feel a personal connection with him the way she did with Gavin. A pair of blue eyes came to mind and her heart fluttered. She needed to find Gavin.

"Please excuse me." She curtsied. He bowed.

Serena stepped around the laird, but didn't see Gavin in the crowd. A flutter of motion with colorful gowns, tall gentlemen, and swirling couples hindered her view. Where had he gone? She sidestepped others and made her way to the wall. Standing on her tiptoes, she recognized the back of his red head departing for the double doors. Was he leaving or merely seeking a bit of fresh air?

Her stomach balked at the thought of missing him. All morning she had imagined what it would be like to dance by his side and swing upon his arm as they had practiced on the cliff to the ocean's beat. She dashed around another couple. He reached for the doorknob.

"Gavin!"

He paused, standing still as if listening for her voice a second time.

"Gavin!"

A gentleman stepped back, bumping into her and stomping her toes.

"Och!"

"Pardon me, lass. Are ye all right?"

"Aye." She nodded, biting her bottom lip as the pain shot through her foot. Numbness set in her sore toes.

"I'll take care of her." Gavin appeared by her side and took her arm, allowing her to lean upon him for support. He guided her to a nearby chair in the corner. "Are ye hurt anywhere else besides yer feet?"

"Nay." Serena sat in a cushioned chair with a sigh. "I daresay, I shall feel fine in a moment." She glanced up into his concerned blue eyes. She loved the warmth in his gaze and the protection she felt around him. Gavin was the first man to tempt her heart with trusting him.

His grasp lingered, and she didn't pull away as he bent close. He smelled of leather and pine in his navy blue and dark green plaid with thin red-and-white stripes. His white tunic had tight-fitting cuffs with pleated shoulders over brown breeches laced to the knees where his leather boots covered his calves. Serena's breath hitched in her throat. The man was well-dressed and handsome, to be sure.

"I could examine yer feet if need be." He raised a red eye-brow as his forehead wrinkled in question. "Or I could fetch Tomas."

"Please . . . I'm feeling much better." Serena gripped his arm. "May I have that dance ye promised me? I've been look-ing forward to it."

"Are ye sure ye're well enough?" He wavered. She not only wanted to dance for her own merriment, but because she sensed how much it would please him. His happiness mattered to her. The realization of how much she cared for him hit her with unexpected force.

"Aye, I'm verra well." She stood to her feet.

Gavin's eyes sparkled and his skin glowed in a rugged hue from the torchlight and candles. His muscles beneath her fin-gertips showed strength. Serena trembled with excitement.

He led her among the circle of dancers, and she stepped to the beat of the music just as he had taught her. "Why were ye leaving, Gavin?"

"I'll be honest with ye, lass. I thought Iain had secured my place. The same thing happened at the village dance. He beat me to ye, and I didn't wish to watch a second time."

"But we danced that day." Serena rushed to the center, meeting the other lasses, and hurried back to Gavin. "I'm a woman who keeps her word. It's the Highland way." She cir-cled around him as the other women did with their partners.

"Ye're right and I'm sorry. I value yer honor. Serena, ye've a quiet, hidden strength in ye that I'm coming to admire—verra much."

Her cheeks blushed, warming her whole body. Serena glanced up at his strong profile. Gavin and his men had given her a glimpse of how things could be with people outside their village. Right now they treated her with kindness and respect. Would their behavior change once they witnessed her fits, or would they be like the villagers who accepted her without thinking her evil and possessed?

Before their arrival, Serena had accepted her life. Now, she longed for more—to be cured of her fits, to be a wife and mother, to experience the love of a husband and child. She wanted this life with Gavin, a man who could never wed a village lass even if she were perfect. Why did God allow them to come here? It was too cruel.

She blinked, attempting to clear her mind as she matched Gavin's steps. The burning desire for more was now ignited in her heart—and it ached. Somehow she had to find the strength to discourage Gavin. Otherwise, her heart might become so woven with him that she would never again find peace when he left.

"That color of green is a perfect match to yer eyes." Gavin leaned toward her ear, his breath warm upon her neck. His voice lowered a timbre. Serena's skin prickled in tiny bumps and her heart bounced inside her chest.

The music ended and they stopped to face each other.

"Make no mistake, Gavin MacKenzie, I chose this gown because ye did."

"Lass, I'm relieved to hear it." A slow grin brightened his expression. "I'm forced to part from ye for the moment, but I'd be honored if ye would accompany me to town on the morrow. I must return for the rest of the supplies we ordered."

More than anything Serena wanted to go, if only to spend the day with Gavin, but the cold reminder of why she must resist him now pressed her. Nothing had changed—only the knowledge of her feelings. A whole day in his company would not only risk him seeing one of her unexpected fits but also feed her heart more of what it craved—time with Gavin.

Serena dropped her gaze, staring at her new slippers.

"What's wrong?" Gavin lifted her chin, trying to see her better.

"I'd love to go with ye, but I canna. Too much work to be done. We'll have to set this place back in order after tonight."

"I thought ye might need to pick up supplies."

"We usually send one of Iain's manservants." Serena noticed Lady Fiona coming toward them. Her nerves tensed at the thought of having to deal with that arrogant woman again. The stress could be enough for her strained nerves to bring on one of her fits. She must make her escape while she could. "Mayhap, ye could ask Lady Fiona. I'm sure she'd be delighted to have an excuse to visit town."

Gavin turned, following the direction of Serena's nod. She chose that moment to slip away.

11

*G*avin welcomed the cool morning air. As he guided the wagon into the cover of the forest leading through the village, his thoughts wandered to Serena. It would be quite tempting to stop by her cottage. He had timed his departure at an hour he'd hoped to meet her while on her way to the castle.

His mind drifted back to last night. Even while Serena had danced with Iain, and he with Lady Fiona, they had sought each other. Gavin respected her for keeping her word to him. A certain air of mystery concealed Serena's past and kept her at length from him. He wanted to know more about her.

The sound of a laboring beast distracted Gavin from his thoughts. He looked up. Gavin squinted to make out the motion in the distance, but the dark forest veiled the image in a black shadow. A moment later, two yellow eyes glowed in contrast to the dark. A growl echoed.

The horse grew nervous and reared. The wagon lurched. Barking ensued.

"Whoa! Easy lad." Gavin pulled on the reins.

"Gavin!" Beacon's voice carried in worry. "Is it ye?"

"Aye." Gavin glanced down at Beacon running toward him. "Can ye calm that wolf so my horse will stop balking?"

The dwarf took deep breaths and laid over Phelan's back, stroking him between the ears. He whispered to the animal who promptly sat on his hind legs. "I promised Serena I'd find ye before ye leave, then I've got to hurry to the castle and tell Iain she won't be coming today."

"Why?" Alarm seized Gavin's chest as a bolt of fear shot through his gut. "What's wrong with Serena?"

"Serena's fine. 'Tis Gunna. Tomas says she needs some medicine that's only available at market. She wanted me to ask if she could go with ye today."

While Gavin had wanted Serena to join him on his trip, he had hoped the circumstances would be much different. "Aye. I'll go to the cottage while ye take the news to the laird."

"Good. The lass will be pleased." He brushed his blond locks to the side and out of his eyes. "Serena's always been so kind to me an' Quinn. I don't like to see 'er fretting."

Beacon tapped Phelan on the head and they were off in the direction of the castle. A bird whistled in the trees above Gavin, a reminder that the morning would progress without him if he didn't get moving. He smacked the reins and the horse lunged forward. The wagon wobbled over the tree roots. Gavin wished he could travel faster, as eagerness pressed against his concern for Gunna. He had grown fond of her these past few weeks.

By the time he arrived, Serena paced outside. She wore a brown dress with a plaid wrapped around her shoulders in thin stripes of red and white on woven wool. Her black hair tumbled around her worried face and down her back. She chewed her bottom lip as her wide green eyes presented a striking contrast to her pale skin.

He set the break and started to climb down to help her up, but she shook her head. "Nay, I can get in by myself. We must hurry. Gunna is bad off."

Once she was seated beside him, Gavin motioned his horse forward. He gave her a sideways glance, noticing how red-rimmed her eyes were. "It doesn't look like ye've had much rest."

"I'm fine. Gunna's breathing is growing much worse by the hour. Tomas says her heart is failing." Serena dropped her gaze as her voice cracked. She folded her trembling hands in her lap, and he fought the desire to cover them with his own—to comfort her.

"Will the medicine help her heal or only ease her pain?" Gavin asked.

"'Twill only ease the pain." Serena sighed. "Gunna insists on having her wits about her, which is why she won't take aught from Tomas. He's known for giving people sleeping potions to help them sleep in comfort until they quietly pass."

"I see." Gavin let silence fall between them. He wondered if he should try to talk about something else to distract her.

"Gavin, please don't think bad of me for refusing to come today and then changing my mind. I hope ye understand."

"I could never think bad of ye, Serena. I know ye had to work, but this is different." He kept his gaze ahead. "I understand, and I'm sure Iain will as well."

"Good, because I don't think I could bear it if ye thought bad of me." She pulled her plaid tight. "I realize I've been reserved, but please believe me when I say that my reservations regarding strangers are truly warranted."

"I imagine people here aren't treated verra favorably by the townsfolk in Braighwick, especially since they dub ye as the Village of Outcasts."

"There's much ye don't know. There are outsiders who would love to destroy us."

"Serena, I realize everyone here is different, but I find it hard to believe that people would want to destroy ye for no good reason." Gavin hoped he could somehow open her eyes to see the world in a less frightening way. "Someone is trying to frighten the villagers, but don't make the mistake of believing all outsiders are like that."

"Never mind." She turned away, observing the land.

He hit a bump. The wagon tilted, sliding her toward him. On instinct his arm wrapped around her. She felt perfect against his side, as if she belonged. Her soft frame brought a heated warmth that he found inviting.

"Are ye all right?" Her hair tickled his chin and reminded him of junipers.

"Aye. Just startled is all." She brushed her hair out of her eyes, and to his surprise, relaxed against him, as if welcoming the comfort of his protection.

Gavin held her a moment longer, not wanting to let her go, but propriety required him to do so. He closed his eyes to savor the moment and then released her. She shifted away and straightened her back. They continued riding in silence.

When they reached the market in town, Serena was pensive and quiet. Concerned he had overstepped his boundaries, Gavin didn't try to force her into conversation. He kept a respectable distance from her as they hurried from vendor to vendor. They found the herbal merchant, an elderly woman who was busy helping a man.

While they waited, Serena sighed. He glanced down. She licked her parched lips. He should have noticed how dry they were earlier. Dark circles now bordered her eyes. Guilt tugged at him.

"Ye look tired. I'm sorry if I've made ye walk too much. Mayhap I should have let ye wait on the wagon."

"Nay." She shook her head. "Ye've made me do naught that I've not chosen to do. I didn't get much rest last night and I'm not quite feeling myself. I wouldn't have wanted to be left alone."

Gavin offered his arm. She accepted, leaning upon him more than usual. Her behavior troubled him, but he didn't know what to do about it. She kept pressing her palm to her forehead.

The herbal merchant finished with her other customer and came over. "What do ye need this morn, lass?"

Serena pulled out a written note from Tomas and handed it to her. The woman's gray hair was pulled back in a ribbon. Lines around her eyes narrowed, increasing the wrinkles as she held it out at arm's length to read it.

"I beg yer pardon, but I'd tell ye what it says if I understood most of the terms," Serena said.

"Even though my eyes aren't what they used to be, I can make it out well enough." She laid down the parchment paper and opened a container, dipping several wooden spoonfuls of a powdered substance into a pouch. "Ye must have a verra ill person." She glanced at Serena, then at Gavin before tying the pouch into a tight knot.

"Aye, my auld nursemaid is dying. We want to ease her pain as much as possible, but she wants to keep her wits about her."

The woman shook her head with a firm frown. "Sorry, lass, but to keep one's wits about them is to endure the pain. Ye'll have to choose one or the other." She handed Serena the pouch. "This'll definitely dull the pain, but 'twill also make her sleep. There's naught better."

Next, she poured a small vial of brown liquid and another vial of light yellow. She set it down on the table in front of Serena. "That will be three pence."

Serena dug into her skirt pocket and pulled out the coins. Instead of dropping them into the woman's outstretched palm, the coins tumbled in separate directions as Serena shook, her legs gave way, and she fell.

Gavin lunged, catching Serena in time to keep her from hitting the table. Her body stiffened in spasms so violent that it brought Gavin to his knees as he tried to maintain hold of her seizing limbs.

"Serena! Lass, what's the matter? Speak to me." Gavin turned her over to see her face. It was like someone had punched the breath out of him. Her green eyes rolled under the top of her lids until only the white part showed. Serena's pale skin faded into a purple-blue color. Her chest heaved in gasps as she chewed her tongue. A combination of blood and white foam leaked from the corner of her mouth, staining her beautiful pink lips.

The woman screamed throwing up her hands and covering her cheeks. "'Tis a demon, I tell ye! Never seen naught like it."

"Serena!" Gavin shook her. "Lord, help me."

"It's a demon!" The woman shouted. "No other explanation to describe it."

A crowd gathered around them, but no one offered to help. "Someone go for a clergyman!" A man yelled from the crowd.

Serena's color grew worse. Her throat made a strange noise, and he feared she might choke to death. Gavin leaned her over his arm and beat her back to dislodge whatever it was.

"Look!" A middle-aged woman pointed. "The demon is killin' her!"

Serena gasped, sucking in her first breath of air since the fit began. Gavin gathered her against him in relief. More blood dripped from her mouth. He pulled his sleeve down and gently wiped her lips. His heart paced so fast he could hardly keep his wits, but he realized the danger she could now be in.

"Go on. She's fine. Only choked is all." Gavin waved them away. Many cast doubtful glances at each other.

"'Twas more 'n that. I tell ye, I saw it with my own eyes. The lass wasn't eating or drinking to choke. She was fine one moment an' possessed by somethin' evil the next." The woman turned in a circle, determined to beguile an audience who would support her claims.

"My lad went for a clergyman. We'll let the kirk decide her fate."

Gavin needed to get Serena out of there—and fast. He reached for the liquid vials and held them up. "Ye sold her yer mixture before it happened. How do we know it wasn't something ye did to cause this?" He turned to the crowd. "Did any of ye see what she gave the lass?"

Some shook their heads. Others mumbled "nay."

"This lass was perfectly fine before coming here. I'm taking her back home where she can recover in peace."

"There's a demon in 'er." A man pointed at Serena.

"I hope for yer sake this lass suffers no lasting effects." He glanced at the woman, mustering a firm expression. Gavin lifted Serena in his arms.

"I've done naught." She set her chin and crossed her arms.

"And neither has she." He turned and rushed back to the wagon. Gavin hoped to gain a good head start if they decided to raise a mob to come after them.

Strong arms lifted Serena, stirring her from a blissful sleep. Bright light warmed her face, and she realized it was the sun, but she couldn't open her eyes all the way. A man grunted as he jostled her against his hard chest. He smelled of leather and pine. Her senses grew as she remembered falling at the market, the old woman's startled expression, and Gavin's timely rescue—as usual.

"Gavin?" Her throat felt hoarse and dry. She licked her lips, wincing from her sore tongue, swollen and awkward. The iron taste of blood still lingered in her mouth.

"Shush, I've got ye now. I won't let aught happen to ye." His smooth voice held none of the reproach she had feared. Instead, he tried to comfort and protect her.

He bounced her in his arms as he lifted her to knock on the door. Evelina answered, her eyes widening in concern. She stepped back and swung the door wide to let them in. Gunna still lay in her bed, asleep and oblivious to their arrival.

"Put her here on my bed." Her mother threw back the blanket from the corner of her box bed. "Now, tell me what happened."

She waited while Gavin laid Serena on the straw bed.

Gavin cradled her head on the feathered pillow. His hands were warm and gentle upon her face, sure and steady. He didn't shake in disgust after witnessing her horrible fit. When he leaned back, his eyes were filled with compassion, not speculation or accusation.

"Serena, did ye have another fit?" Her mother clasped her hand.

"Aye." Hot tears blinded her vision, as humiliation set in, and she worried how upset her mother would be once she realized the full extent of who had witnessed it. Her lips trembled. She struggled to breathe, her chest burdened by the news she was about to deliver. "I'm sorry, Mither!" Serena's voice broke as she rolled to the side, trying to will her tears away. "Everyone saw it. They all know about me now. I've ruined all yer hard work in trying to protect me." A sob burst forth from her like a dam breaking free, her shoulders quaking.

"Don't worry, lass," her mother soothed, gripping her arm in an attempt to comfort her. Serena finally gazed up at her. "Ye canna live like a hermit. We knew this day would come."

Serena sniffled and wiped her wet face. Her eyes were swollen, like heavy rocks in her sockets. Some of the pressure in her chest had released, but guilt still languished in her heart.

"I didn't hear everything they said, but I heard enough to know they think I'm possessed of the devil." Fresh tears brimmed until she wanted to slip beneath the covers and cry. Instead, she took a deep breath and dabbed the edge of the blanket against her tired eyes, drying up the excess moisture.

"'Tis true," Gavin said, rubbing his hand behind his neck with a worried frown. "I tried to defend her, but they didn't appear to be satisfied. One man sent his son after the local clergy, but I took her away before he arrived."

"Let's hope they'll drop the matter, then." Her mother tightened her hold on Serena's hand with an encouraging smile. "Mayhap, I've been overly worried all these years for naught."

Serena wasn't fooled. She knew her mother too well, but she kept silent. Her gaze drifted to Gavin's tall frame pacing at the foot of the bed. She longed to know his thoughts. Even though he had protected and defended her, he must be thinking something after witnessing one of her fits. What if the images haunting his mind made him regret helping her? His apparent distress increased her concern. Her stomach twisted.

Gavin whirled, his disturbing gaze meeting hers. Serena ignored the aching heaviness threatening to claim her body and pushed to a sitting position, bracing herself.

"So this is what ye meant when ye said ye're no different from the rest of the villagers?" He shook his head in disbelief, rubbing a hand over his face. "I've never seen aught like it. Ye should have told me, Serena. I thought ye were going to die." He turned and folded his arms.

"I'm sorry, Gavin, but I didn't think ye'd understand." Serena glanced at her mother for help. She shook her head and walked over to stoke the fire.

"I still don't understand. How am I to help ye if it happens again? I worried ye'd stop breathing all together." He looked up at the dark rafters. "Does Tomas know of this condition?"

"Aye." Hope sparked in her chest. He had called it a condition, not a demon. "Ye don't think I'm possessed, then? Like the others?"

He crossed the short distance to her bedside and bent toward her. "I could never think evil of ye. I may not understand this . . . condition ye've got, but there is naught but goodness in ye."

Someone pounded on the door. The wood rattled in the framed threshold. "Serena! I came to warn ye, lass. Ye don't have much time."

"Beacon?" Serena started to rise, but Gavin laid a hand on her arm.

Her mother set down the pitcher she held and hurried to answer. Beacon stormed inside. He stopped in the middle, turned in a circle, his gaze resting on Gavin, then Serena.

"A friend of mine rushed from town to tell me the news of the fit ye had."

"What did he say?" Serena clutched the blanket in her fists, blinking in worry as she studied Beacon's brown eyes. His blond hair stood in disarray, she assumed from the wind.

"They got a clergyman and are on their way to examine ye. They've gathererd a mob," Beacon said.

"If they plan to examine me, then mayhap, they only intend to ask a few questions and naught more." She looked from Beacon to Gavin, seeking confirmation. Her throat swelled at their sad expressions.

"He's right, Serena. We need to get ye out of here. If the clergyman only wanted to question ye, he wouldn't need to arrive with all those angry people." Gavin dropped a hand on Beacon's shoulder. "Thanks for the warning, my friend."

"Where will ye take me? I won't leave Mither."

"Ye have to, lass. Gunna isn't well enough to travel or take care of herself," Evelina said, linking her fingers in front of her. "Come now. Make haste."

"Help me unhitch the wagon." Gavin turned to Beacon. "We'll make better time on horseback."

"But where are we going?" Serena now stood by the bed. Blood pumped through her heart and brain so fast, she felt faint. She clenched her jaw, resolving to keep herself steady. "Lord, help me. Don't let me be separated from Mither for long," she whispered.

"I think Braigh Castle may be the safest for now. My men are there and can lend their support to the laird," Gavin said.

"What if Iain sides with the others to hand me over? The kirk can be quite compelling, ye know. He wouldn't want to lose his place in the shire over a woman reported to be evil."

"To my constant torment these past few weeks, I can safely wager that ye're much more than a simple woman to the laird. They'll have to to prove that ye're evil," Gavin said.

"Well, he hasn't yet seen one of my fits, has he?" Her hands flew to her hips. "That may be all the proof he needs."

"Serena, Beacon said we don't have much time. Roll up a couple of gowns and please stop rebelling against us." Evelina's voice took on the sternness she had often used when Serena was a child. "My nerves are getting the better of me." She sat down and took a few deep breaths.

Guilt tore at Serena, as the door rattled shut behind Gavin and Beacon. She didn't want to cause her mother unnecessary worry and pain, but some instinct inside her made her want to defend and protect her life—to keep things the same—the way she liked it.

Without another word she chose two dresses, rolled them up, and secured them. She grabbed her plaid and wrapped it around her. The back of her throat ached and her eyes stung as she made her way to Gunna's bedside. Gunna lay still, her breathing a rattle that frightened Serena. She had not awakened all day.

Serena closed her eyes. "Please Lord, take good care of her. Don't let her feel any pain when the time comes." She lifted Gunna's cold, wrinkled hand to her cheek. A wet tear crawled from her check to Gunna's hand. It had been her desire to be with Gunna until the very end.

"Mither, please don't let her . . . be alone . . . when . . . when . . ." Serena couldn't get the words out. A choking sob claimed her throat.

"Love, she won't be alone." Warm arms wrapped around her. "I promise. I'll stay with her until the verra last breath."

Serena turned and threw her arms around her mother's thin frame in a tight hug. "I didn't want ye to be alone in yer grief either. Promise ye'll send for Tomas."

"I will. He went to check on Philip's wife, but will soon be back." Her mother framed Serena's face, studying her as if committing her features to memory. "Truth be known, I can handle Gunna's passing, even my own, but I fear I wouldn't be able to endure it if aught happened to ye, Serena. The roots of a mother's love run deep."

The door flew open. "The horse is ready." Gavin saw them and dropped his head. "Beg yer pardon." He started to back outside.

"Nay, stay," Evelina said. "Serena, I don't know what will happen now that yer secret is known, but if we're separated longer than we think, do what Gavin says. I trust his judgment."

Confusion and pain swirled inside Serena as she tried to comprehend all that was happening. She leaned toward her mother's ear so Gavin wouldn't hear. "Even over the laird?"

"Aye." Her mother nodded. "Trust me." She kissed Serena's forehead. "Ye know I love ye, lass. Trust God above all things and cling to Him regardless of what they say. Now go. We've no more time." Her mother released her, but Serena didn't miss the tremble in her bottom lip or the tears she tried to blink away.

12

$\mathcal{G}$avin stepped outside. Phelan guarded the front door, his ears up and attentive. The wolf was now a common and comforting sight. On more than one occasion, the animal had proven the value of his instincts. Gavin now trusted him as well as any man.

Mounting his horse, Gavin leaned down and locked elbows with Serena, lifting her behind him. Her arms slid around his waist. He covered her hands with his free one. "Hold on tight."

Phelan jumped to his feet and barked. He paced in a circle, warning them. He growled, his black lips rising to expose sharp fangs.

"Go, Phelan!" Beacon shouted.

The wolf took off toward town.

"They're almost here," Gavin said.

"Phelan will detain them and so will I." Beacon stood on his tiptoes and struck the horse on the rump. "Now go!"

Gavin kneed the animal's flanks and they raced into the opposite direction. He could feel Serena leaning with him to avoid limbs and to distribute their weight in sharp curves.

They rode well together, almost as if they were one. She belonged with him, but circumstances had once again thwarted that possibility. He disliked having to take her to Iain MacBraigh for protection. It gnawed at his insides, but more than that, he would do anything to save her from being condemned by the kirk. Serena didn't deserve such a fate. He had never known a more innocent soul.

As they flew by on horseback, birds fluttered in the branches. Leaves and twigs brushed against them. Sholto breathed heavy, never slowing his pace. Gavin and Serena burst from the woods and slowed as they came to the steep drop. Not wanting to cause any further misfortune, Gavin eased their mount down the incline.

The afternoon sun hid behind dark clouds rolling in above them. A clap of thunder frightened his horse, causing him to neigh. Serena gasped, her hold tightening around Gavin. They stayed seated as the sound rumbled and faded. Lightning streaked the sky in a jagged spike of glowing white.

Once they reached the bottom of the glen, Gavin prompted Sholto to climb faster. Now they were not only running from the town mob but also the storm about to pour upon them.

"I think I'll suggest a long drawbridge like some of the other castles have over their moats. Ye think Iain would go for it?" Gavin glanced over his shoulder, hoping a bit of conversation would distract her mind and ease her fears.

He could feel her head lift from his back as she considered his question. "I've never seen such a bridge. I've read about them, though. He might." She laid her cheek against his back. "I'd like to see it." Her voice sounded muffled against him.

More thunder echoed, gathering in strength, and ending in a loud boom. Heavy drops of rain fell like scattered beads. The air smelled of earth, salty seaweed, and fresh rain.

They crested the top of the brae, and Gavin breathed a sigh of relief at the sight of the black iron gate. He struggled to see into the shadows through the rain, hoping for a glimpse of Philip. If he was nowhere about, they could be in trouble.

"Philip, it's Gavin and Serena! Open the gate!"

No answer. Gavin rode up to the iron bars, his heart leaping in hope. "Philip, are ye there, mon? Open up!"

Water drenched them. He shoved his wet hair out of his eyes. A shadow moved forward, slow and steady. Gavin recognized the wide, thick frame of the elderly man he sought. Relief gushed through him. He covered Serena's linked fingers holding tight around his waist. Her hands were cold, and she trembled against him.

"Philip is coming. It won't be long now. Ye'll soon be safe inside, in dry clothes, and warming by the fire."

Her arms tightened around him and her chin dug into his shoulder. "Don't leave me alone . . . please." The whispered plea against his ear made him ache to comfort her. He rubbed a hand along her arm.

"Lass, ye'll be safe here. I promise. Ye've naught to fear."

The gate rattled and rolled up. Gavin waited until it was high enough and rode through. He pulled the reins and turned. "Philip, a mob of people will soon arrive. Don't let them in under any circumstances. Ye hear?"

"I beg yer pardon, but I take my orders from my laird."

"This is an unusual situation and the laird doesn't yet know we'll soon be under siege. It's for our own good and in the laird's best interest."

"A siege? But why? We're living in peaceful times 'round here." Philip crinkled his brown eyes and stroked his gray beard.

"Trust me on this, my friend. I need to get Serena inside where it's safe and dry." Gavin guided his horse from the stone gatehouse and raced across the courtyard. He dismounted and reached up for Serena. She slid into his arms, her wet body molding to his. He breathed deeply to clear his mind.

"What about my garments?" Her blue lips trembled as she spoke. Serena slipped her arms around his neck. He liked the feeling in spite of her freezing fingers.

"I'll come back for them. They're soaked through right now and won't be any good to ye."

She rested her wet head against his chest, accepting his answer. Yawning, Serena covered her mouth. "I'm so tired. I usually sleep a lot after one of my fits."

Gavin carried her through the side door and to the great hall. Servants were readying the tables for the evening meal. All eyes turned toward them.

A lass hurried over, wringing her hands in worry. As if remembering her manners, she dropped into a curtsy, her brown hair in curls beneath her white head piece. An apron covered her gray gown. She lifted dark eyes to Gavin.

"My name's Doreen. Is Serena all right?" She touched her hand to her stomach.

Serena lifted her head and turned to her friend. "Aye, but I'm verra tired. Gavin brought me here to stay. I'm in a bit of trouble."

"What kind of trouble?" Doreen blinked brown eyes and wrinkled her brows in concern.

"Gavin, ye can set me down now." He tilted her and she landed on her feet. "Thank ye."

In spite of the ache in his throbbing arms, he was sorry to release her. The empty feeling felt strange. Serena did things to him he couldn't understand. "Why don't ye go get settled in a chamber, while I find Iain and explain everything?"

"Aye." Serena brushed her wet strands behind her ears, her pale face a stark contrast to her black hair. "I appreciate ye telling him for me. I need some time to deal with things." She turned to Doreen and linked arms with her as they left the hall. "I'll tell ye what I can."

Gavin headed to the library and knocked on the door. "'Tis Gavin. I need to speak with ye."

"Come in." Iain said.

Opening the door, Gavin saw Iain sitting in a chair reading a book by a candelabra. He looked up, snapping it closed. "Sit down." He gestured to a chair across from him.

Gavin told him what happened in town, about Serena's history of fits, and how the townspeople were on their way. When he finished, Gavin steepled his fingers. "Can we count on yer protection for Serena?"

"Of course, I'll do my best. Like ye, I don't believe in this evil claim. It's rubbish!"

A knock sounded at the door. A servant peeked in. "My laird, please forgive me for the disturbance, but a crowd of people are at the gate demanding entrance. Philip would like to know if ye wish him to let them in."

Iain met Gavin's gaze. "Too bad the storm didn't delay them a wee bit longer. 'Twould appear this mob is quite determined."

℘

Evelina wiped Gunna's feverish forehead with a wet cloth. Her breathing was worse as she languished on the box bed shivering in spite of the warm summer day.

After waving Serena and Gavin off, Evelina had recognized a brewing storm in the distant sky. Her heavy heart had lifted in hope. Mayhap the rains would do more than cool the air and would hinder the mob from continuing on their quest.

"Gunna, the rains are coming to cool ye off a wee bit." Evelina covered her limp hand with her own. She kissed the cold, hard knuckles, already the shade of powdered ashes. "Hang on if ye can. Tomas will soon be here. Let him bless ye one more time before ye go."

She laid her forehead against Gunna's arm, her skin now clammy. Evelina closed her eyes and let the grief flow freely. Warm tears slipped through her eyelids. With Serena away, she had no need to hide the swirling pain.

Not only had Gunna been Serena's nursemaid, but she had first taken care of Evelina during her childhood. When Evelina's parents had forced her into an arranged marriage, she refused to part with Gunna. She may have been young, but she knew her marriage would lack love, passion, and tenderness. Gunna's friendship was all she had until Serena's birth.

Thunder shook the cottage, much like the crumbling foundation of their lives with Gunna's passing and the town's discovery of Serena's secret. Things would never be the same again. They had been happy here.

At first, settling in a wee cottage had been hard. Evelina had grown up in a large manor with plenty of servants to attend her. She had been surrounded with a multitude of stylish gowns and jewelry and had an education. Evelina had done her best to protect Serena from that world, while preparing her for the unknown—to live by faith. Serena would now be in the Lord's hands.

She lifted her head, realizing her tears had puddled on Gunna's wrinkled arm. She mopped them up with the sleeve of her gown and traced her fingers to Gunna's elbow. In the past, Gunna would pull her arm away in laughter, saying, "Dearie me, lass, but that tickles, it does." Evelina longed to hear her laugh again.

A determined knock sounded at the door. Evelina straightened, wiping away the evidence of her grief, and sighed. She rose to her feet.

A second knock rattled the door.

Tomas would have already called out. It had to be someone else.

She braced herself and strode to the door. Another rumble of thunder echoed. It must have kept her from hearing her visitor ride up. The door squeaked as she cracked it open and peered through. At least twenty men sat on horses staring at her with grim expressions.

Rain pounded their heads, flattening their hair to the scalp. It hit the ground like small pebbles. A clergyman holding a plaid over his head stepped forward, his gray eyes unreadable. "We came to see the lass that fell down in a fit earlier today at the market."

"She isn't here." Evelina clutched the door until her knuckles turned white.

"Does she not live here?" He tilted his dark head, regarding her with doubt. Stepping closer, he lowered his voice. "My name is Jamieson Kendrick, vicar of St. Gilbert's Cathedral. I only wanted to talk to her and put to rest the fears of these townspeople."

"Aye, she lives here, but she isn't here." Evelina glanced at the other men behind him. "I'd offer ye shelter from the rain, but I fear the place isn't big enough for all of them."

"Nay." He shook his head. "There's no need. Will ye not tell me where she is?"

"Nay. I see no women among ye and there's a good number of men to be chasing a simple lass." Evelina faced him, determined to stay strong and show no fear. She willed her heart to beat steadily.

Vicar Kendrick blinked and set his jaw at an angle. "The people who witnessed her falling fit believe she may be demon possessed. I agreed to come and check out their claims to keep them from storming yer home and causing unnecessary harm."

"There's not an evil bone in her body." Evelina forced herself to swallow, keeping her tone even. "Ye can ask Father Tomas. He's known her from infancy."

"And where is Tomas?" His eyes flickered like hard flint. "It's been a while since I've seen him."

"He should be here soon. I've sent someone to fetch him." Evelina tried to control the trembling in her voice. "An auld woman who has lived with us for many years is dying, and I hoped Father Tomas would arrive in time to say the last rites over her." She looked away before he could further witness her distress.

Vicar Kendrick glanced up at the sky, blinking as drops of rain slipped beneath the plaid he held. "He may be detained by the storm." A thin trail of water rolled from his moving lips, down his chin, and dripped onto his chest. "I could say her last rites. I'd consider it an honor for the inconvenience we've caused."

Evelina opened her mouth to reject the offer, but paused. What if she could win this man's favor and influence him into believing Serena's innocence? Would his word carry weight with the local kirk? She needed to consider every possible option. Father Tomas had always said, "The Lord's ways are a mystery and higher than man's ways."

"The others would wait out here, of course." He leaned forward as if sensing her willingness.

"In the storm?" Lightning lit the sky in flashes of white. "Father Tomas will come in spite of the weather. I've no doubt of it."

He grinned, revealing slight lines around his gray eyes. "They'll be in the rain whether we remain here or carry on our journey. 'Twill only detain us a wee bit."

Detain them? Wasn't that exactly what she wanted? It would give Gavin time to get Serena behind the safety of the castle gates to explain the situation to the laird and devise a plan. "Where will ye go from here?"

"To Braigh Castle. The Earl of Caithness says she's a servant there."

Evelina worked hard to keep her expression free of her thoughts. She stepped back and held the door wide. "Ye're welcome to come in."

Vicar Kendrick turned and explained to the rest of the men that they would continue on to Braigh Castle after he gave the last rites to a dying woman. Their expressions ranged from frustration to confusion, but no one dared speak against the vicar. They murmured among themselves.

"Good day, gentleman!" Tomas said behind them.

Evelina breathed a sigh of relief. The men parted. Tomas made his way through them. Vicar Kendrick continued holding the plaid over his head and turned. Tomas paused. As the men faced each other, instant tension clung in the air like thick smoke. Evelina folded her arms, even more uncomfortable than before.

"F-father K-kendrick." Tomas acknowledged him with a nod. His confidence vanished and stammering replaced it. Evelina's heart turned over in fear. He had to recover his nerves. She needed him right now. "What brings ye this far from t-town?"

"I'm glad ye've come," Evelina said. "I don't know how much time Gunna has."

"Then I'm not too late?" Tomas stepped around Vicar Kendrick.

Evelina shook her head.

"Father Kendrick, ye coming in?" He glanced over his shoulder.

"Tomas, we need to talk. I was hoping ye'd help me with a difficult matter," Vicar Kendrick said.

"Indeed, just as s-soon as I've taken care of Gunna." He stepped to the bedside and took Gunna's stiff hand in his. Tomas bowed his head and began praying.

It was the longest prayer Evelina had ever heard. She smiled to herself, knowing Tomas intended to give Gavin and Serena more time. Finally, he made the sign of the cross. "Amen."

"I hope that long prayer wasn't meant to stall me. Besides the men waiting for me outside, another group traveled straight to the castle and didn't stop here," Father Kendrick said. "Even though we had no proof that Serena is there, the Earl of Caithness is with them. As Iain MacBraigh's cousin, he believes he might have some influence on the laird."

⟡

Hogan Lennox stormed into the great hall where Iain and Gavin waited in matching chairs carved of oak with tall backs. Gavin stretched his long legs, crossing them at the ankles. He gripped the armrests and braced himself for the earl's anger.

"Iain, what is the meaning of this?" His cloudy eyes first rested on the laird and then slithered to Gavin. His lips twisted in obvious contempt. Resting one hand on the hilt of the sword at his side, he dropped his other fisted hand on his hip. "Why won't ye let my men at arms gain entrance? 'Tis an insult that ye hold them at the gate with strange men from another clan."

"I realize it may seem untoward, cousin, but I've my reasons. To what do we owe yer unexpected visit?" Iain kept his mild expression calm, to Gavin's relief. Yet he noticed Iain didn't offer the earl a seat, and he'd never before witnessed the laird's lack of manners.

"Yer cold greeting is verra distressful." Hogan stroked his thick gray beard, glancing at Gavin. "I would speak privately with ye."

"Gavin and I haven't finished our business as yet. He's trustworthy. Ye may speak in front of him."

Silence lengthened between them. Gavin kept still as the two of them stared at each other. Hogan blinked first, folded his arms, and adopted a warrior's stance. "Verra well. I came to warn ye about Serena, the lass that works for ye, but it looks like I didn't make it in time."

"What about her?" Iain kept a steady gaze.

"She was at the market this morn with him," Hogan pointed at Gavin. "I'm assuming ye've already heard the news of what happened—or at least their version of it."

"Aye." Iain launched into the description Gavin had related to him. When he finished Iain crossed his ankle over his knee and raised an eyebrow. "Does that sum up everything for ye?"

"Indeed." Hogan nodded his gray head and straightened his shoulders. "A clergyman from St. Gilbert's Cathedral will soon be here with several townspeople who witnessed how the lass behaved. Do ye intend to deny a man of God entrance into yer home? I'd advise against it. They'll all think she's bewitched ye. Such an action could seal her fate before she even has a chance to stand trial."

"Trial?" Gavin repeated, not liking the direction of this conversation. "Have ye already determined she's to stand trial, then? No one from the kirk has seen her as yet."

"Too many people witnessed her falling fit to question their word against hers. The matter will not be ignored." Hogan's menacing glare boiled Gavin's temper. He gripped the chair arms.

"I was there and only a handful of people really saw what happened. The rest could see naught for the bodies that bent over her. The majority could only hear the boastful screams of the woman selling medicine herbs."

Hogan ignored Gavin. "Iain, I've counseled ye before on the foolishness of keeping this Village of Outcasts. They've been naught but trouble for yer uncle and now ye. The land where they live is fertile. With hard-working souls, it could turn a nice profit for ye. But these vagabonds living there now will do naught but drain yer coffers."

Gavin felt the color drain from his face as his heart paced. Iain must have sensed his anger for he held up his palm to keep Hogan silent.

"Ye surprise me, cousin. For one so determined to cast off evil, ye take no delight in holding those dear to God in value. Those outcasts or vagabonds as ye've called them, have a soul and deserve as much compassion for their conditions as those worthy of praise for achievements."

Hogan's face darkened as he looked down at the floor. After a few moments he took a deep breath. "I've compassion for those who canna help themselves, but ye must admit there's evil in the village. Have ye not heard of the strange things happening of late? Cattle reiving is a common thing among feuding clans, borderlands, and the poor trying to sustain themselves, but pure killing and the laying to waste of good beef? What would be the witless purpose unless it's a sacrificial offering? And the attack upon the blind lass? Or the fire outside the kirk, locking people inside? These are the works of evil."

"I'll have ye know that Serena and her family were locked inside with the rest of us." Gavin shook with anger. "If ye expect yer argument to hold merit, ye need to do better."

Taking a couple of steps toward him, Hogan glared as if he wanted to pierce him with a bow and arrow. "Nay, but none of these strange acts took place before ye arrived. Should that be ignored? I think not."

"If ye've an accusation to make, mon, then make it. Otherwise, 'twould be prudent of ye to examine yer thoughts before sharing them. I was in the kirk as well when the fire was set, as were most all my men."

"Most . . . but not all." Hogan grinned like a man who had caught his prey. "Mayhap, ye have a traitor among ye, one who is angry with a ruling ye gave or feels overlooked next to yer favorites." He gestured to Gavin. "What say ye to that?"

"Only this, if I do have a traitor, Serena Boyd canna be guilty of the sorcery ye claim."

"Maybe not the strange events in the village, but there still remains the matter of her falling fit. Try and explain that one."

"Women swoon often enough." Gavin waved his hand to dismiss the issue.

"Aye, but they don't stiffen in spasms like a mad animal, or foam at the mouth and roll their eyes into their eyelids. What that lass did was no simple female faint."

A servant rushed in. "My laird, more men have arrived at the gate. Two clergymen are demanding entrance."

13

Doreen led Serena to the east wing. She carried a single candle in a brass holder and shielded it from the draft as they walked. Serena yawned and covered her mouth. She hoped she could stay awake long enough to properly prepare for bed.

"I thought ye might like to be on the same hall as Gavin for protection. Though the laird doesn't have many overnight guests, the castle has a lot of strange noises. Having someone nearby will be a comfort."

"Ye're so thoughtful, Doreen. Why did ye not put me with the rest of the servants or near ye?"

"I've a verra strong feeling the laird would prefer ye to be treated as a guest. It might be less comfortable with the other maids," Doreen said, moving ahead.

"Why?" Serena blinked, confusion mixing with her weary mind. "Have I done something to offend the others? Do they already know about this morn at the market?"

"Nay." Doreen shook her head. "I've yet to hear that tale. I'm talking 'bout how the laird favors ye. Have ye not seen the way he looks at ye? 'Tis odd that ye were invited as a guest to the feast—to be served by those ye normally work with."

Serena gulped. She had realized it. Mayhap she should have been more firm in her protests to Iain. Shame crept through her. Should she have not accepted the gowns, even for the benefit of the village lasses? Doubt invaded her mind until her temples throbbed. She rubbed the side of her head as if the simple act would ease the pressure.

"Doreen, please, ye must know there is naught between us. I'm of too low birth for him to consider marriage and I'd never consent to aught else. The thought of dishonoring my mither or my Lord is too much."

"Serena, I trust ye, but men are different from us. King David of Jerusalem had a heart for God, but his lust for Bathsheba overcame his good reason. The laird is a mere man as David was, with more power than ye." Doreen paused in front of a closed door on the left. "Ye'll be two doors down from Gavin's chamber."

"Aye, and I remember Craig is across the hall." Serena clutched Doreen's arm. "What an imagination ye have. Ye could be a gifted storyteller. The laird may have shown me special favor, but that's the extent of it."

Doreen paused in front of the chamber where Serena would be staying. She inserted a key and turned it. The lock snapped and the door opened. Doreen strode across the chamber and set the candle upon a corner table. She laid her hands on her waist. "What do ye think? Will this do?"

Glancing around the chamber, Serena noticed the large bed in the center. It looked so grand compared to her thin mattress in the narrow loft at home. While running the castle, Serena had seen many beds like this, but never once considered that she'd have the good fortune to sleep in one. A carved double-door wardrobe stood against the entrance wall. The mantle fireplace faced the foot of the bed.

"We can bank a warm fire for yer bath since the storm cooled off the summer heat. If ye don't mind, I can bring ye one of my nightgowns." Doreen pointed to the far wall. "If ye open the shutters, ye'll see a beautiful view of the sea. On warm nights ye can sleep with it open and hear the lulling sound of the ocean waves upon the rocks below. I'm in the east wing as well, a floor above ye in the servant quarters."

Serena had never needed to be on the servants' floors as her duties were in the main part of the castle. She nodded. "Aye, a warm fire and a bath would do me good. Then I'll tell ye what happened at the market, why I'm in trouble, and a wee bit about my sordid past."

Doreen lit more candles around the chamber. Serena shivered in her wet garments, eager to donn a warm, dry nightgown, even if it was borrowed.

"Have ye eaten?" Doreen asked.

"Nay." Serena shook her head. "But I would delight in some nourishment."

"I'll see to everythin'." Doreen left the room.

Serena built a fire. Her damp clothes were heavy as she spread out her skirt around her to dry. She rubbed her hands together over the flames. Doreen returned with a tray of black bean soup, some cider, and a chunk of bread. She laid a white nightgown on the bed.

In between bites, Serena told Doreen of the day's events and her falling fit. Once she'd had her fill, Serena pushed her plate aside. Doreen continued to sit in silence.

"Do ye think me evil?" Serena asked.

"Nay! Of course not." Doreen looked at her as if offended. "I wish there was a way to get ye out of this mess. Gavin MacKenzie and the laird may have a lot of pull with the town, but not even they can defy the kirk. No one can. Even the King himself must relinquish some power. It represents God's sovereign authority." She grabbed Serena's hands as moisture gathered in her eyes. "I'm verra worried for ye."

Someone knocked on the door.

"Come in," Serena called.

Two men servants carried in a tub. Four maids followed with buckets of steaming water.

"Over here by the hearth," Serena directed.

The men grunted as they set the tub. The maids poured the water. Warm steam clouded the room, causing Serena to look forward to a relaxing bath. She rubbed her hands like a child waiting for a sweetmeat.

When the servants left, Doreen stood and picked up Serena's discarded tray. "I'll go and let ye bathe in peace. Is there aught more I can do?"

"Nay, thank ye for everything." Serena gathered the nightgown in her arms.

"Ye shall always have it. I won't soon forget how ye taught me to write my name and ye came to care for my mither two years ago while I worked in Braighwick. She might've died if not for ye." Doreen smiled, before turning and quitting the room.

Serena sighed as she undressed and laid her garments by the fire. She dipped her hand into the water. At first it scalded her skin and then she adjusted to the heat. She pulled it out. Her pink skin glistened in the firelight, now cool in the air.

Is this what burning at the stake felt like? Until she was too numb to feel anymore? Fear slithered through her body. Trembling, she slipped to her knees, hanging onto the side of the tub.

"Oh, God!" she cried, her chest heaved, and the tears freely poured. "Please help me. I don't want to die like that. Please—"

Gavin stood over the rocky cliff listening to the constant waves below, letting the salty air open his lungs. The unseen wind brushed his face and neck. Could he be feeling the very breath of God? At home Father Mike had a Latin Bible, and Gavin remembered a passage in the book of Genesis saying, "And the Spirit of God moved upon the face of the waters."

Surely, if ever there was a place for God to hear a man this would be it. An orange orb lifted from the gray sea, ever so slowly, lighting the sky from the dark night to a new dawn. The sun continued to rise, every second transforming the image to a bigger, brighter view until its color no longer mattered—only the magnificent light.

An overwhelming feeling of awe wrapped around Gavin. He fell to his knees. It was as if he had God's personal attention, the audience of the Most High. Gavin trembled, struggling to form words from his thoughts. Burdened for Serena, words burst from his heart to his tongue without thought, and faster than he could have ever dreamed possible. After a while he fell silent, more at peace than he had felt in a long while.

Footsteps approached from behind. "I thought I might find ye out here." Leith's voice was still hoarse from sleep. He settled beside Gavin. "I prayed for her."

"Thank ye," Gavin said.

"Was it as bad as they say? Her fit, I mean?"

"Aye, but not the way they would have ye believe." Gavin draped his elbows over his knees and linked his fingers. "She stopped breathing. Her body shook, gasping for air. I thought she was dying. I was afraid of losing her. I've never felt so helpless."

"Well, it doesn't sound like she would have made it without ye. That witless mob would have tied her to the stake without an inquisition of any sort."

"The vicar plans to question her today. Both he and the earl stayed the night." Gavin rubbed a hand over his face. "I hope she got plenty of rest. She'll need to be clearheaded."

"Father Tomas stayed as well," Leith said. "After the mob grew weary of the rain and finally left."

"How is the work on the wall?" Gavin asked.

"One more month and we should be finished with the outside repairs facing the sea." Leith grabbed his shoulder. "Ye ready to go in and break yer fast?"

"I suppose I'd better get it over and done with. The earl and I didn't part on friendly terms. I've yet to hear him utter aught that doesn't benefit him in some way." Gavin rose to his feet and stretched his arms high above his head.

"What do ye think he wants?" Leith asked.

"Not sure. But I don't trust him." Gavin walked toward the castle. "He seems to have no tolerance for the villagers."

"Aye." Leith walked beside him. "I've gathered that."

They entered the side door from the courtyard. The tables in the great hall were already full of biscuits, ham, eggs, and pastries. Candles were lit everywhere. Servants bounced here and there. Both Father Kendrick and Tomas sat across from each other in amiable conversation.

The laird appeared from the direction of the solar and took his place at the table on the dais. Gavin and Leith settled beside the two clergymen. The only one missing was the earl. Gavin hoped he wasn't searching for Serena.

"I trust everyone slept well last night." Iain glanced around the room.

"Aye, verra well." Vicar Kendrick nodded.

Gavin studied his brown hair and facial features. While he was plain, Gavin guessed him to be in the mid-thirties.

"And the rest of ye?" Iain glanced at Tomas, Leith, then Gavin.

"The beds were quite comfortable." Leith said. "I think Gavin enjoys our view of the sea."

"Oh?" Iain raised his eyebrows. "So ye're in the east wing, then? It is a bonny view."

The earl strolled in and took a seat beside Iain at the table on the dais. He was well dressed in his dark blue and purple plaid. He looked down upon them from his perch like a king ruling over the underclass.

"Good morn, gentleman." His cheerful tone was very unexpected after their awkward parting yestereve.

"Father Kendrick, as our guest, would ye bless the food?" Iain asked.

Gavin glanced in Tomas's direction, hoping he wouldn't feel slighted, but all he saw was the top of his bald head in a bow.

Father Kendrick said an honest prayer that was nothing like the recited Latin Gavin expected. When he included Serena and Evelina, Gavin snapped to attention. The man kept his face down, hiding his expression. Afterward, they plowed into the food, dipping healthy portions onto their plates.

"Speaking of the lass, when will we begin questioning her?" Hogan asked. "I'm assuming she's here . . . somewhere."

"Only Father Tomas and I will be present," Father Kendrick said. "I'll be the one questioning her. There's no need to drag her through a public inquisition at this time. If my interview discovers aught, then we'll schedule something more formal."

"I'd still like to be there," the earl said.

"It's as Vicar Kendrick says," Iain interrupted, putting the matter to rest.

Gavin sighed in relief, thanking God in his heart that Serena would at least have a fair clergyman.

☙

Someone kept hammering until Serena reached up and covered her temples. She rolled over, burrowing deep into the comfort of her bed.

Wait. This wasn't her place in the loft.

She blinked, allowing her eyes to adjust as an unfamiliar chamber came into view. The stone walls were like a drafty cave even in the midst of summer. No wonder she had burrowed beneath the covers. She lay in the fortified walls of Braigh Castle.

"Serena! Can ye hear me?" Doreen called through the door. She knocked again.

"Aye!" Serena choked on her hoarse voice. She needed water. The door flew open and Doreen strode in with a tray. "Goodness, but I thought ye'd never wake up."

"I'm sorry. I'll hurry down to the kitchen." Serena threw back the covers and swung her legs to the side.

"Nay, not today ye don't." Doreen set the tray on a nearby table. "My laird gave strict orders that ye're to break yer fast in yer chamber."

"But," Serena raised a brow, watching her friend, "I feel so lost and out of sorts. I'm used to serving, not being served."

"After ye retired last night, Father Tomas and Vicar Kendrick arrived from St. Gilbert's Cathedral. Ye're to have a private inquision with them."

Serena sat in silence, absorbing this piece of news. She had hoped the mob would be discouraged by the storm and give up.

"Tomas will be there, ye say?" Serena hated how she sounded like a hopeful child, but she couldn't help it. He knew about her condition. She had no doubt that he would defend her and find a way to tell them what they wanted to hear. Tomas understood the kirk, and what would be necessary to save her life.

"'Tis my understanding. He'll serve as witness and be there for propriety's sake. Father Kendrick says either the matter will be dropped or ye'll suffer a public inquisition with his superiors."

Serena tried not to allow despair to steal her peace, but it was hard. Her shoulders sagged.

"I'm sorry 'bout this," Doreen said. "At least the laird forbade their entrance and the MacKenzie men stood by Philip to enforce it." Doreen giggled. "Truth be known, I think it made Philip feel like he was commanding a troop of his own."

"I imagine it did," Serena said, a bit of mirth easing her heavy heart. "So they left? Without the vicar?"

"Aye. 'Twould appear so. I think they have the vicar's promise to examine ye." Doreen pushed the tray at an angle. "Now eat. Ye'll need yer strength and wits about ye."

In obedience Serena turned, bending one leg under the other in better comfort. She leaned forward and peered over the tray, a thick slice of ham, a chunk of bread, and steaming porridge. Serena grabbed the goblet and swallowed the smooth, refreshing cider. She wiped her mouth with the back of her hand.

"I feel better already. Thank ye."

"Ye're welcome. I hung yer gowns up to dry last night, but they're still damp this morn. I'll bring ye something chaste from my chamber." Doreen turned and strode from the room.

All too soon Serena finished her meal and Doreen returned with a dark blue gown. It was simple as she'd promised. At least the two of them were similar in size. The only uncomfortable thing that kept annoying Serena was the sleeves. She tried to tug them down at the wrists, but the material would rise when she moved.

Serena dropped her hands at her side, reared her shoulders and lifted her chin in a mask of confidence she didn't quite feel. "I'm ready." She headed for the door.

"God be with ye, Serena," Doreen said behind her.

Afraid to look back lest she falter and lose her courage, Serena didn't acknowledge her friend's parting farewell. Instead, she charged out of her chamber, down the hall, toward the laird's study.

The door stood ajar. Men's voices carried. One she didn't recognize and the other belonged to Tomas. Her racing heart slowed in relief, but she still had to gulp the rising bile and will the churning of her full stomach to steady herself.

"Lord, please be with me," she whispered before stepping across the threshold. The door hinges creaked. Both men stopped talking, looked up, and stood.

She entered, forcing what she hoped was a pleasant smile. Serena resisted the habit of twisting her fingers. Instead, she bent into a curtsy.

"Serena, I'd like to introduce ye to Vicar Kendrick of St. Gilbert's Cathedral of Braighwick," said Tomas, nodding to the gentleman to his right.

The man bowed. Unlike Tomas, he had a full head of brown hair and wore a purple robe of higher quality. He straightened, meeting her gaze with inquisitive gray eyes as if seeing into her soul. His skin was quite pale compared to most men she'd seen.

His mouth lifted into a smile, but his eyes remained the same. "Lass, thank ye for joining us," Father Kendrick said.

His tone sounded neutral and ready for business. "Ye do realize why I'm here and we've called ye?" He raised a dark eyebrow.

"Aye, because of the fainting incident at the market in Braighwick."

"Serena, please sit down." Tomas gestured toward the wooden chair across from them. "We want ye to be comfortable while Father Kendrick asks ye some questions."

"Aye, please relax," Father Kendrick agreed.

She sat on the edge, keeping her back straight. Serena hoped she gave the impression that she was an honest Christian woman.

Father Kendrick launched into a series of questions about the event and her spiritual beliefs. His manner didn't frighten her as she had expected. Tomas eased the discussion by clarifying things.

The first hour passed. Serena's spine began to ache. She sat back in the chair trying to ease her discomfort. She had tried to be as truthful as possible, but she didn't want to reveal or say anything that could be misunderstood. Guarding each spoken word proved to be tiring.

"Now that we've discussed what happened and yer Christian beliefs, do ye believe ye're possessed? A possession is the only answer that could explain yer strange behavior at the market and yet allow ye to be this calm now." Father Kendrick scratched his chin in thought. "Ye do understand that demonic possession takes over a person's goodwill, do ye not?"

"Aye, but Father Kendrick, I'm not possessed. We believe this to be some unexplained condition in the body. Father Tomas has been studying the matter."

"There does seem to be a connection as some individuals who experience the falling disease do so after a head wound," Tomas said.

"Ye never mentioned a head wound. Have ye had an injury, lass?" Father Kendrick asked.

"Aye, she did over a month or so ago. Gavin MacKenzie and his men came upon her. Serena's head struck a rock. Ye can ask them about it," Tomas said.

Serena kept silent as she looked from Tomas to Father Kendrick as he considered this piece of news. Inspiration lifted in her chest as she realized what Tomas hoped to do for her. If they could prove the act was from an injury, then demon possession would be dismissed.

"Lass, have ye ever had a similar thing happen before the accident?" Father Kendrick leaned forward as if willing her to say "nay."

His gentle expression tempted Serena. She didn't want to ruin Tomas's story. She didn't want to die, but neither could she lie.

14

*A*fter the morning meal, Gavin followed Leith to the outside wall where the men worked. The clergymen had refused to let him or Iain attend Serena's inquisition. He couldn't pace outside the door in the hallway as he wanted. It would have drawn unwanted suspicion. If they learned of his deep feelings for her, it could ruin his word as a credible witness on her behalf.

Handing over the leadership of the men and the castle repairs to Leith left Gavin with more free time. He crossed his arms and glared at his brother. "I promise to stay out of yer way and not resume command, but give me an occupation before I lose my senses."

Leith rubbed his eyebrow in thought. "I could use yer help in starting the new floor in the servants' hall by the kitchen. Take a hammer and beat up the uneven bricks. 'Twill be just the thing to conquer yer frustration right now."

"Aye." Gavin nodded, bending to pick up a discarded hammer and held it up. "This ought to do." He hauled the tool over his shoulder and stomped off in the direction of the kitchens.

For the next hour Gavin beat the old brick floor in pieces. The brick crumbled as it had been doing with age. Some pieces proved to be more difficult, jarring his shoulder like a ship sailing into a rocky cliff. Blisters wore out his hands, and he finally dropped the tool and sat down to catch his breath. He wiped the beads of sweat from his brow.

While he'd passed the time, he couldn't hold back his thoughts of Serena. She had risked her life by going into town to buy medicine for an elderly woman who was already dying— to make her last hours more comfortable. Serena had done this knowing she could have another fit. She had explained that sometimes the headaches were a warning sign. Tiredness, stress, or an illness could bring on a sudden fit. Gavin knew her heart. Serena was a caring lass who acted on principle just as she did the night Iain wanted to steal the first dance. All the signs were there, but in spite of the risk, her only concern had been for Gunna.

The thought of anything happening to Serena was enough to send a fresh wave of anger through him. He swallowed and stood, dusting off his hands. This idle restlessness would do him no good, and neither would his worry. Mayhap the questioning was now over.

Gavin abandoned his task and sought the well to wash off the grimy dirt and sweat from his body. The water felt cool and refreshing, easing his foul temper. He ran his fingers through his wet hair, hoping he now looked presentable and smelled better. To his relief, some lye soap had been left by the well for the working men and he made use of it.

Afterward, he found Iain pacing in the great hall, his hands linked behind his back. His hazel eyes were drawn in a worried expression. The poor man looked as sorry as Gavin felt.

"I take it they haven't come out and ye've heard naught?" Gavin asked.

Iain shook his head. "I canna imagine them asking her that many questions. How many ways can they ask the same thing?" Iain paused and sighed. "They must be wearing her out. I'm tired simply waiting and thinking about it."

"Aye, I thought they'd be through by now." Gavin kneaded the corded muscles at the back of his neck. "I'd imagine they all need a break by now."

Silence fell between them.

Iain took a deep breath. "Gavin, what do ye think of Serena?"

The question took him by surprise, and Gavin had to brace his guarded heart and mask his expression. "Ye mean about this idea of her being possessed? Pure rubbish—that's what I think about it!"

Gavin twisted his lips in anger. Iain could think his ire was over the inquisition if he wanted, but Gavin had been suspecting Iain's feelings toward Serena for quite some time. Right now such a thought writhed his gut so tightly, he feared he might spring like a bow thrusting an arrow. Instead, he clenched his jaw and watched Iain.

"I agree." Iain waved a hand, a grin easing his pained expression. "Nay, I was referring to Serena as my wife. I'm not a titled gentleman, only a man who owns this estate. I'm aware she has no dowery or connections that could elevate my own status, but none of those things are important to me. She is. Mayhap her life could be one of ease and comfort with the protection of my name."

Gavin wanted to throw up. His stomach swirled. His hands grew cold and clammy. The taste in his mouth soured, feeling dry and numb. He tried to swallow, but it felt like a grape had lodged in his throat.

"I'm aware of Serena's strong attachment to her mither, and I thought to offer her a home here in the castle with us,"

Iain said. "What do ye think? I know my offer would be entic-
ing to most lasses in her position, but Serena isn't any simple
lass. She's special—different. And she seems to hold yer opinion in high regard."

Gavin could feel Iain's gaze upon him, but he couldn't meet
the man's eyes—not now when he was about to offer Serena
all that Gavin had dreamed of offering her. Leith had been
right. He'd fallen in love with Serena, but felt duty-bound to
his family and clan. Iain didn't have family intentions burden-
ing him or a clan chieftainship in his future. Yet, he had all
the other comforts of a grand estate, a castle home, significant
wealth, and he seemed to care for her. What right did Gavin
have to take all that away? Even if he wed her, there was no
promise she'd be happy if his family or clan refused to accept
her. Would she want to leave Caithness?

"Gavin?" Iain leaned forward, his eyes narrowing. "Ye're
awfully quiet, and I'm not sure what to make of it, mon."

"Sorry. I was merely considering what ye said." Gavin
finally met his gaze. Everything within him ached, grieving for
a future he could never have. "I wanted to give ye an honest
answer. I think the man who weds Serena will be well blessed
and favored by God."

Relief gushed in Iain's face, a wide grin lit his whole coun-
tenance. "Good! I've come to trust Serena's opinion, and if
she thinks so highly of ye, then so do I." Iain rubbed his hands.
"I need something to do while we wait. I thought I'd go for a
ride. Care to join me?"

"Nay." Gavin shook his head, ignoring the pounding blood
in his temples. "I've other issues to address." The first being
how to reconcile himself with what he'd just discovered.

Serena left the private inquisition feeling as if her mind were bruised. She worried she had told too much, but she had been honest about her condition and at least she could rest in that if nothing else.

Father Tomas had tried to assure her that all would be well, but she wasn't fooled after hearing some of Father Kendrick's comments. She wanted to find Gavin, share her concerns with him, and see what he thought. Right now she didn't need people to shield her delicate feelings. Serena needed honesty.

The whole time Father Kendrick had questioned her, Serena maintained her dignity while providing the same answers over and over. Her nerves were stretched beyond the limit and her entire body taut as if she had been in chains.

As she walked on trembling legs, Serena feared she'd soon fall apart. She quickened her pace, hurrying to get away, as far away as possible from Father Kendrick. She disliked the quiet way he watched her, studying her every expression and move. It seemed as if he waited for her to make a mistake or say the wrong thing to confirm her guilt. Yet, his tone of voice had been gentle, his manners calm and respectful.

She stumbled into the courtyard, the bright sun forcing her to blink. Serena shielded her eyes as they adjusted to the light. Following the sounds of hammering and construction, Serena found Leith discussing an issue with Craig. They both paused and greeted her.

"I'm sorry to interrupt, but I was looking for Gavin and wondered if ye might have seen him?" She bit her bottom lip hoping they could send her in the right direction.

"Earlier he was working on the floor in the servants' quarters by the kitchen," Leith said. "He'll be glad to see ye. He's been worrying. We're all concerned. Are ye all right, lass?"

Serena dropped her gaze, determined to hold onto the rest of her control. The grass felt like it was rushing at her, but she closed her eyes to steady herself. Her silence must have been answer enough for Leith as he wiped his hands on his lein and turned away.

"I think he took a break earlier," Craig said. "I saw him at the well."

"He must be alone." Leith rubbed his chin. "All the men are accounted for at their assigned tasks. I know Iain isn't with him. He stopped to speak to me on his way out for a ride. Try the tower." Leith pointed up. "At home he'd often paced the tower if he was distressed about something—the one over-looking the sea. I think he likes the open, endless view of the ocean."

"Thank ye." Serena dipped into a curtsy and hurried to the nearest tower with a spiral staircase. By the time she reached the top, she clutched her stomach, out of breath. After a few seconds of rest, Serena stepped from the shadows out onto the walkway where a light wind greeted her skin, brushing her dark hair from her face and shoulders.

Gavin leaned over the wall, one foot braced in front of the other. His hands gripped the stone in tense silence. The wind blew a lock of red hair to the wrong side. It gave him the look of a lad and made her heart swell with affection. She'd always thought him handsome. This past week when he had witnessed her fit, defended her, and continued to treat her the same, he'd earned her trust and loyalty.

He didn't hear her soft footsteps as she approached, for he remained wrapped in his thoughts. There was something compelling about him in such an exposed state, unaware of her presence. It gave her a chance to see the distress in his unguarded expression.

A host of feelings overwhelmed her. Serena wanted to run to him for protection, seeking his comfort and understanding—all the things she knew he could and would give. But then he dropped his chin to his chest and her heart lurched as if reaching out to him.

"Gavin?" She closed her hand around his forearm.

He pulled her in his embrace. His arms tightened around her, keeping her close against him. He smelled of lye soap and the sea, a fresh combination that left her savoring the moment. His hand stroked her long hair down her back.

"I've been worried," he said, resting his chin upon her head. "I know I should not hold ye like this, but I'm too selfish to let ye go." He sighed.

"I came to tell ye what happened. It isn't my wish to burden ye, Gavin, but I trust no other." She spoke against the folds of his plaid draped over his chest. "Father Kendrick hasn't made up his mind about me. He says he's relieved and believes I'm not a witch, but he's still concerned I might be possessed. Tomas and I told him that it's a condition in the body, but he plans to stay and observe me further."

"For how long?"

"I know not." She clutched his plaid. "I'm afraid, Gavin."

He leaned back and placed a gentle finger under her chin, tilting her face. "Ye've every right, but I'll be with ye." He gripped her face between his warm hands. His voice faded into silence and his blue eyes gathered moisture and reddened. He gulped. Beneath her hand on his chest, she could feel his heartbeat gallop.

His concern for her was real. He thought she was in serious trouble. Gavin had not given her false hope nor had he tried to pretend all would be well. "Gavin, thank ye for not pretending things are better than they are or for making promises ye canna keep."

He closed his eyes and leaned his forehead against hers. His warm breath fanned her face, and she smiled in spite of her situation.

Moaning, he pulled her close, lifting his hands to cradle her head as if she were the most delicate thing in the world. His lips graced hers, tickling and making her yearn for more. Serena stood on her tiptoes leaning against him, hoping. She knew the moment he gave up the resistance. His entire body relaxed, and he buried his lips against hers. It was like an intense fever burned between them that left her breathless. Her heart pounded.

He pulled away. "I'm sorry."

She silenced him with a finger upon his lips. "Please, don't apologize for something that I'm thankful for. In the next fortnight I may have verra little to comfort me. Father Kendrick will document our inquisition, watch me, and send a recommendation to his superiors. From there, my fate is out of his hands."

"But not out of God's hands," Gavin said.

"True, never out of God's hands." She reached up and cupped his face in a loving way. "I'm reminded of something my mither once said. When she realized Da didn't want me, she knew she'd have to take care of me on her own without family, lest he find us. At first she prayed for God to deliver her, but then realized her problems wouldn't go away. There's no heaven on earth. God would have to guide her through the problems. He brought people in our lives who helped us and told her about the Village of Outcasts. God uses people to help others. I only pray my faith will be strong enough to get me through what I now have to face."

"Serena, I hope that He'll show me a way to help ye, lass. I canna stand the thought of what could happen to ye."

"Shush." She kissed Gavin, silencing him. "I'll endure what I must. Tomas says there is a verse in the Latin Bible. *For the gifts and calling of God are without repentence.* Each of us has the gift of free will. We may use it for good or evil, but God will not take away the gift once He's given it. Tomas taught me this when I was a wee lass trying to understand why the Lord made me so different. I was angry at God until I came to understand that it isn't God's fault when people mistreat me. I still have my doubts at times, but I try to remember God has given them the same free will that He's given me. God can work through people like ye. I won't be forsaken by Him."

Gavin stared at her in silence, his blue eyes devouring her face. She waited for him to process her words. He blinked as his face turned a shade darker.

"Yer faith puts my own to shame," Gavin said. "How anyone could ever believe ye're possessed is beyond me. By heaven's breath, I'll pray for the wisdom to help ye out of this mess. My free will is to help. Mayhap, God will use me."

He lowered his head, their lips molding like melted wax that never hardens, but continues to soften and reshape. Serena lifted her arms around his neck, drawing from his warmth and security. She laid her head against his chest, burrowing in the comfort of his embrace.

Dark smoke pumped through the thick trees where the village lay. Fear sliced through her. She pulled away and pointed. "Gavin, the village is on fire!"

The smell of burning wood grew thick and heavy as Gavin raced Sholto toward the village. He ducked low-hanging limbs and ignored shrubs with jagged branches nicking his arms and legs. He knew by the pounding hooves and panting breaths of the destriers behind that his men kept up the fast pace he'd set.

Only half the group came with him, while the others stayed behind to defend the castle if need be. Serena had fought him hard, wanting to come and see to her mother and Gunna, but Iain, Tomas, and Kendrick had defended his position that she stay. The betrayed look she gave him slit his heart like a dagger. He would not soon forget the memory.

Shouts echoed as Gavin reached Serena's humble home. The cottage was consumed in flames, each blaze snapping in the air like the wind. As Gavin drew near, a wave of heat pressed against him.

Quinn fell to his knees, breathing heavy, and lowering Evelina to the ground. Tears streamed down his face beneath singed eyebrows, leaving a streak through the soot upon his ruddy cheeks. Fear plunged down Gavin's neck and throughout his body as he pulled Sholto to a stop.

Girard and Cara's father beat at the flames to no avail.

"Evelina!" Quinn shook her shoulders. His hands and arms were covered in sweltering blisters. "Evelina!" He sniffed and wiped his face to see.

Gavin leaned over her. A portion of her hair had dissolved from her scalp. What was left of her darkened skin on the left side of her face and neck had melted. He checked for a pulse on the undamaged side of her neck. A faint beat pulsed against his finger. Relief washed through him, and he sighed.

"She lives, Quinn! Ye got to her in time," Gavin said.

"I did?" The giant looked over at Gavin with innocent hope, his eyes searching.

"Aye." Gavin nodded. "Ye saved her life." Gavin checked over the rest of her, but only Evelina's long gown had suffered.

"She needs Tomas," Quinn said.

"I'll take her to him at the castle." Gavin glanced at the burning foundation. "What about Gunna?"

"I couldn't get to her." Quinn dropped his gaze to the ground and sat back, his large shoulders sagging. "I wanted to, but the roof had fallen on her."

"Ye risked yer life to save Evelina. Serena will be so thankful and proud of ye." Gavin pointed to Quinn's hands and arms. "Ye need to come with me so Tomas can attend yer burns."

"Nay," Quinn grunted as he pushed to his feet. "I need to help the others stop the fire. They've gone to the loch. We've got to save our village. Take Evelina to Tomas and tell Serena I'm sorry."

Quinn rushed over to the wagon of barrels Beacon carried on a cart.

Evelina groaned, but didn't awaken. Gavin feared the pain would be too much for her when she became fully conscious. Mayhap it was better this way. Gavin called Sholto. The animal obeyed the summons, but neighed and pawed the ground in restlessness.

"Ye want us to stay and help contain the fire?" Craig appeared at his side, bending over his shoulder.

"Aye." Gavin nodded.

"Will she be all right?" Craig asked.

"I hope so," Gavin said. "I need to get her to the castle where she can be cared for. I'm going to mount up if ye'll hand her to me."

"Aye." Craig nodded and bent to gather Evelina. "I questioned the cobbler and his daughters. No one seems to know how it started, but I suspect it wasn't by accident."

"I agree." Gavin settled himself, rubbed Sholto to calm him, and reached for Evelina. Slightly heavier than Serena, he strained a bit lifting her from a higher angle, but succeeded as she still wasn't a large woman. Gavin gestured to the flaming cottage. "We've got to stop this madness."

"What could be the reason?" Craig raised his hands. "These people are harmless and they bother no one. They stay to themselves and have naught that anyone would want."

"Find out what ye can. The next attack could be worse if we don't find a way to end it now." Gavin turned his horse to leave when he remembered something. "Gunna didn't make it. We'll need to prepare for a burial once things cool down."

On the way back Gavin tried not to jar Evelina's body, but the difficult ride jostled her awake. He knew the moment she realized the extent of her pain. She gasped and a low moan escaped her lips, a deep wail that grieved one's soul. The sound of it made him ache in the pit of his stomach.

"Hang on, Evelina. Soon we'll be at Braigh Castle. Tomas and Serena will take care of ye."

"Hurts . . . to breath."

Her croaky voice didn't sound like her. A surge of concern raced through his mind. Could the smoke have damaged her lungs and voice? He glanced down at all the dark soot that layered her skin. How much of it could a person breathe in without smothering? It was a miracle she'd survived.

They reached the gate where Iain and Philip let him through. Serena paced in the courtyard. Father Tomas and Kendrick were close by. As soon as she saw them, Serena ran to them.

"Mither! Oh, thank God ye're alive." Serena's face reddened. She swallowed and blinked back tears at the sight of Evelina. "Tomas!" She turned.

"I'm here," Tomas assured her.

"She's in pain." Serena gulped. "I can tell. Even if she doesn't say it."

"I'm . . . fine," Evelina said.

"Hand her down, Gavin." Tomas reached up. Gavin did as he asked. The priest faltered, but with determination he gritted his teeth and kept his balance.

"Take her to my chamber," Serena said, following them.

Gavin dismounted as Iain hurried across the courtyard toward him.

"What happened?" Iain asked, almost breathless.

"Where is Leith?" Gavin glanced around, perplexed why his brother hadn't joined them when he arrived.

"Up there. Keeping watch." Iain pointed to the tower. "I don't want a surprise attack from the town mob in case they return."

"I don't think it's the town mob we need to worry about." Gavin said.

15

*O*nce her mother lay on Serena's bed, Tomas ordered a servant to return to his house for his herbal medicines. Then he turned to Serena. "We must to be careful in removing her clothing. The material could have melted to her skin." He looked at Doreen. "We need several bowls of fresh water and cloths to wash the soot from her."

Doreen nodded and vanished to retrieve the items.

"There's an aloe plant outside in the herbal garden," Serena said, hoping to do anything to ease her mother's discomfort.

"Send someone else for it. I need yer help to see if there are other burns. If not, I'll give ye privacy to bathe and change her."

Serena stepped out into the hallway. A row of servants waited. They straightened to attention. "We heard about yer mither, lass. We thought that mayhap we could be of some assistance," said Mary, one of the maids.

Mary was a few years older than Serena, but always did as Serena instructed. Yet, she had never been overly friendly. She treated Serena with indifference—until now. Serena wondered if she was one of those who had talked about her.

No matter. If she was willing to help, Serena would accept her offer with grace.

"Thank ye. Father Tomas requested the aloe plant. I canna remember what else is in the herbal garden, but if ye recognize aught that would be good for burns, please bring it."

"Aye, we'll take care of the duty, lass. Don't ye worry none," Mary said.

Serena closed the door and hurried to her mother's bedside. Her green eyes followed Serena's movement in silence. A glimpse of fear and worry etched her features, but Serena knew that no complaint would utter past her lips—at least not while she was present in the chamber.

"While ye were out, Evelina had the presence of mind to ask about scarring. I told her there would be some, but it's too soon to tell how much. She requested the looking glass, but I told her she should wait until we clean her up. I checked her scalp and while the hair was singed to the skin, it doesn't look as if the roots were destroyed."

"What does that mean?" Serena asked.

"The hair may grow back." He waved Serena over to his side. "We must check the rest of her." A thorough search proved her gown ruined, but the rest of her skin remained uncharred.

After Father Tomas left the chamber, Doreen entered with water and more cloths. "I found a few strips of silk in the sewing room. I thought these might feel better against her skin."

"Doreen, ye're always so thoughtful. I doubt I would have thought of that." Serena pulled out the two nightgowns Doreen had let her borrow. "I'm afraid these will be too tight."

"I'll find something better." Doreen let herself out again.

Serena sat on the box bed next to her mother. She dipped a cloth in the cool water and wrung it out. Picking up her mother's hand, she began to wipe her clean.

"It's a miracle ye weren't hurt worse. How did ye only get burned here?" Serena gestured to the left side of her face and neck.

"A piece of the roof fell on me, but I was able to shake most of it off and crawl under the table." Her scratchy voice sounded painful. "It caved in front of the doorway or I would have run out. There was so much heat, I couldn't get beyond it."

"How did the others know there was a fire? I imagine the entire cottage caught fast, especially with a thatched roof."

"Phelan. He barked until I heard Quinn's voice. Then I passed out."

Serena swallowed her tears and tried to steady herself before speaking. "I'll have to remember to thank him. Phelan too." She moved to clean the right side of her mother's face and neck. "A few more minutes and ye might not have made it."

"But I did. Let's not think about what might have happened," Evelina said.

"What about Gunna?" Serena finally worked up the courage to ask. Her trembling chin betrayed her. "Did she suffer? Tell me the truth."

Evelina grabbed Serena's wrist with her good hand. "Ye know I'd never lie to ye, lass." Serena dropped her gaze to her lap, properly chastised. "Look at me," Evelina demanded. She nudged Serena's chin up. "Gunna had already passed when the fire started. She went peacefully just as ye prayed she would. I was there by her side. Father Tomas stopped by and read the last rites and prayed. She didn't wait to acknowledge him, but it was done. The fire consumed her body, but she didn't feel aught. I promise."

"I believe ye. I didn't mean to imply that ye'd lie to save my feelings," Serena wiped at the hot tears stinging her eyes.

"Maybe not to save yer feelings, but to save yer life I would. It's how I escaped yer father so many years ago. I told him I was visiting my parents. I'm not proud of what I did, but I was a desperate mither and I'd do it again if I had to."

"Ye're the best mither, giving up everything for me when ye could have stayed and had other bairns. Ye would have had yer parents, too."

Serena kissed her forehead.

"I've no regrets. One day when ye have yer own bairns, ye'll come to understand how deep and precious a mither's love is."

Her mother was trying to change the subject as she always did when it came to Serena's father. One day Serena hoped to at least learn his name. Today, she wouldn't press her mother. Serena leaned forward. "Be still. I'll try not to hurt ye, but I must clean the burn. Soot is everywhere."

Evelina closed her eyes and braced herself. Serena wrung out water from a clean cloth over the festering burn, letting it wash the dark film away. She repeated the action several times, trying her best to keep from having to touch it and cause her mother further pain.

"Thank ye," Evelina said, relaxing. Her fists eased. "I thought it would be much worse when ye wiped the cloth over it."

"I couldn't touch the burn. The thought made me cringe and then I realized I could do it this way."

Someone knocked at the door. Doreen walked in carrying a white gown. "Mary was kind enough to offer this one. I hope 'twill do." Doreen held it up by the shoulders as she approached.

It was simple, long sleeved, and made of soft linen as it had been well-worn and washed several times. Mayhap this would be better than a new linen gown made of crisp material.

"This is fine." Serena nodded. "Mither, if ye'll sit up, we'll try to slip it over ye without touching the burns. Looks like the neckline is plenty wide enough."

Once Evelina was dressed and settled, Doreen went to retrieve Father Tomas. He walked in mixing a healing salve in a wooden bowl. "The servants were kind enough to bring some herbs from the garden. While it doesn't contain all that I'd like, it'll have to do until my other medicines arrive."

"What is it?" Serena asked.

"Aloe, honey, comfrey, and olive oil."

While they applied the salve, Evelina looked up at Serena. "I haven't forgotten why ye came here. What happened after the mob arrived? Are Father Kendrick and the earl still here?"

Serena glanced at Tomas, unsure how much she should tell. Her mother had already been through so much. He nodded. She met her mother's gaze. "Aye, they're both still here. My laird never allowed the mob entrance to the castle and the MacKenzie men helped to ensure it. As to the other, I survived my first private inquisition with Father Kendrick, but the whole ordeal isn't over."

"Neither is the fire in the village," Gavin said from the threshold. "I'm sorry, Father Tomas, but this time the culprit succeeded in burning the kirk. The villagers were so busy keeping the other fire from spreading that they didn't learn that the kirk was in flames until it was too late."

❧

Gavin didn't like the idea of Serena leaving the safety of the castle, but she finally persuaded Iain that she needed to see what had happened to her home and that Gunna deserved a proper Christian burial. Now she rode between Gavin and Iain on her own mount while Tomas followed close behind. They brought twenty men in case of an ambush, determined to be as prepared as possible.

During the last thirty-six hours, Serena tended to her mother. Dark circles cradled her eyes. While she had written a short speech to honor Gunna, her grief began to take root, and she feared another fit would soon follow from all the stress she endured.

The cool weather and wet dew layered the green leaves, pine needles, and grass. Sunlight filtered through the branches above, casting spots of shade in various areas. Birds chirped and fluttered from branch to branch.

As they drew closer to Serena's home, the stench of burnt wood and the residue of soot drifted in the air. It stung Gavin's nose and made his eyes water. He blinked as they rode to a pile of black rocks and the remnant of a foundation. The structure had burned to a pile of rubble, but the stone chimney stood like a tower fortress that refused to go down. They slowed to a stop. Serena gasped, took a deep breath, and dismounted. Her steps were slow and steady as she gathered her plaid around her. Stopping where the front door used to be, she dropped to her knees.

"Gunna!" Her voice broke into a sob, her shoulders shaking. "I'm so sorry."

Her weeping tore a gut-wrenching hole inside Gavin. He longed to comfort her as he slid from his horse. Both Iain and Tomas wore similar expressions of discomfort. Gavin understood their concern. There was naught any of them could do. This kind of pain could only be diminished with time and God's mercy and grace. He couldn't take it away, but he could be there for her and that he would do.

Gavin went to stand on one side of her, Iain on her other.

"Serena, I'm right here with ye." Gavin kept his voice low.

Her breath hitched. She turned and threw her arms around his neck. "Gavin, there's no trace of her. Ye'd never know she was ever here."

"Sure there is—there's ye. Serena, her memory resides in ye."

Serena clutched his plaid and dropped her head against his chest and sobbed. He stroked the back of her hair and met Iain's confused gaze above her head. If he'd expected Gavin to turn her away, Iain would be forever disappointed. He couldn't do it.

The thought of Iain asking her to wed him still irritated Gavin. In his heart, he sensed she preferred him over Iain. Hadn't she sought him as soon as the inquisition ended, just as she turned to him now? Iain kept watching them.

"Ye see any trace as to how it might have started?" Gavin asked, hoping the question would spur the man into action and give them a moment of privacy.

A look of defeat settled upon Iain's face. "I suppose someone should check around." Iain's jaw tensed and his eyes held a lack of trust that wasn't there before.

"I've seen enough." Serena pulled back, wiping at her eyes. "Let's go bury her now."

None of them reminded her that there was no body to bury. Gavin understood that Serena felt the need to give Gunna a proper ceremony and a stone carving to mark Gunna's life. He helped Serena mount and then he waited upon Sholto for Iain and Tomas to return.

"We couldn't find any evidence," Iain said. "Serena, did yer mither hear aught before the fire started?"

"She didn't mention it." She shook her head, her eyes now dry, but red and swollen. "Mither would have told me if she'd noticed something unusual." Serena looked around and bit her bottom lip. "I've never lived anywhere else. Seeing it like this makes me feel so sad." Her chin trembled, but she lifted her head. "I'll always cherish my memories here, but I'm ready to go now."

"Lead the way, Tomas," Gavin said. "I've never been to the graveyard before. Is it near the kirk?"

"Aye. Follow me." Tomas pulled ahead of them. "'Tis on a brae in the woods behind where the kirk was. Ye canna see it from the front. It's a good distance, which is probably why ye've never seen it."

They formed a line as they rode. The villagers were already at the kirk cleaning up the rubble left from the fire. They had made a pile of stones in one area and were dismantling burnt wood and hauling it to the side on a wooden cart that belonged to Quinn and Beacon. Quinn paused with a load of stones in his arms and looked up.

"We're going to rebuild the kirk, Father Tomas." His deep voice sounded hopeful and full of determination.

"We sure are," Lavena said, dragging a black log. Birkita, her sister, scooped ashes into a bucket.

"Sorry 'bout yer home, Serena. How's yer mither?" Girard asked, his voice too loud. "Speak up now, ye know I canna hear like I used to."

"Thank ye. She's going to be fine," Serena tried to raise her tone.

"What?" He turned to his youngest daughter, Rosheen. "What'd she say?" He shouted.

Rosheen repeated Serena's words, even louder. He nodded in understanding, scratching the side of his gray head. "I'm glad she made it. We're sorry 'bout Gunna, though."

Gavin glanced at Serena, worried how she'd be at the reminder of Gunna. She gave Girard a smile of gratitude and dropped her gaze. He rode up beside her, hoping his presence gave her comfort.

"We'll visit the graveyard and when we return, we'll help," Father Tomas said. "I agree. The village must have a new kirk."

"One bigger and better than before," Beacon dropped a stone half his size on a pile.

They road on and climbed the hill. The smell of pine surrounded them as their horses' hooves crushed pine needles. Dark pinecones lay scattered about the forest floor. Soon headstones and wooden crosses appeared, about twenty graves in all. Some were marked with field stones containing no dates or names. For a brief moment, Gavin wondered who they were.

"Over there by the purple heather," Serena pointed to a patch of tiny flowers banked near a mid-sized pine tree. "Since we don't actually have to dig a grave, we can place the wooden cross there. Gunna loved Scotland's heather. 'Tis the perfect spot." Her voice drifted to silence.

Iain dismounted and untied a large item wrapped in a plaid. "I've something even better for Gunna. I had one of the servants carve her name on this tablet. Stone won't wither and rot as easily as wood. I hope it meets yer approval."

Serena gasped, covering her mouth in pleasant surprise. She dismounted and rushed over to view Iain's thoughtful gift.

Gavin slid down the side of his horse at a much slower pace, his heart aching for her. He closed his eyes, fighting a legitimate fear that he could still lose Serena to Iain. Gavin swallowed and waited by Sholto.

"Gunna Moore," Serena read. "Our dear friend now rests in peace." Tears slipped down her cheeks as she turned to Iain and threw her arms around his neck. "Thank ye for being so thoughtful."

As he wrestled with feelings of gratitude on Serna's behalf, Gavin's gut twisted like a spike, more jealousy that he wanted to deny taking root.

Serena willed her body to keep going as they rode through the gate to Braigh Castle. Her heart still ached with each beat, but it no longer burdened her with the same weight she'd endured before Gunna's burial ceremony. The prayer Father Tomas had prayed eased Serena's mind and the stone tablet showed that Gunna was loved in life.

A black carriage sat by the courtyard door. Serena glanced at Iain, but he showed no outward reaction that he knew who it might be. Curiosity gripped Serena with a tide of fear. She couldn't see an inscription from the kirk on the side. If they intended her harm, wouldn't they haul her away in a wagon with bars rather than this nice piece of equipment?

Leith had stayed behind with the other men. His brown eyes were guarded as he stood with his arms crossed waiting for them. His mouth slanted in a frown and his chin set at an angle that reminded her of Gavin when he was cross about something.

When they pulled to a stop, Leith strode to Iain. "Lady Fiona arrived with her maid and enough trunks for a lengthy stay."

"I don't remember extending an invitation. Is her da here with her?"

"Nay," Leith shook his brown head. "She said he told her about the fire that got to Evelina. As soon as she learned the news, she set out to comfort her friend."

"Friend, indeed. I'd just assume friend a snake," Serena mumbled, turning her head to the side to keep from being heard.

"What was that, Serena?" Gavin asked, always in tune with her mood swings and ever aware of her. Bless his dear soul. If ever there were a true friend, Gavin would be it. He had no reason to be so kind to a village lass or to risk his life and reputation to try and save her from a mob, yet he had. Not once had he expected anything in return. Gavin had earned her friendship, her respect, and even a secret love she would continue to harbor in her heart.

"Naught of importance." She glanced at Iain. "I'd like to retire now. I'm weary and I'd like to go to my chamber if ye don't mind."

"Of course," Iain said. "I could have a tray sent up for both ye and Evelina."

"Serena, I think ye should know that Lady Fiona is with yer mither. She wanted to keep her company while ye're gone," Leith said.

Alarm crashed into Serena as Lady Fiona's haughty comments came to mind. She didn't trust the woman—no matter how well-bred her family claimed to be.

Serena slid from her horse. She landed on her feet and shook out the soot and dust in the folds of her skirts. Her eyes burned from crying and her temples had begun to throb while on the way back, but she couldn't worry about that right now. She needed to save her mother from Lady Fiona's arrogant tongue.

Stepping around the others, Serena touched her palm to her head as she hurried.

"Serena, are ye all right, lass?" Gavin asked, walking away from Leith to follow her. "Ye kept pressing yer head that same way the last time ye had a fit."

"I'll be fine since I'm going to my chamber to rest," Serena said over her shoulder. She rushed inside and into the dark hallway. By the time she reached the great hall, someone called her name.

"I need to warn ye." Doreen caught up with her. "Lady Fiona's here."

"Leith already told us." Serena slid her hand along the rail as they climbed the stairs.

"I'm sorry. I tried to get her to wait in the great hall, but she insisted that she was 'ere to help yer mither an' ye."

"It's fine." Serena touched Doreen's shoulder when they reached the landing. "Lady Fiona is used to having her way. I'll take care of things from here—providing I'm able."

Serena turned the doorknob and stepped inside her chamber. The window was open, allowing the afternoon sun to cast light upon the corner shadows. Her mother's veiled form lay on the bed, her chest rising and falling with each breath. Serena swallowed, her pulse easing with relief.

A woman's voice paused. Lady Fiona sat in a shimmer of green satin with a purple and green plaid draped over her shoulders. She laid a handwritten journal down in her lap. It was a set of Scriptures from the book of Psalms Tomas had given them after the accident.

"Good. Ye're back." She scratched the side of her face. "I didn't realize yer mither would want to hold kirk right here in her chamber."

"Ye didn't have to stay if it bothered ye so much." Serena walked forward, folding her arms over her chest. "The Scriptures comfort her and after what she's been through, I daresay, it's the best thing for her."

"Which is why I chose to stay." Lady Fiona sat back as if settling in for a while. "How bad are her burns under that veil?"

"Bad enough." Serena rubbed the back of her neck. "Lady Fiona, I thank ye for coming to visit, but it's been a long day and I'm tired. I'd like to retire now." Serena opened the door.

"Ye're asking me to leave? After I've traveled here to see ye?" Gray eyes sparkled like coal on fire. Her pink lips thinned in a straight line. She stood and dropped the book on the chair. Rearing her shoulders back and lifting her chin, Lady Fiona glided toward her. "Ye're upset, so I'll overlook yer behavior tonight, but remember this. I've offered to be yer friend and ye'll need all the friends ye can keep if ye have another one of those fits I've heard about."

✑❧

Serena bent over an aloe plant and snapped a branch off. She measured its thickness between the pad of her thumb and forefinger. The best she could estimate was the width of a good half inch. With a stem of six inches in length, she'd have enough to mix twice as much salve as Father Tomas had made.

The sun brightened the day with a few white clouds dotting the blue sky. These warm days wouldn't last much longer with August approaching. Mayhap it would be a good time to go for a walk in the courtyard. She would prefer a longer walk, but Gavin and Iain had warned her to stay within the confines of the castle walls for safety. Lately, even the castle seemed like a new kind of prison with Lady Fiona's arrival.

Serena and her mother took most of their meals in their chamber to avoid the woman. When Serena did venture out, she kept to the servants' areas where Fiona would never venture. Gavin soon learned of Serena's habit and often stopped by the kitchen or asked Doreen for her whereabouts. He complained of Lady Fiona's vixen ways, making Serena laugh at his attempts to mock her.

Serena drifted through the herbal garden. She dropped an aloe branch in the fold of her apron with the other herbs she had picked and stood. Turning, she nearly collided into someone. She gasped, juggling her load to keep from littering the ground. Once she had gained a semblance of balance, she looked up, shielding her eyes from the bright rays.

"Pardon me, Serena. 'Twasn't my intention to frighten ye, lass." Iain rubbed his mustache at the corner. He shifted his feet and she wondered if something bothered him as he stared off into the distance.

"Iain, is everythin' all right?" She held her breath, dreading more bad news. They had certainly experienced their share of late.

"Nay." He shook his head. "I was hoping I could talk to ye, but I didn't want to keep ye from yer mither." He glanced at the bundle cradled in her arms.

Serena followed his gaze and realized his concern. Touched by his thoughtfulness, Serena felt compelled to hear him. "Actually, she's sleeping at the moment. I had planned to make more salve to apply to her burn when she wakes."

A disappointed expression crossed his features as a crease marred his red eyebrows and his mouth dropped in a frown. "In that case, it can wait until another time."

"Ye mistake me. While she is resting would be a fine time for a walk in the courtyard. The thought just crossed my mind." Serena pulled the strings free at the back of her apron, careful to keep the herbs wrapped inside. "Allow me a moment to set these aside."

"Of course."

She laid the bundle on the ground by the gated fence to the herbal garden and turned back to Iain. "I'm ready."

He led her around the corner into the wide courtyard. They strolled in leisure. He cleared his throat. "How is yer mither healing? Does she need aught?"

"She's better each day. I must admit, she's far more comfortable here at Braigh Castle than she would have been at home. I canna thank ye enough for that." Serena gave him a sideways glance. He kept his gaze down toward his laced brown boots as they walked. The color of his skin had darkened to match the shade of his hair.

"I'm sorry about yer home. As soon as ye're both up to it, we can send for Kyla to make new gowns. The two of ye canna keep going around borrowing from the servants."

The back of Serena's throat stung. How would she ever repay the kindness of so many people? For herself, she didn't mind going without, but she couldn't bear to see her mother suffer one more discomfort.

"As for the cottage, I was hoping ye wouldn't rebuild." Iain said. "I'd like ye to remain here at Braigh Castle, both ye and yer mither."

"But we must rebuild!" The idea of not having their own private home filled her with apprehension.

Iain stopped and touched her arm. Serena paused to face him. This time the sun was at an angle behind her so she could clearly see his expression. He took her hand in his. Iain's hazel eyes searched her face as he squinted.

"Serena, these past several months of having ye work in my home, getting to know ye, and coming to care about ye has made me realize I never want to be without ye. I don't want ye to be here as a servant, but as a wife. Share my life with me. Everything I own would be ours." He paused and rubbed his face. "I realize ye may not love me, but I'm hoping in time ye'll come to care for me as much as I do ye. I can give ye security in a nice stable home, the protection of my name, my body and heart will be yers . . . all that I am."

Stunned, Serena stared at him trying to absorb his words. She realized her mouth hung open and quickly closed it. No words came to mind, but Gavin's face appeared in her memory, the kiss they'd shared. She tried to imagine the same kind of closeness with Iain. Her heart revolted, weighing heavy against her chest like a large field stone.

Father Kendrick's words from their private inquisition filled her head . . . the pressing questions . . . the accusing warnings. How could she be any man's bride? The thought thrust her into a pool of agony when she considered Gavin, not Iain. Still, she didn't want to hurt him.

"Iain, I wish I were free to accept such an honorable proposal, but I canna—not when the kirk believes I could be demon possessed, and I've no idea what my fate could be."

"Ye must have faith, lass. God delivers the innocent and reveals truth," Iain said, clutching her hands in his. "I don't speak on religious matters often, but I know ye to be a woman of God and I've always admired yer faith. Didn't I once hear ye say that to a servant?"

"Aye." Serena nodded. "To Doreen when she thought ye would believe another maid's lies about her."

"It isn't my desire to preach to ye, Serena." Iain grinned. "For I'm hardly an authority on such matters, but I only wanted to offer some encouragement."

"Thank ye, Iain. But being practical doesn't mean I'm faithless. Even if the kirk declares my fits acceptable, my future husband will need to witness them before we wed. I must be sure before taking a chance of binding that person to me for the rest of our lives."

"Promise me ye'll at least consider it." He tucked a finger under her chin and lifted her face toward him.

"I canna . . . not while things are so hectic." Her aching chest grew heavier. She could never consider wedding Iain as long as Gavin was around to remind her of with whom she longed to spend the rest of her days. "I don't want to mislead ye. I think a lot of ye, but I don't love ye—not in that way."

"I know," Iain's voice lowered. "I think we suit well, and I'm willing to accept that if I have a chance of at least changing yer mind."

16

*G*avin wiped his sweating brow and blew out a deep breath. He'd been working on the hallway floor by the kitchen all morning. His thoughts withdrew to Lady Fiona cornering him in the great hall. She wanted him to describe Serena's fit. Gavin refused to oblige her. Instead, he asked about her activities in town. The plan worked as she was more than delighted to discuss herself.

A woman's figure appeared at the hall entrance. Sunlight from behind cast her face in a shadow. With the torn-up floor, he feared she would stumble and fall. He straightened, standing to his full height.

"Be careful. The floor is uneven with broken stone," he warned.

"Gavin? Is it ye?" Serena's innocent voice increased his pulse. He dropped his tool and went to her, stepping over the scattered pieces. Once he reached her, Gavin stopped within arm's reach. He had to clasp his hands together to keep from touching her.

She wore her long black hair draped over her shoulders with a simple headpiece behind her ears, but it didn't conceal her shaking. Worry kicked him in the gut, and he feared Father Kendrick had made a terrible decision regarding her fate.

"Ye're trembling. What is it?" He tried to lower his voice, hoping she would bestow her trust in him. He waited, but she kept silent. "Serena?"

She pressed her hand against her forehead. "I was just in the herbal garden when Iain came and proposed to me. I canna fathom what makes him believe that a woman in question by the kirk would make a proper mistress of this grand place." Serena swung her hands in a wide circle. "I'm so addled."

Gavin swallowed. It felt like a large walnut had lodged in his throat. He reminded himself to keep breathing. Bracing for the news he didn't want to hear, Gavin folded his arms across his chest and adopted a warrior's defensive stance.

"What did ye say?" The words strained past his tight lips, every passing second a moment of torment.

"What else could I say?" She threw her hands up and paced. "I reminded him of the inquisition and that my trouble with the kirk is still eminent. A woman of my reputation could only hurt him. As much as it pains me to admit, I could be wife to no one." She leaned back against the wall and closed her eyes. Fat, round teardrops slid beneath her lids and down her smooth cheeks.

Gavin's chest tightened, disappointment flooding into the pit of his stomach. "Ye care that much for him?" The back of his throat ached, but he ignored it and forced his thoughts in an honorable direction. He should at least try to find the right words of comfort to ease her pain. The sight of her misery only added to his own. "I'm sorry, Serena. Mayhap this ordeal with the kirk will soon be over and ye'll be free to wed. I dislike seeing ye so upset. I've no doubt if ye both love each other, and ye're meant to be together, God will provide a way."

Her bottom lip quivered until she bit it. She sighed, wiping her wet face. Gavin averted his gaze to the outer courtyard. The sunlight bore a direct contrast to the clouds in his heavy heart.

"I didn't mean to imply that I'm in love with Iain. I care about him, to be sure, as I care for everyone in our village. What bothers me is that I'd like a family of my own some day. Iain may be fond of me now, but what about after he sees one of my falling fits? Will he think me demon possessed? If not, will he grow weary of forever defending me? Will he be shamed or offended by the gossips? Any man who musters up enough courage to wed me will have to face these issues and so will the children I bear."

"Then he doesn't deserve ye. I've seen yer fits and it hasn't changed the way I feel about ye. Serena, ye deserve a man who'll love ye regardless of yer fits and who will defend ye until his dying breath. Ye're a special lass because ye're different. As yer friend, I caution ye in making yer decision."

Their eyes met and silence and lingered between them. He longed to know her thoughts, but more than that, he longed to share his.

She was the first to break eye contact and looked down. "Gavin, I wish it had been ye to ask me, but I understand why ye wouldn't. I've lived here in this small village my whole life. I canna go anywhere because of my condition. If I do survive this ordeal with the kirk, I'll not likely receive a better offer. Is it so wrong to marry for security, the chance at a contented life for myself and Mither? Iain has been good to me and now he's offered to shelter Mither. Mayhap love could develop between us over time."

Gavin ran his hand over his jaw and approached her, leaning both hands against the wall on each side of her head. He lowered his head and brushed his lips against hers. The tender kiss held the promise of what already existed between them. She melted against him, no resistance in her gaze or response. He pulled back and tilted her chin. "Nay, it wouldn't be so bad if ye didn't already have another choice." He lowered his voice. "I love ye, Serena. I can offer ye the same things as Iain, but beyond that, I pledge my love. Marry me, lass."

❧

Serena blinked, staring at Gavin in stunned silence. Her heart hammered against her ribs. Gavin leaned so close, she could feel his warm breath fan her face. Light freckles spread across his nose. She imagined they had faded with age and were more profound in childhood. Rather than detract from his appearance, it added to his charm. Serena loved him all the more.

"Lass, don't leave me hanging. Tell me what ye're thinking." He leaned his forehead against hers. "Will ye wed me?"

"Gavin, ye'll leave Caithness when the repairs on the castle are finished. I canna leave my mither and how will yer family and clan react when they learn of my fits? I'll end up going through the same accusations there as I'm enduring here, only then, ye and yer whole family would be involved."

"Nay." He shook his head. "They'll accept ye and I'd want ye to bring yer mither. I've grown quite fond of Evelina. She's given me the impression she approves of me."

"When?" Serena searched her memory.

"'Twas the morn ye were hanging the laundry. I stopped by offering to fetch supplies for ye." He touched the tip of her nose. "Ye said nay, but yer mither gave me a request. She recognized my need to have a reason to return. Even then, I think she knew I was smitten."

"Aye." She smiled. "I wanted to resist ye, but ye're too much temptation. Ye have a way about ye that grips one's heart and won't let go. I knew that about ye from the first day we met. If ever there was a man for me, he would be ye." She gulped, hoping she wouldn't choke. A throbbing began to drill a gaping hole in her heart for what she was about to say. "I love ye, of that ye can be sure, but I canna wed ye. I love ye too much to saddle ye with my fits and kirk problems."

She braced herself against the wall and used it to push him away. Slipping beneath his arms, Serena took advantage of Gavin's moment of stupor.

"I'm sorry, but I don't want ye to resent me years later when yer family still won't accept me and the whole family is shunned—possibly even yer chieftainship stripped from ye because of me."

Serena backed away, breathing hard, and unable to halt the tears flowing down her face.

"Ye embellish. No one will shun us." Gavin stepped closer, reaching for her.

"Won't they?" Her voice rose. "Ye don't know what it's like to go to market and have people stare, point, and play tricks on ye because ye're from the Village of Outcasts!"

She wiped her eyes. Gavin watched her with a dazed expression. How could she make him understand? He had always been accepted by his clan and a leader among them. He had influence, authority, honor, and the admiration of others. In one sweeping move to wed her, all of it could be taken away. How could she do that to someone she loved? She couldn't.

"I canna make ye understand, Gavin." Serena held up her palms, keeping him at length. "Ye need to trust me." She lifted her hem and turned to run across the courtyard.

With her chest heaving from sobbing, Serena could hardly catch her breath when she sailed into Father Kendrick by the herbal garden. He caught her by the shoulders. "Lass, slow down! Has someone harmed ye?"

"Nay." She shook her head. Salty tears slid into her mouth as she took a deep breath. "Please . . . I need to be alone." As she would no doubt be for the rest of her life.

Not true. At least she had her mother.

"If ye're certain ye'll be fine?" Father Kendrick lifted an eyebrow.

"Aye, I'll go to my mither where I belong."

Father Kendrick released her, and Serena rushed to her chamber, passing by servants who paused to stare at her. She knew it was out of concern, but it didn't ease her discomfort or shame. Once inside her chamber, Serena sagged against the door.

"Serena?"

She whirled. Her mother peered at her from the box bed.

"Why are ye weeping? Is it the kirk?"

"Nay." Serena wiped her eyes and cheeks. She relayed the proposals she'd received from Gavin and Iain—and her response to both. By the time she finished, Serena sat on the edge of the bed and her mother leaned up against two feather pillows.

"I thought both of them might be interested in ye, but I feared the kirk's inquisition would change their minds. It appears I may have been wrong."

"Gavin has seen my fits and still claims to love me. Once Iain witnesses it for himself, he may think me evil as everyone else does."

"I doubt that, lass, but ye're right. We canna possibly know his reaction until the time comes." Her mother reached for her hand. "Serena, it's my desire that ye accept Gavin's proposal if ye truly love him. Ye've got to take what moments of happiness ye can get out of life. Plenty of disappointments will find ye without ye looking for them."

"This is my home. The village is all I've ever known. Ye've always said I must stay here where I'm safe. Ye told me what could happen to me out there in the world with my condition."

"Aye." Her mother nodded. "Since my accident, I've had a lot of time to reflect on things. I've been praying for understanding, and I've come to realize that I've been raising ye out of fear, not trusting in the Lord."

"Other than Tomas, ye're the one who taught me about the Lord."

"Things have now changed here in the village." She covered Serena's hand. "Ye've been discovered and it's no longer safe. Mayhap God has brought Gavin MacKenzie as a means to secure both yer safety and happiness. Do ye not see the protection ye'd have as the wife of a chieftain?"

"I thought no one could defy the kirk—not even the King himself."

"That's true, but there are limitations to the kirk's power and ways around it." Evelina tightened her hand on Serena's. "If I would have had a more supporting husband, our lives might have been different. Ye wouldn't have grown up here in the village. Ye would have known my parents, other family, mayhap been affiliated with my clan and known some of yer father's English family."

"Did ye love him?" Serena asked.

"Nay, I did not. Mine was an arranged marriage. I hardly knew him. I prayed Da would change his mind, but he'd given his word to yer father's father and wouldn't go back on it—not even for me." Evelina sighed and looked away. "So I resigned myself to make the best of things, but it wasn't to be. Yer father was an evil man, and I took it upon myself to protect ye at any cost." She brushed a lock of hair from Serena's eye. "I wish I could advise ye better, but I've never been in love. I don't know what it feels like. If ye and Gavin both love each other, don't let it fade. Trust God and give it a chance."

"But the kirk could destroy my future."

"The kirk doesn't control yer future, God does, if ye let Him. It may be time for ye to leave the village. For everything there is a season and it may be that our season in this place is now over."

"Ye'll come with me?" Serena heart leaped with hope. She couldn't imagine leaving her mother here. Ever since her secret had been discovered at the market, her faith had wavered, testing her through temptation and confusion.

"Aye. My home is where ye are, Serena."

A bold knock warned them that someone was at the door. Doreen's head appeared, a bright smile on her face. "Serena, ye've guests downstairs waiting in the great hall."

Gavin rode Sholto toward the site where the new kirk would be built. He planned to check on the villagers' progress and offer to help them, and see if he could discover any trace as to who could be behind all the recent actions. He needed to think of something else besides Serena. She frustrated him. How could she admit to loving him and then refuse to wed him?

He arrived, expecting to see villagers cleaning and rebuilding, but the place was deserted. Much of the burnt timber had been removed. Patches of soot covered the area where the kirk used to be.

A rustle of leaves caught his attention. He turned his horse to the left and noticed a narrow path in the woods. Gavin motioned Sholto forward. He ducked under a low branch, keeping a slow pace, ever mindful of the unexpected.

Low voices carried through the trees. Gavin dismounted and tethered his horse nearby. Continuing on foot, he unsheathed his sword. He stepped lightly on the ball of his toes, careful not to reveal his presence.

"Tell me where it's hidden. Ye know this land rightfully belongs to 'is lordship—an' everything in it. When the estate is legally his, he'll remember yer loyalty. Ye can stay 'ere an' farm the crops all ye want."

Gavin didn't recognize the man speaking, but he leaned against a branch to listen.

"Iain McBraigh owns this land," Quinn said. "I don't believe it belongs to ye. Show me the deed. Why do ye not live at Braigh Castle? None of it makes sense."

Gavin imagined Quinn scratching the side of his large head as he often did.

"Forget the estate. How about I help Serena prove her innocence to the kirk?" Another male voice asked.

"How?" Quinn asked.

"Ye don't need to know how." The other man sighed. "That's for me to 'andle. All ye've got to do is trust me."

"But ye said Serena is possessed and I know she isn't. Ye told everyone that the village is full of evil spirits and that is why all the bad things have been happening." Quinn coughed.

His response concerned Gavin. He stroked his chin, trying to decide the best way to approach them.

"I'm not sure I can trust ye," Quinn said.

Gavin had heard enough. Someone was trying to take advantage of Quinn's slowness. Whoever it was had gone too far. With deliberate purpose, Gavin struck his sword against the leaves. He stomped and thrashed around to announce his approach.

"Tomas? Quinn? Anyone around?" Gavin raised his voice.

"Over here," Quinn answered.

Gavin broke into the clearing where Quinn towered over two men. One was short and stout, the other, tall and slender. Quinn held an ax where he'd been chopping wood. Two horses grazed nearby. Quinn grinned, a gaping hole replacing his front teeth. The men turned, their eyes widening in surprise. The thin one offered a smirk. The short one pursed his lips in a frown.

"I came by to see yer progress on the kirk. Where is everyone?" Gavin asked, looking at Quinn.

"We took a break today to catch up on some of our own household chores. The women went to the castle to visit Serena and Evelina. They've been working into the wee hours, sewing new gowns to replace what they lost in the fire."

"That's verra thoughtful," Gavin said. "Serena and Evelina will be thankful."

"Beacon says we're all family, an' family helps and supports each other."

Gavin swallowed in unexpected discomfort. These people really acted like family. They pulled together in hard times, defended one another, and shared their faith. He'd witnessed them caring beyond themselves and their immediate families to sacrifice for each other.

"Have we met?" Gavin turned toward the men, raising an eyebrow.

"My name's Donald and this is Kenneth." The thin man gestured to his friend with his thumb. "We work for the earl, who sent us to offer Quinn and Beacon some business. The earl would like another supply wagon." He reached up on his toes and laid a hand on Quinn's large shoulder. "Isn't that right?"

"Aye, an' we can definitely use the work. They asked 'bout the cave, but I canna tell them about it. 'Tis a village secret." Quinn puffed out his chest in pride.

"What cave?" Gavin let his gaze drift from Quinn to the men.

"'Tis naught but a legend. We're only teasing 'im." Donald's lips thinned as he glared at Quinn. He waved his hand to dismiss the subject.

"What's going on here?" Beacon sneaked up behind them, his hands fisted on each hip. His brows wrinkled in concern as his gaze traveled to each of them.

"I didn't tell 'im about the cave, Beacon. I promise." Quinn held up his hands in surrender. "Honest."

"Who's asking 'bout a cave?" Beacon asked.

"Donald and Kenneth." Quinn pointed at them.

"Never mind what I said," Donald interrupted. "We heard there was a cave nearby. I only asked Quinn if he knew aught 'bout it. 'Tis all." They walked past Beacon and grabbed their horses' reins. "Let's go." They climbed upon their mounts and vanished through the woods.

Once they were gone, Beacon turned to Gavin. "And what about ye?" Beacon crossed his short arms, a scowl upon his face.

"What about me?" Gavin stood his ground not easily threatened. "I came upon them when I stopped to see the progress on the kirk and heard their voices. Ye're right about them trying to trick Quinn. That Donald fellow made quite a few promises from the earl that I doubt he'd keep."

"I'm not surprised." Beacon looked back to where the men had gone, his expression a frown. "I've never trusted the earl or his men."

"What's in the cave? In spite of what they tried to make me believe, Donald seems to believe it exists, and whatever it is—he wants it—bad enough to make false promises."

"There's no cave!" Beacon met Gavin's gaze, his dark eyes narrowing. "Come on, Quinn." Beacon stomped away and Quinn followed, his shoulders slumping.

Gavin followed. "Beacon, tell me, someone is trying to murder the people in this village. Let me help before it's too late."

"I'm aware of that." Beacon snapped. "Ye think I need remindin' of it? In this village we stick together and take care o' our own. We're fond of ye, Gavin, but ye're still an outsider."

Gavin walked back to Sholto and mounted him. Serena would be the one who would most likely tell him about the cave. Too many strange things were happening, and somehow, he had a feeling that the cave was involved. At least he now knew the earl was up to something, but he had no proof he was behind the other things.

A while later Gavin arrived at the castle. He walked into the great hall and stood in stunned silence at all the chaos. The cobbler's daughters were all in tears, wiping their eyes and faces. Lady Fiona stood with her arms folded, glowering. Father Kendrick and Iain were bent over a lass lying on the floor. Kyla paced, wringing her hands in distress. Cara edged around them, reaching out to feel for the lass on the floor.

Gavin's heart lurched. Was it Serena? He strode over and bent beside Iain.

"We'll have to exorcise it out of her. I've no experience in such matters. I'll have to send for help from the local bishop. In the meantime, we'll need to tie her down to keep her from hurting herself." Father Kendrick pressed her quivering shoulders against the floor.

"Tying her up won't be necessary," Gavin said. "I've seen this before. It's a physical condition, not a possession. In a few moments she'll be fine and calm again. She isn't a danger to herself or anyone else for that matter," Gavin said.

"Ye jest!" Lady Fiona said. "'Tis the most horrible sight I've ever seen. Something is definitely controlling her." She pointed at Gavin. "She's bewitched ye! I know she has."

"Ye're a liar!" Kyla whirled, stomping toward her. "A fever controls one's body an' ye don't claim the person to be possessed."

"That isn't the same thing." Lady Fiona retreated, leaning her head back from Kyla's reach. "The people in Braighwick were telling the truth."

"Iain, get these people out of here. Ye don't want it jumping from Serena to another weak soul," Father Kendrick said.

Gavin reached over and pulled the vicar's hands from her and met his gaze. "With all due respect, Father, ye canna cast out something that doesn't exist."

⟡

"Serena, wake up." Gavin spoke softly in Serena's ear as he knelt by her bedside. He shook her shoulder. Her head hurt as she protested and pulled free, rolling over.

"Ye must wake now!" Her mother's stern voice echoed near her face. She pinched Serena's right cheek. The pain jolted through her head. Serena's eyes flew open. Her mother lay beside her, perched on an elbow. Her green eyes were full of worry . . . and tears.

"Do ye remember having another falling fit?" Evelina asked. "Father Kendrick believes ye're possessed. He wanted to tie ye up and lock ye away. But for the grace of God, Gavin was able to encourage Iain to defend ye."

"We've got to figure out a plan," Gavin said. "Father Kendrick is appealing to the local bishop for an exorcist to cast out a demon that ye don't have." He rubbed his eyes. "Iain can only resist the kirk for so long before he too becomes a target for sheltering and defending someone they consider to be possessed." Gavin stood and paced around the chamber. "I'll write my da to see if he has any connections who could help us."

Serena rubbed her eyes. Every muscle in her body felt like a heavy stone. When she tried to sit up, she might as well have been hauling logs across the bed. She brushed her tangled hair from her face.

"We shouldn't involve more people. Gavin, I don't wish yer family to resent me. Helping me could ruin their reputation and cause people to choose sides," Serena said.

"Ye're more important than our family reputation. Besides, ye don't have a choice." Gavin leaned over her. "The bishop will have to act when he receives Father Kendrick's request. Yer fits will become so well-known that people will take sides regardless. Ye'll need some people with power to speak up for ye. I intend to make sure ye get whatever support we can gather."

"Will yer family and clan have that much influence?" Evelina asked, her voice hopeful.

"I'm not certain, but we must try. When Doreen comes with yer meal, ask for some parchment paper with quill and ink. I'll not only write to my da, but I'll also write to my sister's husband, Bryce MacPhearson. He's chieftain of the MacPhearson Clan. They both have favor with the King."

"Verra few have any favor with King James the Third," Evelina said. "Yer family has achieved a rare feat, indeed."

"True. The King isn't known for his compassion or justice, but he does reward loyalty at times." Gavin paused at the foot of the bed. "I need to ask ye both about a specific cave in the village. Does it exist?"

This was the last question Serena expected from Gavin. She glanced at her mother for a sign of how to answer.

"How did ye hear about the cave?" Evelina asked.

"I overheard the earl's men trying to trick Quinn into telling them the location. Beacon arrived before he could give it away." Gavin leaned his knuckles on the bed. "I saw the two of ye exchange a look when I asked ye about it. I need ye to be honest with me. Does this cave exist? If so, could we use it as a hiding place for Serena?"

"Nay!" The single word escaped her lips before she could stop it. The idea of being stuck in that cold, dark place where she couldn't easily come and go filled her with fear. Wouldn't she be better off here in Iain MacBraigh's protection?

"So it does exist!" Gavin leaned forward, his expression intense. "It could be the perfect place to hide until I can form a plan to get ye home to MacKenzie land." Gavin paced again. He snapped his fingers, whirling. "What's in that cave to make the earl seek it out?"

"Mayhap he's only curious about it," Evelina said, shrugging.

"I think it's more than that. I suspect that cave has something to do with the strange things that have been going on in the village, only I canna prove it yet."

"What I'd like to know is how the earl even knows about the cave," Serena said.

"More important than the cave, I want to figure out a way to save Serena. How much time do we have before the bishop sends an exorcist?" Evelina shifted and adjusted the cover.

"I'll meet with Iain to find out what I can about the process. Then I plan to go to the village to see if anyone has any ideas." Gavin strode to the door and turned to meet Serena's gaze. "I'll do my best."

17

$\mathcal{G}$avin paused at the sight of a guard stationed outside Serena's door. The man stood with his back against the wall and his arms crossed over his chest. He eyed Gavin, his jaw set at a superior angle.

This new situation would make it harder for him to escape with Serena. Gavin nodded in greeting and strolled away, keeping his steps steady. He didn't want to do anything to raise the guard's suspicion.

Voices echoed from Iain's study. Gavin knocked on the door and was granted entrance. Inside, Iain and Father Kendrick sat in wide-wooden chairs with embroidered cushions facing each other. Both men looked up with expectant gazes in Gavin's direction.

"Serena is now awake. She's calm and herself again. Her mither is keeping her company." Gavin forced himself to maintain a casual tone that wouldn't be mistaken as a challenge. "I noticed the new guard outside their door."

Iain sipped from his goblet and glared at Father Kendrick over the rim. His silence surprised Gavin, but he refused to be alarmed. Iain may still lend his support on Serena's behalf.

All Gavin had to do was remain patient, hope and pray God would give him the right words to turn things around in Serena's favor.

"It's unfortunate," Father Kendrick said, "but I insisted on a guard for Serena's own well-being. These things are unpredictable. I didn't want to take a chance."

Gavin strolled further into the room and swallowed. He felt like pacing, but kept his feet planted and his hands at his sides. "I promised I'd stop by for a visit on the morrow. I'd like to keep my word." He raised an eyebrow, waiting to see if his request would be denied.

"Since she's possessed, I'm concerned that the demon could try to transfer to others," Father Kendrick said.

"I've been around her twice now during a fit and have seen no evidence of such things," Gavin said. "I'm sticking to what Father Tomas has thought all these years. I believe she has a condition in the body, not a demon."

"Well, ye've no knowledge of spiritual matters. I understand yer point of view, but I happen to know better." Father Kendrick paused, tapping his chin. "Mayhap this is why everyone in that village is so strange."

"I'm not sure what to believe," Iain said. "I agree that caution must be exercised on Serena's behalf, but I'm not in favor of making her a prisoner here in her new home." Iain pointed at Gavin. "Ye may visit her if ye choose. I don't wish to deprive her of company as well."

"Thank ye." Gavin bowed his head in a slight nod. He glanced at Father Kendrick to see if the man begrudged Gavin's triumph in their small battle of wills, but he showed no sign of it. His expression remained the same.

The mention of company brought Lady Fiona to mind. She'd claimed to be here as a friend to Serena, but she had turned against Serena at the first opportunity. Gavin wasn't fooled. What did the woman want? "Where's Lady Fiona?" he asked.

"She excused herself to her chamber," Iain said. "I believe she mentioned something about writing her da."

No doubt to inform the earl of Serena's latest fit. Then he knew why Fiona was there. She had been sent by her father as a spy. But why? Did they think Fiona could earn Serena's friendship and trust in order to learn the cave's location?

"I presume ye've already written to the bishop and someone will arrive in a fortnight?" Gavin asked Father Kendrick.

"Indeed, I took the liberty of sending one of the servants with a message. The sooner this matter is settled, the better." Father Kendrick crossed his ankle over a knee and adjusted his robe. "About a month ago, I heard that an exorcist was visiting the nearby shire of Wick. With divine assistance, the clergy may reach him before he leaves the area."

A wave of fear dashed across Gavin's flesh, raising the hairs on his neck and arms. They wouldn't have much time to come up with a plan. He'd have to send a messenger to his father and Bryce. His mind raced, grasping at fleeting ideas. *Lord, help me help her.*

"When did ye do this?" Iain stared at Father Kendrick, tight-lipped. Gavin had to commend Iain, he contained his anger well.

"After ye and Gavin carried Serena to her chamber," Father Kendrick said.

Iain set down his goblet and linked his fingers. "Gavin, ye may have a seat and join us. No need to stand." Iain nodded toward an empty chair.

"Thank ye, but I need to visit the barracks." Gavin glanced from Iain to Father Kendrick. "Father Tomas will be by in the morn to check on Evelina's burns. He may want to see Serena as well."

Gavin turned and strode from the room. After stopping by to visit with Leith and Craig to update them, Gavin set out on Sholto for the village.

As he approached the site of the new kirk, he reined in Sholto. All the villagers bowed on their knees. Kyla was the first to see him. She stood and walked toward him. Without a word, he raised an eyebrow in question.

She raised up on her tiptoes. "In times of a crisis, we fast and pray as a whole," Kyla whispered, glancing back at the bent heads. "This is how we fight our battles."

The realization of what she meant blazed against Gavin's chest like a flaming torch. Humbled, he swallowed. He had been mentally tormented trying to figure out a plan to save Serena. Other than the day he had prayed upon the cliff, when else had he bothered to pray? Fasting never crossed his mind, not that he truly understood the purpose in it, but right now he'd try anything. Not since his sister's kidnapping years ago had he felt so helpless. In the end, God had made everything all right. Why couldn't he trust that things would be fine this time?

A restless burden raged in his heart, distressing him and robbing him of peace. This wasn't a battle he could ride into and claim victory with a sword. The enemy was invisible, but real.

"*We do not wrestle against flesh and blood, but against principalities and darkness,*" Father Mike's words came from a childhood memory. Strange how the right scripture sometimes came to mind when he most needed it.

"May I join ye?" Gavin bent toward Kyla.

A fortnight passed as Serena adjusted to the changes in her life. Father Kendrick only allowed Gavin, Father Tomas, or himself to accompany her outside the chamber. He claimed it was for her safety, but she knew the truth. He wanted further evidence to condemn her. Whenever she occupied her chamber, a guard was stationed outside her door and all through the night.

She couldn't even take consolation in her work as she wasn't allowed to be around the other servants, lest she transfer a demon. Serena considered reading, but it gave her a headache. She had never had so much idle time. At least she and her mother kept each other company.

Unlike Gavin, Iain had not repeated his wish to wed her. His reaction to her secret had been as she'd imagined—distant and uncertain.

Serena fastened her mother's veil around her head. The black netting hid her healing scars well. They continued to apply the salve, hoping for the best.

"I think it will do us both good to stroll about the courtyard and take the fresh air," Serena said.

"I've never considered myself a vain woman, but the idea of people seeing me look so hideous turns my stomach." Evelina touched her middle as if she were already ill. "This way, no one is uncomfortable."

Serena opened the door and gasped as booted footsteps charged down the hall like an army of knights. She peeked around the corner and caught a glimpse of Iain and Father Kendrick hurrying to keep up with two men who resembled warriors on the frontline of battle. They wore grim expressions, as their sheathed swords rattled against their sides. Their broad shoulders were wide enough to discourage the average man, let alone two defenseless women.

Where was Father Tomas? He usually visited about this time of day.

She stepped back and braced for their entrance. With Gavin away, she could only assume they were here for her.

"What is it?" her mother asked, stepping closer, and laying a hand on Serena's shoulder.

"I don't know," Serena whispered, looping her arm around her mother's. Footsteps drew nearer and Serena's throat went dry.

"Gentlemen, please allow me to break the news," Iain said.

A few moments later, he appeared, wearing a scarlet, purple, and dark blue plaid draped over his shoulder. His mustache had been trimmed, but his red eyes spoke of little rest. Surprise flickered in his eyes at seeing the door open and Serena and Evelina waiting.

"Were ye expecting us?" he asked, glancing uneasily at the men behind him.

"Not at all. Mither is feeling better and we thought to take a walk in the courtyard when Father Tomas arrived," Serena said. She forced a smile as she met each man's gaze, willing her nerves to remain calm.

Father Kendrick stepped forward. "Serena, I've heard from the local bishop. He was able to reach the exorcist with a message before he left the area. He's agreed to come to St. Gilbert's Cathedral to meet ye and work to set ye free."

"Who are these men then?" She gestured toward the large men with their muscled arms crossed over their chests.

"They were sent by the town's magistrate to escort ye. Be assured ye've naught to fear as long as ye come peacefully."

"What if she wishes to stay here in Iain's care?" Her mother tightened her grip on Serena's arm, refusing to let go. She swung her attention from Father Kendrick to Iain, who dropped his gaze to his feet.

Alarm rose in Serena as goose pimples forced a shiver throughout her body. If Iain wouldn't look her in the eyes, then guilt plagued him for a reason.

"I'm afraid she doesn't have a choice." Father Kendrick addressed Evelina. The men behind him stepped closer, their presence a demanding threat. He turned to Serena. "As soon as Devlin Broderwick delivers ye, these men will escort ye back here."

"Devlin?" Her mother whispered, her grip on Serena faltered. She swayed.

"Mither?" Serena reached for her, but she slipped through her grasp. "Nay!"

Iain rushed to her, his arm slipping around her back. "I've got ye." He swept her into his arms and carried her to the bed.

Serena followed, bending toward her mother. "We need to call Tomas. Please." She pulled the veil back and brushed her mother's hair off her forehead. Familiar green eyes blinked.

"I'm fine. Just a weak moment is all. Mayhap I tried to go out too early." Evelina's voice didn't sound as solid as before, but she laid a hand over Serena's.

"Ye know I'll take care of her," Iain said.

"I'm not leaving her," Serena wrinkled her brows, a low determined tone passing through her tight lips.

"Ye must, Serena. Ye're expected at St. Gilbert's Cathedral and we canna detain Devlin Broderwick longer than necessary. Too many people need him in other places," Father Kendrick said.

"I'm not leaving!" Her heart hammered against her ribs, and she fisted her hands at her side, turning toward Father Kendrick. "My mither needs me. I'm all the family she has."

Father Kendrick stepped back and inclined his head toward the two large men. "Take her."

One of them came at her. Serena searched for a weapon. Tears stung her eyes in desperate fear. How could she fight them or outrun them? She was cornered in this chamber.

The man's hands seized her shoulders, swung her around. He bent and threw her over his shoulder.

"Nay!" Serena kicked and beat his back. Tears blinded her as his shoulder dug into her lungs. The worst thing they could do was separate her from her mother. She couldn't imagine a worse nightmare.

"Don't hurt her!" Evelina's voice drew near. "Let me tell her goodbye."

Soft hands gripped Serena's checks. Her mother stooped to look into her face. "Don't give them a reason to harm ye. Confess to naught, but the Lord Jesus Christ. Keep yer faith." Evelina lowered her voice. "I promise I'll think of some way to set ye free. I love ye, my child."

The tears in her eyes made Serena's heart weep. Evelina kissed Serena's cheek. As they carried her away, Serena prayed it wouldn't be the last.

"I love ye, Mither!"

"I love ye, lass!" The agony in her mother's tone tore at her heart as the beastly man hauled her away against her will.

After several hours helping construct the kirk walls, Gavin sought an afternoon bath and looked forward to some refreshment. He rode Sholto into the stable yard and slid to the ground, patting the animal's neck. A vigorous ride from the village felt great.

The stable lad hurried over and took the reins. Gavin rubbed his hands together, pleased to have completed a good day's work. "Give him some extra oats. He worked hard for me."

"Aye." The lad nodded.

"Gavin!" Leith rushed toward him, his tone full of alarmed concern. Gavin strode forward to meet him.

"Were ye in a fight?" Gavin pointed to his dark eye now swollen and bruised.

"If only it were that." Leith stopped in front of him, nearly toe-to-toe. His jaw angled in a grim expression. Narrow brown eyes watched Gavin at eye level. "I've bad news. The town magistrate sent a couple of men here and they took Serena. She's gone."

Gavin's ears burned and the heat spread to the base of his neck. His chest throbbed like an arrow pierced him. He cleared the lump in his throat. "Gone? Where did they take her?"

"St. Gilbert's Cathedral. Father Kendrick left with them. I tried to stop them, but they threatened to send an army from town," Leith touched the side of his head. "One of them has a powerful punch."

"What about Evelina? Did she go as well?" Gavin paced, circling his thumbs over his temples as if to spur more thoughts.

"Nay." Leith shook his brown head. "She remains here with Iain. The servants in the castle say she's verra worried, and Iain is trying to comfort her."

"Aye, I would imagine so." Gavin marched toward the courtyard with Leith following close behind. Anger rooted inside him. How could he have prevented this? He should have ignored her protests and taken her to the cave as soon as he found out about it. Gavin swung open the side door.

"What will ye do?" Leith asked as their booted footsteps pounded against the floor.

"I don't know. How long ago did this happen?" Gavin glanced over his shoulder, but all he saw was the outline of his brother's head in the darkness.

"Less than an hour."

"Why didn't I see them?" Fear for Serena loomed over him like a drenching flood.

"I heard Father Kendrick say they would have to go around the village to avoid resistance."

They entered the great hall. Iain paced with his head down, his fingers tracing his brow. At the sound of their footsteps he turned, his face eased in hopeful relief.

"Gavin, thank goodness ye've returned. I could use some wise counsel. Iain glanced at Leith and back at Gavin. "I'm assuming ye've heard they've taken Serena? 'Tis no easy feat to go up against the kirk. The clergy is too powerful in all of Europe."

"Aye. If ye couldn't stop them, ye should have sent for me." Gavin clenched and unclenched his fists at his sides. *Be calm. Iain is not at fault.*

"And what would ye've done?" Iain lifted his palms up, shrugging his shoulders. "The local bishop had already appeared to the town magistrate. He sent two well-armed men to escort her from here. If we'd resisted, I daresay an entire army would have soon descended upon us." He shook his head, walking closer. "Some could argue that we're protecting her guilt and resorted to such lengths with no other options. Is that what ye want? To strip away Serena's claim of innocence before she even has a chance at a public inquisition?" Iain's voice rose.

"Nay, of course not." Gavin, properly chastised, stroked his chin in worry as he dropped his gaze from Iain. He needed to think things through rather than accuse others. When his sister had been kidnapped by the MacPhearsons, many had encouraged him to go with his brother against his father's wishes, but he'd refused. Instead, Gavin considered the potential consequences their actions could have on the entire clan. Avoiding war and unnecessary bloodshed became the goal . . . for everyone.

Now, his goal would be keeping Serena alive without her captors breaking her spirit. Although he had no idea how to accomplish the task ahead of him. He prayed God would give him wisdom and favor.

"I need to speak with Evelina." Gavin strode out the door leading to the staircase.

"She's in her chamber, recovering," Iain said, following him. "'Twas verra sudden and unexpected. Evelina fainted. Serena refused to leave her, so one of the men carried her out on his shoulder. Afterwards, I gave Evelina a goblet of water, but she asked to be alone."

"They manhandled Serena?" A flash of anger bolted through Gavin, breaking out a new line of sweat upon his forehead. "Did they hurt her?"

"She put up a fight, but she wasn't injured."

"This is unnecessary. She's lived all these years among the villagers with no problem. She's a poor, defenseless lass who has never harmed a soul in her life. Why make up lies?"

"Gavin, ye must admit that her fits are like naught we've ever seen," Iain said. "Did it not frighten ye the first time ye witnessed it?" Iain rubbed his tired eyes with his knuckles. "As ye've pointed out, I can accept it, but that is because I know her. People in town rarely see her. They don't understand something they canna explain."

"They canna explain the weather, the sun, the wind, the vast mysteries of the sea, but they accept it. Why must she be evil just because she's different?" Gavin whirled, shaking with fury. Letting out a slow breath, Gavin tried to imagine the peaceful ledge by the sea where he enjoyed praying. Images of him dancing with Serena branded his aching heart.

Without another word, he stomped up the stairs.

Gavin knocked on Evelina's door. He waited. No response. He knocked again.

"Please . . . let me alone," a weeping voice called.

"Evelina, it's Gavin. I need to talk to ye."

A few moments later, the lock clicked and the door creaked open. She wore a black veil over her face. "Are ye alone?"

"Aye," Gavin inclined his head to the left.

"Come in, then." She swung the door wide. "Doreen's here. She's trustworthy." When he stepped across the threshold, Evelina closed the door and leaned against it.

"The kirk has chosen the wrong man as Serena's exorcist." She stepped forward and clutched his plaid. "Ye have to do something. We've no time to spare."

"I will. But first tell me everything that happened. What do ye know about this man?"

"His name is Devlin Broderwick. He's Serena's father . . . and my husband."

❧

Twice Serena tried to escape. Now her wrists were bound as she rode in front of the burly man who had carried her over his shoulder. She had learned his name was John. He was quiet and ignored most of her questions. It was just as well, since talking eased her frayed nerves and she'd probably say more than she should.

Serena prayed they would encounter Gavin, some of his men, or the villagers, but they took a narrow path through the woods leading around the village road. A few hours later, they rode into Braighwick. She would never feel the same way about this town again. Growing up, Briaghwick gave a glimpse into the outside world that had tempted her curiosity, but was forbidden. Here, she and her mother had bought and sold goods, learned of new inventions, and made a few friends—or so she had thought.

"There's the possessed lass I've been tellin' ye 'bout!" The herbal merchant pointed at her.

Conversations faded as they passed. People stopped to stare. Some faces were familiar, others were not. Serena wanted to hide, but the inclination was foolish. She would have to endure the agony of their public humiliation as best as she could.

Serena gasped as a slimy tomato shattered against the side of her face, leaving a sodden trail as it slid onto her lap. She pinched the soft vegetable and dumped it on the ground, as the horse continued to clip-clop forward.

"If ye miss the lass an' hit me, I'll string ye up to a tree, I will!" John raised a threatening fist above her head.

Serena pulled a mess of seeds from her hair. The thick strands were now matted together. A rotten stench lingered. She gritted her teeth, determined to maintain her dignity. Her mother's inspiring words came to mind, and she lifted her chin, ignoring their mocking jests. At least, no more tomatoes were thrown at them.

By the time they reached the gray stone towers of the kirk, relief contrasted her remaining fear. Was her trembling evident? Her insides were as unsteady as a stomach illness that wouldn't allow one to eat. She gulped air as John dismounted and reached up to set Sereena on her feet.

It took a moment to gain her balance. She straightened and glanced up at the towering fortress. A silent prayer escaped her whispering lips. Only God could help her now.

John led her by the elbow, following Father Kendrick up the stone steps. She counted each one, twelve in all. He opened one side of the double oak doors, holding the heavy structure for their entrance.

A long aisle faced them down the center to the altar, with rows of wooden benches on each side. Serena stared up at the ceiling that seemed to be miles high. Plain candlebras hung from the rafters with unlit candles. The only light radiating throughout the sanctuary was from the lit candles on the walls and at the front altar. Three confession booth doors were on the left side behind the pulpit.

She had always wondered what grand images lay behind these stone walls. Now she knew. A painted mural of Mary, the Mother of Jesus, kneeling by the cross where her son was being crucified covered the front wall.

The hundred or so benches were empty, but a priest stepped out from behind one of the confession doors. He was young, mayhap Gavin's age. The priest wore a black robe with a silver cross around his neck, resting on his chest near his heart. He greeted Father Kendrick with a smile and a nod.

"Good evening, Father George." Kendrick said. "I'll escort Serena Boyd to the guest chamber on the second floor beneath the bell tower. That room has a door with a lock. Would ye tell Father Devlin Broderwick of our arrival?"

"Aye." Father George nodded. He left through the confession booth.

Father Kendrick led Serena and John through a small door on the other side of the pulpit to a dark staircase at the end of a hall. A cool draft brushed her face. She blinked and kept walking as a shiver passed through her.

They stopped outside a door and Father Kendrick sifted through a set of keys hanging on his rope cord belt. He pulled out a long, thin key and unlocked the door.

"Do ye have further need of me?" John asked.

"Aye. Stand out here in case she tries to escape again."

Father Kendrick walked to a far corner, struck some kindling, and lit a candle. He then lit two candelabras on the walls and another candle on a dresser. The furniture was simple, but more than Serena was used to having. A wardrobe sat in one corner, a dresser on the other wall, a simple fireplace, a small table and chair was by the box bed. It would serve well as a writing desk or a place to eat a meal. No windows. At least, they hadn't brought her to a dungeon—yet.

Footsteps marched toward the room as the door still stood ajar. A tall man entered also wearing a black robe and a silver cross on a chain around his neck. He rubbed his hands together.

"So, you must be the girl I've been hearing about. Are you Serena Boyd?" His English accent surprised her.

"Aye." An eerie feeling swept through Serena along her spine. She tried to hide the tremble, but her shoulder shook.

The man leaned close. He had black hair with silver streaks throughout his head. His eyes were dark and piercing as he watched her. She longed to look away, but dared not.

"Are you sure?" He raised a thick black brow. "I've an idea that you might have another surname."

This was the last question she expected. "That is the only name I've ever been told." Serena gave him a questioning look.

"Who's your father?"

"I don't know. My mither refused to speak of him."

"What do you know of him?" he asked.

Serena glanced at Father Kendrick, wondering what these questions about her parentage had to do with her fits. He bent his head in a small nod, and she turned her attention back to the man questioning her.

"I know he didn't want me when I was born and so my mither took me and left. She refused to give up her only child."

"So you may have inherited a rebellious streak from your mother." It wasn't a question, but a statement. He folded his hands behind him and circled around her, taking measure.

Serena closed her eyes and swallowed, wishing this would soon be over. Devlin Broderwick was the name Father Kendrick had mentioned earlier.

"They tell me you're possessed. Do you agree?"

"Nay, I do not. I love God. I've always loved the Lord. Satan cannot love God and be Satan."

"So your fits are unwanted." He raised a dark brow.

"Aye." Serena looked down at her feet in shame. She had always hated her fits. They shamed her, ruined her life, and made her an oddity among others.

"What of your mother?"

"What of her?" Serena met his gaze.

"Where is she and how has she handled your fits all these years?"

"She wanted to come, but they left her at Braigh Castle with Iain MacBraigh, the laird. Please . . . will she be allowed to visit? May I write her?"

"Perhaps I'll benefit from speaking with her as well. The better I understand these fits of yours the better I may rid you of them. I make no promises. If we don't succeed, you'll have a public inquisition. If you're convicted, you'll die by burning at the stake. Let's hope it doesn't come to that."

18

Evelina told Gavin the tale of Serena's birth. Reliving the horror of trying to save her newborn from a murdering father brought fresh tears to her eyes and renewed fear she thought she'd overcome.

"I'm amazed ye were able to escape," Gavin said, shaking his head in disbelief. He folded his arms as he stood facing Evelina and Doreen sitting side-by-side on the bed.

"I couldn't have done it without Gunna. She hid and fed Serena until I was well enough to travel."

"Do ye think he'll figure out that Serena is his daughter?" Gavin asked.

"'Tis possible, if he remembers her given name. The Boyd name may throw him off a wee bit. He'll be thinking of my maiden name—Anderson. Boyd was my mother's maiden name." Evelina smiled, remembering her mother's goodbye kiss on the top of her head at Evelina's wedding. Neither of them had known it would be the last time they would see each other. "Serena is named for my mother's mother. She was Spanish."

Tilting his head, Gavin gave her a curious glance. "Are ye from the Boyd family connected to the royal family?"

"Aye." Evelina nodded. "My great-grandfather was a duke."

"Oh my, a duke is a grand thing, to be sure," Doreen mumbled in admiration.

"I thought it best if Serena not know these things. I feared the temptation to discover more of her kin would overcome the logic of staying here where it's safe." Evelina sighed, and looked out the window at the sea. "But all that has changed now. She's no more safe here than anywhere else."

Gavin approached Evelina, bending to her eye level. "Ye're all the family Serena has. Ye may be the only one they'll allow to visit her. Would ye be able to do that knowing ye might come face-to-face with Devlin?"

"Aye, I've naught to lose. He already has her." Evelina licked her bottom lip in thought. "Mayhap I'll be able to help change his mind—to help her. Twenty years is a long time to dedicate to the kirk. I'd like to think that some of God's word has taken root in Devlin's heart and softened him."

"Do ye think ye're well enough to ride?"

"Aye." Evelina nodded.

"Good. Then ye're coming with me." Gavin turned to Doreen. "Can ye occupy Iain for a while and give us time to escape?"

"I'll do my best." Doreen nodded.

"Take only what ye can carry," Gavin said.

A few minutes later, they were ready. Evelina hugged Doreen. "Thank ye for everything."

"I wish I could've done more," Doreen said. "Take care an' let me know when she's safe."

They left the chamber, keeping quiet as they passed through the hall. With Serena gone, no guard watched the chamber. Gavin led Evelina through a back entrance that Leith had discovered a fortnight ago. She waited outside the stable by a cart so she wouldn't be seen. Gavin prepared Sholto and walked him out to where Evelina stood. He mounted, and lifted her up behind him. Once she was settled, they were off.

Philip would be their only obstacle at the gate. An idea came to him and Gavin guided Sholto toward the barracks. He hoped the men would be heading toward their quarters now that most of the day was gone and they would be ready to wash and clean up for the evening meal in the great hall. A few were walking in pairs and threes from the well to the barracks.

Gavin pulled up beside three young men not much older than Leith. "Have ye seen Craig or Roan?"

The taller one tilted his dark head behind them. "Roan is waiting for a turn at the well, but I canna recall seeing Craig."

"Nay, me neither," said the one in the middle.

"Thank ye," Gavin said. As he approached the well, Roan noticed him and stepped out of line to meet him. Gavin leaned over. "I'm taking Evelina to see Serena, if they'll allow it. I don't want Iain to discover our absence for awhile—I need enough time to give us a good head start."

"Ye think he'd try to stop ye?" Roan raised a wrinkled brow.

"I don't know, but I canna take a chance. He seems awfully concerned about losing favor with the kirk. He's given Serena his word to protect Evelina, so he might demand to travel with us. I'm afraid he'll slow us and I'm concerned he wouldn't deny the kirk information if pressed. I plan to stop and discuss an escape plan with Father Tomas since he's been to the cathedral. So try to detain Philip so we can get past the gate. I'll wait about twenty minutes. Send someone to raise and lower the gate and tell Leith."

"Aye." Roan reached up and slapped Gavin's arm. "I'll take care o' it. Ye can count on me."

"I know it, mon."

To his relief the wait didn't take long. Gavin rode out of the cover of a low-hanging tree and into the shadow of the gatehouse. The bars groaned against the stone casement as Roan cranked the rope wheel. Gavin rode through to freedom. As soon as they were beyond the huge drop in the hill and back over to the other side, their ride would be smooth.

Evelina clutched him tight as they descended, a gasp slipping past her lips.

"Ye'll be fine." Gavin assured her as he glanced over his shoulder. "I've never lost a rider—yet."

"I usually ride the wagon," came a muffled voice against his back.

The afternoon heat had cooled as the sun drifted lower. Gavin wondered if Serena could see this same view or if they had locked her away in some dark chamber. Sholto eased them up the steep incline. Once they made it, Evelina sighed and relaxed her grip around his waist.

Soon they arrived at Father Tomas's cottage. Tender meat roasted over a fire. The aroma drifted through the open front door, luring them inside.

"Tomas?" Gavin called, not wanting to barge in on him without an invitation.

"Come in. I'm preparing the evening meal."

Gavin gestured for Evelina to enter before him. He followed close behind.

"Have a seat and make yerself at home while I get two more plates." Father Tomas glanced between Gavin and Evelina. His expression sobered. "What's happened?"

Gavin told him about Serena being taken. "I was hoping ye'd be able to help me plan her escape."

"First, we'd have to know where she's being held, if it's locked in, guarded, and bound."

"I'm hoping Evelina will be allowed to see her and then she can report back to me all that we need to know. Could ye draw a map of the inside of the cathedral from memory?" Gavin asked.

"Mayhap, but I'd prefer to go with ye. She may need some spiritual counseling by the time they're done with her."

⌇

Serena woke with a start. Her dreams had been disturbing with a dark shadow chasing her through the woods. Her heart raced at a frantic pace as if it had been real.

She blinked, trying to open her tired eyes wider, but the chamber was cast into complete darkness. Cold hovered in the air, chilling her nose. She had slept in her clothes. No one had given her any other garments, and she wasn't given time to gather any of her own.

Sitting up, she ran her fingers through her tangled hair. She pushed aside the cover and smoothed her wrinkled dress. Serena slid her bare feet to the wooden floor and winced as her toes curled up at the biting air. Soon every morning would bear this chill as fall set in.

Her throat swollen and dry, she swallowed, wishing for some water, but they hadn't even supplied a wash basin. Reaching out her arms, Serena made her way to where she thought the door was located. She bumped into the wall, felt around until her fingers touched the iron handle. She twisted and pulled. It was locked.

Disappointment and frustration assailed her. Even though she knew it would be locked, she had hoped. . . .

She stumbled over to the table and then the dresser, seeking a candle, but felt naught. Had Devlin taken it with him? Was she to remain in this bleak darkness until someone returned?

Serena stifled a sob and inched back toward the bed where her right knee hit the hard box bed. She smoothed her bruised flesh, blinking back stinging tears. Lifting her chin, she crawled onto the bed and wrapped her arms around her legs.

"Lord, please help me." She let the tears flow. "What have I done to be plagued with these horrible falling fits? Why me? Please take them away!" She dropped her head onto her bony knees. "Please . . . please," she whispered. "I don't want to die upon a burning stake. I'm a child of God. Save me."

After a while her tears faded and her wet cheeks dried. Serena's stomach churned with hunger, but she tried to ignore it. Instead, she thought of the sea below the cliffside of Braigh Castle, willing her nerves to calm.

A key turned in the lock, startling her. She clutched her plaid at her neck, mentally preparing herself for the unknown. If only they were bringing food, her belly rumbled again.

A burning candelabra with five lit candles appeared around the door, and Devlin followed with a menacing scowl upon his face. He squinted, his mouth slanting as his gaze landed upon her curled up in the corner.

His soles made the only sound in the room as he walked toward the table and set down the candelabra with a tiny clink.

"Today begins your exorcism." His harsh tone sent a shiver up her spine as it had yesterday when she'd first met him. "For the time being, you'll receive no food or water. I find it best to weaken the flesh during these difficult moments. If the flesh is weak, then it'll not fight the Holy Spirit so hard, and we can work faster to remove the evil spirit taking residence inside you."

Serena stared at him. He was mad! Her fate was in the hands of a madman.

"As long as there is no violence on your part, you'll remain unbound. Is that understood?"

She nodded.

"Now, let me give you a bit of my background. I think it may be important to you." He paced back and forth, touching the tips of his fingers. "I was once wed to a young girl who bore me a child, a daughter, who had fits similar to yours. When I made it clear that I wouldn't tolerate any kind of evil in my household, my wife left with the child—along with the nursemaid."

Serena choked and her chest ached as icy fear twisted through her heart. Her mind went numb with the mental chant, *Lord, please don't let this man be my da.*

"Brokenhearted by my wife's betrayal, I set out to find them to no avail. When it became clear I wouldn't find them, I dedicated my life to battling the evil that took my wife. I joined the church, became ordained, and worked hard to set other families free, sparing other men from my fate."

He stopped talking and Serena sat still, afraid to move. Devlin strode forward, towering over her. "My daughter would be about your age. So you see, I'm determined to succeed in this. The first thing you'll do is write your mother. Ask her to come visit you."

"Why?" Alarm prompted her heart as it beat faster. If he was her father, could he harm her mother? Make demands upon her? After all, he was still her husband, wasn't he?

"Because I want to meet her." A mischievous grin slid across his face. "It often helps to meet the families of the person I'm trying to set free. Family members often reveal secrets about a loved one that the individual themselves will never give." He leaned forward. "But in this instance, I've more to gain. Would you not agree?"

Serena lifted her chin and met his gaze. "I know not. There's naught my mither can tell ye that I canna. She may be unable to come. She's suffering from burns on her face and isn't well."

"If she's who I think she is, I want her here." He pointed a finger at the floor. "Would her name happen to be . . . Evelina?"

Serena gulped, never straying from his gaze. She couldn't let him see her fear. It would only give him the upper hand in this battle of wills.

"I see ye've been askin' around about us." She lifted her chin.

"You'll write that letter, and I'll oversee every word of it. The writing will be in your hand, and if I know one thing about mothers, they'll come to the aid of their children—no matter their age—especially Evelina."

Serena wanted to weep. Regardless of how much of a mad monster he was, she knew he was right about her mother.

❧

With unwavering determination, Father Tomas induced Gavin to let him come along. Gavin hitched Sholto to a small wagon Tomas kept in a shed behind his cottage. Once they arrived in town, Gavin was glad he'd succumbed to the idea. They arrived in Braighwick in better spirits than they would have been on their own.

Gavin secured a tavern inn with two rooms, one for Evelina and the other for himself and Father Tomas. Throughout the night, he slept little as Father Tomas snored like rumbling thunder.

The next morning, he and Tomas consumed a plate of eggs and a chunk of bread as Evelina finally appeared, wearing a black gown and a matching veil. She glided toward them with a straight posture and floated into the chair opposite them.

"I trust ye slept well?" Gavin asked.

"Hardly at all." Her quiet voice drifted through the netting. "I couldn't help thinking about Serena. All sorts of things vexed my mind. I'm sure the Lord is disappointed in my lack of faith."

"Not at all," Father Tomas said. "That's why God established grace. He's strong when we're weak. 'Tis one of the greatest blessings—to have a Savior we can depend on."

Silence followed as Evelina and Gavin processed Tomas's words. Gavin lifted his cup of water and noticed Evelina still had no food.

"Please forgive me for not offering sooner, but would ye like me to order somethin' to break yer fast?"

"Nay." She shook her head. "My stomach is tied in knots at the thought of having to face Devlin again."

"A wee bit of bread might settle yer stomach, and besides, ye need to keep up yer strength. Serena may need ye." Gavin held out a chunk of bread from his plate.

"I'll try." Her trembling hand reached for it. She slipped it beneath her veil and chewed in silence.

"I've been thinking about our approach—whether we should all arrive together and ask to see Serena, or if we should try alone at different times," Tomas said.

"Aye. Such thoughts have been on my mind as well." Gavin glanced between the two of them. "While Evelina is

Serena's mither and would have the best chance at seeing her, she could also be in danger from Devlin as his long-lost and disobedient wife. I don't think she should risk going alone."

"True, but from what Evelina has said and the level of respect he's achieved in the kirk, I'd imagine him a verra prideful man. He may be too ashamed to reveal her as his wife. 'Twould make him look like a failure in his own household, and he would lose his priesthood."

"Aye." Evelina coughed, touching her chest. "He's prideful, but that's naught compared to his need for revenge. If he's like the man I remember, vengeance will weigh him down, and he'll somehow justify it through his idea of religion."

"Then that settles it. We'll attempt to visit all together at once," Gavin said.

Evelina sighed. "I must admit, that does make me feel better."

Less than an hour later, the three of them were shown into the sanctuary at St. Gilbert's Cathedral and told to sit upon the front bench. Inside, the building looked quite similar to other cathedrals Gavin had visited in Edinburg, Galloway, and London. The eerie silence thickened around them. Gavin's nerves twitched until he desired to pace. He had to grip the bench on each side of his legs to stay seated.

Father Kendrick appeared through a door behind the pulpit. A slight grin chiselled deep lines into his expression. He first greeted Father Tomas, then Evelina, and at last, Gavin.

"I knew it wouldn't be long before we had a visit from all of ye." He scratched his chin. "Serena is doing well, but I'm sorry to say that she canna receive visitors while Father Broderwick is in the process of an exorcism. It can last weeks . . . even months."

"What about a supervised visit where ye or Father Broderwick is present?" Gavin asked. Hope beat with each pounding pulse that pumped throughout his body.

Father Kendrick glanced down at his feet, shifted his weight back and forth as if considering the question. "I'm sorry, but we canna. Too much risk is involved."

"May we write her and receive letters from her?" Evelina asked.

"'Twould be permissible." Father Kendrick's eyes lit in obvious relief to offer some good news. "Though I must warn ye, the correspondence will be read to ensure no planned escapes or persuasion of the mind are present in the letters."

"Thank ye, Father." Evelina released a deep breath.

"There's one exception." Father Kendrick raised a finger and turned to face Evelina. "Father Broderwick has requested a private meeting with ye, Evelina. He asked Serena to write ye, but now that ye're here, he'd be pleased to meet with ye now if Father Tomas and Gavin will wait." Father Kendrick stepped back and tilted his head to the side.

Determined to learn what he could of Serena's situation and condition, Gavin leaned over and touched Evelina's arm. "We'd be happy to wait for ye."

"It's time," Father Tomas agreed.

Evelina stepped forward, straightened her shoulders, and lifted her veiled head. "I'm ready. Lead me to him."

As Gavin watched her leaving the sanctuary, he glanced up at the painted mural on the wall where Jesus lay on the cross with Mary bowed at his feet. *Lord, be with her. Give Evelina lots of wisdom and strength.*

Father Kendrick led Evelina down a dark hall. His black robes blurred into the shadows surrounding them. Their footsteps were soft, steady clicks against the stone floor.

Evelina thought of her flight from Devlin twenty years ago and her courage returned with each step. God had not forsaken her then. He would not forsake her now.

He paused by an open door. "I've brought Evelina Boyd as ye requested."

"Good. Send her in and you may leave us," a deep voice said in an English accent. Even after all these years that voice had tormented her dreams and hovered upon her mind like a ghost—something that wasn't supposed to be, but still lurking. Evelina didn't believe in apparitions, but the perception still applied to her past with Devlin.

Father Kendrick stepped aside and waved her in. With her head held high, her chin lifted, and her spine straightened, Evelina strode into the study.

A small fire burned in the hearth, giving the air the smell of burning wood. Lit candles graced his dark wood desk littered with an open book, parchment paper, ink, and several quills in a container. Two candelabras permitted more light on opposite walls of dark panel.

Devlin stood and walked around the desk. Evelina wasn't expecting so much gray in his once-dark hair. He still kept it cut straight around his head like an upside down bowl and trimmed around the ears. His dark eyes sparkled through lined circles she didn't remember. He wore a black robe similar to Father Kendrick's with the exception of a silver chain around his waist. A silver cross hung from his neck and lay mid-length of his chest.

"Please sit." He pointed to the two brown chairs at angles facing the fire.

Evelina disliked the mischievous grin that slid across his face making his age lines even more visible. To make the best of her opportunity, she'd humble herself, bargain and beg if need be—anything to save Serena. Her gown swished as she walked further into the room and sat. She linked her black gloved hands in her lap.

"Where is Serena? May I see her?" At least her voice sounded steady.

"At the moment, she's fine. And no, you may not see her. I do not wish her to be influenced during the exorcism." He leaned forward. "I'm afraid you're at an advantage and I at a disadvantage. After twenty long years, you have the opportunity to see how I've aged. Must I continue conversing with you through that abominable black veil?"

His quick denial in letting her see Serena stung like a whip. A deep ache burdened her heart, so much that it was impossible to ignore.

"Please . . . must ye do this? Serena is a good lass. She loves the Lord with all her heart. No evil lurks inside her. What can I do to make ye believe her innocence?"

"There is naught you can do. The whole situation is dependent upon Serena. The good news is that she's confessed the Lord Jesus Christ as her Savior. Now all she must do is stop having those evil spells that seem to possess her entire being."

"And if she does not?" Evelina's chin trembled and she was thankful he couldn't see it.

"I think you know the answer." His voice lowered to the dangerous pitch she remembered when something had angered him.

Even after meeting Serena and talking with her, his own daughter, Devlin possessed no feeling or warmth toward her. Evelina closed her eyes, fighting the pain. She should have known not to hope for such a change of heart.

"She's yer flesh and blood . . . yer verra own daughter. Do ye have no depth of feeling for her at all?"

"Evelina, she's the cause of your leaving me . . . the ruination of the family I would've had. She's the root of our humiliation. We could have had more children, but you were too stubborn." He stood and paced around her chair like a hungry lion on the prowl. "No, I feel nothing."

"I didn't want other bairns. I wanted Serena. Ye're wrong about her. Ye always were." She let the contempt in her voice carry, trying not to lose her courage.

"Careful Evelina, after all these years, her fate is now in my hands." He grabbed her shoulders from behind, his grip so hard he bruised her flesh. She swallowed the wince that rose up in her throat. "'Twouldn't be wise to provoke me," Devlin threatened at her ear. "I asked to see you out of curiosity, not to give you some false hope that you've any power to change my mind. I wanted to know how you've supported yourself all these years. Coming from a family of high standing with plenty of servants, it must have been hard to adapt to doing everything yourself, living so humbly, and raising a child on your own."

Devlin shook her, snapping her head back. "At first I was so angry at you, I feared what I would do to you once I found you." His hands slid to her throat under her veil, tightening until it was difficult to breath, then he released her. "But after I joined the church and matured, I realized what you had undergone, and I admired your determination." He leaned to the side as if trying to see her eyes beneath the veil. "I've always thought highly of your character, Evelina. I could've never taken vows if I had not."

She shifted in her seat. "Ye won't allow me to visit her?"

"No, I will not." The words sliced through the air.

"How long shall this . . . process last?"

"That depends," Devlin stepped in front of her, linking his fingers, watching her, "on whether or not she has another fit."

"And how long will ye wait?" Evelina clenched her jaw, hoping he wouldn't wait long.

"A month, maybe two."

Her heart plummeted. Serena was likely to have another fit by then. She had to get her away from Devlin before then. "Please . . . let me see her!" Evelina wanted to beg, but she knew it would do no good. She had to depend on her faith—now more than ever.

"No!" His harsh tone grated on her nerves. "You're wasting your time asking. After what you've put me through, I'll not give in." He gripped her by the elbow and pulled Evelina to her feet, against him. "You're still my wife, Evelina. I could have you punished, but this is better." An evil grin framed his face, and he ripped off her veil. His eyes widened in horror. Devlin stepped back, his lips twisting. "My . . . my . . . you're ruined." He tossed the veil back at her.

"I've done no wrong against ye, Devlin." Evelina caught the veil. "I've lived like a nun, but I won't stand by and watch ye murder our child."

"I won't have to. The church will condemn her. She'll be turned over to the magistrate."

"So ye've already decided her fate, have ye?" Evelina straightened her shoulders. "That decision belongs to God, not ye!" She strode from the room and hurried down the dark hall.

19

A sennight passed without any word from St. Gilbert's Cathedral since Evelina's meeting with Devlin Broderwick. Gavin stood outside the kirk, staring up at the bell tower as it chimed the hour. Somewhere inside those gray, stone walls, Serena heard the same bells. His heart ached like an empty hole.

He unfolded the parchment paper containing the drawing Father Tomas had made for him of the inside of the cathedral. As helpful as it was, Tomas could only remember the main hallways and floors. He'd never seen the remote areas of the kirk. Father Tomas had guessed Devlin was holding Serena in a chamber on the third or fourth floor—no doubt, well away from the sanctuary and visiting kirk members.

Over the last few days, Gavin had watched who entered the cathedral, which entrance doors they used, and the hour of each visit. He noted the clergymen who departed on errands and town visits. It appeared that the kitchen had the most people coming and going and would serve as the best opportunity for him to slip into the cathedral. A tall man about his size brought fresh logs and coal each morning at dawn. He was given entrance, as none of the female servants could carry the load and set piles out back. Gavin asked around town about the man's identity and character. Mayhap he could bribe him into letting Gavin take his place for a few days.

"Still out here forming a plan of action?" Father Tomas walked up from behind.

"Aye, and I think I'm beginning to get somewhere. Thank ye for these drawings." Gavin refolded the parchment and shoved it inside a folded pocket he'd created out of his plaid. "How'd ye know where I'd be?"

"We knew ye'd be out here studying a way into the cathedral."

Evelina approached, holding out a cup. "I thought ye might like a wee bit of goat's milk this morn."

Gavin nodded, accepting the fresh cup. He wiped his mouth with the sleeve of his ivory colored lein. "Ye sweetened it."

"A bit of honey can make a world of difference."

The sound of cantering horses brought their heads around to the north. A small army of men rode toward them—Highlanders. Gavin walked toward them, squinting to make out their colors. "Is that Leith and the MacKenzies?"

"Aye, and I believe Iain McBraigh rides with them," Father Tomas said, shielding his eyes from the morning sun slanting at an angle.

"About time he showed up. I canna believe the man wanted to wed Serena and he's done naught to assist her thus far." Gavin tossed the rest of his drink down his throat and handed Evelina the empty cup. "Thank ye."

Gavin crossed his arms over his chest. "Well, I won't do the gallant thing and stand aside this time. He doesn't deserve her." He clenched his jaw, preparing a litany of ideas for a proper tongue lashing.

"Gavin! Is that ye?" Leith called as they neared.

"Aye! What is it?" Gavin strode forward, recognizing the concern in Leith's voice, his anger at Iain forgotten for the moment.

They slowed their horses when they reached Gavin's side and Leith wiped sweat from his brow. "They took over McBraigh Castle. Lord Lennox and Lady Fiona have produced a new will and persuaded the magistrate that it's a legal document. He seized Braigh Castle and ousted Iain like some common criminal."

The rest of Leith's men slowed their horses, gathering around. The animals breathed hard from the trip.

"Did ye know aught about another will?" Gavin looked at Iain, whose eyes were bloodshot and a day's growth of a beard shadowed his face. He shook his head.

"I doubt the inn could put up the lot o' ye." Gavin rubbed his eyebrows. "Have ye set up camp somewhere? Have some of the men tend to yer horses while we talk. Let's go to the inn and take refreshment."

"Aye, good idea." Leith nodded and dismounted.

"How's Serena?" Iain moved much slower. "I wrote to Father Kendrick, but he didn't return a response. My letters to her were returned unopened."

At least Iain hadn't completely abandoned her. Gavin cleared his mind, searching for a reasonable response. "They won't let any of us see her, not even Evelina. We have some ideas." Gavin gripped his shoulder in an offer of a friendly gesture. "But first refreshment. Ye look a sorry sight, my friend."

"So do ye." Iain said.

He imagined he did. Ever since Serena had been taken, he couldn't eat, sleep, or think of anything else.

Inside the inn, they secured another room for Iain and Leith and sat down at a wooden table in the tavern. A burly middle-aged woman with stringy brown hair sauntered over and glanced down at them. "What'ya havin'?"

"Some eggs, a chunk of sausage, and whatever ye have for drink," said Iain.

"We've some fresh goat's milk."

"That'll be fine. Thank ye." Iain nodded, rubbing his jaw.

"I'll have the same," Leith said.

She nodded and left through a side door. Only one other patron sat at a table in the far corner, a lone traveler who had arrived the night before.

"When was this new will proven?" Gavin asked, looking first at Iain and then at Leith.

"Not sure, but they arrived two days past to seize the castle." Iain rubbed a hand through his hair making his auburn locks stand up on end. "I fear his intentions. He's never been kind to those beneath his station. I'm concerned for the villagers."

Leith leaned his elbows on the table and linked his fingers. "We finally discovered the secret about the cave."

"What about it?" Gavin asked.

"According to Quinn, the cave is full of diamonds. He took me there. Ye can only get to it by being lowered by a rope over the rocky ledge above the sea. It goes way deep, but I didn't have time to follow the tunnel. The villagers claim there's a tunnel under Braigh Castle and another one that leads under the village."

"Did ye know about this?" Gavin turned to Iain. "Could that be why Lord Lennox is so determined to claim yer property?"

"I thought it was an auld legend," Iain said. "I never imagined it might be true. Aye, I suppose Hogan might think there's some truth to it. 'Twould explain his deceitful behavior."

"Did ye truly see diamonds, Leith?" Gavin gave his brother a direct look.

"Aye. A whole lot o' them." He produced a hard stone from his pocket. "It shines in the sun like a brilliant rainbow and I've been able to cut nearly anything with it."

Gavin examined the stone. In the tavern light, it didn't shine so bright, but he didn't doubt his brother's word.

"Evelina, did ye know about this, too? Did Serena?" A bit of hurt layered his heart at the possibility that neither of them had trusted him. They knew about all the strange things happening to the villagers. "Why would ye not share something so valuable? It could have explained everything."

"Aye." Evelina took a deep breath and nodded, her black veil bobbing. "But we agreed as a village that none of us would tell—not even the laird. We didn't want strangers pushing us from our homes. Greed does that, ye know. Look what's happened to Iain. If a laird could be ousted, imagine what could happen to poor defenseless villagers that no one wants around." She paused. "We were content and happy. We accepted each other when no one else would. If word got out about the cave, greed would have gone wild. We knew Lord Lennox suspected something and it made us even more determined to say naught."

"Then what made Quinn break his silence?" Gavin asked.

"When Iain lost Braigh Castle, Quinn grew scared and came to me," Leith said. "Beacon found some important papers in the cave, but he canna read and didn't know what they were." Leith pulled out a folded parchment from his plaid. "It's an original will from Iain's uncle and a journal with entries of how the Lennox family has tried to claim the property. We need to have this will proved by someone in power, but who isn't a cohort of Lord Lennox?"

Gavin realized his brother was right, but he didn't know who in this shire they could trust. Most of their connections were further south.

The front door opened and a man walked in looking around. He glanced over at them and scratched his brown beared. "An' who might ye good people be?"

"I'm Gavin MacKenzie."

"MacKenzie, ye say?" He dug his hand into a leather pouch around his waist and pulled out a letter. Stretching his arm out, he squinted and read the name. "I was told to find Gavin MacKenzie at Braigh Castle. Don't know what to think of findin' ye here."

"I was at Braigh Castle, but now I'm here," Gavin said.

"A lass by the name of Akira MacPhearson paid me to bring ye this message from her own 'and. She said it's important."

"I'm much obliged, sir." Gavin stood, walked over, and accepted it. He recognized his sister's bold penmanship. Not wanting to worry Akira, he'd only written her husband, Bryce, and their father. Like an eager lad, he broke the seal.

⟡

Serena woke with her face pressed against the cold stone floor. Something wet trickled down her chin. She pressed her finger to stop the dripping as she attemped to sit up. Blood stained her skin. She frowned. The slight movement made her realize how her lower lip had become stiff and swollen.

Her stomach heaved, but the starvation from the last few days left her weak and empty. Dizziness made her head swim until all she saw was black. Serena waited and her sight slowly returned. She groaned, her joints protesting as she moved to her knees, preparing to stand.

"About time ye came to," Devlin's voice boomed over her.

Serena froze, carefully concealing the dread she felt at having to face Devlin Broderwick yet again. He must have been sitting behind her. She turned in slow motion, gritting her teeth.

"Do ye know what happened?" Devlin sat in a wooden chair, his voice a taunt. The crumbs from his meal sat on the table beside him. She licked her lips, forcing her gaze away. Her hollow stomach churned in hunger.

She remembered being asked question after question. No answer satisfied him. Her silence enraged him. Naught she did pleased the man. She believed he was determined to sentence her guilty. She endured hours of him speaking Latin verses over her, chanting prayers she didn't understand.

"I'm sorry. I do not." Her dry voice shook, sounding much like an aged woman.

"You had another fit, just as I knew you would. You busted your lip when you fell. After all the effort I've put into you, Serena, you've resisted the cleansing. There is naught more I can do." He folded his arms and twisted his lips until lines showed around his mouth. "Believe me. It pains me to do this, but I've no choice."

Her heart raced. "Do what?" Tears stung the back of her eyes, but somehow she swallowed them. "Whatever it is, please have mercy on me."

"I've already given you mercy." His harsh tone bit into her and left a chill racing down her spine. "I've turned you over to the town magistrate. He'll see that you're given a public inquisition. Your fate is now in the hands of the town."

God, I thought my fate was with You?

"Not the town! They already saw my fit at the market and will have plenty of people to testify against me. Ye canna do this. Have mercy and give me sanctuary in the kirk. I've done naught to hurt anyone."

"You know the church will not abide any sort of evil. This thing you have . . . it isn't normal, and I'll not fool myself into believing it is. I'm not weak like you're mother. I serve God."

Serena fell silent, at a loss for words. No amount of begging would change this man's hardened heart. Was this how Jesus felt—utterly lost? Forsaken?

"What will happen now? Will ye escort me there or will they come for me?" she asked.

"They're on their way. I thought it best to get the matter over and done."

"Will I be allowed to see my mither one more time?" Her lip trembled.

"It's up to the magistrate. My understanding is that you'll be held in a cell."

Like a criminal.

She stood in silence a while longer until footsteps in the hall grew louder. Chains rattled on the other side of the door. Someone knocked.

Her breath caught in her throat and she clenched and unclenched her fists. She looked down at her feet and hands, cherishing her last few moments free of chains.

✍❤

Dearest Gavin,

I've been concerned as I haven't heard from you in a while. Leith hates letter writing, but I always look forward to my letters from you.

By the time you receive this, we will be on our way. I'm coming with Bryce and Da. I've arranged for a nursemaid for my wee one. As you're probably guessing, if I'm willing to leave my bairn, I must have good reason. I believe

God has spoken to me in another dream and I will be needed. I overheard Bryce and Da talking about Serena. Based on what you say, I believe no evil exists in her heart. Many could claim my dreams are not from God, but we know the truth. It sounds as if she and I have much in common.

Dear brother, I don't know how to say this, but I dreamt of a woman burning at the stake. A crowd of people were around her and a cloud of darkness covered her face. I'm not sure if this darkness represents the evil around her, or if it is meant to conceal her true identity since naught has yet happened.

Keep in mind that my dreams do not always come true. Yet, I do know that it is a warning.

Da has appealed to the King on Serena's behalf. He wrote back that he would ask his physicians and the pope. In the meantime, we must find every legal means of delaying Serena's trial. The King's inquiries could take a while. Da will arrive with the King's letter, and, hopefully, that will be enough to delay further proceedings until we hear from the King.

I will pray for everyone involved and see you soon,

Love, Akira

An eerie warning swept through Gavin as he looked up at the expectant faces sitting at the tavern table. He met Leith's gaze. "Da and Bryce are on their way. Akira is with them."

Should he tell them about the dream? He didn't want to worry Evelina. The knowledge of it was enough to dash his own hopes of gaining Serena's freedom.

"Akira's coming, too? What about the wee bairn, Evan? Is he not still nursing?" Leith asked, suspicion crossing his brow.

"Aye, but she has left him with a nursemaid. She's with her husband, Bryce, and ye know how much she loathes being away from him when he takes overnight trips."

"Even though wee Evan is now weaned, Akira is even less likely to leave him behind." Leith narrowed his gaze on Gavin. "Ye're not telling us everything. What have ye left out?"

Gavin sighed. His brother wouldn't leave the matter alone, so he walked over and thrust the letter out to him. "Here, read it for yerself. But I warn ye, some contents are a private family matter so ye may not want to share it with everyone." Gavin kept his gaze averted from Father Tomas and Evelina.

"I understand." Leith's eyes flickered, as he took the letter, sat back, and read in silence. A moment later he looked at Gavin, equal concern in his eyes. He cleared his throat. "Um, they've already left so they should be here soon."

"And that's not all. Our da has appealed to the King on Serena's behalf. He carries a letter that the King is checking with his personal physicians and the pope," Gavin said. "But that will take some time, so we don't know how much we may rely on that. The sooner our da arrives with the King's letter, the better."

Evelina's mouth dropped open and she lifted her fingers to cover it. "I don't know what to say. Yer da would go through this much trouble for people he's never met? Indeed, he must be a mon of some great importance to have the King's counsel."

"I'm blessed to have a father who trusts my word so well." Gavin could not mistake the tears of gratitude in her voice.

"And only Gavin. If I'd written him, he would have written Gavin in turn to verify my account," Leith said, crossing his arms and rolling his eyes.

"Trust comes when ye earn it, Leith." Gavin glanced over at his younger brother, willing maturity to soon take root in the lad's wayward thinking.

"Well, I'm thankful to both of ye, for all ye've done," Evelina said.

"Do ye think yer father might have a recommendation for who I may contact concerning my plight over Braigh Castle?" Iain asked.

"Mayhap." Gavin went over and retrieved the letter from Leith before the wrong pair of eyes could see it. He folded and placed it back into the pocket folds of his plaid. "We can ask him when he arrives, which I'm hoping will be within the next sennight."

The wood door swung open, the hinges squeaking like a wailing cat. Booted footsteps rushed toward them. Roan and Craig charged into the room. Their eyes were wide and their faces grim with anger. Roan's lips were in a straight, thin line, his hand upon the hilt of his sword at his side. Gavin straightened, prepared to diffuse the man's temper, which often barreled out of control at the slightest provocation.

"Gavin, we've bad news." Craig spoke first, his expression one of sympathy as well as anger.

"Aye?" Dread crawled through Gavin, but he contained it as he folded his arms and took a warrior's stance. He prayed whatever it was didn't concern Serena. Akira's written words echoed through his mind, haunting him.

"A notice was just nailed to the outside door of the courthouse. Serena is to have a public inquisition in two days' time."

Serena lay on a narrow wooden bench that rocked against the uneven stone floor with each move she made. Her cell was the size of two privy closets. The stench of decay, mold, and urine lingered in the air like rotten fruit, but no longer stung as hard as the first day.

She covered her face with her elbow, the chains around her wrists jingled against the floor and bench, cutting into her flesh. Her ankles were now raw from the iron shackles.

For two days she had endured the shrewd comments from other prisoners held within earshot on the same hall. Having new female blood in the area amused their time.

Only one other person shared her cell—a thin woman about a decade Serena's senior, but she looked much older. Her bones bulged through her skin. Serena guessed she hadn't bathed in a while. Dirt smudged her face and she lived on a bed of straw in the corner, talking to the rats as if they were her friends. The sight had reduced Serena to tears on her first day making her forget her own miserable circumstance. She wondered if she would be reduced to a similar state before it was all over.

"Lord, however long I must be here, please don't let me lose my wits. Help me keep a presence of mind, and the determined will to not denounce ye or confess to anything evil regardless of the agony I may be forced to endure. End my suffering early."

A shiver passed through her and fresh tears gathered, trailing a hot path down to her hair. "God, have ye forsaken me? Whatever happens to me, have mercy on my mither. Give her someone that will be a true friend to her. Now that Gunna is gone, and I'm separated from her, I fear how alone she must feel." Her shoulders shook as she wept into her sleeve.

Thoughts of Jesus praying in the garden before the Romans came filled her mind. What had Tomas said? Something about Jesus asking God why He'd been forsaken. In that moment, she understood what He must have felt. A deep connection rooted inside her and a presence overcame her, bringing a peace she couldn't explain.

A door at the end of the hallway creaked open and prisoners began yelling and calling out, whistling to someone who must have been female. Serena sat up, the chains prohibiting too much movement as she tried to wipe her face. A guard led a woman to her cell. She carried a tray of food and wore a brown cloak with a hood covering her head.

The guard unlocked the cell door. "Mind both of 'em," he warned. "The one is naught more than a witch if ye ask me. Don't look her in the eyes lest she cast a spell over ye. I'll wait right here."

"Thank ye, kindly." A familiar voice answered.

As she walked closer, Serena tilted her head trying to peer beneath the hood to see the woman's face, but the torch on the far wall outside her cell didn't shed enough light. The woman adjusted the hood so Serena could see her face. She gasped. The woman held the tray in one hand and lifted a finger to her lips. *Praise God, it was Doreen!*

"I've brought ye a bite to eat," she said aloud then lowered her voice to a whisper. "There's a veil beneath the tray from yer mither. If ye receive a guilty sentence, ask to wear it."

Serena's cell mate scrambled toward them after the food. Doreen picked up a chunk of bread, tore it in half and threw it at her. "Here, that should satisfy ye," she said aloud for the guard's benefit. The woman caught it and crouched in the corner, content to devour the meager portion.

"What do ye know?" Serena asked.

"Yer public inquisition is to begin within the hour," Doreen said. "I'll pray for yer soul." She set the tray down on the bench and backed away. "We'll all be there," she whispered.

"Mither?" Serena's bottom lip trembled, and she fought the ache in the back of her throat.

"Aye, she's fine. She's with Father Tomas and Gavin. Don't worry none. We'll take good care o' her."

Serena breathed a sigh of relief, breaking into a flow of silent tears as she watched her friend go. She'd wanted to hug her, but knew it would make the guard suspicious, so she remained still. God had not forsaken her. He was taking care of her mother just as she'd prayed. Serena picked up the other half of the bread. She lifted the wooden cup, surprised to taste mead. Doreen had slipped her something better than the stale water she'd had since her arrival. She washed the bread down, thankful to have something strong against her parched throat.

She saved a wee bit for her cell mate and set it on the floor between them. The woman waited until Serena sat back on the bench, and darted out like a wild mole and grabbed the cup.

A while later another guard came for Serena. He unlocked the shackles at her feet and led her down the dark hall. The chains on her wrists weighed her arms down as she followed at a slower pace. They turned down another hallway. He stopped before a closed door, motioning to her. "Hurry, lass!"

When she reached him, he opened the door wide, revealing a courtroom full of people. The judge wore a black robe and sat at the front center of the room.

"Go . . . stand before the judge," the guard said, pointing ahead.

As Serena made her way, she noticed Gavin, her mother, and Father Tomas sittng on a bench near the front. The rest of the villagers were in the back or standing on the sides. She couldn't see her mother's eyes through the black veil, but she could imagine her sorrowful expression. Gavin's blue eyes looked red and swollen. He hadn't shaved in a while. The red beard he'd grown looked different. To her dismay, he'd lost a lot of weight. She turned from them to face her judge. Serena lifted her gaze to the elderly man frowning down at her with hard charcoal eyes.

"Witch!" a man cried.

"Devil worshiper!" a woman yelled.

The judge pounded a rod against the counter. The people quieted. "First, I'd like to call her accuser forward. Devlin Broderwick."

Her inquisition began. For the next five hours, they called witness after witness from the market. They told falsehoods and embellished the truth. When given an opportunity, Serena tried to defend herself, but they twisted her words and everything she said was used against her.

Father Tomas spoke on her behalf, but he was dismissed because of his speech problems. Father Kendrick said Tomas couldn't keep up with a whole parrish and had been relieved of his duties and only allowed to tend to the spiritual needs of the villagers.

Unwilling to give up, Father Tomas pulled out a petition signed by all the villagers, but the court and the townspeople laughed saying the Village of Outcast signatures didn't count since they weren't members of the town. When it came to Gavin's turn, he was accused of being a love sick fool who had been cast under her spell. They complained of the same thing regarding Iain MacBraigh.

Hot tears slipped past Serena's lashes. It was no use. They were determined to persecute her regardless of the lack of evidence. Her legs were sore, her body tired, and a headache pounded against her temples.

The judge repeated a short litany of complaints against her. He pointed down at her. "Serena Boyd, I pronounce ye guilty of evil, being possessed by the devil. Ye refused to give up the evil spirit dwelling within ye during the exorcism Father Broderwick tried to perform. This is a God-fearing town and we'll not tolerate evil persons in our midst. Ye're hereby sentenced to death, by burning at the stake tomorrow morning at dawn."

Serena's knees gave way, and she slid to the floor in a mixture of tired disbelief. "God save me!" she whispered, closing her eyes.

20

*R*age exploded in Gavin when Serena shuddered and sank to the floor. Her unfair sentence threw the courtroom into chaos. Cheers and moans burst at the same time. People stood and poured into the aisle eager to spread the news. Others hovered in conversations.

Gavin lunged forward, thrusting anyone who stood as a barrier out of his way. His heart pounded in his ears, blocking out the noise around him.

"Serena!" he called, wanting her to know he was there and that he wouldn't desert her no matter what.

"Gavin!" Leith called him.

Unwilling to heed his brother's warning, Gavin continued forward as the guard hurried over, gripped Serena's elbow, and snatched her up. Her head snapped back on her neck, and she cried out in pain.

Before Gavin could seize the guard, someone grabbed Gavin's shoulders from behind. The person used his entire weight to pull Gavin down. He fell to one knee, but struggled with all his might, dragging his attacker with him.

"Gavin, stop!" Leith shouted in his ear. "They aim to do a lot more harm than that before it's over." His brother lowered his voice. "Ye canna help the lass if ye get locked up. Now be reasonable."

Breathing hard, Gavin watched in helpless frustration as Serena was hauled away. At the door she glanced back one more time. She found his eyes. He knew she'd told him how much she loved him. When she vanished, strength left him, and he sagged upon the floor like a flower in darkness.

Leith must have known the fight had left him, for he released Gavin and pulled on his arm. "Come. Everyone is staring."

"I don't care!"

"Well, for Serena's sake, ye might. If we're able to save her life somehow, ye don't want her virtue to be a topic among all the other accusations, do ye?"

"See!" A woman pointed in his direction. "The mon is under a spell, he is. The witch 'as cast a spell upon 'im, she 'as."

"These people are awful," Gavin said through clenched teeth. "They're so driven by suspicion that they make things up even when it doesn't exist."

"I've an idea, but ye've got to come with me." Leith shoved him toward the door.

"Ye should listen to the wise counsel of yer brother, lad." Devlin Broderwick's deep voice cut through the air. He stood a few feet away, glaring at Gavin with disapproval.

"I don't take advice from murderers, even those garbed in robes." Gavin stood to his full height and strode over to the man until he was a few inches from his face, eye to eye. "Now I know the true meaning of what the scripture means by wolves in sheep's clothing."

Gavin turned and strode down the aisle, ignoring people as they quietly moved to the side. Leith hurried after him, the villagers falling in line behind them.

Outside, Evelina stood weeping by Father Tomas, who wore a grim expression. He kept patting her back, unsure how to comfort her. When she saw Gavin, she lifted her black gown from the ground and ran to him.

"Gavin, please help me. I must see her one more time . . . before . . . before . . . ." Evelina couldn't finish her sentence. She burst into fresh tears.

"I'll do what I can," he promised. Gavin turned to Father Tomas. "Mayhap they'll be more generous if ye're with me."

"Verra well, but remember a kind word turns away wrath." Father Tomas lifted a finger at Gavin as if he were tempted to give a lecture. "If it wasn't for Leith here, I'm not sure what might have happened in there. Ye lost yer head, lad. Ye canna afford to do that at a time like this."

"Aye, I'm sorry for it." Gavin rubbed his weary eyes. "Leith, stay with Evelina until we return."

"We'll be at the inn," Leith said.

He and Father Tomas walked down the street to the magistrate's office, passing the baker. The scent of fresh bread and pastries lingered in the air. Rolling carts and wagons passed by in both directions with wheels crushing against the dirt road and horse hooves clopping. The world continued on as usual, while his world crumbled like many of the stones at Iain's castle.

At the door, Gavin paused, stepping to the side. "Father Tomas, I caused such a scene in the courtroom, I doubt any favor I ask would be granted. Mayhap yer best chance is to go in alone."

He nodded and stepped inside. Gavin leaned against the limestone structure with a thatched roof. He crossed his arms and closed his eyes.

"God, please don't let this happen. She's innocent of what they accuse her. Ye're our only hope. I promise, I'll continue to do everything in my power to stop it. Please help me. Give me wisdom and ideas."

A while later, Tomas stepped out.

"Well?" Gavin bent to read the clergyman's expression.

"Only one person is allowed to see her before she's placed on the stake—and that's her mither." Tomas sighed, shaking his head. "I'm sorry, Gavin. I tried."

"I'm glad she'll at least have that. When will Evelina be allowed to see her?" He swallowed the rising disappointment, blinking back moisture.

"We're to bring Evelina before daybreak. She'll only get about ten minutes."

"Will ye bring her?" Gavin asked. "I'm going after my da. He's carrying a letter from the King that could make a difference, if I can reach him in time."

"Of course, but are ye going alone?"

"Nay, I'll take Craig with me," Gavin said. "But Leith will stay here and help ye with Evelina. We must leave right away. We're losing time."

"Go with God's speed, Gavin." Father Tomas gripped his shoulder in a gesture of support.

"Pray." Gavin lifted a hand and touched the clergyman's arm.

Evelina spent most of the night on her knees weeping before God. She wrote a long letter to Serena on some parchment paper with ink she had borrowed from Father Tomas. She feared she would run out of candle wax before she was done. While the ink dried, she dressed in her black gown. She pulled her hair up and fastened it in a bun and covered it with a long black veil. This one was the darkest one she owned and it reached beyond her chin.

Stepping out into the dark an hour before daylight, Evelina made her way to Doreen's lodgings, where she had taken work in the kitchen at the inn now that Iain no longer possessed the castle. She was often required to take meals to the prisoners down the street, which allowed her to take the veil to Serena.

This time Evelina had a very different favor to ask of Doreen. Evelina climbed the stairs and stopped at the second room on the right. She knocked on the door and waited, hoping she didn't wake anyone else.

A muffled groan sounded on the other side. "Who is it at this 'our?" a sleepy voice asked.

"It's Evelina. Please, I need to speak with ye.'

The lock clicked and the door opened. "Evelina, I'm so sorry. Come in." Doreen swung the door wide, blinking from Evelina's bright candle.

"'Tis I who's sorry to wake ye at such an hour, but they've granted me ten minutes with Serena before daybreak . . . before . . . before they take her out." Evelina nearly choked, but caught herself.

She pulled out the folded letter from her plaid. "I've a plan, but if aught goes wrong and something happens to me, give this letter to Serena."

Doreen's eyes flickered in concern. Further awake now, she stared at the letter and back at Evelina. "What do ye mean? It isn't a foolhardy thing ye plan, is it?"

"She's my daughter, Doreen. I'd never be able to forgive myself if I didn't try everything within my power." Evelina's throat cracked and she paused. "Please, promise ye'll find a way to give her this letter."

"I promise." Doreen took the letter and cradled it to her chest. "I'll guard it with my life."

"Thank ye." Evelina sighed with a relieved smile.

Doreen's lip trembled. Tears sprang to her eyes. She stepped forward and raised her arms around Evelina's neck. "I'm so sorry. I'll be praying." Her weeping voice came out into a whisper.

"Shush, none of that now. I've been weeping most of the night, and I'm saving the rest of my tears for later. Thank ye for yer prayers, lass." Evelina hugged her back and stepped away. "I must go. I don't want to miss my allotted time."

Evelina turned and made her way back down the stairs and stopped by the fourth room on the left. She knocked on the door. A haphazard Leith swung it open and ran his fingers through his brown hair.

"Have ye heard from Gavin?" she asked, hope harboring in her heart.

"Nay, not a word." He shook his head, leaned out into the hall and glanced up and down and then back at Evelina. "Is it time already?"

"I came a wee bit early. I've a favor to ask of ye."

"Aye?" He raised a dark brow.

"I need ye to have yer horse ready and saddled. I only get ten minutes from when I enter her cell. Serena will come out, and when she does, mount up with her and ride out of here as fast as ye can. Get her out of the shire. Take her to Gavin—to yer family. Will ye do that for me?"

"What are ye plannin' to do?" He folded his arms and stroked his chin, watching her with interest.

"I won't tell ye and we don't have much time. Please . . . if I succeed and Serena walks out, will ye take her away from here to Gavin?"

"Evelina, I don't wish to consent to a plan that will end up with both of ye hurt."

"If I do naught, Serena will die." Her voice came out harsh. "What happens to me doesn't matter. She's young, in love, and has her whole life ahead of her. I'm getting auld and I've already lived half my life, and it will amount to naught if she dies like this . . . today." Evelina swallowed back the threatening tears. "Please . . . help me."

Leith let out a deep sigh. "I'll do as ye ask. Give me a moment." He grabbed his broad sword, a knife, and a few items and tucked them in his plaid and followed her out.

While Leith went for his horse, Evelina hurried to the courthouse prison. A guard carried a large round ring with several keys that jingled at his side. He held a torch and whistled as he made his way past the cells. Most prisoners were asleep, a few snored.

He reached Serena's cell and clicked the lock open. "Only ten minutes."

"My daughter will die shortly. Would ye grant me some time alone with her...please?"

He paused and finally nodded. "All right, but only ten minutes an' no more. I've a daughter, too." He locked the cell door and whistled down the hall, the sound fading as he lengthened the distance.

"Mither!" Serena rushed forward.

"They already took yer chains off?" Evelina touched her hand to her chest. "Oh, thank God, the Lord is with me in this."

"Aye, when they brought me my last meal this morn."

"Listen. I don't have much time. Take my clothes and I'll take yers." Evelina began undressing.

"What? Nay!" Serena protested.

"Do as I say and keep yer voice down." Evelina used the tone she'd needed when Serena was younger. "We'll switch places." Evelina talked as she worked. "Once I know ye're safe,

I'll reveal myself. They may put me in prison, but they won't burn me at the stake."

"Are ye sure this will work?" Serena began to undress. "I'll never forgive myself if aught were to happen to ye, Mither."

"And I'd never forgive myself, if I didn't do it," Evelina said.

They exchanged gowns.

"Do ye still have the veil Doreen gave ye?" Evelina asked.

"Aye." Serena nodded.

"Did ye ask if ye could wear it on the stake?"

"My request was granted. They decided it might be best for the wee children who'll be present. There hasn't been a burning at the stake around here in years."

Footsteps sounded down the hallway with the whistling.

"Hurry! Get the veil," Evelina said.

Serena grabbed the veil. Evelina helped her situate it on her head and down her face.

"I'll be over at the bench weeping with yer plaid over my head, pretending to be ye." They hugged in a tight embrace. "Go with Leith and don't ask questions. He's waiting outside," Evelina whispered in her ear, slipping the plaid over her head.

"Time's up." The guard appeared at the cell door.

"Bye, Mither." Evelina burst into tears. "I love ye." She sat on the bench at an angle and listened for Serena to play her part.

"Bye, my sweet daughter." Serena had to stifle a sob that Evelina knew wasn't real. "Thank ye, kind sir," she said in a muffled voice beneath her veil.

"As soon as I escort yer mither out, I'll be back for ye, lass. 'Tis time." The guard closed the door and clicked the lock. Evelina listened as their footsteps faded down the hall. Her heart beat lighter with each footstep they took.

Once they were gone, she dropped to her knees and thanked God for allowing this plan to work. She prayed for Serena's safety. Now the true test of her own ability of endurance would come. "God, I meant it when I said I'd take Serena's place. Give me the strength to hide myself until she's well away and safe. Then if it's yer will to save me, so be it. Regardless of what happens, in the next hour, I love ye. I'm a child of God, and I commit my body and spirit to ye, my Lord Jesus Christ."

The door opened at the end of the hall Evelina dried her tears with Serena's plaid. She pulled it down over her shoulders and set the black veil in place. Standing in the center of the cell, Evelina folded her hands in front of her and waited.

"God be with ye, Mither." For the first time, Evelina noticed the auld woman sitting in the dark corner, hiding on a bed of straw. Evelina prayed the woman wouldn't give her away.

*

Gavin raced Sholto across the moorland and around the peat bogs. He and the army of MacKenzie and MacPhearson sliced a path through the fields of purple heather that now looked gray in the moonlight. Gavin glanced across the starry sky, measuring the minutes left until dawn.

His father had stayed on familiar roads that most travelers took and then cut across the lands of the overlords he knew until he reached the MacPhearson holdings north of Inverness where they joined forces. Unaware of Serena's new death sentence, they were settling into camp when Gavin came upon them. He prayed they hadn't lost too much time.

As they rode into Halkirk, Gavin's heart pounded with fear. The sun broke through the clouds. "Please, God, save Serena. Slow them down somehow. Bring obstacles against them. Don't let them harm her," Gavin prayed, knowing he wouldn't make it on time.

The others kept pace with him. The one thing he could always count on was the Highland code of conduct. Highlanders were fiercely loyal to their clan and leaders as long as they were treated with respect and honor. Bryce and Birk achieved that status with their clansmen. Gavin hoped he would one day follow in his father's footsteps.

The crisp morning air blasted his face, keeping him wide awake. His pulse pumped through his body, giving him more energy than a person in his sleepless state should contain.

They reached Dunnet and rounded the loch with less than two miles to go. "Almost there!" He called out to his Da and Bryce. Akira rode behind her husband. The four of them led the rest of their combined armies.

When they finally rode into Braighwick, the main street lay quiet and eerie. The usual morning bustle of the market wasn't taking place as the vendors were often out by daybreak. It could only mean one thing.

He glanced up at the rising sun, slanting across the purple-gray sky. "If they've started a fire, make it rain, Lord!"

Beyond town, dark black smoke swirled from growing flames. A crowd had gathered in a half circle around a tall stake, well away from buildings and homes.

"Nay!" The word ripped from Gavin's throat.

He cringed at the mental image of what Serena must be enduring. Grief wedged through the brittle pieces of hope that had kept his heart beating with spirited energy. Their thundering horses pounded the ground in threatening speed, but in spite of their valiant effort, it looked as if they had arrived too late.

Many turned and pointed. Some scattered and ran from fear of attack. Gavin rode right past them, straight to the burning stake. An armed man went after Gavin, but he paid the man no heed. Bryce lifted his bow and arrow and shot a warning that came two inches from the man's nose.

"I wouldn't touch 'im if I were ye!" Bryce motioned the men to take command of the town's soldiers, outnumbering them two to one.

"Who's the magistrate in charge here?" Birk MacKenzie asked, slowing his horse to a halt. "I've a letter from the King that concerns ye and the local kirk."

"Serena!" Gavin called as their voices faded into the background. He hurried to her. The veiled figure high on the stake didn't move. Was she already dead? The fire had now risen.

He almost didn't see the others hugging the bottom of the stake as the flames closed in on them. Some of the villagers had refused to leave her side. His heart swelled with even more fear as he realized he had more than one person to save. "Help me! More people are in there!"

"We warned them to leave, so we built the fire in a wider circle around them," Devlin Broderwick said in his English accent. "They only succeeded in prolonging the inevitable. We thought they'd have enough sense to move once we set fire."

Gavin turned. A roar rumbled from deep inside his chest as anger overcame his good sense. He balled his fist, reared back, and bolted his knuckles straight into Devlin's nose. The man swayed to the ground. His hand flew to his face as blood exploded. "And that was inevitable!"

"We need water!" Akira gestured to the others, trying to gain their attention from the chaos.

"Ye need at least twenty barrels of water. We don't have time for that. It's too far away," Craig said.

"Gavin . . . hurry." Quinn's voice rose from the blaze. "Canna . . . hold on . . ."

Another scream ripped through the air. It sounded like Father Tomas.

"We only need to break through a small path to get them out. I know we canna put the whole thing out, but we've got to give them an outlet of escape." Akira pointed to an area where the flames weren't as high or thick.

"She's right," Gavin said. "A path will work."

"Gavin watch out!" Akira's gaze lifted over Gavin's shoulder and widened.

Gavin whirled in time to see Devlin lunging toward him with a dagger. An arrow flew through the air piercing him with solid aim. His expression shifted from anger to surprise as he halted in slow motion and sank to his knees, then crumbled.

"He had a dagger strapped to his leg." Bryce lowered his bow. "I'm glad I saw him pull it out."

"So am I," Gavin shook his head in disbelief.

"There are barrels stored at the loch in case of a town fire." A woman called out. "I'll show ye where. I didn't like them burning the lass. I'm glad ye're here to stop it." She handed a wee bairn to her husband, lifted the hem of her skirt and ran over.

"Come on." Akira slid. She flicked the reins and they were gone.

"Serena!" Gavin called. No movement. "Quinn, can ye hear me?" The giant hugged the post, keeping his face from the fire.

"Getting closer . . . so hot!" Quinn said.

Gavin motioned to Roan and another man. "We can use those shovels on the wagon to dig up dirt and throw it in the fire and start a path until the others get back with the water."

"Good idea." Roan grabbed the shovels and handed them out. They dug and threw dirt in the area Akira had pointed out. By the time the others arrived back, a dent had been made in the fire, but not as much as Gavin had hoped. They lifted the barrels and hauled them as close as possible.

"Throw it here." Gavin directed where he and Roan had been piling dirt. It took four barrels of water, but they finally cleared a path. "Wet yer plaids and soak some extra ones."

"Keep dumping dirt and make the path wider if ye can." Gavin said.

Covering himself with a wet plaid, Gavin ran into the burning midst. He covered the giant with the other wet plaid as best he could and Quinn stumbled out on unsteady legs. He collapsed once free, coughing. Beacon had already succumbed in a heap. Gavin went back in, picked him up, wrapped his plaid around them both, and carried him out.

"I'll get the next one!" Craig ran inside.

Gavin laid Beacon down and went to soak his plaid again. Pulling out his knife, he ran inside after Craig came out carrying Father Tomas.

Gavin wiped his sweating brow, pulled out the knife, and chipped grooves in the stake. He climbed to cut Serena's hands free. Her limp body fell over his shoulder. He suffered splinters as he climbed back down and choked on the swirling smoke. Gavin cut the rope at her feet. He wrapped her in his wet plaid and raced through the cleared path, marveling that the fire had not yet consumed the center where the stake stood bold and tall.

Breathing heavy, Gavin fell to his knees, settling her on a bed of grass. He coughed, trying to ignore the scratching pain in his lungs and throat. The stinging smoke lingered in his eyes and nose.

Akira lifted the black veil and gently tapped her cheeks.

Gavin gasped. "Evelina?"

21

Serena held onto Leith as they rode into Halkirk. He'd taken an unfamiliar path, avoiding travelers on the main road who might have recognized them or heard of Serena's escape. "I think we're far enough away from Braighwick to stop in Halkirk," Leith said over his shoulder. "If I know my brother, he'll come through here."

A sturdy black carriage with red trimming rolled toward them heading out of town. Six beautiful stallions pulled the large carriage surrounded by riders dressed in royal clothing. Half an army traveled ahead of them and the other half followed in the rear.

As they passed, Serena glanced at the royal inscription painted on the side and wondered if it contained the King himself or other members of the royal family.

"Stop!" A man's voice called out the window. The driver pulled the reins, halting the prancing stallions.

Serena clenched Leith tighter, worried she'd been discovered. He patted her hands. "Don't be afraid. He may help us."

"You there!" The door opened and a thin man with reddish curly hair and a long thin nose stepped out. He wore colors of black, red, and gold. Thick chains hung around his neck, one carrying a cross pendant, and solid gold rings adorned his thin fingers. "Is that the MacKenzie crest on the hilt of your sword?"

"Aye." Leith said, dropping his head in a bow.

Serena didn't move, too afraid of attracting his attention. If she could have slipped off Leith's horse without being noticed, she would have done so—and escaped.

"And what is your name, lad?" The King asked.

"Leith MacKenzie, the youngest son of Birk MacKenzie, Clan Chief."

"Ah." The King raised a finger and grinned. "That explains it. You've the look of your father. He's been a loyal and dedicated subject. I may have need of his influence in the near future. I've heard some alarming reports that Braigh Castle has been taken over in a wayward manner. I received a letter from your father stating his sons were there. Do you know aught about these claims?"

"Yer Highness, I'm afraid the report is true," Leith said. "I believe Iain MacBraigh was pondering how best to contact ye. I doubt he's aware that ye know about his plight."

"I'm aware of everything. It's my duty . . . as King." He glanced at Serena. "And who is this lass in mourning?"

"Serena Boyd. She's the one with the falling fits my da wrote ye about. They sentenced her to die upon the stake this morn, but she and her mither dressed alike and switched places. They may be coming after us as we speak."

"Who? The magistrate of Braighwick?" The King waved a hand. "I had my secretary draw up a pardon for Miss Boyd. Even though we're not on the best of terms, I have Boyd relations, you know. Are you kin to any of the royal Boyd line, Miss Boyd?"

"I . . . I wouldn't know, yer Highness. I've never met any of them."

"Well, I often wish I'd never met any of my Boyd relations, but that's another matter." The King glanced back at Leith. "I questioned my physicians about her fits. They tell me it's been known as the falling desease for centuries and remains unexplained. Hippocrates, a Greek physician, wrote a book claiming it's a brain disorder. I'm told Julius Caesar also had the condition and it was named for him—a 'seizure.' They warned me there's naught to be done."

"We thank ye for the pardon," Leith said.

"If none of her fits have caused anyone harm all these years, and she's fine after having one, I'm inclined to believe my physicians. The pardon has my written signature and the royal seal. I brought a copy with me as I've other business here in the north."

"Your Royal Highness, may I see it?" Serena asked.

"Indeed, you may." He turned and snapped his fingers. A servant hurried to the carriage to retrieve it. The King turned to Leith. "You're welcome to return to Braighwick with me. My next order of business is the true ownership of MacBraigh Castle and the estate grounds. I'd hoped Iain MacBraigh's connections in London would aid me in an alliance I'm trying to build. He must remain part of the landed gentry for my plan to succeed."

"Yer Highness, Iain MacBraigh discovered another will from his uncle naming him as heir. I believe he plans to show ye the document," Leith said.

"Good. I'll ask to see it when I arrive." His servant brought a rolled parchment bound by a scarlett ribbon. The King handed it to Serena. "May my trust be proven well, Miss Boyd."

He turned and snapped his fingers. "Let's make haste. Onward!"

"Are ye goin' to open it?" Leith asked over his shoulders.

"Nay, I don't wish to ruin it while riding, but I did want it in my possession."

Leith turned his mount around and they kept to the brisk pace that the King's men set. A while later, they arrived in Braighwick to the smell of burning wood and black smoke clouding the sky. A wave of despair assailed her as a painful ache seared her heart.

"Nay! This canna be!" she cried.

"Serena, it may not be what ye think," Leith said.

As soon as he slowed to a stop, Serena slid from the horse and pushed her way through the crowd. "Mither! Mither! Where are ye?"

Gavin bent over a woman covered in black soot, wearing Serena's clothes. She thought of the day they brought her mother to her from the house fire. If her mother could have survived that, she could also survive this. Hope swelled in her chest as Serena lifted the hem of her black gown and ran to them, sliding to her knees.

"I tried, Serena." Gavin looked up. Tears gathered in his red eyes, dashing her hopes. "I really tried. She'd already smothered from the smoke under the veil before I could get her down. I thought she was ye."

Serena ignored his words. "She's not dead, Gavin. She only passed out." Serena grabbed her mother's shoulders and shook her. "Mither! Mither! Ye have to wake up. The King pardoned me. I'll never be in danger again. Mither? . . . Please, wake up."

"Serena, she's gone," Gavin said, touching her shoulder.

She shoved his hand away. "Nay, she's not! It's like the house fire. She'll be fine." Serena pulled her mother's limp body to her chest and wrapped her arms around her, but there was no heart beating against her. No warm breath leaving her nose or mouth. "Mither, wake up. Ye canna leave me. Not like this. Wake up!" She rocked back and forth, cradling her mother's body.

When no response came, her situation began to take root in Serena's mind and heart. She let out a deep wail that ripped through the air and lingered like a gut wrenching tide. "Nay! Ye canna leave me all alone!"

Gavin felt like he'd failed Serena. The way she had looked at him before she came to realize the truth, pierced him through the heart like a dagger, thrusting him each time she cried out in pain. He tried to comfort her, but she rejected him. Unable to leave her, he sat by Serena's side, grieving in silence with her.

Not far away, Quinn leaned over Beacon trying to wake him, but his wee lungs hadn't been able to handle the smoke. When the giant finally realized his friend would never wake again, he let out a long moan that shook the ground beneath them.

Birkita broke through a crowd of people and dropped by his side, wrapping her thin arms around his huge, awkward frame. "I'm here, Quinn. Ye're not alone."

"Birkita?" Quinn looked up, his face wet with tears.

"Aye, it's me." Birkita wiped a lock of brown hair from Quinn's forehead and pressed his round cheeks between her palms. "Beacon is no longer suffering. What ye did was brave— more so than any noble knight I've ever read about."

"He's gone!" Quinn took her in his arms and buried his face against her shoulder. Birkita's long hair hid his grieving expression as she stroked his head like a child.

"Lock him up!" The King pointed at the town magistrate. "I want a full investigation conducted on the seizure of Braigh Castle, the crimes against the villagers, and the murder of this innocent woman." He gestured to Evelina.

The King's men grabbed the magistrate.

"It was all a mistake. I didn't know she was the wrong woman," the magistrate said.

"Did no one bother to look beneath her veil before you set the woman on fire?" The King raised his voice as he walked toward him. "Such negligence is unpardonable." The King braced his fists on his hips and whirled around to the crowd. "Is this murdering priest the only one involved?" He pointed at Devlin lying on the ground.

People stepped aside to reveal Father Kendrick, who linked his hands in front of him and bowed his head. Father George stood beside him, also bowing his head.

"Come forward. Both of you," the King commanded.

The priests inched toward the King as if they expected to be whipped.

"Was an exorcism attempted in this case? And on whom was it conducted?" the King asked.

"Father Broderwick tried to cast out a demon from Serena Boyd, the lass weeping over her dead mother." Father Kendrick pointed from Devlin to Serena.

"That's the girl's mother?" the King asked, raising a dark eyebrow. "How is it one cannot see the difference between the two? Did you help with this exorcism?"

"Not in the exorcism itself, but I was notified of her strange fits and stayed at Braigh Castle to observe her for a fortnight. After witnessing her fits, I wrote a report and recommended the demon to be cast from her. Father Broderwick is well known for his successful excorcisms."

"I want to see that report. Have it sent to me at Braigh Castle on the morrow," the King said.

"Permission to speak, Your Highness?" Gavin rose and bowed before the King.

"Granted."

"This man they call Father Broderwick was Develin Broderwick, an English subject. He was Serena's father and the husband of her mother, Evelina," Gavin said. "He had a personal grudge against them for leaving him."

"Interesting." The King laid a finger on his chin. "A married man who lied to the church to become a priest? Such an odd predicament. I'd like to hear the tale when I've more time. Right now, prepare the dead for burial, put out this inferno, and the rest of us will take our leave to Braigh Castle where more business is to be done."

Gavin and Bryce laid Evelina and Beacon on a wagon bed, while the town took care of Devlin's body. Serena sat beside her mother, and Quinn took his place on the other side of Beacon. Gavin drove the wagon with Akira sitting beside him. On the way back to Braigh Castle, no one spoke. The tense silence was hard to bear as Serena wept as quietly as she could. Once in a while her breath caught on a sigh and she'd cough, trying to catch her breath.

Iain warned the King of the steep incline so he made provisions to leave the royal carriage in town and mounted a horse. Now he, Iain, Birk, and Bryce rode ahead, leading the rest of the King's army, as well as the MacPhearsons and the MacKenzies.

When they arrived at the castle gate, Philip leaned against the gate for support. He peered through the black bars, straining to see. "Who goes there?"

"King James the Third of Scotland, if you please, and I accompany the rightful owner of Braigh Castle, Iain MacBraigh."

"Oh, the King and Iain, ye say?" Philip bowed in an awkward manner. "An' a whole army 'twould seem. Just a moment, yer Highness. My bones don't work as fast as they used to." Philip hobbled over and pulled on the rope that raised the gate inch by inch. It groaned and squealed. When it was high enough, they rode through.

Leith showed the men to the barracks. Birk and Bryce followed Iain and the King inside the castle. Gavin trailed behind the women, watching as Serena withdrew and appeared to move on instinct without any conscious thought. She wouldn't look at Gavin, which made him ache all the more for her.

Akira paused and turned, offering Serena a warm smile. She draped an arm over Serena's shoulders and led her down the dark hall. To Gavin's relief, Serena didn't refuse Akira as she had him. Mayhap Serena needed female company now that she'd lost her mother. Content that she would be fine in Akira's care, he moved on around them to catch up with the others.

Iain and the King stormed into the great hall. Startled, Lord Lennox bounced in his seat knocking over a chess piece. Realizing the King stood before him, the earl grunted as he stood in a bow. Lady Fiona gasped and rose. She curtsied, allowing her eyes to peer at her father as she adjusted her plaid skirts.

"Yer Highness, I wasn't expectin' ye," Lord Lennox said.

"I suppose not since this isn't your rightful home. Braigh Castle and all its lands will be restored to Iain MacBraigh. He holds the original will. I've seen it with my own eyes. What you've produced for the town magistrate is false. I'm verra disappointed in you, Lord Lennox. I've a good mind to strip you of your title."

Alarm came to Hogan's eyes. He glanced at Iain and then Gavin. "There must be some mistake. Please . . . I haven't forged any documents."

"Be careful," the King's voice took on a hard edge. "I intend to have experts examine both documents and compare them to the signatures on other documents signed by Iain's uncle now in possession of the crown. Do you insist on digging deeper troubles?"

"Nay, of course not," Hogan said, bowing again. "But they haven't told ye everything. Iain's hiding a cave on the estate. It contains valuable diamonds that would be verra important to the crown." Hogan pointed at Iain. "He didn't want to pay taxes to the crown so he kept it a secret."

"I knew naught of it. Indeed, I thought it was a myth— some legend the villagers might have made up," Iain said. "If I'd have known, would I have not filled my coffers?"

"Lord Lennox, gather your things and be gone from here. I'd better not hear one more word concerning the ownership of this estate or you'll not only lose your title, but your lands. Your children will have no inheritance. Be gone within the hour." Lord Lennox and his daughter hurried to collect their belongings.

"Your Highness," Iain stepped forward. "We've reason to believe that Lord Lennox may have had men attack the villagers in an effort to frighten them."

"For what reason? What did he do?" the King asked.

"A lass was attacked and beaten, a cow butchered, and someone ran a burning wagon into the church Sunday morning while everyone was inside. While we've no proof, would an attempt to murder an entire village be worth a royal investigation? He would have stopped at naught to discover the cave's location." Iain glanced at Lord Lennox and back at the King.

"Indeed. Lock him up in the dungeon below. I'll have my men begin on the morrow." His Highness waved a hand at his men and turned to Iain. "Call your servants and have chambers readied for us." He stepped back and gestured to everyone else. "But even before we all rest, I'd like a warm meal. I've been traveling awhile and I'm hungry."

"Of course, I'll see to it posthaste." Iain strode away.

"What about Lady Fiona?" Gavin asked.

"She may be confined in a chamber upstairs until we can question her. One of my men will stand guard," the King said.

Serena stood with her hands linked in front of her and burst into tears. She looked down at the floor as her shoulders trembled. Gavin strode to her and tried to take her in his arms, but she stepped away.

Akira met his gaze over Serena's head, a look of sympathy in her eyes. Once again she wrapped her arm around Serena's shoulders and wasn't rejected as he'd been. "Come . . . show me yer chamber. We'll order a warm bath for ye. I know that cell was filthy."

Serena sniffled. "My mither shared my chamber while she was healing from the first fire." Her voice broke again.

Gavin turned away, unable to bear it. The women's soft footsteps faded across the great hall. Each step compounded his grief and vexation. He paced in a circle, rubbing the back of his neck. "I need to make sure they remember to take a tray up to Serena."

"And one for Akira as well," Bryce said. "I doubt she'll leave Serena's side this night."

"Nay, I wouldn't want her to." Gavin stroked his chin. "If she'll not allow me to comfort her, then I pray she would at least let Akira keep her company."

"Son, the lass only needs some time," Birk said. "She'll be back to herself again after she grieves. Besides the death of her mither, she's been through a terrible ordeal."

"I know, Da." Gavin closed his eyes. "But what concerns me is that she might blame me. How can she forgive me for being there and not saving her mither?"

ℋ

Serena woke to the sounds of a maid building a peat fire in the hearth. The scent of burning wood revived her senses, reminding her of a new day, God's gift of a fresh beginning. Her mother used to say that God's mercy was new every morning.

Her mother!

How could the smell of burning wood be welcome after what her mother had endured? Despair consumed her, sinking Serena into a pit of devastation. An image of her mother's smiling face came to mind as she had sat by the fire beside Gunna in their comfortable cottage, listening to her read *The Canterbury Tales*. She'd never see them again, hear their encouraging voices, share a warm and comforting embrace. An empty ache pressed against her until she turned her face into the pillow, desperate to drive the horrible feeling away. She moaned against the pain, drowning in distress.

Her stomach lurched in protest, and Serena laid her hand upon the area as if to smooth it down. Memories of yesterday flooded her mind barring any escape. Sickness claimed her. Having skipped the midday meal yesterday and dinner last night, there was naught to release, only the churning of a restless soul and a rolling stomach.

She leaned over the bed, the dry heaves making her weak until she wished she could vomit and be done with it.

"Oh, I'm sorry to wake ye, miss," said Mary, the maid.

Serena couldn't find her voice to greet Mary. She crawled out of bed and sank to the floor, still heaving. Her mouth watered, but naught came to the surface. Tears filled her eyes. What a wretched existence she had now that Gunna and her mother were gone.

"Lass, are ye ill?" The maid ran to her and bent down.

"Serena?" Akira stirred from sleep and moaned. Sitting up, she stretched a hand out feeling the empty space.

"I'm afraid she's verra ill," Mary said.

Akira rubbed her tired eyes, threw the covers back, and knelt by Serena's side. "Quick, some water!" She pointed to the basin.

"Aye, that should 'elp," Mary said.

"Mayhap, yer stomach is revolting at being so empty." Akira wrapped her arms around Serena. "Ye're naught but bones to begin with."

Serena couldn't answer, as trembles quaked through her. Under Devlin's merciless care, she'd been starved and her mind oppressed. Losing a bit of weight had been the least of her worries.

Fresh tears flooded her eyes and she sank back on the bed, rocking. She deserved no sympathy, no kindness. Serena had allowed her mother to take her place. If she had not agreed to trade places, her mother would still be alive. Nay, she was a rotten daughter.

Akira lifted a goblet of water to her lips. Serena turned her head, content to remain miserable. "Please . . . 'twill help. It breaks my heart to see ye this way."

Gavin's sister was too kind. Ever since she'd arrived, Akira had stayed by her side encouraging her to keep going. She took care of her needs as if she were a child. Serena no longer cared about her own comfort, but she still cared about those around her—Gavin and his family. Out of respect for them, she sipped, not wishing to be a further burden.

The cool water smoothed her parched throat so she drank more, suddenly craving it. The liquid swirled in her belly and settled down with each breath she took. Her lungs were sore from all the smoke she had breathed yesterday.

"There, is that better?" Akira asked.

Serena nodded, not yet trusting her voice.

Akira turned to Mary. "Go to the kitchen and ask the cook for some fresh warm milk with a dash of ginger. Tell her it's for Serena's hurting stomach."

"Aye, I'll do it right away." Mary bobbed her head and hurried from the chamber.

"Do ye have enough energy to sit by the fire? There's a wee chill in the room and ye look cold." Akira touched Serena's arm.

"To tell the truth, I don't know if I'll ever want to see another fire again." Serena leaned on her palm. She used her other hand to shove her tangled hair from her face.

Akira smiled. "I'd feel the same way if I were ye. However, our whole lives are built around the warmth of a fire. Try to think on good thoughts the fireplace used to bring before yesterday. The sooner ye get over this, the better. We canna have ye freezing all winter. It simply won't do, lass." Akira covered her hand with her warm one and tightened her hold with encouragement.

"That's what happened this morning. I woke to the wonderful smell of the fire, and I was happy—because for a moment I'd forgotten. I could understand if it had been a fortnight, or mayhap a month, but she only perished yesterday. Her burial hasn't even taken place yet." She looked away and wiped her eyes. "One would think I'd run out of tears by now."

"Serena, I'm no stranger to grief. While both my parents still live, I've lost a brother, one in the prime of his youth. I thought he'd died by my hand. We were sword playing, and I accidentally stabbed him. I know firsthand the guilt ye're feeling. Yer grief will take time, but yer ability to wake up this morning with such a bright outlook is a promise, a slight glimpse of the happiness that is still available in yer future if ye're willing to grieve and then heal."

"No wonder yer brother thinks so highly of ye. He's told me much about ye." Serena attempted to smile through her tears. Her chest felt like it would soon burst with all the pressure building inside.

"I've missed him, both he and Leith." Fondness lit Akira's eyes.

"How did ye know I was referring to Gavin?" Serena asked.

"Because Gavin's last seven letters have all been about ye. Leith rarely writes me, and when he does, I get a few sentences. Gavin is thoughtful enough to write me pages."

While Serena didn't laugh, the way Akira stated it made her feel better. Akira had a natural gift of lifting one's spirits.

"I'm cold," Akira said, sifting her hands together and blowing on them. "Let's move closer to the fire. I promise, it's the best thing for ye right now." Akira rose to her feet. She bent and took Serena's elbow, tugging her up. Serena could not in good conscience reject her kindness, so she allowed Akira to lead her across the chamber. Her friend made sure she was settled in a chair before relaxing in one beside her. The warmth did feel much better.

"I've been thinking . . . I'd like my mither to be buried beside Gunna. She was my nursemaid and died recently, a dear sweet soul she was. I think Mither would like that."

"Of course. I'll tell Gavin and Iain so they can see to the preparations." A short silence fell between them and then Akira cleared her throat. "Ye know, ye and I aren't that much different. I've had my fears of being burned at the stake, too."

Of course, why hadn't she realized it before? After Gavin learned of her seizures, he'd confessed about his sister's dreams. It wasn't like her to miss such a connection. "Ye mean yer prophetic dreams?"

"Aye." Akira nodded. "I've had a few people call me a witch in the past. But I'm no such thing. I love God dearly, and I give Him full credit for my gift."

"I wish what I had was a gift." Serena glanced at her lap and wrung her hands. "All my fits have ever caused is hardship and heartbreak. It tore up my mither's marriage, forced us to live our entire lives in hiding, kept us in fear, and made us outcasts. I could go on, but what's the point?" Serena bit her lower lip. "In the end, it killed my mither."

"I've seen some of the people in yer village. Do ye love them any less for their differences?" Akira asked.

"Nay, of course not. But they aren't considered possessed by demons for their problems. No one wants to burn them at the stake. Only me."

"Mayhap, but they're looked down upon. Some people believe they have their infirmities because of an evil deed they might have committed or as punishment for the evil deeds of their parents and earlier generations." Akira lifted her bare toes toward the fire. "Either way, it's all thought evil in varying degrees. And . . . they're all wrong in their superstitious presumptions."

Someone knocked on the door. At Akira's permission, Mary came in carrying a steaming mug. "Here ye go, lass. Fresh and warm."

"Thank ye." Serena accepted it and took a slow sip. "Mm." The warm drink felt good on her dry throat and filled her belly making her all warm inside.

Mary linked her hands in front of her and stood beside Serena. "I nearly tripped over the mon out in the hall. I believe he must have slept by yer door. He seemed verra distressed that ye're ill. He wanted me to ask if there was aught he could do."

"Who is he?" Akira asked.

"The red-haired one. If ye ask me, he sort of favors the laird, but seems a bit more brawn of muscle."

"Sounds like my brother, Gavin," Akira said.

Serena closed her eyes. Now her heart felt as warm as her stomach. A blush of pleasure washed through her from head to toe. "Please tell him I'm much better. Ask him if he would mind making preparations for my mither's burial. I plan to lay her to rest beside Gunna. If Father Tomas is well enough, I hope he'll say a prayer."

"Aye, I'll tell 'im."

As the maid reached the door, Serena turned. "And tell him . . . I'm verra thankful."

"Ye're doing well." Akira smiled.

"I know yer brother. His mind will do better if he has a task to keep him occupied." Serena sighed. "As for me, I'll do what I must to bear this. I keep hearing my mither's voice in my head, instructing me as she did all my years of growing up." Serena looked at her new friend. "Do ye think that's what they mean when they say a loved one who has passed on remains in one's heart, I mean besides the love ye still feel for them?"

"Aye, I would think so." Akira searched her face.

A feeling of understanding passed between them.

"Gavin is so blessed to have such a loving and loyal family," Serena said. "I've always wondered what it would be like to have a father and brothers and sisters."

"We may not have been born as family, but sometimes God brings us family like He brought ye Gunna." Akira paused. "I believe Gavin still wants to wed ye. Now that ye've met us, don't ye see that we would all welcome ye with open arms?"

The back of Serena's throat ached and her nose and eyes stung with more salty tears. "That's easy to say when ye haven't seen one of my fits," she whispered, her lips trembling.

22

A sennight later, Gavin sat on the ledge by the castle overlooking the sea, his elbows propped up on his bent knees. It had become his favorite place to pray in the mornings. He would miss Braigh Castle when he finally got up the courage to leave.

His father and Akira and Bryce were ready to go home. The King had left after a couple of days, needing to conclude other business in Caithness. He left men in charge to investigate Hogan Lennox, the strange events in the village, and to work out a tax for any diamonds Iain mined from the cave.

Leith and the men had started back on the restoration to Braigh Castle. He had taken their father around for a tour, showing him all the changes he'd overseen and plans he'd drawn up. Their father was proud and impressed with Leith. He thought the lad would be fine finishing the restoration without Gavin. Birk wanted Gavin home to take over some of the estate duties. Gavin couldn't leave without first speaking to Serena.

She had shown admirable courage throughout Evelina and Beacon's funeral. While she openly grieved, she had shown kindness to everyone and a clear state of mind. She'd had little sleep, and he could only imagine how much it must have pained her, but she made it through like a true leader. Serena would be the perfect wife for a chieftain—for him.

Two days after the burial, a distant coldness still lingered between them. Couldn't she see that he loved her no matter what? He would never leave her unless she desired it? She had once told him she loved him. Could her grief drown out her love for him? He prayed not. Mayhap all she needed was time. Would he be able to persuade his father to delay their departure a little longer?

Footsteps approached. Gavin turned. Serena walked toward him. A dark purple and navy plaid wrapped around her. She pulled it tight against her. Serena's long black hair blew over her shoulder in the wind. She sat beside him.

"Akira told me they're all leaving on the morrow," she said.

"Aye."

"She also said ye might go with them." She searched his eyes.

"Da wants me to, but I haven't given him my answer yet."

She scraped her teeth over her bottom lip and looked out to the sea, avoiding his gaze. Something was on her mind. Hope elevated his battered heart. Why did she insist on healing alone? Why wouldn't she share her heart and thoughts with him? How could he help her if she wouldn't let him?

"Ye mean ye're actually considering it?" She paused and took a deep breath. "I thought ye would be staying with Leith and the men until the restoration was complete."

"He can handle it. I'm only here to guide him in getting started and my real duty was to protect the castle estate. Now that the mysteries are solved and the danger over, I'm not really needed."

"I see." She gulped.

No other words. If she wanted him to stay, why wouldn't she ask? He folded his arms around his knees and linked his fingers to keep from pulling her into his arms and making a fool of himself.

"Serena, naught has changed regarding my feelings. I love ye now more than ever. I still want ye to be my wife. Please come with me."

Her midnight hair blew around her face, hiding her expression. Serena wiped at her eyes, as she sniffled.

"I canna." She turned away.

"Why not?" Her rejection cut him to the quick. In spite of his trembling insides, he forced himself to remain calm. He had to show consideration for her wounded feelings. His selfish desires would have to wait—if he could be strong enough.

"Don't ye see? This is the place she chose for our home," Serena said. "It's where I've always been safe. It's where Mither and Gunna are laid to rest. I canna leave her . . . not now . . . not ever. After she sacrificed her life for me, I'll stay here and live the peaceful life she tried to create."

Gavin clenched his jaw. She needed to hear the words he was about to say, and he prayed she wouldn't hate him for it.

"She's not in that grave, Serena, only her body. Yer mither is in heaven enjoying a much more peaceful life than she ever had here with us."

She broke into sobs then, her shoulders shaking as she turned her whole body further way from him.

"Her life is over. Yers isn't. That's what she sacrificed herself for—ye to be happy wherever yer life may lead ye." Gavin crawled toward her and draped his arms around her.

"Serena, this place isn't yer sanctuary like it once was. Yer secret is out, and they tried to kill ye for it. Ye've a pardon from the King that will enable ye to go anywhere in Scotland. Yer home, mither, and Gunna are all gone. There's naught to keep ye here. But there is me. I love ye, lass. Please . . . let me love ye for the rest of our lives. Come with me."

"Even if I have a pardon from the King, my fits would shame ye, Gavin." The tears in Serena's voice nearly choked her, but she cleared her throat. "It could ruin yer chieftainship and yer ability to rule. People may lose respect, distrust ye. How would our children feel? I don't want my fits to ruin the happiness of anyone else I love."

She wiggled away from him. He crawled after her and grabbed at her plaid. Serena let him have it as she ran off. Gavin clutched her plaid in his hand, the scent of jasmine reaching his nose. His heart swelled with hope. Did she just say she loved him?

⁂

Serena paced in her chamber. She and Akira had already said their good-byes in the privacy of her room, but she couldn't bear to tell Gavin good-bye. It felt too permanent.

At least she had a window by the sea, and she wouldn't have to endure watching them leave the courtyard and through the gate. If ever she had a sister, Akira would be the one. They had grown quite close over the last sennight and had promised to write each other.

She longed for the kind of passionate love that Akira and Bryce shared. Whenever she witnessed a kiss between them or a stolen glance, Serena's mind went to Gavin. His rust-colored hair, intense blue eyes, and his ruddy complexion warmed her heart as he often gazed at her with a mischievous grin. How could he leave her like this? He didn't have to go, he was choosing to go.

Gavin had asked her to come with him. The man had tenderly expressed his love and shown how much he cared these past few months. What more would she require of him?

To stay! That's what.

She turned, repeating the path across her chamber. How could she let him go? Why did it feel like she was betraying her mother's memory if she left?

Someone knocked at her chamber door. Mayhap Gavin didn't leave after all!

"Come in," she called.

Doreen opened the door. Even though Serena was glad to see her friend, she was disappointed that it wasn't Gavin. Her shoulders sagged. She swallowed, determined to give her friend a proper greeting.

"Doreen, are ye back for good?" Serena asked, forcing a smile she didn't feel.

"Aye." Doreen nodded. "I wrote to the laird and asked for my old position back. I hated that place in Braighwick."

"Well, I'm glad ye're here." Serena recovered her manners and held out her arms, welcoming Doreen back with a hug. "Did ye happen to see anyone leaving?" Serena asked.

"A whole clan it seemed. They were passing through the gate as I was coming in." Doreen linked her free arm through Serena's. "Come sit by me."

Serena's hopes plummeted as she allowed Doreen to guide her to the edge of the bed.

Doreen pulled out a folded parchment letter from her plaid. "I'm sorry 'bout yer mither. She gave me this the morning she died. I was only supposed to give it to ye if somethin' happened to her."

Serena accepted the letter, speechless. Her mother's familiar penmanship was on the front with Serena's name. She glanced at Doreen. "Do ye mind if I read this in private?"

"Of course not." Doreen rose and went to the door. "I still need to get settled back into my auld chamber." She slipped out.

Serena broke the seal with trembling fingers.

My Dearest Serena,

No mother could be more proud or feel more loved than me. Every mother raises their children to have the morals and values they want them to have as adults, but not all parents get to witness the product of their labor and the fruit of their love as I have. Thank you for being who you are.

If you're reading this letter, then my plan worked and you're alive and well. Do not keep mourning me, dearest. I am in a safe and happy place with my heavenly Father, the final destination for all of us who love Him. My love for Jesus and you is why I had the courage to do what I did. One day you'll understand the strength of a mother's love. It is no more than what Jesus did for us when he went to the cross and sacrificed himself in the hope that we might live. If we could only grasp the absolute power of our heavenly Father's love, we'd never fear again.

We have a choice to resist His sacrifice as many do or accept His gift and live to the fullest. Please, don't reject my sacrifice, dearest. Now that you're free, live to the fullest with God's blessing. Go where you desire to go. Love whom you desire to love.

I'm certain Gavin loves you. Don't be afraid to go with him if you love him. I could have lived anywhere as long as I had you. A true home isn't a place. It's wherever you're loved.

I fear I have planted in you a false sense of security in the village. As long as your secret was unknown, the truth is you would have been safe most anywhere away from your father. I'm sorry I made you fear the outside world. Don't live trapped in the fear I allowed your father to create in me. Break free and put your trust in God. He is your true sanctuary, and He is everywhere.

Love you always and forever,
Mother

Serena wiped away the tears streaming down her face. A fierce determination rose inside her. She would not let her mother's death be in vain. Many men had died fighting for their freedom and that of their family and clansmen over the years, for the generations to come. Her mother had done no less—for her.

Gavin!

He's leaving!

She pulled on her plaid, wrapped it around her arms, tucking it tight. She hurried down the hall and found Iain talking to Leith in his study.

"Please, may I borrow a horse from yer stable?" she asked.

"Aye, but are ye well enough to ride, lass?" Iain eyed her with indecision. "I thought ye didn't come down to see everyone off because ye didn't feel well."

"I feel better. Thank ye." She rushed out to the stables and ordered the lad to saddle a fast horse.

A few moments later, Serena rode out of the gate. Once she advanced beyond the huge dip in the hill and entered the pine forest, she increased her speed. She ducked low, keeping behind the animal's head. Knowing the curves well, Serena leaned to each side to keep from losing pace.

She caught up with the travelers at the site of the new kirk. "Akira! Akira!" Serena called, not seeing Gavin among them.

Akira rode her own mount beside her husband. She turned. Concern entered her expression as she rode to meet Serena.

"Where is Gavin?" Serena asked.

"He couldn't leave ye. He separated from us before we came to the first house. Has something happened?" Akira tilted her head.

"Nay . . . Aye . . ." Serena shook her head. Tears gathered in her eyes, but she blinked them back. "Please . . . I canna let him leave without me. I just came from that way and didn't see him."

"Mayhap he went for a ride to think. Serena, I've never seen him like this. He's verra worried ye won't have 'im. He doesn't understand why ye rejected him if ye love him. And for the first time ever he's willing to defy Da and give up his entire inheritance."

"Yer da didn't give his permission?" Serena's hopes lay buried in the cage of her heart, her entire future depending on Akira's answer.

"Da didn't forbid yer union but expressed his concern and doubts that it was the best match for Gavin." She reached out and grasped Serena's hand. "Don't let it worry ye. Our da is a wise and sensible mon. He's already lost one son and nearly lost me once, he'll gain his son back by giving him the freedom to chose his future."

"I hope ye're right because I came to tell Gavin I've changed my mind. I'm going home with him." Her heart pounded so hard, she feared it would bruise her ribs.

"Then we'll truly be sisters?" Akira asked.

"Aye." Serena grinned.

Birk and Bryce rode up to join them. "'Bout time ye came to yer senses, lass," Bryce said. He elbowed Birk. "Right? Gavin deserves to be happy. Ye both do."

The MacKenzie Chief said naught, only jutted his chin at a defiant angle and looked away. He swallowed and when he looked back his eyes were red. "Aye, I agree."

"Mayhap he's with Father Tomas," Serena said, happiness rooting inside her. She turned her horse and galloped in that direction.

Gavin sat across from Father Tomas at his wooden table. A small fire blazed in the hearth.

"Would ye like something to eat? Sure looks like ye could use it." Tomas leaned on his hands, poised to rise.

"Nay." Gavin shook his head. "I wouldn't be able to eat it. She's taken my appetite. I canna sleep. My brain is like mud." Gavin rubbed his tired eyes. "My whole life is on hold, waiting for this woman to come to her senses. What if she never does?"

"Then I guess ye'll be miserable for the rest of yer life." Tomas grinned.

Gavin wasn't amused. He glared back. "Mayhap she doesn't love me." He shoved a fisted hand into his palm. "This is worse than an illness."

"From the confessions I've heard over the years, it must be an illness." Tomas scratched his bald head and stared at the table.

"I came here for good counsel and some inspiration." Gavin said, allowing his annoyance to show.

"Lad, I can counsel ye on most any religious thing or health-related issue ye wish, but women are out of my league.

Sometimes they confound me as much as they do ye." Tomas shook his head.

A timid knock caught their attention. "Excuse me." Father Tomas stood and answered the door.

A female voice spoke, but Gavin couldn't make out the words. He wasn't in the mood for entertaining. He hoped whoever it was wouldn't stay.

"Come in," Tomas said.

Gavin rolled his eyes. He sat up, prepared to make his excuses to leave. Serena stepped around the door. Gavin froze, his jaw dropped open.

"Gavin! I've been lookin' for ye." Her red eyes widened in pleasant surprise. "I couldn't let ye leave without telling ye how I feel. Please forgive me. So much has happened. I've been so mixed up. It's hard to think beyond all the pain."

The words tumbled from her tongue so fast he hardly had enough time to process them. Gavin didn't move. He was too afraid to hope again, so he merely listened.

"After ye left, Doreen brought me a letter my mither wrote to me the morning she died." Serena twisted her hands as she moistened her lips. "Somehow her words gave me the strength to finally leave this place. I want to go with ye, if ye'll still have me."

"Ye want to be my wife?" He raised an eyebrow as if he didn't believe her.

"I do." She nodded, wincing and shrinking back. "Thank ye for not leaving me." Her voice fell to a whisper. .

"Um, I think I'll go for a walk." Father Tomas said. His footsteps were the only sound across the wooden floor as he closed the creaking door behind him. Voices greeted him outside, but Gavin and Serena ignored them.

"Serena, ye canna get my hopes up and dash them again. Please, ye don't know what it's doing to me." He rubbed his eyebrows and swallowed. "I pray ye mean what ye say. I don't think I could bear it if not."

"If it's ripping ye up as much as me, then I've an idea." She walked toward him. "Gavin, I never lied to ye. I really do love ye. I've been afraid to leave the village. It's hard for me not to fear the unknown. And after my mither died, I felt like I was betraying her if I left the safety of the home she'd created for me here. These villagers have become the only family I've ever had. They would sacrifice their lives for me. Beacon did." She pulled out the folded letter from her plaid and handed it to him. "Here, read this. Mayhap it will explain what I canna seem to find the words to say. It has released me from my fear."

He reached out and took the letter. "Are ye sure ye want me to read this?"

"Aye." She nodded. "From this day forward, I want no secrets between us."

Gavin unfolded it and read the looped handwriting. He had to blink back tears. While he didn't understand a mother's love, he did understand God's love. He could see how Serena would feel free to leave the village after reading this. Her mother had given them her blessing. He stepped forward and took her in his arms, pulling her tight against him, never wanting to let her go. "Serena, from this day, never let fear come between us again." He kissed her forehead and stroked her hair, resting his chin upon her head. He closed his eyes. *Thank ye God, for this precious gift.*

She wrapped her thin arms around his chest. "I won't." Tears lingered in her voice and she sniffled.

Gavin leaned back, cupped her chin, and lifted her tear-stained face to his. With gentle restraint, he lowered his lips to hers. The soft touch soldered them together, kindling a passionate warmth that flowed through his body like a current. He dug his fingers into her silky black hair, savoring every moment.

When they finally pulled apart, both of their hearts beat in rapid succession and they breathed in short breaths. He waited until he could speak. "Do ye want a large wedding in a kirk?"

"Nay, that isn't necessary. God is everywhere." She laid her head against his chest.

"Do ye have any reason why ye'd like to wait before ye become my bride?"

"Nay, I've no reason at all." She leaned up on her tiptoes and pressed her warm, soft lips upon his.

"Good," he said against her, taking her hand and pulling her to the door. Gavin swung it open. "Father Tomas, we're ready to have a wedding."

Gavin paused, surprised to see his clansmen all gathered around the yard. Everyone clapped.

"It's about time!" Bryce roared with laughter. "I take it ye were so engrossed in each other, ye didn't even hear us ride up, did ye?"

Serena and Gavin met each other's gaze, their red eyes now sparkling. "Nay!" they said together.

"I want to be the first to welcome my new sister!" Akira pulled her husband forward, weaving in and out of their clansmen, making their way to the front of the cottage.

Cara stood beside Craig, her arm linked with his, and a bright smile. "Serena, we'll both have our verra own clan."

"This is so wonderful." Serena laughed, covering her hand over her mouth in awe. "I've always dreamed of a family like yers."

Gavin looked down at her and grinned. He kissed the tip of her nose. "And now yer dream has come true, for now they're as much yer family as mine."

Dear Readers,

Highland Sanctuary has a special place in my heart and there is a reason I've dedicated this book to my daughter, Celina. Even though I didn't know it at the time, this story began with my daughter's birth, specifically within the first thirty-two hours of her life. Celina was born with a life-threatening seizure disorder, much like *Highland Sanctuary*'s heroine, Serena.

Unlike Evelina, I had a very supportive husband and a community of healthcare professionals who rallied behind our family. We had the benefit of medical technology with medications that controlled my daughter's seizures. Celina didn't have to worry about hiding her condition since people have a general understanding about seizures these days and few think of them as demonic behavior.

As we learned to cope with Celina's condition, I couldn't help thinking about how different her life would have been if she had been born in the late medieval period. The next thing I knew, my story grew into a whole Village of Outcasts. As with everything, the maturity of this story needed to be in God's timing. He knew I needed healing from the emotional trauma and time to let go of my fears.

Celina's doctors told us she may grow out of her seizures, but we know she's been healed. I'm pleased to report that Celina is now seizure free and no longer taking seizure medications. The descriptions of Serena's seizures came directly from my experience with my daughter.

Even though the word *seizure* was in existence by 1477, many people, especially those in remote areas of Scotland, wouldn't have known the word. Those who did were still skeptical and had very little experience with them. For this reason, I tried to use the word as little as possible.

I hope you enjoyed *Highland Sanctuary*. I pray you were somehow touched and inspired by this story. Thank you for traveling back in time through the flight of my imagination to bonny Scotland.

Blessings,

Jennifer Hudson Taylor

Discussion Questions

1. In order to save her baby's life, what other choices did Evelina have? Did she make the right choice to leave her husband? Why or why not?

2. Other than demon possession, how else might a person with seizures have been viewed in 1477?

3. Once Serena's secret became known, Evelina was forced to place her faith in God, not in the remote location of the village. How did this change her?

4. What made Serena finally trust Gavin?

5. Back then, the church and king had a power struggle. Was there anyone else who could have helped Serena besides the king? What other options did she have?

6. Do you think there are unique places in the world where people with similarities gravitate toward one another? What did you think of the Village of Outcasts?

7. What role did Phelan, the white wolf, play? Do you think of him as the protector of the village?

8. I chose not to drag out the details of the inquisition and trial, but to give you a glimpse. How do you think it might have really happened?

9. Gavin faced the obstacles of coming from a wealthy family and convincing his clan to accept Serena's seizures. How did his faith play into his ability to overcome this?

10. Would you have made the same sacrifice for your daughter if you were Evelina?